SINS OF OUR FATHER

SON OF SYN

Written by Christopher R. Mix

Robert,

Thank you so much for buying the finale to this trilogy. We really hope you enjoy it and you find a bit of an escape. I appreciate your friendship and all the laughs we share. Lets keep it going for years to come!

ISBN: 9798343369892
Imprint: Independently published

Cover & Art design by: Ben Moran & Thomas
Beswick

Logo Design: Dan Le
Edited By: Stacey Mix & Zachary Johnson
Proofread By: James Urban & Daniel Glover
Printed in the United States of America

Dedicated To:

Justin Camden
Gregory Ehlinger
Christian Stogryn
Vincent Quintanar
Noah Eden
Robert Fattouch
Collin Pedroza
Katie Sabin
Robert Hicks
Frank Bruno
Dan Le

And all Son Of Syn fans that have pushed this endeavor forward. Thank you.

Contents

BOOK 2 SYNOPSIS 7

CHAPTER 1 - Shattered Will Begets Bravery 12

CHAPTER 2 - When It All Crumbles Down..........................34

CHAPTER 3 - Washing The Blood Away 48

CHAPTER 4 - Take Me For A Ride.......................................66

CHAPTER 5 - Mystery and Arrival 85

CHAPTER 6 – You Are Safe Here.......................................104

CHAPTER 7 - Meet The Illuminaries 123

CHAPTER 8 - Escape From New Beam City 138

CHAPTER 9 - Reflections as Sweet as Honey.....................166

CHAPTER 10 - Let Bygones Be Bygones 181

CHAPTER 11 - Healing 201

CHAPTER 12 - To Slay A Demon...215

CHAPTER 13 - Club Nis...236

CHAPTER 14 - The Alluring Eyes Of A Demon..................269

CHAPTER 15 - Surprise..297

CHAPTER 16 - A Message 317

CHAPTER 17 - Campfire Condolences 327

CHAPTER 18 - Airways to Mayhem 341

CHAPTER 19 - Return To New Beam City...........................352

CHAPTER 20 - Phantom Rider...366

CHAPTER 21 - Toying The Edge Of Control.......................382

CHAPTER 22 - Throne Of Atonement 398

CHAPTER 23 - Farewell For Now..412

NOTE FROM THE AUTHOR

Modern society drifts through illuminated screens, with daily life scattered across endless tasks and distractions. Humanity has unknowingly shifted its focus, coveting devices while neglecting real-world connections. As we stare into the digital abyss, time slips away, leaving us isolated in the glow of our machines. New generations now have unprecedented access to information—answers to any question just a click away. But what was once a thirst for knowledge has been tainted by a lack of discipline, leading to a shallow consumption of data. The early days of the internet offered a vast, uncensored archive to anyone willing to explore it. Today, the youngest among us can outsmart seasoned historians with a few keystrokes, yet their depth of understanding suffers in a world where information is cheap and context is lost.

In this hyper-connected age, those who fail to adapt are left behind, swept away by the relentless current of technological advancement. To survive, we must conform. But how far is too far in a world that continuously rewrites its own rules? The threats of militarized technology and weaponized data loom large as we create new realities, evolving within them at breakneck speed. Modern ideas will shape our future, but at what cost? Someone must bear the burden of leading us into these uncharted digital landscapes. How will you adapt to the rapidly evolving ecosystem of ones and zeros?

Value is a concept we learn from a young age. Is it wealth, love, or resources that determine what is truly valuable in life? Many societies have agreed on these measures, but one commodity remains consistently undervalued, even though it can determine the success or failure of individuals and entire nations: information. Information stands at the apex of value in our world, rising higher with each technological leap. In both its real and fictional forms, information is potent, easily manipulated, and endlessly powerful. It fuels media, advertising, propaganda, and governmental control—tools that can both enlighten and deceive, depending on who wields them. This duality suits those seeking power, twisting truth into dark fictions to serve their agendas.

In New Beam City, the struggle over information is no different. The most reliable intel is found not in public broadcasts, but within the shadowy underground street networks. Here, knowledge flows without a central authority, fueled by hackers, independent personalities, and rogue journalists. No single source controls this information pipeline, yet it is vital to those who live in the shadows. These are the unsung heroes of truth, risking everything to push back against the megacorporations and authoritarian forces that seek to enslave the masses through deception. Among them are brave journalists, like Mitt of Mittcast News, who put their lives on the line to deliver unfiltered stories to a public starved for truth. Mitt collects verified news from around the world, presenting various perspectives and offering commentary on how each can impact society.

But recently, New Beam City has been thrust into the global spotlight. A sudden lockdown has paralyzed the city, triggered by the spread of an illegal street device known as FreqyD. Authorities are scrambling to contain its distribution, yet they can't find the source— or a way to stop it. As chaos spreads and the city becomes ground zero for a war over information, Mitt and his underground network of truth-seekers must navigate dangerous waters. In this battle for control, where the line between fact and fiction blurs, who will emerge victorious?

BOOK 2 SYNOPSIS

Tower of Phantoms left Clain bloodied and broken, alone in the rain-soaked streets after a devastating clash with Synric, the world's first self-aware AI. Though Clain previously defeated Synric, smashing it to pieces with a manhole cover, the danger is far from over. As the plot around Clain thickens, the premonition realm inside him grows stronger, threatening to break free and wreak havoc. Meanwhile, FreqyD devices—the mysterious contraptions that allow users to communicate with what they believe are the dead—have spread throughout New Beam City. Are these devices truly connecting people to the afterlife, or is something far more sinister at play?

This dilemma weighs heavily on young Fila, who discovered a bag of FreqyD devices and locked herself away to use one. Believing she had reached her deceased mother, Fila found herself holding hands with a dark entity known as Tia. Her father, Mr. Le, found her sobbing, and the sight of his daughter in despair shook him to his core, fearing he had lost the only thing he had left to love. He removed the device from her head whilst she fainted in his arms repeating a few short words: "I saw Mommy."

Meanwhile, Honey and Dawn barely escaped the violent chaos at the Pit Pig headquarters, a desert stronghold. The leader, Kruger, had captured a phantom wearing Clain's face, believing it was the real Clain. Dawn was forced into a deadly duel with this impostor, suffering a brutal wound after being impaled during the savage fight. Honey intervened just in time, whisking Dawn away on her cutting-edge C9X speed bike. As they escaped, Dawn planted a landmine, blowing Kruger's mechanical legs to pieces and leaving the enraged leader vowing murderous revenge.

With Kruger's words ringing in their ears and the looming threat of a mechanical kaiju built using the head of the fallen Hux, the stakes couldn't be higher. Honey races toward Eagle's Equinox to find help for Dawn, as the fate of New Beam City hangs in the balance.

Welcome to Son Of Syn: Sins Of Our Father. For this third entry in the series, we invite you to partake in a musical adventure with us! Throughout the book you will be treated with hand-picked dark synthwave style music coordinated by the author. These tracks best fit the tone and emotion intended for each scene and offer a fun addition as you experience your read through. The QR codes are strategically placed throughout the chapters, so we suggest having a smartphone or tablet handy to scan the codes which lead directly to songs on YouTube. Enjoy them as you read along!

This QR above is an example of what you will come across. This track is by ALEX & TOKYO ROSE, called "CURSED." They were kind enough to allow the lyrics to be a part of the book's plot, as this song is pivotal to the story. If you enjoy these tracks, please support the musicians and leave them a comment. Let them know Son Of Syn sent you.

CHAPTER 1 - Shattered Will Begets Bravery

 "I saw Mommy..." Little Fila lies limp in an empty booth of her father's restaurant. Mr. Le strokes his teenage daughter's hair with trembling hands, suppressing his panic and holding back a tearful scream as his fingers touch the cold sweat on her brow. Her eyes open and shut, open and shut. They're not focused on anything. Wherever she is, it's not here, and it's not safe. She's repeating the same thing over and over again.

"I saw Mommy..."

Mr. Le looks down the nearby corridor. The light from Clain's old room in the garage casts a soft, orange glow on the walls. He can't remember if her door was already unlocked or if he smashed it open. The aches in his head, arms and legs could just as easily be from his struggle to stay composed as from punches and kicks landing on a hard, wooden surface. Sirens ring out in the distance, growing louder. Within seconds of him hearing the sound, red and blue flash through the windows across his and Fila's faces. A heavy knock on the front door rings through the dining area. Mr. Le's head snaps towards the main entrance to his restaurant. He blinks, trying to focus his vision and shake his thoughts loose. He can't quite seem to get up and move towards the sound.

"Mr. Le?" a baritone voice asks from behind the door. Mr. Le moves his mouth to answer, but nothing comes out. The next knock is much more aggressive. "Mr. Le! Emergency services! Open up!"

With a couple more strangled bobs, his throat finally opens just enough to force out a choked "Yes! Yes, just a moment! My daughter...she..."

"We're aware sir; you provided details to the dispatcher. Open the doors, please. We can't help her from out here."

Mr. Le silently obliges, gingerly placing Fila's head on the booth cushion and moving to the door. She's speaking at a whisper now, but he can still hear her haunted repetitions.

"I saw Mommy…"

The next few minutes fail to make it into Mr. Le's long-term memory. He's trying desperately to drown out Fila's fading cries, detaching from the present almost completely until questions from a medical emergency responder bring him back to the moment.

"Mr. Le?"

"Oh," Mr. Le replies, shaking his head to clear the fog in his mind once again. A tall, wiry man in a paramedic's uniform stands in front of him. "Um…yes. How can I help?"

"I know you're scared, Mr. Le, but I do need to gather some basic information from you and the police will need to take a statement. Can you handle that?"

The members of the SWAT team bark orders and updates to one another in the background.

"Secure the contraband."

"Secured. Confirmed 17 units of illegal virtual reality device, street designation 'FreqyD.'"

"Any indication where she got them?"

"Still looking, sir."

"Mr. Le," the paramedic says again. Mr. Le runs his hands down his face, trying his best to hear what the man is saying. "Do you think you can handle all that?"

"Yes," he responds absently.

"Very good. Just a few questions and the medical team should have what they need. Bear with me." Mr. Le nods. "Let's start easy. Her name?" the paramedic asks.

"Fila," Mr. Le responds. "Fila Le. One e in 'Le,'" he clarifies.

"Age?"

"Thirteen."

"Any family history of mental or physical illness?"

"Nothing physical. She received a diagnosis of PTSD when her mother died."

"I saw Mommy..." Fila whimpers again. Mr. Le's eyes shut and his jaw tightens.

"Stay with me," the man reminds him. Mr. Le nods again. "You have my condolences," the man says.

"Thank you," Mr. Le responds.

"Cursory examinations showed she has a cybernetic arm. Is this correct?"

"Yes."

"So she's suffered the loss of a limb as well?" Mr. Le exhales shakily, remembering the night he found his daughter bleeding out in front of his restaurant, her arm having been torn off and thrown into his chest by the raging, hideous pig mutant Hux. He can only nod to confirm once again.

"May I ask how?"

Mr. Le bumbles his way through an explanation, but there's no good way to convince the man his parenting isn't to blame for her injury. No matter what words he strains to compose into a coherent sentence, ultimately what the man questioning him hears is that his young daughter was left to her own devices in a nearby alley in a less-than-safe neighborhood and brutally attacked and spent an inordinate amount of time in his garage with a poorly vetted stranger. The skepticism on the man's face is all Mr. Le needs to know exactly what's been written down on that clipboard about his parenting. The next question is no better.

"Do you have any idea how she obtained these illegal devices?"

Mr. Le is grateful the man doesn't mention them by name. Even the faint echo of the tactical officer saying it moments ago conjured images of Fila on the floor, screaming, sobbing, convulsing with the demonic machine strapped over her eyes. Overcome by frenzied panic, he'd ripped the thing away and tossed it aside, only to remember a split second later the recent public advisory that warned sudden removal could cause fatal neural shocks. If the user was lucky. Reports of less-fortunate victims essentially getting lobotomized by improper deactivation have started to circulate recently as well.

"I saw Mommy..."

"Mr. Le?"

"Uh, yes, I...I mean no! I...no, I don't. She..." Mr. Le suddenly remembers Kiva, that strange animal that stalks the nearby streets every night. "She said something about a cat..." The paramedic raises an eyebrow. "I-I don't know! I-I'm sorry, I just..."

"Was she left alone prior to obtaining these devices?" Mr. Le opens his mouth to speak. His jaw hangs open as his voice fails him. Yet again, he just nods.

"Understood. Again, with regards to your daughter obtaining these machines, you're certain you've no idea how?"

"Yes!" Mr. Le snaps. He immediately regrets his failure to stifle his distress.

"Very good. That should be everything I need."

"Will she be alright?"

"Well, by some near miracle the abrupt removal of the device didn't cause extensive damage. But for the time being she appears catatonic. We can't say how long that's going to last."

"What happens now?"

15

"The police will approach shortly to take a statement. In all likelihood you'll retain custody of Fila for the time being. However, given the frequency and severity of recent incidents involving your daughter, that's likely to be on a probationary basis. Sergeant Neda will tell you more. Anything else?"

"No. Thank you." Mr. Le answers. The paramedic walks back towards Fila, asking questions to the EMTs taking vitals.

The Sergeant's questioning passes by quickly. She's no more impressed with Mr. Le's fathering than the medical team. Much of Mr. Le's statement is devoted to answering her questions surrounding Clain. Her glare seems to intensify with his every response.

"You're claiming he displayed no violent or even concerning tendencies prior to your evicting him?"

"Not exactly, he wasn't always the most responsible I suppose but he was a good man."

"Was this the man your daughter was with when she lost her arm?"

Mr. Le's face falls as he answers.

"Yes," he pinches the bridge of his nose as he stifles a defeated sigh. "He was, but..."

Sergeant Neda looks back over her shoulder at the massive hole in the ceiling left by Clain's colossal blade, the Motherboard.

"Did you evict him after your daughter was injured?" she asks.

"Almost, yes."

"So, no?"

Mr. Le swallows.

"Correct," he replies.

"And he was also responsible for the damage to your ceiling?"

"Yes."

"Was he evicted at any point prior to the incident that caused the damage?"

"No. He was evicted because of it."

"Can you describe the incident, please?"

Again, Mr. Le obliges, and again he can feel his claim to fatherhood weakening in the eyes of the local authorities.

"Alright, that's everything Mr. Le. Before you ask: Your daughter is going to be questioned separately if and when she recovers. You're not to speak to her or communicate with her in any capacity until we do. If you violate this order, custody will be revoked immediately. If we're satisfied with her answers, you'll be assigned a social worker to monitor your case until they deem it safe to end your probation. If she never recovers, then I suppose the point is moot. Do you understand?"

Mr. Le keeps his expression composed, trying to stifle the volcanic rush of justifications, clarifications, and context trying to erupt from his mind. He knows it will only make things worse. He can hardly believe what's happened these past few weeks himself.

"I do. Thank you, officer."

The Sergeant walks away without so much as a nod. Mr. Le watches Fila as she's wheeled away to the ambulance. Each of her pained whimpers is like an ice pick to his eardrums.

~~~

Mr. Le rests his head against the trunk of his flame tree. The dense clusters of heavy branches and bright, red-orange leaves cast a near-perfect blanket of shade, allowing only the thinnest streaks of the rising sun through. From his vantage point atop what remains of his roof, Mr. Le can see the police barricades and checkpoints that have been in place for the last week. Ever since he called them. Door-to-door raids have been a regular occurrence for at least the last two days, and the searches have, unfortunately, been entirely founded more than once. He saw two take place just today. Both times, the tactical officers emerged with duffle bags full of the accursed things and the

17

drooling husks of their users on stretchers. Whoever is distributing FreqyD, they're making absolutely certain that it's reaching all of the most vulnerable populations in New Beam. Addiction to it has reached epidemic levels, and at the rate the problem is worsening, it's poised to spread to other major cities alarmingly soon.

Fila's catatonia was mercifully short, but the barrage of questions from police, doctors, and social workers was almost more torturous. His little girl was isolated in her hospital bed for days. She was barely 12 hours out of her ravaged mental state when the first ones showed up and started asking questions. Of course, not one of them explained why she couldn't see her father. If they had revealed what exactly it was they were asking about, they would have risked biasing her answers in his favor, and leaving her in the custody of what they could only conclude based on her missing arm and reckless use of illegal brain-altering technology must be a dangerously irresponsible father who isn't even possessed of the means to fix his own place of business.

Can you tell us how you lost your arm?

Where did you find those devices?

What made you decide to try them?

Are there more?

Did your father give them to you?

Can you tell us a little bit about Clain?

Each and every question Fila has been asked – at least those she's told him about since returning home – is on loop within Mr. Le's mind. The last two have been playing especially loudly. They're easily the most decisive blows to any argument in favor of his fathering. The latter could only have led to a string of answers about the events that led to Fila's hospitalization. None of which would have made him look good. The former? If they're even asking it, that tells him everything about what they think of him. Their assigned social worker has already made her first visit. It's likely probation is going to last quite some time.

Mr. Le attempts to meditate in the warmth of the rising sun, trying to restore some semblance of calm so that he's properly

18

prepared for the next inspection, but the soft crunch of gravel intrudes on his practiced tranquility. With an exasperated sigh, he looks towards the source of the noise. His eyes land on the gravel, and he follows a trail of tiny indentations to the edge of the roof. There sits Kiva, Fila's favorite stray cat. The obsidian black feline gently waves its tail, staring right at him. He's about to get up and shoo the animal away when a soft voice rings out from behind him.

Mr. Le's attention is immediately drawn away from Kiva. Behind him stands his daughter, wrapped in a thick quilt. He turns to face her.

"Fila! You're up awfully early. Are you ok? Do you need something?"

"I'm ok," Fila replies with a yawn. Her stomach grumbles as if to disagree with her statement. Mr. Le smiles.

"Hungry?" he asks.

"Yeah," Fila chuckles shyly.

"Alright, let's get you something to eat," Mr. Le says, pushing on one of his knees to get to his feet. His back cracks and pops as he stands. He winces as a nerve in one of his hips pinches. "Ah!" he hisses.

"What's wrong, Daddy?"

"Oh nothing. Just a chance for me to remind you that sitting on concrete for three hours is a bad idea," he grumbles, rubbing his calf to work out a Charlie horse.

The pair nears the bottom of the rooftop staircase and Mr. Le opens the door to the dining room. A sparrow is perched on the bottom step. It cocks its head and flies away as they near it. Right up through the giant hole in the ceiling. Fila laughs and watches it fly away. Mr. Le. Pinches the bridge of his nose, more concerned with any droppings it might have left behind on the steps.

"You're not gonna look, Daddy?" Fila asks. Mr. Le smiles gently and obliges, seeing it fade into the purple and orange clouds.

It would almost be beautiful if I wasn't watching through where my roof used to be…

He turns back towards the dining room, taking Fila's hand. Paths are carved through piles of carefully shifted rubble, allowing the two to move about the space, albeit with some difficulty. It's been long enough since Clain's sword wrecked the Pho King that Mr. Le and Fila have gotten used to walking the narrow paths blazed through the trail of destruction.

*Not something one should ever have to get used to…*Mr. Le laments.

A carefully folded letter still sits in there. It's a promise from his neighbors. When they heard about what had happened to Fila, they'd gotten together to send their sympathy and promise to help him rebuild. Mr. Le read the letter three times before the words sank in. It was the first time he'd smiled or cried in weeks. He's still holding onto hope that one day they'll be able to make good on the promise. He's met enough of his neighbors to know that at least a few of them aren't the sort to go back on their word. But citywide lockdowns, constant raids, and a widespread new addictive craze are hardly conducive to local solidarity. He goes over the letter in his mind. He can still see the signatures. Still remember the names. His thoughts turn to the recent busts in the neighborhood

I hope none of them were involved…

The two work their way through the wreckage to Fila's favorite booth. It sits near the front door and overlooks the sidewalk and street out front. She used to draw on it with crayons and markers, much to her dad's dismay. She'd insist the haphazard scribbles were Vietnamese lotuses and she wanted to make the tables prettier. Eventually Mr. Le had gotten the real things carved into the corners of this particular table as a birthday present. It's been *her* booth ever since. Mr. Le walks to the kitchen that has miraculously escaped the surrounding devastation. He returns with two big plates of spring rolls and peanut sauce. Fila's favorite. Considering the week Fila had, Mr. Le finds himself forced to acknowledge she's probably earned the right to demand them whenever she wants for the rest of the year.

I'll just have to hope for the sake of her health she doesn't suddenly become an expert negotiator, thinks Mr. Le.

The two enjoy their meal in silence for a few minutes before Mr. Le finally tries to start a long overdue conversation. He slides his plate aside and places his hands on the table, folding them thoughtfully. Fila immediately gives him her undivided attention when she sees the gesture. Mr. Le smiles.

"Fila…" he begins. "I am truly sorry that I had to send Clain away."

"I know, dad," Fila replies.

"Well, I hope one day you can understand why. Please know it wasn't an easy decision."

"I think I do understand, Daddy."

"You do?"

"I was spending all this time being mad at you. But I never thought about how you just want to protect me…" she says, hanging her head. Mr. Le's brows rise in disbelief. "Those officers were so mean! I couldn't believe they asked me if you were a good dad. And then I had to think about why they would even ask that…." She tears up. "And then I realized this was all my fault! You kept trying to tell me to think before I did anything. And I didn't! And I caused this because I didn't listen!" The tears turn to sobs. "I should have never run into that alley that night. And then I snuck out because I was worried about Clain…" she pauses. "The city is such a scary place, Dad. I hate it."

"Part of growing up is learning to think before you act." Mr. Le manages a smile. "It's a lesson I always knew you'd have to learn. One I knew that, at least in part, you'd have to learn on your own. But I never wanted you to come to understand it the way you've been forced to. No child should have to suffer what you've had to. Ever." He looks at Fila's artificial arm. "But the bravery you've demonstrated in the face of it all is more than I could ever muster. And I'm so proud of you and who you are. Never forget that. I've been remiss in reminding you of that. And I'm going to try and do better, too, Fila. You deserve to know what a wonderful daughter you are, and you deserve to hear it from me."

Fila grins.

"You always know how to make me feel better, dad."

Mr. Le smiles, swallowing the rock in his throat as he tries to determine how to ask the question burning in his mind.

Do I just ask her about FreqyD? About what she saw? No. I can't ask her to relive that.

Eventually he decides now isn't the time.

Best to give her a few days. She's lived through enough for now.

He puts on his best fatherly smile, focusing all his attention on how grateful he is that Fila is even alive and conscious. The two enjoy their food in companionable silence for a while before Fila finally pipes up.

"Hey, Dad?" she asks.

"Yes?"

"None of that was real, right?"

"None of what?" Mr. Le asks, dreading her answer.

"What…what I saw? You know, when I was using the…" she trails off.

"I understand," Mr. Le interrupts. His thoughts return to that dreadful day.

I saw Mommy….

"Yeah," Fila continues. "Like…Clain was there. And he was falling. There was a yellow bunny for some reason and…and Mommy was holding my hand." Fila's speech becomes more pressed as she recalls her grim vision. "He was fighting this weird robot guy and he looked hurt and he was throwing metal stuff around like he had superpowers or magnet hands or something, and then Mommy squeezed my hand and she looked so sad and when I looked back…I think I saw him die, Dad! I saw Mommy and I watched Clain die and I don't know what to think anymore!"

Mr. Le rushes to Fila and hugs her as she starts to cry.

"It's alright Fila. It's over. And I'm here. You know that I wish every bit as much as you Mommy was still with us. And I'm so sorry she isn't."

"She was right there, dad. It was like it was real and I can't stop thinking about it!"

"Anyone would feel the same after what you saw. But no, it wasn't real, and I'm certain that, at the very least, Clain is absolutely alright."

Fila's distress eases just a little.

"You really think so?" she asks. Mr. Le wipes her tears away.

"Do you remember when I sparred with him?"

"Yeah."

"Do you remember how tough he was? How well he held his own?"

"Yeah."

"Well. I can tell you for certain that, even as impressive as he was that day, he was holding back. Far more than I care to admit."

Fila's eyes go wide.

"Really?"

Mr. Le nods.

"I think if he'd wanted to, he could easily have hurt me. Badly. Maybe even killed me if he weren't being so careful."

"But he didn't. You beat him. I saw it!"

"My point exactly. Do you remember when you snuck out to see him fight in that tournament?"

Fila nervously shifts in her seat.

"Yeah…" she reluctantly answers. Mr. Le holds up a reassuring hand.

"No need to worry. I'm not asking because you're in any kind of trouble. You've had quite enough of that this past week. I'm asking you to remember what you saw of him that day. Did he fight the same way as he did with me?"

Fila looks down and scrunches her brow, summoning the memories as vividly as she can. Eventually, the creases in her forehead relax and she looks up, the answer written on her disbelieving face.

"No," she whispers, awe carrying on her voice. "He didn't."

"I thought so," Mr. Le replies. "So that would mean?"

"He was holding back. He's even stronger."

Mr. Le nods.

"So, we know two things: He's a strong man. And he's a good man, right? If anyone can survive out there amidst all this, it's him."

Fila sniffles, but she smiles a little.

"I guess I just hate to think of him out there all alone," she says. "I hope I can see him again someday." Mr. Le lovingly clasps her shoulder.

"Well, we'll just have to make sure we keep doing our best right here. We'll stay careful, stay smart, and stay hopeful. If we do that, we just might get that chance. Can you do that for me?" Fila smiles and nods. "Good girl. How about some tea?"

"Yeah!" Fila says. Mr. Le stands up and quickly returns with a steaming kettle, two bags of tea leaves, and an ornate pair of porcelain teacups and saucers reserved just for those times he shares tea with his daughter. Fila eagerly grips her cup with both hands as her dad pours the hot water. She giggles as steam rises from the cup.

"What's so funny?" asks Mr. Le.

"It's just kinda funny how I still grip the cup with both hands when I can only feel warmth in one," she explains. "Is that how life is, Daddy?"

"What do you mean?"

"Is life just getting older and forgetting how to feel?"

Mr. Le freezes when he hears the question, forgetting that he's pouring boiling water until Fila yelps in pain.

"Ouch! Dad, that burns! You overfilled it!"

"Oh! Oh no I'm so sorry!" he exclaims. He turns and runs to the kitchen. "I'll get a towel and an ice pack."

Mr. Le reaches the freezer just as Fila calls out to him.

"Uh…Dad?"

"Yes, sweetheart?"

"Is the table broken? Like, leaning or something?"

"I don't believe so. Why?"

"Well…my cup is moving."

Mr. Le scowls, uncertain he's heard her correctly. He starts back. "I'm sorry. Did you say your cup is…" He stops in his tracks as Fila comes into view. She's watching her cup and saucer intently, unease plain across her features. It is, indeed, moving to her right. Towards the edge. On its own. She looks up at him when she hears his footsteps. Only then does Mr. Le realize the ground has started to rumble. Fila grips her teacup, holding it in place right as it nears the edge of the table.

Mr. Le looks towards the window. It too has started to vibrate. It's not a constant movement. The vibrations pulse. Then stop. Then pulse again. And they're getting louder, longer, and angrier each time they do.

"Fila," he says. "Stay here. I'm going to go see what this-"

"Dad! No!"

"Please just listen to me, Fila."

"Dad, you just said to think ahead before you make a decision. So you rushing out there would be no different than if I did!" she shouts.

Mr. Le stops partway to the front door. He looks back over his shoulder, then turns back around and rejoins Fila at the booth. As the quakes intensify, he finds himself glad he's done so.

"You're right, Fila," he admits. "Let's just stay hidden for now." The pair crawl under the table, hiding themselves underneath the large front window and angling themselves so that they can look up and out of it while staying minimally visible.

The earth-shaking thuds continue, one after another, louder and louder.

"Are those footsteps?" Fila asks. Mr. Le shakes his head.

"I can't imagine," he says. "If they are, whatever's walking this way would have to be the size of a kaiju."

Fila just gulps. Mr. Le follows suit. The two stay deathly quiet.

The ground stops shaking. The crunch of metal rings out from somewhere that sounds like it's only blocks away. A faint scream echoes down the street.

And the compacted remains of an armored police tank bot come sailing through the air, right towards the window.

"Move!" Mr. Le yells, grabbing Fila and diving away from the glass. Arcs of electricity emanate from the wreck as it impacts the ground. One of the high-explosive shells wedged in its cannon detonates. Screams reverberate from the police barricades as shrapnel ravages the area. The wave of air pressure from the blast cracks the front windows of the Pho King.

An ear-splitting screech rings out as the crumpled vehicle grinds to a halt with a shower of sparks, stopping just short of the front wall of the dining room.

The rumbling resumes, and a towering, bipedal monster stomps its way into the intersection.

God help us all if it actually was footsteps, Mr. Le realizes.

Fila is flat on her back. As she starts to sit back up, her eyes suddenly go wide and she starts to scream. Mr. Le lunges toward her and wraps a hand over her mouth and places a finger over his lips.

"Don't scream, Fila," he warns. "We have to stay hidden."

"But Dad!" Fila whispers. "Don't you see it?"

"I can't make out more than a silhouette through the fog, honey."

Fila's jaw trembles as she struggles to speak.

"Dad…" she finally manages, her eyes glued to the scene outside. "It's Hux!"

~~~

Mitt does his best to suppress his sheepishness as Zaria looks at him with wide, indignant eyes. He's only recently reunited with his old friend. Zaria. An ex-combat medic and just the person to bail him out of trouble. Or so he hopes. Right now, she looks like she'd rather ditch him. Given the danger involved in fulfilling his request, he can't really blame her.

"Mitt, what the hell?! You can't be serious! We're surrounded by police drones and you want me to go pick up some random crap?!" Zaria shouts. The drones swarm overhead, seemingly oblivious to their presence. She's holding an electronic device in her hand and watching the battery indicator intently.

"These Faraday fields last five minutes, tops! If we waste time, those drones are gonna know we're here!"

"Zaria, we might need it! I saw him using it to fight that android!" Mitt gestures to a lifeless Clain, laying motionless in a pool of his own blood in the middle of a rain drenched street.

"If anyone comes after him, he'll be defenseless! Here, it's not far!" Mitt insists. He flies his camera drone away from Zaria's vehicle, a small urban cargo hauler she's borrowed from Mitt. Her eyes narrow. She looks increasingly annoyed as she watches the distance counter in the lower right of the drone's camera feed keep ticking up. Finally, the object he's looking for comes into view. It's the hilt section of Clain's sword. It looks far worse for wear, missing the much larger parts of its upper half which were shattered all over the street. "Here!" Mitt shouts. "This thing here!"

Zaria looks back at Clain. One of his arms is mangled, and he's bruised all over. She looks up at the drones. Then at the pool of blood on the concrete where Clain hit the ground just minutes ago. It seems to be sparkling and almost glowing, but she passed it off as an oddity within the neon lights shining down around her as sunlight was just creeping through the dark clouds above. She struggles to load his body onto the cart, her eyes fixating on the immense wounds and shattered bones protruding from his right arm. His body seemed to sizzle with steam as she flops him onto the bed of the cart.

"He's bad, Mitt. Even if we grab that thing, he could die if we take too long."

"Please just trust me, Zaria. This thing is important to him. I know it."

"Fine. But if the field goes down before we're home I'm throwing you out here as a bullet sponge!" Zaria floors the gas.

"Love you too, Zar," Mitt retorts.

It doesn't take long for the pair to reach Clain's discarded weapon. Shortcuts through a local all-glass storefront or two shave crucial seconds off the trip. Even then the battery indicator on the field projector is just shy of turning red. Far more worrisome is how long it takes to load the thing.

"What the fuck is this thing made of?! It's heavy as shit!" Zaria grunts.

"Just keep pushing! We got this!" Mitt encourages. The low battery warning sounds just as the broken sword is finally tossed into the cargo bay.

The two rush to their seats. Mitt has barely buckled his seat belt when Zaria once again guns the engine, speeding back to their hideout.

"How long do we have?" Mitt asks, eyeing the field projector.

"Two minutes. Maybe." Zaria responds, her expression grim and her eyes dead set on the road in front of them.

"Hold on," Mitt says. He pilots his drone into the swarm of police bots and presses a red button on the remote control. A blue pulse emanates from it as it explodes. All the police drones fall to the ground, sparking and smoking as their circuitry melts.

"You could've done that the whole time?!" Zaria asks.

"Well yeah, but, you know…" Mitt replies, rubbing the back of his neck.

"I know what?" Zaria prods. Mitt shrugs with a nervous grin.

"I liked that drone."

~~~

A few days have passed since the rescue, and Zaria has done her best to nurse Clain back to health. However, Mitt's insistence on taking in such a bizarre stranger is testing her patience. He's refused to allow Clain to be admitted to a hospital; he's deemed the possibility of an obvious digital footprint too risky for their operation. So, Zaria has had to use her knowledge to care for Clain's more severe injuries. Oddly, Clain's eyes have remained wide open even as he's lain comatose this entire time. Odder still, an X-Ray scan run by one of Mitt's service bots has revealed that Clain's shattered arm was already beginning to heal, albeit incorrectly.

Mitt excitedly rambles on about how he had heard of people with accelerated healing and insisted Clain might be one of them as an attempt to convince Zaria into helping him break Clain's bones again to align them correctly. It is not an experience either wishes to repeat. Watching Clain's utterly unchanging dead-eyed expression as sickening cracking, splintering, and squishing sounds reverberate through their makeshift infirmary is singularly disturbing. Whoever this man is, he seems to be, at least sometimes, completely impervious to pain.

And possibly the vilest sounds ever made by a human skeleton, Zaria thinks. Her combat medic experience is all that's keeping her from sharing the trash can Mitt is currently using as a vomit receptacle.

"Alright, he's been tended to for the day," Zaria flops into one of Mitt's swivel chairs, heaving an exhausted sigh. "Got sick of looking at his blank stare, so I taped his eyes shut," she snickers.

"Seriously? That's pretty messed up." Mitt shakes his head.

"Dude, I have used three bottles of eye drops now in just a few days. Although last I checked, you don't have an abundance of those here in the bunker," Zaria shoots back.

"Yeah, I guess that's a good point," Mitt nods. He turns back toward his console.

"What's up today? Anything new?" Zaria asks.

"Nah. I have one lead I'd like to look into, but it seems like a dead end."

"Oh, yea? A lead for what?"

"Possible source of FreqyD, but it doesn't add up… plus doesn't seem worth the risk."

"Why not?"

"It's in a hazardous neighborhood on the city's east side. It doesn't make sense geographically."

"The east side? Yea, screw that noise. Who would be crazy enough to even go there?" she scoffs, sidestepping toward the city map pinned to the nearby wall. Mitt smirks.

"I can think of a few people."

"What? Me?!" Zaria scoffs. "I'm crazy, but not that crazy."

"Well, if you're going to stay here, you'll have to help out," Mitt admonishes, waving his finger like a dad straight out of the 1950s. She laughs.

"I don't know who you think I am, but I can assure you I am not nearly as cool as you're assuming I am."

"Ex-infantry medic with advanced energy shield training? Seems pretty useful!"

"Yea, but that was all just training. I've never seen any actual combat, and I am certainly not some badass vigilante prowling the streets in search of evildoers." She drags out the last word with a dramatic flourish.

"Well, you sure looked like you knew what you were doing when you rescued Clain."

"That was all spur of the moment," she insists, waving her hand to silence him. "I'm not going out there to investigate your hunches. Especially when you said it was a dead end anyway."

"I said probably," Mitt reiterates. "We won't know unless we check."

"Send one of your bots over there," she suggests. "Those are more expendable than my life, ya know?"

"I already did," he admits.

"You did? And what happened?"

"I'm not sure. The first one stopped transmitting for a while and then just kept sending dead battery alerts. I sent a second to retrieve it and that one just vanished completely."

"So your next best idea is to send your childhood best friend over there alone?" Zaria smacks the back of Mitt's head, sending his beanie flying forward onto his keyboard.

"Hey! That hurt! You don't have to be an asshole, Zaria. Sheesh." Mitt complains, putting his beanie back on as he glares daggers at his friend. He stands up and walks to the kitchen. "Seriously though, I do need your help around here. Unless you want to beg your dad to crash on his couch again?"

"Oh, so what you're telling me is risking my life for some random stranger you claim is super important with zero explanation, all during an "arrest on sight" lockdown, then nursing him back to health isn't enough for you?" She motions her hand like a box, as if to frame her point. "When you put it that way it makes my dad's couch seem downright appealing. At least there I can get away with just doing the dishes. I thought we were friends, Mitt."

Mitt hangs his head and sighs.

"Dammit. You're right. It's a shitty suggestion. We are friends. I promise. Not an excuse or anything, but this whole 'imminent career collapse' as a guerilla journalist is getting troublesome. Nothing newsworthy is fucking happening' and this whole situation has had me on edge for weeks. Tracking down the distributors of FreqyD might be the only thing that keeps me afloat, you know?"

"I do, Mitt. I am entirely aware of how your world works. But you've gotta give me time to adjust. I got home just a few weeks ago, saw you for the first time in years, and then the city went to shit and now I'm stuck in a bunker with you. I missed you and everything, but…not exactly the reunion I was hoping for."

"Yea… it really sucks." Mitt sighs. "Keep an eye on the drones while I cook us something to eat. You remember how, right?"

Zaria rubs her hands together and plops down into his chair, eagerly tapping commands into the console.

"Oh yea! Now this I can do!"

Mitt rolls his eyes.

"Don't touch anything but the drones. I mean it!"

"Yea, yea. You worry too much," she jests, already absorbed in scrolling through his camera feeds throughout the city.

~~~

Clain lays on the bottom of a bunk bed in one of the side rooms. Snuggled firmly within blankets, a small computer monitor displays his vitals. His mind keeps replaying the last few minutes of his fight against Synric. His fingers twitch as his body reintroduces itself to his brain. Flashes of him tumbling down the side of a building, noticing his reflection in the glass panes of a skyscraper. He's in a different realm, away from this earth, among an army of terrifying beings, including Tia, the multi-faced monster holding hands with some warped approximation of Fila. A female voice calls out, jolting Clain awake.

"Mitt!"

He springs into an upright position, smacking his head into the bunk boards above. He realizes that he can't see and his hands fly to his face, searching for the cause. After a few seconds, his frantic, scrambling movements calm as he finds the tape keeping his eyes shut. He removes the strips, rolling them into balls and flicking them aside with a grimace. As he gets his bearings and his vision clears, he realizes his right arm can't be moved, securely nestled within a sling that was tied firmly onto his torso. His throat is dry. He feels nauseous, and the world spins like a tumble dryer when he moves his head. He groans, struggling to vocalize through parched cords. "Mitt?" he mutters. He vaguely remembers asking the man for help, but the rest of the last twenty-four hours is still a concussed haze.

"Mitt, get in here!" the female voice shouts again.

"What? Did you find something?!" A familiar voice yells back. Mitt. Clain struggles to come to, the fog finally clearing when he hears the woman shout: "You won't believe this shit! A giant pig robot is attacking a noodle shop!"

CHAPTER 2 - When It All Crumbles Down

Clain struggles to sit up within the cramped bunk bed. He's still dizzy, and the pain in his arm scolds him as he scoots to the edge, allowing his feet to flop onto the cool ground. He rubs his head as a calm glow illuminates the floor beneath him. An automated lighting system helps his eyes focus, clearing his head within a flurry of blinks. Faint, muddled voices murmur outside the room.

The walls are bare. Only a tiny dresser sits nearby. A doorway in the corner of the space opens into a dark room. A bathroom, perhaps. As Clain turns to get a better look, he feels a pinch in his wrist. He looks down, seeing an IV taped firmly in place, connected to a bag of fluids hanging from the upper bunk bed. He tears the tape away, removes the needle, and braces his arm beneath the sling on his right. Slowly, he pushes pressure onto his feet, the cool floor seeming to grow colder as he struggles to stand. His injured arm throbs intensely, the rush of blood seeming to scream at him to lie back down. He falls to a knee and grits his teeth as his head pounds with each thud of his heart. His muscles tense as he braces for another wave of pain. It never comes.

His eyes dart open as he breathes in deeply.

What was that? he wonders. Slowly, he stands up. His muscles are still tight, and his arm still sore, but the agony he felt moments ago has vanished. He looks at his broken arm and attempts to move his fingers. Only his pinky responds. Barely. He limps toward the door nearest the bunk bed, leaning into it with his shoulder. He presses his ear to the door, doing his best to listen, but the voices have gone silent.

He places his hand on the small lever to unlatch the door and tries to push it forward. It takes multiple attempts for his tired brain to realize that this door doesn't swing open. It slides. He does his best to open it quietly, wincing as he trips the motion sensors on the hallway lights. Lucky for Clain, no one seems to notice. He shields his eyes as the brighter light assaults his dilated pupils. A draft wafts across his ankles from the hallway. He shivers and looks down, realizing he was only in his underwear. He reaches back toward the bed, retrieving a small throw blanket and draping it over his shoulders. He shuffles gingerly down the hall as silently as he can. His muscles and bones vehemently protest any sudden movements. The comforting glow of computer screens immediately grabs his attention. He stops once he notices shadows dancing across the opposite wall, accompanied by a female voice.

"What do you think they're talking about?" she asks.

"I don't know, but it doesn't look good," a familiar male voice responds. He moves closer to the end of the corridor, kneeling to keep himself hidden as he eavesdrops on their conversation.

"Don't you have long-range mics on these drones?"

"Not this model. Of course," Mitt grumbles. Clain can practically hear Mitt rolling his eyes. "And the closest drone that does is halfway across the city."

"Well shit Mitt, fly in closer!" she demands.

So, this is *Mitt's studio* Clain realizes.

He peers around the edge towards the two staring at the screen. He couldn't help but notice Zaria's attractive figure, leaning energetically over the console in a pair of rather short shorts. Appearing maybe five foot eight with deep auburn red, curly hair. His eyes then glance toward the camera feed she was smitten with as half of the feed is displaying a small building. He isn't quite able to make it out, but he's almost certain he recognizes the neighborhood. The other half isn't visible from his position. He edges forward slightly, squinting to try and make out the image on the screen. The camera angle shifts and a familiar cherry blossom tree comes into view on the roof.

Pho King?! Why are they filming that?

He leans even more, struggling to coax the rest of the screens into view. He succeeds just in time to see a colossal metal foot stomp

35

into the frame. It's supporting a 100-foot-tall mech. And it's looking right at the Pho King. Any concern for staying hidden evaporates, and Clain stumbles into the room.

"What the hell is this?!" he shouts, his voice raspy and hard to understand.

Mitt tumbles out of his chair. Zaria's head whips around as she assumes a combat stance, fumbling for a nearby handgun just out of her reach.

"Zaria, don't!" Mitt shouts, scrambling to his feet and standing in Zaria's line of fire. He holds up a placating hand to both of them. "It's cool, Clain. You just spooked us. Put the gun down, Zaria. I told you what this guy can do, remember? Shooting him would most likely not do anything." Reluctantly, Zaria lowers the gun with a grin.

"Jesus! Don't sneak up on me like that!" Zaria scolds. "I could've shot you!"

Mitt shoots Zaria a glare, then turns back to Clain.

"Sorry about that, man. How are you even up right now? It seemed like you'd broken pretty much every bone in your body when we found you."

"I'm fine," he says. His tone is clipped. He waves his hand at the monitors. "You gonna tell me what the fuck is going on there?!"

"Oh, uh, this. We found this while cycling through the feeds from my drones." Mitt explains.

"This is a live feed?" Clain asks.

"Yes."

"What is that thing there?" he asks, moving closer to the console and pointing toward the giant robot.

"We don't know, but they seem to be conversing."

"They?"

"Yea, look closely down there on the rooftop." Mitt adjusts the console to focus on the roof. Clain's eyes widen, seeing Mr. Le trying to hold back a tempered Fila who is shouting at the mech.

"Move in closer!" Clain demands.

"Dude, I can't! If I do, that thing will for sure detect us."

"You don't know that! Now move in closer!" Clain slams his fist on the console, glaring at Mitt.

Mitt lifts his hands.

"Woah dude, ok." Mitt stands up from his chair and gestures to it, inviting Clain to sit down. "How about you pilot it yourself for a bit? You can try and take it in closer." Clain glances across Mitt's console and notices a manual control option. His hand wraps around the joystick on the armrest and he pushes it forward. The drone moves inward with a bit of jank from Clain's untrained hand.

Mitt slides up next to Clain, glancing at him, then to the video feed, then back at him, eyes wide and brow furrowed.

"Dude, you've got to fly it smoothly," Mitt comments.

"Yea," Clain replies, his attention mostly on the drone.

"This isn't a simple thing to control. And it's custom made. Nobody else has one."

"Custom made by me. You ordered it from *my* shop."

"*Your* shop?"

"Yup. GG Shop."

Mitt just stares, struggling for words.

"I've ordered from GG like, a lot."

"Yeah. You're a good customer. Thanks"

"So you know all my systems?"

"Pretty much. That's the problem with online orders. Never know who you're ordering from. This one doesn't have a speaker, right? I made you a few, but it was a while ago. Can't remember all the features on each."

"No, unfortunately. Just a camera. We can't say anything to them. But…"

"That better be a 'but I have a solution' kind of 'but.' No time for bullshit."

"But there is a mic. So you should be able to hear them if you can get close enough."

Clain speeds up the drone and flies downward and around the side of a building, trying to keep it concealed. The Pho King is on an empty, exposed street making it difficult to be very discreet. He zips it up to the top of the closest building as the upper half of the mech finally comes into view.

"Holy shit!" Zaria screams. "That's… that's…". She fumbles with her words. "I know him!" She aggressively points at the black-haired man sitting atop the robot.

"Who is it?" Clain asks.

"He was pretty famous in the ranks. um..."

"What ranks?"

Mitt interjects.

"She was in the military. Was he a high-ranking officer, Zaria? Is that what you're trying to say?"

"Not exactly. But he was practically a celebrity in the military when I was serving. General Kruger. About twenty years ago he designed some of the most vicious tanks the army's ever used. Like "too brutal for the public" kind of stuff. He and his whole squad were dishonorably discharged when it got out they were keeping secrets. Apparently, he had a whole set of designs that were so nasty they were just short of humanitarian war crimes on treads. I never knew what happened to them."

38

"What the hell is someone like that doing here?" Clain asks. He moves the drone in closer. Kruger sits atop a rusted throne with a set of glowing controls at his fingertips, flanked on either side by a complicated lever system. Beneath him is a container with a thick glass window, but they can't see what's inside. Clain switches the engine to low power, hoping to silence it enough to stay hidden.

"How far away are we from here?" Clain asks.

"Like geographically?" Mitt asks.

"Yeah."

"Oh, man. Miles."

Clain sets the drone to standby. It floats in place in a nearby alleyway, a periscope camera extended just high enough above the dumpster it's using for cover to continue to monitor the situation. He turns to an adjacent monitor, pulling up Mitt's GPS display. The Pho King is an estimated three miles away.

 "Shit," he bites out, turning to Mitt. "You have to get me over there. Now."

"What? Are you crazy, dude? You can barely stand."

"Just get me over there!" Clain snarls, shooting to his feet and towering over Mitt.

"Wait, listen!" Zaria shouts. "I hear something."

Their eyes snap back to the screen as Mitt raises the volume.

Kruger's raspy voice vibrates through the speakers.

"Seriously, little girl... what are you looking at?"

Clain zooms in to get a better look at Kruger's target.

"Fila. Don't blow out cover. Please." he murmurs under his breath, realizing she had spotted their drone spectating them.

"No, nothing! It's nothing!" she pleads. But it's too late. Kruger Follows her gaze, eyeing the area until finally spotting the eavesdropping drone.

"Well, well, well, who might that be?" He cocks his head with sinister curiosity. His mech lumbers towards the drone.

Clain's eyes widen as Kruger steps out of the fog, his walking tank coming into full view.

"What the fuck!" he exclaims, having never seen such a horrific monstrosity.

"What? What's wrong?!" Mitt asks.

"Hu... Hux!" Clain stammers. "How? How is that even possible?!"

"You talking about that demonic-lookin' pig head in the glass orb?" Zaria asks. "That's probably just some sick decoration."

Hux's head twitches as its mechanical eyes glow. Clain grimaces. "He didn't always look like that."

"You mean that was a person?" Mitt asks.

"Yea, one of his thugs. One that I saw die a while ago."

"Holy shit. The rumors were true!" Zaria exclaims.

"What rumors?"

"Remember those blueprints I mentioned? The next generation of tanks he was designing were human-machine hybrids. He was rigging up ways to integrate human brains into machines."

"Hey!" Kruger shouts toward the drone. "You gonna stop ignoring me anytime soon?!" He stomps the mech's foot, tipping the dumpster over and sending cracks through the asphalt. Silence follows, hanging over the scene as thick as the fog.

"Guess that's a no, huh? Good. Fuck it." He points toward the drone. "Take care of it Hux."

A rumbling cannon shot follows Kruger's order, and the feed goes dead. Clain turns back to Mitt, fists clenched and poised to strike.

"Take me there now!" Clain shouts. Looking at both of them frantically as his eyes swell with tears. "Or I can bust this place up and *then* you can take me there." he pleads desperately.

"Dude, the city is literally in lockdown." Clain shoves him to the side, barely resisting the urge to smack him. He looks to Zaria instead, grabbing her shoulder.

"Those people are my friends, and that freak is about to fucking murder them!"

"You... You know them?" she stutters. His grip trembling as a tear runs down his cheek.

"I *lived* with them. My shop was attached to that building! Now let's. Fucking. *Go*. Please!*"

"Mitt, we have to try and help," Zaria insists. She rushes to a nearby cabinet and retrieves a bag, tossing it over her shoulder.

"Look, Zar, I'd love to, but the streets are swarming with police drones and I'm really not in a position to blow any more of mine up to get past them! We go outside, we're dead!"

"When did you become such a pussy?" Zaria snaps.

Mitt's eyes narrow.

"Excuse me?" he goads.

"The Mitt I grew up with would never turn his back on people in need. Whoever the hell you are just sits holed up in here like a bitch, staring at screens all day." Zaria admonishes.

"Yeah, bravery will do me all sorts of good against a giant fuck off robot with a *mutant pig head on it!"* Mitt retorts angrily.

"What if that was me out there? You wouldn't do it to save me, Mitt?"

"I don't have time for this," Clain interrupts, storming into the hallway, clueless which direction to go.

"Wait, I'm going with you!" Zaria catches up with Clain, hoisting his arm around her shoulder to help him walk. "The garage is this way." She points toward a doorway further down the hall.

Mitt rolls his eyes, grabbing a nearby backpack.

"Fine, but I'm driving. And I'm *not* losing another drone. That's five now just this month! No drones, no living. No living, no hideout. No hideout and we're all fucked. Got it?"

Zaria just waves her hand dismissively.

"Whatever Mitt. Just drive the damn car and try not to bitch out at the first sign of trouble, yeah?" Zaria throws open the door to the garage, helping Clain inside the cargo hauler.

"Here," Zaria urges, pressing a small black bag to Clain's chest. "It's not much, but you need something in your stomach. Make sure to hydrate, too. You're no good to them if you're dried out and starving." She smiles warmly and grabs some clothes hanging to dry in the garage. "And put something on. Doubt you want to do this in your underwear," she winks.

"Ugh, I just washed those," Mitt complains. He scowls at Clain. "You owe me," he grumbles. "A lot."

"Uh, right. Thanks," Clain replies, trying to fit inside the cramped vehicle. He winces as he rests his splint on a small armrest. With the other hand, he rummages through the bag, retrieving a bottle of water. Mitt and Zaria enter the front seats, looking back to ensure he's secure.

"You ready?" Mitt asks Clain.

"Yea."

"Zaria, pull up the maps. I have an idea."

"What's that?"

"I'm betting the police are flocking to the place after that blast, which means we know where they're all going."

"Right, so they'll all be focused on Kruger. Good thinking!"

"I've been around this city long enough to know the best time to travel is when the police are distracted."

The garage door slides open, and Mitt floors the gas pedal.

"Next left!" Zaria shouts.

"Already?!"

"Yea, there's a whole pack of them that way. We'll have to take a wide detour. It looks like they're trying to form a perimeter, but it isn't in place yet. Kruger probably knows they're moving in, so we don't have much time."

"How much of a detour?" Clain asks.

"Maybe 45 seconds."

Suddenly an explosive shockwave rips down the street, shattering windows and leaving the fragments strewn across the street.

"What the hell was that!?" Mitt yells, doing his best to keep control of the vehicle.

"Smoke over there!" Zaria points toward the sky.

"Oh no." Clain moans. "Go faster. Now!"

"Dammit, I'm beginning to regret meeting you!" Mitt curses him before slamming the gas again.

"They're all moving away!" Zaria reveals.

"What do you mean?"

"Look!" she insists, showing them her screen. "The police are all leaving! Kruger's probably on the run. Or he scared the shit out of them. Either way they are leaving. Quick."

"But that explosion…" Clain begins.

"Don't jump to conclusions," Zaria warns. "We don't know what happened yet."

"One more turn," Mitt announces nervously as smoke clouds the windshield and a fire comes into view.

"No…" Clain gasps. The Pho King is in ruins. The beautiful flame tree that used to sit on its roof is burning to cinders.

"Let me out!" Clain screams as Mitt pulls to the curb.

Zaria rushes to help him, but he shoves her to the ground and scrambles toward the front of the devastated building.

"Fila! Mr. Le!" he screams. "Can you hear me?!" He stumbles, falling to his knees. His arm swells, firing off a sharp bolt of pain as reality sets in.

"No, no, no, no, this can't be happening," he shouts toward the sky. "Why!?" he yells at the top of his lungs. A purple aura radiates from him. His head pounds. A memory of another fire flashes through his mind. He can feel the heat from the fire in front of him and the fire in his mind all at once. Memories begin rushing by, one after another, each hitting harder than the last. He pounds the sidewalk with his bare fist. The concrete cracks and crumbles from the force of each strike. The skin on his knuckles is scraping off. Bloody imprints start to appear on the concrete, deeper, redder, more and more numerous. He notices neither his injuries, nor the fact that the impacts of his fists have spread to the nearby wall, sending webs of hairline fractures up its baseboards.

"Watch out!" Zaria screams, rushing to pull him back as the wall comes crashing down onto the street. Narrowly missing them both.

"Try to breathe, ok? I know this is hard, but you need to breathe homie."

Racked with shivers, Clain tries to remain calm as tears stream down his face.

"We have to search for them!" he demands.

"We will. Just breathe right now. Mitt, check the maps."

"Already on it! We're still good. No police are coming, but ambulances are close. We won't be alone for long."

"Help me up, please." Clain insists to Zaria, wiping his face on his hooded jacket. "I'll be fine; just get me up," he pleads.

"Take it slow."

Clain tries to look inside the restaurant, unable to see through the smoldering wreckage. More tears fall as he realizes nobody inside could have survived this. He moves further down the sidewalk.

"Help me open this!" he begs as he nears the entrance to his GG Shop.

"Do you want the paramedics to tend to you?" Mitt scoffs. Zaria smacks him in the chest.

"The hell, Mitt?!" she exclaims.

"What?! It's a serious question. They're gonna be here in maybe two minutes if we're lucky. You think they'll let someone in Clain's condition just walk away?"

"All my stuff is in there. I just need to look. And I want to grab my main drive."

"Like, hard drive?! The whole building is on fire!"

"The garage was reinforced like a bunker. This side of the building wasn't hit as hard, so my shop might be ok and they could be inside."

Mitt looks up, noticing the GG Shop sign hanging by a corner screw, swaying within the wind and embers.

"Fine, but only because I loved this shop." He rushes toward the door with Zaria. They both kneel to lift the door open as Clain clenches it with his bloodied hand.

"Is it locked?"

"No, the locks are lying over there." Clain points down the sidewalk at the smashed electronic deadbolt. Zaria tries to force the door open, to no avail.

"Well, then it's jammed," she sighs. Clain closes his eyes and focuses on his arm, doing his best to channel any of his power to help force the door open.

"Woah, did you suddenly get stronger?" Zaria blurts out toward Mitt.

"Nah, not me," Mitt replies through gritted teeth. "He can do that."

With a piercing screech, the garage door shrieks open.

"That's enough..." Clain says, panting. He approaches the halfway-open door as Zaria and Mitt fall onto their rears to gather their breath within the smoke-filled air.

"It won't take long," Clain assures them as he ducks inside the garage. Mitt looks inside the dimly lit shop, noticing it actually hasn't suffered any fire damage yet everything within was toppled over and a complete mess.

Huh…he was right, Mitt thinks. He shrugs.

"We might as well wait inside here," Zaria suggests. Mitt climbs to his feet and walks through the debris. Zaria slides in after him. Clain is rummaging in the back.

"Got it?" Mitt calls.

"It's not here," Clain replies.

"What? Really?"

"Someone must have taken it…" Clain growls. "It had my whole life on it!" Sirens are growing louder in the distance. Mitt glances towards the door then back to Clain and Zaria.

"Look, man, that sucks, but we need to go. I'll give you a new drive and whatever you need, but please, let's bounce."

"Wait, one more thing." Clain kicks aside some pieces of fallen ceiling. He squats, sliding his fingers under the hunk of cement. "Help me lift this," he urges Mitt. Mitt grabs the other side of the slab.

"Alright, but after this, we're leaving," he declares.

"Just a little more so I can see underneath," Clain grunts. He lowers his head to peer beneath. "Shit," he exhales, finding the healing tank King had left him now wrecked.

Clain' shoulders slump. "Alright... let's go," he sighs. The three rush back to the utility vehicle and speed around the corner, avoiding the ambulances by mere seconds.

"Back to my place then?" Mitt asks, looking in the rearview. Zaria nudges him to be quiet. Clain sinks down in the back, clenching his arm. Weeping deeply as the emotional pain of losing his friends has begun to sink in.

CHAPTER 3 - Washing The Blood Away

Honey finds herself staring down the barrel of a rifle, surrounded by automated turrets. She is moments away from losing her head when a bloody, gurgling cough from Dawn cries out. "Stand down! Lenny, please." He struggles, still propped onto the back of Honey's bike. His abdomen continues dripping blood off the side of the fender. The exertion of yelling weakens his grip, and he slides off the bike, crumpling into a heap on the dusty desert road.

Lenny shouts, recognizing the voice and the massive size of his Skip Hunter friend. He looks at Dawn momentarily before Honey snatches the rifle from Lenny's grip, knocks her forearms across his shin and drops him to his knees.

"Get up," she commands. Lenny shakes violently, raising his hands and struggling to climb to his feet.

"I'm going to make this real easy, ok, Lenny?" Honey explains with a deadly smirk. "You're going to help your friend Dawn here, and I'll help you by hanging onto your rifle, got it?" Sweat beads on Lenny's forehead as he nods. He starts turning towards Dawn but stops when Honey starts speaking again.

"One more thing." Honey lowers the rifle just a bit and nods towards the turrets above. "Could you be a pal and switch those off?" Lenny glares, but his expression immediately relaxes when Honey's finger twitches over the trigger.

"Sure," he obliges, tapping a few buttons on his wristband. The turrets power down with a low whine. He turns to the entrance wall and gestures towards the gate. "Stand aside, ok?" With a few more button presses, the gate opens and a utility cart wheels through it. He nods toward Dawn's wound. His eyes narrow as he looks back at Honey. "You gonna tell me what happened?"

"Sure, but after we get him loaded on," Honey replies, setting the rifle onto the cart.

"Uh, right." Lenny's tone tightens, but he appears relieved by the offer of Honey's help. Dawn squirms and moans in pain as the two hoist the big man onto the cart.

"He was impaled with a pole," Honey explains as Lenny straps Dawn down.

"A pole? What kind of pole?"

"Ten feet of galvanized steel with an inch and three-quarter diameter."

Lenny raises an eyebrow.

"That's quite specific." Honey grins sheepishly, realizing how strange that spot on of an answer may have sounded.

"Sorry, it was a tetherball pole. I looked up the size on the way here."

"Tetherball pole? How the hell did that happen?"

"Look, there's no time. Can you help him?" she pleads.

"Well, you said it was galvanized steel, right?" he pauses to think. "Means no rust. So at least tetanus isn't a concern." He takes another look at the injury. "Might be able to handle this. No promises, but his chances ain't awful, either." He turns back to Honey, offering a hand. "You coming?" Honey hesitates for a second.

"Is that ok?" she manages.

"Well, I assume you two are friends, right?"

She looks toward Dawn, who lies motionless, barely conscious.

"I suppose so. I just drove his ass here for 2 hours." She climbs onto her motorcycle. "Mind if I park my bike inside?"

"Sure," Lenny replies. "Park it right in there on the side lot." He points just inside the Eagle's Equinox gate. Honey switches her bike to auto drive mode and instructs it to follow her and Lenny to the parking space.

Honey stays in a small dorm room. It's not remarkably comfy but certainly better than the hot desert outside. She is surprised by the cleanliness of her lodging compared to what feels like a rather unkempt community. Lenny has visited her several times with updates on Dawn's condition. He consistently and respectfully requests she keep her distance to minimize distractions as he works on the wound. A sense of relief washes over her when he finally tells her Dawn is stable and resting peacefully.

Over the next few days, Honey finds herself fascinated by Eagle's Equinox. At least for a while. The place feels almost alien. A vacant commune of dusty homes and empty streets nestled in an isolated pocket of the world. Though she is relieved by Dawn's recovery and grateful for the hospitality of the few people that still live here, she soon finds herself missing the crowded chaos of New Beam City.

However, Honey soon discovers a new focus for her attention. A little girl has been lurking in the shadows cast by the buildings and trees, intently watching her and Dawn. Honey's warm smiles, however, haven't managed to convince the young girl she is safe to approach. The child has run away each time their eyes have met. Now, as the sun sets, she leans against the window next to Dawn's bedside. She perks up as she spots the child, hiding behind a barrel across the street. She nods, winking at the kid. And once again, she runs away. Moments later, approaching footsteps echo on the wooden floors of the hallway outside.

Lenny enters, lumbering through the room and struggling to hold a tray filled with bandages and ground-up, powdered medicines for Dawn's wound. Visibly exhausted, he places the tray down before taking a break on a nearby seat, fishing a rag from his pocket to dry the sweat on his face. Honey approaches the bandages and places a gentle hand on Lenny's shoulder.

"You should take some time to rest," Honey insists sweetly. "I can change bandages too, you know?"

50

Lenny rubs his neck with a yawn, cracking it with a grimace.

"I ain't got no help around here if you haven't noticed," he grumbles.

"A bit obvious, yea." She smiles. "You see what I rode in on? I know something about gnarly injuries," she jests. "I can help!"

"Ya can't," he snaps back.

"Why is that?"

"We ain't using the same type of stuff out here that you in the city got."

"Well, that's ok." She reaches into her first aid kit. "I've got some good med gels."

"Nah, that shit sucks," he interrupts before realizing his rudeness. "Uh, yeah sorry, that was a crap way of puttin' it. But look, we ain't gonna be needin' none of that. Thanks." He smiles. A little more softly this time. But no less sarcastic.

"Umm, ok... I'm just offering to help, something you just said you needed."

"It ain't that. Just forget it. Ya, mind steppin' away so I can get to work?"

Honey crosses her arms.

"Look, Lenny. We could get along better if you'd speak straight with me. I am more than capable of helping take care of Dawn, and you need the rest."

"Here's the deal: I ain't got the time or patience to teach you what needs to be done. So the sooner you get out of here, the sooner Dawn can get better."

"I have plenty of experience tending to wounds and treating them," she continues.

"Yea, great, if you want to wait weeks and weeks."

51

"What?"

"Those damn gels take way too long. You city folk rely on all that big pharma shit. It only treats symptoms. Never cures."

Honey stands silent, astonished by the statement.

"Are you suggesting that my supplies are somehow inadequate?"

"Exactly what I'm sayin', miss."

"So then, what are you using..." He cuts her off with a scoff and a wave of his hand.

"I just told you. I ain't got the time nor patience to explain it to ya right now!" he shouts. "Now, would you please leave so I can do this?"

"Alright," Honey concedes. "You got it."

"At least tell me about the kid out there."

Lenny leans forward in his chair, grabbing a book from his tray. Reluctantly, he looks toward her.

"Her name is Cato. She's harmless. It's just..." he hesitates again while flipping the book open to a specific page.

Honey narrows her eyes.

"Speak straight with me, Lenny." He looks up from the book, frustrated.

"She's a mute. Ain't ever heard her mumble a word. She's timid, so just let her be. She only met Dawn recently, so she's trying to understand what's goin' on, ya know?"

Honey nods in understanding. As she exits, he shouts after her.

"One more thing!"

"What's that?"

"The Elder will be seeing you tonight."

"The Elder?"

"He's calling the shots around here," he mumbles. "Feel free to wander around. He'll find ya."

Honey closes the door behind her, pondering his odd choice of words. *He'll find me?* Her eyebrows furrow as she begins to walk down the hall. Having passed through here maybe three times total, her eyes can't help but fixate on the impressive wall decor. Framed artworks depict mankind through the ages. Some show antiquated, often grotesque, medical practices. Others are more modern, portraying recent advancements. Pinned newspaper clippings announce significant breakthroughs of the last century, with post it notes mocking the headlines. Still, more images also seem to show other worldly creatures. She ducks out of the doorway, passing through an archway onto the dusty road. She raises her arm to shield her eyes from the setting sun. The sweet aroma of something cooking nearby catches her attention as she notices a small stack of smoke rising from the center of the community.

She rounds another corner, seeing a large courtyard filled with rows of wide wooden tables. Several chairs are neatly tucked underneath them, covered in dust and clearly having not been used in months or even years. She runs her fingers along the top, intently leaving her mark atop the caked-on dust while admiring the character they portray with scuffs and scratches signifying decades of use. One table, however, was decorated with a few empty glasses and bottles strewn about. It has been used more recently. She smirks, lifting one of the bottles to inspect.

"Grape soju, huh? At least they have good taste out here."

"Of course, we do!" a husky voice echoes across the courtyard. "Would you like some?" the voice continues.

"Uh, hello?" she calls back, anxiously surveying the courtyard. A slow electronic hum vibrates down a nearby corridor as a burly man makes his entrance, a big smile on his face. He sits atop a peculiar, hovering vehicle that appears to be floating. He wears a baggy brown cloak that drags along the ground behind him.

"Well, hello there!" He greets her with a smirk, placing a bottle of soju on the table for her. "Is watermelon ok?"

"Uh?" she stammers.

He chuckles, cracking his bottle open.

"My apologies for the abrupt greeting." He pauses to sip. "I am The Elder," he smiles with a charming sense of gusto.

"Oh, right. Lenny mentioned you! My name is-"

"Honey, right?" he interrupts excitedly.

"Correct," she laughs. "I suppose Lenny already mentioned I was staying here."

"He did, and I couldn't believe it! We don't get many visitors here, as you can imagine. But someone of your status? Unheard of," he jokes, taking another drink. Honey smiles.

"Oh, you've heard of me then?"

"Absolutely! I've seen you in some of the magazines that make their way here when traders visit. Imagine my surprise when my boy Dawn showed up half-dead with you."

"I see. Well, I'm sorry it was under such dire circumstances."

"No need to apologize. I hope he wasn't a terrible amount of trouble?"

"Dawn? Oh no, not at all. His life was on the line, and I did my best to keep him alive. We ran out of options in the city, and he insisted I bring him here."

"I see." He turns from her to consider the situation.

"I hope that was ok?" Honey asks.

"You made a good call by honoring his request," he assures her. "However, bringing visitors here unannounced is against our code."

"Right. Dawn mentioned that on the ride over, but all his gear was busted, and he couldn't send word to you. All your comms here are well encrypted, and I couldn't get a message through, either."

"Well, then, I guess our systems are still working, at least!" He snickers before continuing. "I'll have to commend Lenny for that, but perhaps we should have an emergency channel," he ponders, stroking his chin.

"I'm just thankful your son is ok. I really thought I might lose him."

"My son? Dawn, you mean?" He smiles brightly, "He is not my son, although I think of him as one."

"Oh, my apologies. You referred to him as your boy, so I assumed."

"Quite alright, my dear. I raised him from a very young age, but we share no blood. Only spirit."

"Oh? Dawn is an orphan?"

"A story better suited for another time, I'd say." His smile turns to a stern frown. "Would you mind telling me what happened?" She pauses to collect her thoughts.

"Well, we were involved in a nasty confrontation with a gang of thugs called the Pit Pigs. I was there before he arrived, and we were both shocked to see each other there, but…." He cuts her off.

"Why were you with the Pit Pigs?" he asks, his tone laced with dread.

"You know about them?"

"I do, unfortunately." He sighs. "Please continue."

"Well, things didn't go well, as you can imagine. Dawn got into a deadly battle with…." She pauses, struggling for the words to explain Synric. "With someone resembling a friend of his? I'm sorry, it's hard to explain."

The Elder clangs his bottle of soju onto her unopened one, signaling her to join him. "This will make it easier," he smiles.

"Sorry, I'm not really in the mood to drink." She reluctantly declines.

"Not a problem," he assures her, "but please continue. I would like to understand the situation before Dawn awakens if you don't mind."

"Sure. He fought some sort of android with the face of his friend, Clain."

"Clain?!" The Elder sputters, choking on his drink momentarily.

"Wait, you know Clain too?"

"I do! I mentored both boys when they were younger," he declares proudly.

"Really? No wonder Dawn insisted we come here," she smirks, thinking of Dawn.

"Ok, so Dawn fought an android using Clain's face? All within the Pit Pig headquarters? I got that right so far?"

"Yes. Dawn and Clain fought each other in a Pit Pig tournament a while back. It got cut short so the Pit Pig leader Kruger demanded that they fight each other as a sort of rematch."

"Dawn had mentioned that tournament to me and the mysterious android that pestered them in weeks past. But the last time I saw him, he stormed out of here after learning a new technique I had just taught him."

"Wait, that the giant bull he summoned?!" Honey shouts. "You taught him how to do that?"

"Summoned Lasgaire, did he? A mighty beast. Yet the android bested it?"

"I guess? The android impaled Dawn with a pole, and the bull disappeared after."

56

"I see. That is the unfortunate weakness of the channeling."

"Yea, and he doesn't remember any of it." She looks at The Elder, hoping to hear something reassuring about Dawn.

"He will lose all memory of the creature completely. An unfortunate setback for such an ability."

"Well, anyway, I got him on my bike and sped out of there, narrowly escaping those crazies before making it all the way out here."

"And where was Clain during this whole fiasco?"

"He was unconscious, actually, but saved us on the way here."

The Elder's eyes widen.

"Saved you?" he asks.

"I was weaving through traffic, running from that android which was somehow keeping pace with me on foot. It had almost caught us when Clain suddenly slammed onto the freeway and cut off the chase, buying us time to escape. Dawn might not be alive if had not intervened."

"And where is Clain now?"

"I have no idea. His comms have gone dark."

"I see." The Elder pauses to reflect on the extraordinary story. "Something stinks." He furrows his eyebrows.

"Excuse me?"

"Cato! You're burning the stew!" The Elder suddenly shouts. A loud bang rings out. Cato scurries out from under the table, rubbing her head and whimpering. The Elder guffaws. "Silly girl! Eavesdropping instead of minding the stew." Honey snickers.

"I was wondering where that kid was."

"Ahh, you have noticed her lurking around then? She is another troubled youth I am doing my best to raise and teach. Although a much harder task at my advanced age."

"I see. You seem quite selfless."

"I seek only to raise those in need. Guiding them into their strengths and away from their weaknesses."

"Do they all learn to summon giant bulls?" Honey jokes. The Elder lets out a boisterous laugh.

"Not all of them, I promise."

"Well, from what I can tell, Clain and Dawn didn't turn out so bad. They certainly seem to have some awesome abilities, although they are quite thick-headed."

"They possess the drive of a warrior. Both are constantly thirsting for the thrill of battle to test their abilities and push themselves further."

"God, no wonder they're so fuckin stubborn…" Honey mutters, looking up to see the Elder raising an eyebrow and realizing the comment wasn't as 'under her breath' as she'd hoped. "Oh, I meant no offense! Sorry for my language," she nods to Cato with a smile.

"You seem to have a decent amount of history with them. Might you be partial to one in particular?" he smiles with heightened interest.

She grabs the unopened soju and laughs.

"I'd need several of these for you to get that answer out of me!"

"I see. Well, I hate to cut this short, Honey, but it is getting quite late. I thank you for sharing such a wondrous, albeit exhausting tale with me. But now, I must tend to Cato before dinner is ruined. Would you care to join us?"

"Actually, I'm a bit tired. I haven't had much of an appetite through this whole ordeal." Honey yawns. "I think I'll call it a night if you don't mind."

"Not at all! We will speak again soon. I have a feeling Dawn might be awake tomorrow, so we will reconvene then."

"Sounds good. Thank you for allowing me to stay."

"And I thank you for staying by his side. Your concern over Dawn is reassuring. These boys need someone like you in their life," he winks.

She blushes.

"Actually, I uh…" she pauses, not wishing to keep him any longer. "Never mind."

"Alright, and one more thing Honey."

"Yes?"

"Could you wash Dawn's blood off your bike in the morning? It seems to be bothering Cato. She's a bit queasy at the sight of blood."

"Oh sure, no problem."

"Thank you. I'll have Lenny leave a bucket and soap near the courtyard's well. Goodnight, Honey." He gently bows, then navigates his floating chair to the secluded kitchen.

The sun rises differently when you wake in the silence of Eagle's Equinox. Honey is used to the urban cacophony of New Beam City, not the near-total silence of the abandoned complex where she now resides. Her connection to the city's network has also been severed; she's unable to get a signal from within the isolated desert commune. After brushing away the bright menus illuminating her wrist, she stands up, stretches, and enters the small bathroom nearby. She checks her hair in the mirror before looking at her heavy yet sleek bike suit hanging in the small alcove by the shower. She did her best to clean it of the grime, sweat and blood from the trip here and felt saddened it would never again have the new sheen she had so much admired about it.

She has almost nothing with her, and that includes clothing. She is still wearing the same threads for a few days now, a pair of form-fitted black yoga shorts and a matching black sports bra decorated in a subtle hexagon print. She has diligently scrubbed the blood from it, though not before it managed to soak through to the clothes underneath.

The few residents of Eagle's Equinox were all fast asleep, allowing Honey ample time to wash away the rest of the blood without any prying eyes ogling her skimpier outfit. She exits the dirt pathway and down the narrow road toward the front gate. The Hive C9X begins to glow as she nears it. She runs her fingers along the golden yellow paint, wiping away morning dew streaks. Thankfully the bike encloses the rider's seat while it's parked, shielding it from the elements. She throws her leg over to mount the bike before thumbing through its menus to engage silent mode, great for early morning rides, or just those times when she simply doesn't want to be noticed.

She pulls the C9X next to a stone water well in the nearby courtyard. She cracks a smile when she notices a few fresh fruits left in the water pail and a small stack of towels to dry the bike. As she powers the bike down, a deep, resonant hum catches her attention, echoing as though trapped within the walls of a concert hall. She looks around but sees no one.

"Hello?" she calls out.

No reply. She peers through a dimly lit window high above. The glow from inside flickers like flame on a lit candle. Her thoughts return to the strangely familiar hum. It's like a musical instrument she has heard but cannot name. She returns to the C9X and approaches the well. A wooden frame sits mounted over the top. A crankshaft is affixed to it. She wraps her hand around the tattered fabric of the handle, reservedly turning it and spurring the antiquated device into motion. After a few cranks, a pail full of water emerges from the deep shadows, its contents sloshing over its sides.

After transferring the water into the other bucket, she sets it near the bike's rear wheel and lathers the sponge in soap before submerging it in the water. The blood is mainly plastered on the back right fender, but she washes the whole bike for good measure. The ominous buzz turns into soft music as it reverberates through the courtyard. Honey's mind shifts to distant memories of her father and his lessons on the importance of the finer details, on how one must never lose sight of crucial minutiae amidst the bigger picture. They are worn thin by time, cracked and faded, shrouded in the inevitable fog of temporal distance that suggests they may never have happened.

She eventually makes her way to the bloodied areas, squeezing the sponge over the caked-on crimson, watching as it dissolves and drips onto the tire, funneling down treads into the swirling and growing puddle on the ground and fading away, crimson, then pink, then gone.

"Nice view," a raspy voice says from behind.

Honey jumps, whipping around to face the speaker, ready to chew him out. Until she sees who it is.

"Dawn?" she says, eyes wide and a smile growing on her face. He stands across the courtyard from Honey, leaning against a wooden pillar, with a pained smirk on his face. He is shirtless. The bandages on his abdomen are spotted with blood. He's propped up on a single crutch, doing his best to stay upright.

"How are you even standing right now?" Honey asks, concerned.

"I needed some fresh air. That thing was making my head pound." He points up toward the candle-lit window.

"Thing?"

"That damn didgeridoo. It's part of a healing ritual that I have the...privilege...to be a part of," he chuckles.

"Oh, a didgeridoo?" she questions, wondering if she has ever actually seen one.

"This place is filled with ancient secrets, and healing practices are a part of that," he explains.

"Well, I guess it works, huh?" She nods toward his wound.

"Oh, no doubt. Can't deny the old man has his tricks. Crazy to think he's finally handing some of them down."

"What do you mean?"

"Some of his ways just ain't natural. I might not even agree with some, but now he's including...." He purses his lips, wondering if he is about to say too much. Honey kneels to grab some towels to dry her bike.

"Including what?" she persists.

"Not what but who, rather."

"Oh, do you mean Cato? The little girl?"

"Ahh, I guess you have had time to get to know everyone around here."

"Not really," she snickers. "Everyone is pretty closed off, but I get it. I'm a total stranger."

"Yea, tough crowd. How long have I been out anyway?" Dawn rubs his head.

"About 79 hours." She hesitates, wiping the rearview mirrors. "We arrived halfway through the day, and you've been out since."

"Well, aren't you precise," he nods.

She swiftly pulls up her holographic screen and shows him a timer. "Details matter," she winks.

"I was referring to your cleaning routine on the bike," he chuckles, watching as she dries even the tightest nooks of the fender.

"A proper lady always worries about her curves," she laughs as she pours out the bucket of bloody water.

"I'm sorry about that."

"What? The blood?" She slips her finger under her sports bra strap to snap it. "It was harder to get out of my clothes than the bike." She sticks her tongue out and winks.

"Right." He blushes, looking away from her to the bike. "Still, it's obvious how much you love your ride." She runs her index finger down the front fender.

"How couldn't I? This thing is the creme de la creme of hardware! A little blood won't hurt this sexy beast."

"I bet," Dawn mumbles under his breath.

"What was that?"

"Oh, nothing. My mind wanders sometimes."

She approaches him, leaning in with her hands on her hips.

"Wanders where?"

"You heard me, I guess," Dawn rubs his head again, embarrassed.

"You owe me, ya know? I saved your ass from the pigs."

"Owe you, huh?" His eyebrows raise as he adjusts himself on the crutch under his arm. "And what exactly do I owe you?"

She steps back to continue cleaning up her mess.

"Maybe share some of the secrets this place holds with me?"

Dawn scoffs, chuckling toward his shoulder.

"As if."

"What? You don't think I can keep secrets?"

"It's not that. We are sworn to protect this place and what we keep here."

"Aww, come on, Dawn. I already know so much but so little!"

"Yea, what do you know?"

"Well, I know you and Clain trained here under The Elder as kids."

"And who told you that?" Dawn's tone changes at the mention of his friend and rival.

"The Elder! He told me just last night when I met him."

"Is that right?" Dawn spits off to his side.

"Clain still a sore subject for you?" she asks.

"Sure. Or the fact that I just had my ass kicked by something that looked like him." he looks down at his wound.

"Come on now, don't be so stingy. You can share something, at least, right? How about I make you a deal? Show me something cool around here, and I'll give you a lift back to New Beam City?"

He smiles.

"You don't give up, do you?"

"Nope!" she winks again. "Oh, did you notice? The didgeridoo stopped."

Dawn looks up toward the window. The candlelight inside has been snuffed out. The Elder and Cato are probably looking for him. Not wanting to end his time with Honey, he thinks of something quick.

"Take me for a ride," he blurts out.

"Wait, what?"

"You said you wanted to see a secret. I'll show you one, but you have to drive us there."

"You have to be kidding. I can't take you anywhere in your condition."

He hobbles toward her bike, lifting his other arm to show her a small device braced to his forearm. "I'll be fine; this thing monitors and adjusts the pain. Don't worry about me."

Hearing the sounds of someone descending some nearby stairs, Honey quickly deduces why Dawn is in a rush.

"They'll be worried about you," she insists.

"Are you with me," he winces, struggling onto the bike, "or them?"

She smiles with a squinted eye.

"You're dangerous. I like that." She climbs in front of him and fires the bike to life.

"Head out the back, and I'll direct you from there."

"You got it. Now hold on, big guy."

Dawn blushes as he slowly places his hands on her hips.

CHAPTER 4 - Take Me For A Ride

Days have passed since Clain's return to Mitt's compound. If his sudden loss of consciousness in the backseat of Mitt and Zaria's vehicle hadn't worried them enough, his recent outburst certainly did. As he gave into his rage upon seeing the ruins of the Pho King, the two watched as he was engulfed in an aura of purple energy, slamming his fists into the sidewalk with frightening strength. It is evident to them now that there is more to Clain. Something powerful, unnatural, and most of all, dangerous that he doesn't seem in control of. His hands are rebandaged now, with his shattered arm once again reset in his sling, this time even tighter courtesy of Zaria. The two have run multiple medical scans over him at her insistence, looking for any sign of cybernetic enhancements. Yet they have found nothing. Despite every outward indication to the contrary, Clain, at least according to X-rays and thermal imaging, seems normal. With their efforts to understand Clain yielding no results and him returning to a deep slumber, the two have shifted their attention to tracking down the source of FreqyD.

Tensions among the citizens are at an all-time high. Homes have become cages, and more and more people are attempting to escape them. To little avail, of course, they cannot hope to escape the iron grip and advanced technology of their fascistic government. The ones that have tried seem to inevitably disappear by the Police, or worse. Screams regularly echo within the streets and darkened windows. The monolithic Cloud 9 building has deployed an army of drones working around the clock to deliver essential goods to the trapped citizens. Still, supplies are drying up, and the beginnings of panic are setting in.

The Syn network is no exception, working at breakneck speed to organize and manage its resources and personnel, including the field unit Synric. He has also been endlessly trying to track down the source of FreqyD. King has demanded it be his top priority, as it seemed key to an unrelenting scheme within the city. Clain is still their ultimate goal, but all indications are that he will be incapacitated for a long

66

while. Synric is losing patience, grappling with a newfound sense of limitations as it finds itself up against the first obstacle it cannot easily dismantle. He scours the streets of New Beam, even its darkest and most dangerous alleys, including the destroyed remains of Pho King and the cracked pavement out front, a testament to Clain's power. However, King has forbidden further investigation. So far, Synric has complied. Reluctantly.

Clain's mind is locked inside the realm of his premonitions, bristling with a host of macabre creatures. Only one has still ever spoken to him directly: Tia, a grotesque entity emanating motherly energy adorned in amorphous faces, always floating well out of reach no matter how quickly Clain gives chase. Yet, even with its many disturbing qualities, this place feels strangely calming and familiar. There is a sense of ownership about it, however, warped it may be. The surreal qualities of the space render much of it nonsensical, and few of the beings present seem capable of communication. And strangest of all, despite seeming built from the stuff of deadly nightmares, not one of the inhabitants of this realm has attacked him. A melody also calls to him constantly, reverberating across a nearby foggy canyon. The harmonies of an angelic female voice distract Clain from his maddeningly futile pursuit of Tia. Even a herd of nearby imp like monsters seem captivated by the sound, its members rushing toward the source. As Clain steps in their direction, Tia appears in front of him, obstructing his path. "You are forbidden from entering those lands," her voice echoes.

"Oh, now you want to talk?"

"There is no discussion!" Tia surges forward, her teeth bared in a guttural snarl as her ghostly figure passes through him, sending a startled Clain stumbling backward into a bottomless ravine.

The fall jolts Clain from his slumber. He pants, cold sweat drenches his forehead, hands shaking as he feels for something, anything solid underneath him. He calms when he realizes he has woken from a dream and a full-body ache returns. The pain stubbornly persists, as though he has not rested at all. He winces as though hung over when the distant sound of machine gun fire reaches his ringing ears. Summoning every ounce of his discipline, he focuses on a nearby air conditioning vent, letting the cool breeze from it settle his nerves. He slows his breathing, feeling the pounding of his heart subside. He can hear Mitt and Zaria laughing outside, bantering amongst themselves. It is a simple, comforting sound he has not heard in far too long. He groans as his arms throb and sweat trickles down his cheek.

He raises his right hand to examine the bandages around his knuckles before reaching to the bunk above and pulling himself up. His shattered arm thumps, reminding him to move slowly. He notices he is still wearing Mitt's sweatpants, remembering that he has no clothes of his own. Unfortunate, but he is humbled that anyone would take him in after witnessing his primal rage at the Pho King. He trips a motion sensor light as he stands, doing his best to not fumble to the floor which he can barely see, albeit faintly. He braces himself onto the sink at the far side of the room, slowly looking into the mirror. Tia was there, staring back at him, whispering into his mind. *We will speak soon. You shall remain here.* Clain jerks his head to the side, knocking the faucet handle to the "on" position as he flails and gasps, bracing to throw up. It never comes. He has grown tired of the creature, as if his mind was her prison and he could not unlock it.

His stomach was empty and growling back at him. He splashes his face with water before cautiously looking back up, releasing a tightly held breath of relief at the sight of his own face. The cuts and bruises are healing noticeably, but his skin remains caked with cracked dry blood. He looks to his left, thankful to see a bathtub; his own body odor has become more bothersome than the pain.

"Hey, you hear that?" Zaria says, pointing toward the ceiling.

"What?" Mitt responds.

"The water. Sounds like Clain is awake."

Mitt glances at a nearby utility display, noticing the high-water usage.

"Oh, you're right" "Looks like he's taking a bath."

"You must be relieved. It was your turn to clean him next." Zaria sighs, stepping away from the wide computer console.

"Where are you going?"

"Dude's gonna be hungry after, so I might as well start making something."

"Good point. How do you think we should handle this?"

"Handle what?"

"Well, our supplies can't support three people much longer, especially when only two can contribute. That's not even mentioning the city's supply shortage."

"True. The damn mac n' cheese is all gone. Not cool." Zaria exhales, standing up on her toes to check the top shelf.

"Alright, I'll get back to our contacts about the new information. You sure you want to follow through on it?"

"That is your call, Mitt. You know them better than I do, but it is our best lead by far."

"Alright, I'll try to figure it out while you care for our guest."

"Hey, wait a second! You're trying to pin this awkward conversation on me, aren't you?"

Mitt chuckles

"Of course not. Would you rather I do the cooking and you call these guys back?"

"Heck no. Your cooking might actually kill him."

"Oh, real funny Zaria."

"Besides, he's pretty cute. I don't mind chatting with him at all," she winks. Mitt rolls his eyes and makes his way down the compound's main hallway, stopping a moment to listen in on Clain. Hearing only silence, he continues down the hall before pausing at a door and waving his hand in front of the doorknob. An electronic lock releases, and he steps out onto a small balcony overlooking New Beam City. He pulls up a holographic HUD and makes his calls as the sun sets.

Back inside, Clain has just finished drying himself off when a knock on the bathroom door startles him.

"Yo!" Zaria calls to him, smiling. "Thanks for cleaning yourself this time." Clain remains silent, trying to cover himself with the towel. "I'm leaving you some clean clothes out here. Come out whenever you're ready." Clain pokes his head out to ensure the room is empty, noticing a complete set of folded clothes on the bed. He reaches down to grab the garments, but Zaria gasps out behind him, startling him as he bumps his head on the bunk bed.

"Well, this is awkward!" she laughs, holding his bundle of dirty clothes she was retrieving from the corner.

Clain rushes to cover himself.

"I thought you already left."

"I figured you were still soaking in the bath. Sorry bro. Got food on the stove if you're hungry though." She chuckles as she awkwardly shuffles past him.

"Thanks," Clain mumbles. His stomach begs him with a grumble at the mention of nourishment.

Freshly dressed, Clain leaves the room and looks up and down the dark hallway. He can smell food coming from his right but hears Mitt's muffled voice coming from the back end of the hall. Hoping to avoid any more mishaps, he decides against eavesdropping and heads toward the kitchen. Zaria is waiting for him, leaning against the counter with her arms crossed and a smirk on her face.

"There you are," she smiles. "Have a seat and help yourself!" Clain's eyes scan across the table, watching steam rising from a warm bowl of soup as well as a small basket full of bread and fruit.

"Wow, thanks," he nods to her.

"Sounds like I was right on time! You must be pretty damn hungry by now."

"Definitely," he agrees, lowering his aching body onto the chair, looking for a spoon, and finding none. He spots a metal container filled with silverware in the middle of the table and reflexively primes his magnetic powers, stopping when he realizes Zaria is looking right at him.

"Something wrong?" she asks, tilting her head. "Oh, you need a spoon! One sec, I'll grab one." Unwilling to wait, he levitates a spoon from the container and quickly begins to eat. The clatter of the dishes stops Zaria as she turns to see him feasting.

"How did you..." she begins to ask before she sees him scarfing down the food. "I'm guessing that won't be enough." She returns to the stove to heat up more.

"This is so good!" Clain compliments her, grabbing a second roll of bread to soak up the remaining soup.

"Thanks! You're in luck. A lot of those ingredients came from that pho place," she explains. Clain stops chewing.

"Excuse me?" he asks. His face is a mixture of confusion and anger, reminiscent of the expression he made as he pounded the ground outside the Pho King.

"Mitt and I snuck back over there a few nights ago. We were running low on food man, and both remembered all the fresh produce that was just sitting over there. It was all going to waste. Sorry if it pisses you off, but tough times, you know?

Clain's expression softens.

"Right," he sighs, looking down.

"So, eat up!" She slides another bowl of vegetable soup in front of him.

"Oh, you're out here," Mitt calls from the hallway. "We got a solid lead! For real this time," he explains excitedly. "How are you feeling? Think you can help us?"

"Dude, Mitt, chill. Are you serious right now? He barely woke up." Zaria scolds him.

"I know, I know, but this is huge! It sounds like Sigma is real, and we might know where it is."

"Sigma?" Clain asks.

"Operation Sigma, yea. Don't tell me you haven't heard of it. It's been all over the conspiracy forums for years!"

Clain furrows his brow at the word.

"Come on. You gotta know a lot of them are true, right? People in power just weaponize the word "conspiracy" to discredit anything they don't want us to find out."

"I guess. I've never heard of Sigma before, though."

Zaria smacks Mitt over the head.

"Ouch! Dammit, Zar!"

"Slow down and let him eat, alright?"

Clain stares back into his soup, stirring it absentmindedly.

"I was just telling Clain here that we salvaged what we could from his destroyed home."

"Oh, right. I hope you don't mind that. I know the place meant a lot to you, but letting all those fresh tomatoes rot just didn't seem right."

Clain quickly changes the subject. "It's fine. So, what's Sigma?"

Mitt looks at Zaria, worried she might hit him again. She rolls her eyes and throws her hands up in exasperation.

"Whatever. Tell him then. But start with why you were told in the first place."

"Oh, right, sure. I guess that is very important." Mitt scrambles through the menus on his HUD and displays a photo on his largest console monitor. "Check this out."

"A photo of the city?"

"Hold on, let me zoom in. There!"

Clain squints. It's a photo of Kruger on top of the giant Hux robot moments before it destroyed the Pho King.

"Ok, and?"

"Well, my contact -let's just call him Ed- he was at the scene that day. Managed to stay hidden. His drone hung around long enough to even capture when ours arrived. And even your little outburst on the sidewalk."

"Great. What does this have to do with whatever Sigma is?"

"Well, Ed contacted me about it, asking who you were. I tried to cover for you, but he immediately called you by your name. Said he knew you from the fight pits."

"So he's a fan or something?"

"Not exactly. Said he's lost a lot of money betting against you."

"Great."

"Yea...and now comes the bad news."

"Bad news?"

"He's threatened to release the footage. Wouldn't be good optics, ya know?"

"So, he's blackmailing you?"

"Us! He's blackmailing us. You want the whole city to see your outburst?"

"Why?" Turns out he recognized Kruger on that giant ass mech, and it seems he knows exactly what he's looking for. Problem is, he wants you to follow the lead."

"Me? Why me?"

"Operation Sigma is linked to FreqyD, and Kruger is trying to find the source of it for himself. Supposedly he was involved in the project when he was in the military."

"You still haven't told me what Operation Sigma is?"

"Well, like I said earlier, most know it as a long-time conspiracy that never came to be. Apparently, the world's governments conspired to create several pandemics and then tried to force inoculation onto the population. The shots contain transmitters that eventually find their way into the brain and lay dormant there." Clain's eyes widen. "I know it sounds crazy, but governments have done much worse in the past, yeah?"

"I guess so. Anyway, you said that happened a while ago?"

"Yea, so they planned to keep forcing these injections on people until the majority had complied and then activate Operation Sigma when the time was right. Sigma is short for signal machine. Those transmitters enable mind control. They're literally going to program and control people directly."

Zaria laughs at Clain's shock.

"I bet you wish you never woke up now, huh?"

"That's a lot to take in. You still didn't tell me what this Ed wants with me."

"Well, the location could be super dangerous, and he knows you're a damn good fighter. Far more capable than Zar and I. Plus, again he saw your outburst."

"In other words, he's not willing to go himself."

"Exactly. There's no guarantee this lead is solid either so it would be a total gamble for him."

Clain lifts his braced arm sarcastically.

"Well, I'm not in the best shape right now. I'm sure you've noticed."

"Exactly what I told him, but he didn't care. Said if we didn't check the place out tonight, then he would release the footage tomorrow."

"This guy seems like a real prick."

74

"He is, but I think, more than anything, he's scared of Kruger getting his hands on the Sigma system. I could hear it in his voice."

Clain lifts the bowl, gulps down the remaining soup, and then walks back toward the hallway.

"Where are you going?" Zaria asks.

"I need to meditate."

"Oh, you do that spiritual junk?" Mitt jokes.

Clain turns back to look at him, scowling.

"You could probably use it more than me with all this conspiracy nonsense you have cooking."

"Hey man. You're the one almost killing yourself floating over the city on a giant sword to fight some android freak and falling off buildings. You definitely need it more than me."

Clain clenches his jaw, then sighs and looks away.

"You're not wrong."

"So you'll help us?"

"Let him release the footage. I don't even care anymore. I need to find my friends."

"Your friends...they were squashed in," Zaria smacks Mitt over the head again. "I'm sorry about that. I'm just really nervous about this whole Kruger thing. Plus, Zaria and I have been caring for you for a while now, ya know? Maybe you can return the favor."

"So, you're blackmailing me too?"

"No, no, no!" Mitt puts his hands out in a placating gesture. "Look man, we all have goals, right? Yours is to find your friends, and ours is to find the source of FreqyD. Both of those sort of coincide. Kruger was the one that destroyed your home."

Clain pinches the bridge of his nose, slowly exhaling through his nostrils.

"You'll both be going with me?"

"Well, no, but we will control a drone to direct you plus record and gather intel alongside you."

"Only those willing to get their hands dirty ever change anything. You're not gonna make a difference staring at a screen all the time."

"You'd be surprised! Besides, we would only slow someone like you down. From here, we can be much more useful to you."

"If I do this, are we square?"

"Sure."

"Fine, I'll go."

"Yes!" Zaria shouts as she hugs Mitt. "This is a huge deal, Clain; you might save the world!"

Clain opens the door to his room.

"Give me a few hours. I want to try and heal further." Mitt and Zaria look at each other and shrug before rushing back to the computer console to strategize.

~~~

 Honey waits patiently with her finger pressed firmly onto the accelerator of her C9X. Dawn hasn't given her any direction for miles. In fact, both have been silent for most of the trip. It is obvious Dawn is still in pain, though his condition has improved noticeably, and Honey trusts him to know his body well enough if he can endure this journey.

"Just ahead. See that ridge?" Dawn speaks suddenly while pointing up towards mountains on the horizon. "Slow down near that grouping of cacti." Her bike hums beautifully under the setting desert sun.

"You see that, right?" Honey asks, nodding toward brewing storm clouds gathering in the distance. "I just washed the bike.

Wouldn't mind making it back before the rain." He laughs as the pair dismount and remove their helmets.

"Damn, you really love this thing."

"I do." She smiles. "It never talks back." Her hair flowing in the breeze as the scent of rain wafts by. Dawn finds himself distracted by the contours of her silhouette, he blinks, turning to regain his focus while remembering why he wanted to take her here in the first place.

"Who knows what might be out there, though." He cautiously makes his way through the cacti.

"You're serious?" She asks.

"About what?"

She makes a sweeping gesture toward the uninviting landscape.

"You were just on your deathbed and now you want to walk through this?"

"I told you I wanted to show you something, didn't I?"

"Well, sure." She pauses. "I just figured you wanted me to see this beautiful sunset."

"That's a bonus." He smiles. "Come on."

As she powers it down, the bike compacts itself, sealing her helmet inside its protective shell. She examines the sharp plants, trying not to brush up against any of the spines.

"It's not too far," he insists.

"We barely have any clothes on. You do realize that?"

He continues moving forward, his oversized stature making brushes against the sharp botanical spikes unavoidable. Yet he is unfazed even as they inflict the incidental spotting of blood on his arms and legs.

"This must really be worth it," Honey mutters. Impressed with his unwavering demeanor.

"Let me ask you something."

"Sure, shoot."

"How much does your technology define you?"

The question stuns her for a second, and she pauses mid-step. "What kind of question is that?"

"You love that bike more than anything else, don't you?"

"If you brought me out here to psychoanalyze me, it ain't happenin', buddy."

He laughs.

"Guess that's one way of confirming it."

"You're an asshole. You know that?" she barks at him. "I saved your ass and drove you out in the middle of nowhere and you want to talk to me like that?" She turns around, walking back to where they started. "What the fuck am I even doing out here?"

"You're right." He looks back at her, grabbing her wrist.

"Don't touch me." She wrenches her wrist free.

He puts his hands up.

"You got it. We are almost there though, so just humor me, ok?" He turns and continues forward.

She rolls her eyes and continues back toward her bike.

"Good luck getting back," Dawn calls after her. Honey stops, realizing she probably doesn't know the way, and has no signal way out here. Her bike could retrace her path but she clenches her fist and resumes following him.

"Make it quick," she growls.

They pass under a mountain ravine with a natural bridge of sandstone overhead. A small creek runs down its middle. They both hop left to right, avoiding the gentle current. He points up the canyon wall, looking back at her with a smile. She looks up to see an antelope looking down at them.

"Oh, look. Another wild animal, just like you."

He laughs.

"You know, you're actually quite funny."

"Yea, if only I were kidding."

"Right. It's just in here," he nods toward a cave around the bank. "Just follow the creek inside."

She stops, folding her arms.

"You're insane if you think I'd go in there before you."

"Fair enough."

 He walks past her towards the cavern. Even barefoot, he doesn't seem to mind stepping over the rocky ground. Thankfully she has some decent shoes on, although she would have preferred her riding boots. She reluctantly steps into the flowing water. The rays of the sun just barely make their way inside the rocky tunnel, and their light is fading quickly.

"We're here." He steps out of the creek, pulling himself up onto a formation of red rocks. He turns to offer her his hand, but she has already begun climbing.

"You wanted to show me this empty cave?"

He smiles softly, retrieving a small remote from his pocket and clicking a button. A large crate suddenly comes into view as Dawn steps forward to detach the straps fastened to the ground.

"A chameleon tarp, huh?"

79

"First gen too. Before they added all those limitations," he boasts.

"It's hacked?"

"Like you have to ask," he scoffs. He pulls the tarp away. The box now sits bare, its mystery contents tantalizing. "

Ok, now you have my attention," she smiles. "What's in the box?"

"Maybe you can tell me."

"What? What is that supposed to mean?" She furrows her brow in confusion.

"I found this thing on my last hunt," he explains. "I've had it hidden here for a bit. I've been on a sort of side mission trying to figure out where it came from. You being pretty high up with Cloud 9 made me think to ask you about it."

The door creaks open, the accumulated desert dust scattering into the air. Honey's eyes widen. A mechanized battle suit stands inside, its glowing visor staring down at them. Its shell sparkles in the waning light, casting it in a rough purple hue, its texture and shine like obsidian.

"Wow," she gapes.

"My thoughts exactly."

"Where did you find this?" She steps forward to examine it.

"Quite far northwest of here. Small town that runs off alien tourism."

"What?" She pauses. "The one next to the giant meteor crater?"

"Yep."

She laughs.

"So it's some tourist prop? Did you win it at their local carnival or something?"

He facepalms.

"Touch it," he tells her, leaning on the cavern wall. She tilts her head and narrows her eyes at him.

"You first."

His boisterous laugh echoes through the canyon.

"If it's a prop, then why are you scared to touch it?"

She looks back to it, approaching it slowly as she reaches out her hand. She gently slides her fingertips along the surface, registering a texture not unlike sandpaper. The suit glows in response to her touch, leaving a trail of illumination as she traces circles with her fingers. Her breath catches at the sight. Beautiful," she breathes. She studies the intricately articulated joints, realizing how agile it must be. "I've never seen anything like this. Not even at Cloud 9."

"I figured."

"Oh yea? Why's that?"

"I can tell by your reaction."

"I've seen some crazy stuff they're making, but nothing like this."

"Yea, like cyborgs?" he blurts. "You didn't seem to know about that either," he accuses, referring to Synric.

"Yea," she looks away, embarrassed.

"Sorry, not meaning to rag on you," he smiles, "but this is just another piece in my ever-growing puzzle." He groans. Dawn points his remote up toward the cavern ceiling. A set of turrets reveal themselves. All pointed down toward the suit.

Honey jumps away, startled.

"Not cool, man." She ducks behind a large rock. "A warning would have been nice!" she scolds.

"Relax. I keep it under tight security while I'm away. Plus, I've done some stress testing on it."

"What does that mean?"

"These turrets here are pretty old models. I put them up here since it was all I could get for cheap. They were busted, and I had to fix them myself, and of course, I needed to test them." He laughs.

"Does that mean what I think it means?"

"Yup, now duck!" he shouts, diving behind a rock and activating the turrets. All five spin to life, and a flurry of bullets spray out onto the mech before ricocheting like a swarm of fireflies, their metaling echoes pinging off the cave walls.

"Stop it!" Honey shouts. Dawn presses a button, and the barrels start to slow down.

"See?" he yells over to her as the sharp smell of gunpowder fills their nostrils. Honey pokes her head out, her eyes widening at seeing a completely undamaged mech suit.

"No shit." She steps out to examine it further.

"Insane, right? I don't even know if it's man-made."

"Wait, you think it could be alien?"

Dawn shrugs.

"Like I said, another piece of a puzzle."

"You don't know anything about it at all?"

"The room I found it in had a placard on the wall. Some sort of weird hieroglyphics or some shit. If I had my gear, I could show you a picture."

"What did it show?"

"It took me a bit, but I knew a few shamans that helped me decipher it. They weren't certain about it, but they thought it depicted a human getting inside and darting off into the stars. There was one word carved below in Latin."

"What word?"

"Fio."

"Become?"

"My best guess is that if you get in that thing, you also become it. Or worse."

"Worse?"

"It becomes you. Takes over your body."

Honey chuckles nervously.

"You can't be serious."

"You want to test it?" he asks sarcastically.

She looks back at it, her eyes locked on the sharp edges of its head at the top. She can't help but feel drawn to it, the curiosity of being inside of it, taking control. Dawn laughs at her, snapping her out of her trance.

"What's so funny?"

"You're looking at that thing just like you do your bike."

She runs her fingers across the surface of the suit again.

"Maybe it's easier this way," she whispers under her breath.

"What's that?" Dawn asks.

She looks at him blankly. Unwilling to repeat herself. Her eyes slowly gaze down his torso toward his hips. "You're blinking," Honey replies with a flirtatious nod.

"Blinking?" he asks, confused and almost blushing. Then he sees a flashing red light on his remote. "Hm. That's strange."

"What is?"

"It's some indication light. Nothing I've programmed it to do." He presses a side button to see what might happen.

"Hello?" a voice calls out. "Dawn? I know you can fuckin hear me!"

"Lenny?" he responds.

"Damnit, Dawn! Where the hell are you?"

"How are you calling me on this?" Dawn continues to examine the small remote.

"I gave you that thing, remember?! You needed it for some bullshit you were doing and wouldn't tell me."

Dawn looks away from Honey, embarrassed.

"Do you need something, Lenny? I am kind of in the middle of something right now."

"Yea, yea, probably humping around with that biker chick. I don't care what you're doing. I need you back here pronto."

"Why are you yelling? What's going on?"

"There's a vehicle heading toward Eagle's Equinox right fuckin now! They seem to know the exact path here."

"What?!" Dawn yells. "No idea who it is?"

"None. And what's worse, this storm rolling in is messing up our whole system. Get your ass back here now!".

"On our way." Dawn clicks the remote off and looks back to Honey. She grins.

"I guess we better hump our way back, huh?"

CHAPTER 5 - Mystery and Arrival

Clain releases his mediation and rises to his feet, staggered and sore. He grits his teeth, pain ebbing and flowing over his body as the accelerated healing forces its way through his wounds. His mind is still racing, seemingly no calmer even from a few hours of meditation. All he could think about was Mr. Le and Fila, how he had no idea if they were alive, and he relives the boiling rage that punched holes in solid concrete every time they cross his mind. He knew he had to keep it under control but it was torture watching his friends on that computer screen, terrorized by a towering cybernetic abomination of Hux. The fear on their faces seems forever etched into his memory, a scar that angrily pulses each time his mind brushes against it. He can only imagine the agony of losing their home. His psyche seethes with the need for answers. For revenge. For himself. For those he has failed to protect. For the simple satisfaction of seeing Kruger's arrogant grin as he lays waste to innocent lives beaten off of his face. Yet more frustrating is his condition. Even if he had been there, he struggles with the reality that he might not have been able to help.

His shattered arm still throbs, a harsh reminder of what else ails him. His bouts with Synric. He managed to get the better of the android. Barely. Reliving the moment he shredded his adversary's body as he bludgeoned it with a manhole cover gives only small comfort considering the black bruises and splintered bones he took home as souvenirs. It wasn't a total loss, however. He has one lead. Finding the source of FreqyD.

Rest seems determined to elude him, assured to him by Tia so however dangerous this next adventure may be, it is a welcome distraction. He steps out of the room slowly, hoping to not yet catch the attention of his new housemates. The place is surprisingly empty, almost as though it has been suddenly abandoned. Even the bowl of soup from yesterday is still sitting on the table. He lifts the bowl to his face, the aroma of tomato and cilantro evoking thoughts of the Pho King and with them, a smile. Then tears. He drinks from the bowl, unbothered by its cold temperature, unwilling to let the memories contained within go to waste.

"You're up!" Zaria calls from behind.

Clain sets the bowl down and turns to face her.

"Yeah," he murmurs, rubbing his head. "No choice really, right?"

"How are you feeling?"

Clain adjusts his sling, grimacing.

"Like you have to ask."

"How's the pain? Do you want anything for it?"

"Nah, I'm good. Feels like pain is the only thing keeping me going."

"Alright, I can respect that."

"Where's Mitt?"

"In the garage! Said he was modifying your shoes."

"What?"

"Yea something about making it easier for you to get through the city. I told him it wasn't cool to mess with another man's shoes but he didn't care." She shrugs. Clain looks away, trying to hide his irritation. Zaria lifts her wrist to her face, clicking a button to radio Mitt. "Yo man, you done? Clain is waiting."

"Just a second. Tightening these screws and I'll be there," he replies.

Clain quickly turns back around, almost indignant.

"Tightening screws?"

Zaria chuckles as a door at the back end of the compound opens and closes. Mitt jogs up to them with Clain's boots cradled in his arms.

"Yo! Glad you're up!"

Clain immediately looks at his shoes, morbidly curious. To his pleasant surprise, he notices they've been cleaned.

"Why are you screwing around with my boots?"

"Yea, sorry about that. We just don't have a lot of time, and we had to devise a plan while you were resting."

"And what plan is that?"

Mitt approaches the table and slams the shoes down.

"You're going to ride the waylines!"

Clain looks at his boots, confused. The soles have been replaced with metal brackets and grind plates. His eyebrows raise.

"I told you he wouldn't go for it," Zaria sighs. Clain lifts one of the shoes to examine it.

"No, this is actually really smart."

"Really? You think so?" Mitt excitedly joins Clain at his side. "Believe it or not, I was a rail rider when they were still open! You remember them then?"

"Yeah, of course. I was pretty pissed when they closed the waylines down. How long has it been now?"

"Oh shit, almost a decade, I think."

"Why did they close them again?" Zaria asks.

"A few people got careless and died, so of course, the city shut them down for everybody indefinitely."

"More wasted tax money," Clain murmurs.

"Exactly! The waylines were so cool back then, and the convenience was insane. If you were fast enough, you could get across the entire city in 10 minutes."

"7 minutes." Clain smiles.

"Wait, that was you? I thought it was just a myth!"

Clain laughs.

"Sometimes I wish I didn't ruin that guy's camera. He caught almost everything, but I didn't want all the attention."

"Dude! You beat him up and stole his camera? Ahh, man. I wish I could have seen it!" Mitt complains.

"No, of course not. I simply asked if I could see the footage and the phone conveniently lost all its data." Clain smiles while moving his fingers around. "Magnetic powers, remember?"

"I hate to break up your little bromance, but we don't have much time." Zaria urges.

"Sorry, I kinda ruined your shoes, but I didn't have any others in your size. Besides, I had a feeling you'd understand when you saw them."

"It's cool. These were already pretty rough." Clain begins to put them on. "Thanks for cleaning them too." He pats Mitt on the back.

"The least I could do. This could be quite dangerous." Mitt rushes toward the computer console. "Zaria, you mind helping him while I pull up the map?"

"Uh sure." She reluctantly agrees, kneeling at Clain's feet to help him put the shoes on. "Ok, so I guess I am going to have to ask the obvious question. How are you going to ride the waylines when the electromagnetic energy is turned off."

"Good question." Clain smiles as she finishes clamping them in place. "I'll show you." He stands up, cracks his neck, and loosens his eyes.

"Remember I told you he was flying around on that giant sword? Maybe now you'll believe me," Mitt gloats. Clain struggles to keep his balance as he slowly begins to levitate above the metallic floor panels. Zaria's jaw drops.

"Woah. How the hell?" Clain drops back down to the chair. "You alright?"

"Yeah, just a bit rusty I guess. The enamel flooring over the metal frame makes it a bit harder."

"You can feel the metal below your feet?"

"Yes, I can feel or sense all the metal around me. It used to be very difficult, but I've had a ton of practice."

"Now do you believe me?" Mitt asks Zaria with a smirk.

"Sure. I just don't understand how. I did a bio scan on you, and don't have any body modifications."

"I don't understand it myself." Clain shrugs. "But let's get to the mission. I don't want to be out there too long."

"Right!" Mitt retrieves a small hologram device and sets it on the table. It projects a map of the city. "Alright, let me adjust this to only display the waylines."

"Let me guess. East industrial district?"

"Wow, how did you know?" Zaria asks.

"City is in lockdown. There's a ton of dilapidated buildings where the dead heads scavenge."

"Right," Mitt agrees excitedly. He zooms in on the nearest wayline. "I figure you can start here and go southeast to bypass downtown and most of the residential buildings. Of course, you'll need to be careful not to be seen."

"I'll be silent. The only problem I can think of is the shoes sparking. I don't know if I can levitate high enough above the rails to prevent it the entire time."

"We'll use the drone to scout ahead and keep you updated. But we picked this path for a reason. Even the police shouldn't have any eyes on it. And you're the only one in the city that could do this."

"Right." Clain nods. *Except maybe Synric.*

"Alright, once you come around the bend here, you'll drop off at this building." Mitt points at a five-story building nestled in between a few smaller factories.

"Really? That seems a bit obvious."

"What do you mean?" Mitt asks.

"Well, if I remember correctly, all of those have been abandoned for years. I have scavenged out that way for shop parts before. It's not a discreet place to deal something like FreqyD."

"I thought the same but check this out. This is a list of all the places the police have been canvassing. They thought the same and have combed through here at least three times just this week." Clain thinks it over, placing his hand on his chin.

"How do we know this isn't a trap?"

"We don't. That is exactly why this is so dangerous. But Ed has never steered me wrong before. I can vouch for him at least."

"Alright. I want to spend less than an hour out there, so let's get moving."

"Cool. I'll fire up the drone and get it out front to meet you."

Clain makes his way toward the garage but stops when Zaria calls after him.

"Aren't you forgetting something?"

Clain turns around.

"Am I?"

"You're hardly wearing any clothes, dude! Your pale ass skin will stick out and there's a full moon tonight." She laughs.

"Oh, I guess you're right."

"Hey, with abs like those, I wouldn't wear clothes either." She winks at him. Mitt rolls his eyes.

"Zaria, quit flirting with him and give him the outfit."

"Outfit? You have something?"

"I do! Hemmed it up a bit to hopefully fit you better, but it might be snug but it's gnarly!"

"It's one of my old rail runner fits I used to wear. Take care of it, ok?" Mitt asks, frantically typing on his console.

"No promises." Clain smiles, following Zaria.

~~~

Back at Eagle's Equinox, Honey and Dawn have just arrived to meet Lenny and the Elder. Cato hides behind a nearby barrel, her nerves about the new arrivals compelling her to stay hidden, but her curiosity compelling her to spectate.

"Enjoy your joy ride?" Lenny badgers them.

"Jealous?" Dawn leans in with a raised brow.

"We'll see if I save your ass next time then," Lenny snidely remarks.

"Enough. Both of you," the Elder scolds them. "Could either of you have been followed?"

"No way," Dawn assures him. "I had Honey take a staggered path out here."

"I can vouch for that. You're lucky my tires don't go flat," Honey jests.

"They're right. Whoever this is is driving straight here like they know exactly where we are."

"I see it, there." Dawn points toward the horizon as a black car comes into view. "I'll man the other turret."

"Damn, you guys are protective," Honey comments. "How do you know they ain't friendly?"

"We have much we wish to keep concealed from the rest of the world and all visitors are arranged months in advance. We don't like surprises and have already endured your arrival. Certainly, you could understand that?" The Elder asks her.

"Sure, but Lenny here almost shot our heads off when we got here."

"Now I wish I did," he grumbles, climbing into the turret closest to him.

"Look, all I'm saying is keep cool. No need to escalate right away. What if they're lost?"

"Yeah sure, Honey. They drove straight out into the desert in the middle of a dust storm. Right along a path that's supposed to be hidden. Maybe they got lost."

"People are evacuating the city, remember? You never know."

"That is true. We shall exercise restraint." The Elder insists. Cato runs up to his side and grips his robes. "Worry not, little Cato. You are safe."

Dawn adjusts his grip, steadying his aim.

"They're almost here. You ready, Lenny?"

"Yeah, yeah. Worry about yourself." he barks.

The car draws closer. It hovers above the ground, its propulsion system sending dust out around it. The wind picks up. Rain begins to fall, obscuring visibility. They all squint, trying to keep the vehicle in sight.

"That's a..." Dawn begins, but Honey interrupts.

"An air rider. Advanced model too."

"Of course you would know."

"Naturally." She smiles.

"You sure are calm about this."

"Someone has to keep all this testosterone in check."

Lenny triggers the floodlights as the vehicle approaches. "You handle it, Dawn." Lenny urges.

"Fine." Dawn grabs a microphone. His voice booms over the speakers. "Halt immediately! Move any closer, and we will open fire!" The vehicle stops roughly 50 yards from the gate. "Whatever you do, do it slowly! Who are you, and why are you here?"

The moonroof of the vehicle opens slowly. The rain pours harder. A pair of hands slowly begin to poke out of the top of the car, visibly trembling as the forearms of the driver come into view.

"Please don't shoot!" a voice calls out. The shrill cry of a young girl follows.

"Daddy don't!" she pleads. Honey and Dawn look at each other, seemingly thinking the same thing.

"Who are you?" Dawn shouts again. The driver's head comes into view and Honey perks up with shock.

"Mr. Le?!" she shouts.

Fila pops out beside her dad, shouting back.

"Honey?! Is that you?"

"We know them. They're cool." Dawn jumps off the turret, rushing toward the staircase.

"Well, I don't know 'em," Lenny argues.

"Trust me, they're no threat to us," Honey explains, joining Dawn at the staircase.

"Trust you!? I don't know you either!"

"Lenny, calm down." The Elder barks. "Do you not trust Dawn's judgment?"

"Should I, after all the shit he's pulling? It's getting a bit too busy round here." Lenny's aim stays fixed on the car.

"They are the family that Clain has been living with. A kind father and his daughter. I assure you, they are no problem," Dawn insists again. The Elder pounds his staff on the ground, signaling the gate to open. The doors creak as they slowly obey.

"Enough Lenny. Get down from there and take a walk," he demands. Lenny scowls, powers down the turret and exits the seat, walking away without saying a word. "He will get over it. We have deep trust issues around here." The Elder smiles at Honey. "Go, meet with your friends and get them out of the rain."

The air rider slowly drives inside, parking next to Honey's C9X. Fila repeatedly pulls on the car door handle before its lock finally releases and she rushes to Honey, who greets her with a hug.

"Honey, I am so happy to see you." She begins to cry. "Our home was destroyed and we have nowhere to go. I was so scared. Daddy is hurt!"

"It's ok, Fila. Tell us everything, ok?" Honey gently rubs her head as her sobbing worsens, making her words unintelligible.

Dawn approaches the car, noticing Mr. Le struggling to get out. "Are you ok? Let me help you," offering him a hand.

"You don't look much better." Mr. Le comments, nodding towards Dawn's bloodied bandages.

"I'll be fine. What happened to you guys?"

"A giant robot destroyed the Pho King!" Fila blurts out.

"What?"

"It had Hux's dead head on it and a scary man on top of it."

Honey and Dawn look at each other, remembering Kruger and the Hux bot they saw at the Pit Pig hideout.

"Slow down, ok? Just breathe and let's get you out of the rain." Honey pulls Fila back up to her feet. Her clothes are in tatters and she shivers in Honey's arms.

"Why the hell would Kruger attack them?" Dawn asks.

"His name is Kruger?" Mr. Le asks, limping away from the car. "It approached our building, demanding that Clain come outside to face it. We have no idea who it was but he was in no mood to chat. I tried to talk him down, but he refused to believe that Clain wasn't there. It started pummeling our building with its fists before bombing it with missiles. We barely escaped."

"How did you get out of there?"

"Dad had a secret tunnel that went down into the sewers. It was inside Clain's shop."

"Well, it wasn't much of a secret. I had it covered to keep mischievous little girls out of there, but that didn't work now, did it, Fila?" He scolds her, and she looks away, embarrassed. "It was her idea, actually."

"It wasn't my idea though!" she insists, pushing herself away from Honey to run back to the car. She leans over to reach inside, then turns back to face them with something in her arms. "It was all Kiva! She guided us all the way through the sewers and right to this car!"

~~~

Clain sneaks down an alley near Mitt's compound towards the wayline rail. So far, he has been met with only silence; nobody is outside in the district. The moon is rising, seeming tinted in a pale purple hue. The city almost seems to moan with grief. The distant glow of fires illuminates their telltale black smoke plumes, evidence of riots. Citizens are lashing out against the militant police force keeping them inside, their confidence bolstered by the sight of Kruger and his Pit Pigs dominating the northern sector of the city. Everyone, Kruger included, is hunting for the source of FreqyD. The citywide lockdown has everyone curious about what could prompt such drastic measures. Kruger's plans, however, are far more ambitious. He sees the potential it has for control of the masses, the power to transform whoever wields it into a global threat. He relishes the thought, and his patience wears thin as his search drags on and the stakes rise ever higher.

The waylines were a thriving network in decades past. All a citizen needed to avoid the strangled gridlock of the streets was a decent board, fitted chair or pair of suitable shoes. Simple. Cheap. Efficient. But accidents, several fatal from irresponsible residents quickly ruined their public image, and the fear of the masses saw them powered down in short order. Many of the rails still remain, however, a tangled metal memento of the past weaving through the concrete forests of New Beam City. As Clain prepares to ride, he reflects on just how impressed he is with Mitt's solution. The chaos in the streets means nobody will be watching the skies. Nonetheless, speed is paramount. Any unnecessary risks could prove deadly.

"You ready?" Mitt's voice emits from the hovering drone in front of Clain.

"Yea. Feels stable enough."

"I still don't get why you insisted on bringing that piece of junk."

The Motherboard hilt sits securely holstered behind Clain's hip. He wraps his hand around the handle, like a sailor preparing to launch into the water.

"You're not the first one to call it that," he mutters. "You'll see. It'll be like steering the rudder of a sailboat."

"Oh wait, I think I get it. To counterbalance your left side and broken arm?"
"Exactly." Clain leans forward. "Think you can give me a pull to get me started?"

"Sure," Mitt agrees. He maneuvers the drone closer, and Clain grabs hold of it. He propels it forward slowly until Clain lets go, accelerating by channeling his magnetic power down through his feet. Now comfortably balanced, he moves the motherboard's handle left and right to see how much it helps him pivot.

"It's working. I think we can do this."

96

"Sweet! I'll fly ahead and let you know what's coming up."

Clain increases his speed further, the familiar feeling of riding the rails returning to him, albeit under much different circumstances. This guided path of the waylines was far easier to work with than a free-floating sword-turned-surfboard he struggled with in weeks prior. He smiles as the adrenaline hits, and the wind begins to whip past his face and through his hair, evoking memories of rides past and bringing an overwhelming sense of relief at being outside again. "You're enjoying this, aren't you?" Mitt asks.

"I am actually."

"All things considered, it's nice to see you smile, man."

Clain nods to the drone. His eyes scan the skyline, looking for the remains of the Pho King.

"They put the fire out, huh?"

"At your noodle shop? Yeah, a while ago. There's been no movement there since. We've kept an eye on it."

Clain remains silent, looking forward again as they round another bend bearing toward the east of the city.

"What's that?" Clain asks, seeing a scattering of lights ahead.

"Police drones. Not a problem, that's for sure." Mitt exclaims confidently. The drone surges ahead, then stops. A bright light flashes, emanating from its chassis. The blinking lights flicker out, and the drones fall to the ground.

"Woah man, you have mini EMPs on that thing?"

"Of course! This is my best drone. Modified it myself."

"You're a pretty impressive guy, Mitt. Gotta give you credit."

"Says the guy surfing on the waylines by himself. Thanks though. Means a lot coming from someone like you."

"Someone like me?"

"You got superpowers and shit! Plus, you were a repeat champ in the pits. Talk about street cred. I could never do any of that in my wildest dreams."

"Don't discount yourself too much. You've been spreading the truth in these streets for years. That's a superpower in itself. I'd never have the patience to do what you do."

"Sit in a chair yelling at a computer screen every day? It's not all that glamorous, as you've seen." Mitt laughs.

"I suppose, but now you're busting your ass to save the city and..."

"Heads up! A chunk of the rail is missing!" Mitt shouts.

"What?!" Clain shouts back.

"I don't know, man. Looks like a 100-foot gap."

"Shit. I see it." Clain thinks for a split second. "Bank upwards!"

"What?"

"Just do it!"

"Ok." Mitt obliges, swerving the drone upwards. Clain leans his body downward, preparing for the jump. "Hold steady in the middle of the gap."

"You're not planning what I think you're planning, are you?"

"Yep!" Clain shouts, leaping into the air. He winces as his shattered arm sends a bolt of pain up through his shoulder but manages to reach out with his unbroken one. He magnetizes himself, orienting his body on a collision course with Mitt's bot. He swings his legs forward like he is swinging from a rope, rocketing into the air and leveraging the momentum into a backflip, altering his trajectory as he enters freefall.

"You're not going to make it!" Mitt shouts.

"The fuck I ain't." Clain retrieves the broken Motherboard hilt. He channels his energy into it, points it at the rails, and pulls another small surge of momentum out of thin air, propelling him into position as he plants his feet back on the tracks. "Nailed it!"

"You gotta be kidding me."

"Not my first wayline ride," Clain gloats as he speeds forward.

"Wow, that was awesome! I can't believe you never ran with the rail riders."

"They were too slow for me." Clain smirks as he keeps ahead of Mitt's bot.

"Awe come on, man. I am supposed to scout ahead for you!"

"Then keep up," Clain urges as they pass under a bridge.

"Making great time. Way ahead of schedule."

"Told you. 7 minutes."

"Yea, but that was the main line. It's an easy straight across."

"Who said I took the easy path?"

"Alright, enough of the dick-measuring contest." Zaria's voice comes in on the mic. "You both need to focus. We aren't out here for fun."

"She's right," Clain agrees, slowing down to allow Mitt to pass him.

"You hear that Mitt. He said, 'she's right.' Are those words even in your vocabulary?"

"You two have good chemistry," Clain remarks. "Reminds me of my friends."

"Aren't we friends too by now?"

"Zar stop pestering him. You're drooling on the console."

"Oh, shut up. You're just jealous."

"You guys sure do bicker like childhood friends. Reminds me of someone."

"Oh, you have a childhood friend too? What are they like?" Zaria asks excitedly.

"Zar, weren't you just telling us to get serious? Not the time for chit-chat."

Clain chuckles. "Speaking of friends. What is going on over there?" He points a few blocks toward the north as groups of citizens rush across the road together.

"Right, our perfect distraction I forgot to mention! There is a massive block party forming in the inner city and many people are trying to rush there. The hoard is holding the police off as a sort of safe zone in protest of the lockdowns. Pure anarchy if you will."

"Block party huh?" Clain exclaims, seeming impressed.

"Probably a thousand people by now, all surrounding club Nis. No shocker, they probably instigated it."

Clain knew of the place but had never been. It was widely known as a sadomasochism venue often partaking in quite grotesque acts of celebration. A bit out of his scope of grunge, even for his tastes. His mind refocuses to the wayline as the ride starts to become rather bumpy. "We're almost there, aren't we?"

"Yep, should be coming into view soon."

"I think I see it up on the right."

"Now we just need to find an exit for you."

"No need."

"What?" Mitt asks.

"We can use the same move, and I can land on the roof."

"See, that is why I like this guy!" Zaria exclaims.

"That's way higher, though." Mitt's voice quivers with doubt.

"Dick-measuring contest, right?" Clain jokes.

"Alright, I assume you know what you can do, so I'll just have to trust you."

 Clain slows to a stop, allowing Mitt to bring the drone upward into position. He looks again over the skyline, his eyes locking onto the Cloud 9 building. His thoughts race, wondering if the same trick could get him to the top. He reflects back to his time on the motherboard, imagining himself hovering upward into its mysterious clouds to face Synric and whoever might be waiting at the top. His eyes drift further above the monstrous tower, fixating on the hypnotic glow of the purple moon.

"You ok, man? We're ready," Mitt calls over the mic.

"Yeah, sorry. What's up with the moon?" he replies.

"What do you mean?"

"Why is it purple?"

"Oh wow. You're right. I hadn't noticed."

"Maybe it's just weird coloring because of that dust storm out south in the desert?" Zaria suggests.

"Yea or the increasing amount of chemicals being sprayed out of Cloud 9." Mitt snarls with disgust.

"Could be..." Clain replies, doubtful.

"We can worry about that later. The coast is clear over here. No one is on the roof. Ready when you are, Clain," Mitt assures him.

"Got it." Clain rushes forward down into the bend of the waylines as it banks around the side of the industrial factories. He leans into the curve before leaping sideways into a flip. He grapples upward toward the drone and swings himself high above the building.

He retrieves the Motherboard hilt, placing it beneath his feet while freefalling toward the rooftop.

"Shit, you're coming in too fast!"

"I got this," he assures them as his descent quickens. Unable to control the small chunk of the sword, he struggles to slow his momentum. He falls forward into a roll on his spine. His arm screams at him, sending the sword sparking and screeching forward across the rooftop, crashing into a massive air conditioning unit with a loud bang.

"Well, that was subtle. Are you ok?" Zaria asks.

"Sorry about that. Pain in my arm screwed up my landing."

"Drop something?" Mitt asks as the drone brings the Motherboard hilt back to him.

"Yeah, thanks. Can you scan for any movement?" Clain asks.

"Already on it," Mitt confirms as a blue aura emanates from the drone. "Everything seems quiet. Hmm."

"Something wrong?"

"Doesn't feel right. A crash like that should've alerted someone, but it didn't."

"That's a bad thing?"

"Well, if we're looking for the source of FreqyD, I'd assume there would be more fanfare after that kind of arrival."

"Yeah, good point," Clain agrees, climbing to his feet and placing the Motherboard back in its holster.

"Looks like there's a door over there." Mitt's drone floats over to a small metal door, lighting the way for Clain. He approaches it slowly, limping from the rough landing. He tests the door handle.

"It's locked."

"No worries. I can pick it open with the drone."

"No need," Clain assures them as a click sounds out from the handle.

"Ahh, right. Mr. Magnetic over here," Mitt jests.

"Wow, that must come in handy," Zaria comments.

"Only when needed." Clain smiles as they head into the stairwell.

"Welcome to Rolling Sands Mall, Mitt announces. Clain takes a breath, steadying himself.

"Let's get this over with."

CHAPTER 6 – You Are Safe Here

Neon Hills shopping mall stands atop a large incline, overlooking the abandoned remains of a once vibrant and sprawling shopping district. The back of the massive structure faces west, towards the distant, sandy mountain ranges, casting a stark silhouette against the desert landscape, a pinnacle of commerce turned decaying mausoleum overlooking the bones of the buildings below, a long-forgotten piece of New Beam City, a memory so distant not even its name remains, only its image, a dilapidated reminder of human wastefulness.

The waylines do not extend this far out, leaving Clain to hike the remainder of the journey here, with Mitt keeping him company through the drone's speakers. He stands at the base of the steps leading into the mall. Mitt hovers the drone to his right and provides a cone of light forward.

The steps and the surrounding grounds are covered in trash and trees ill-suited to life in the desert, long dead from thirst. The pungent, oily drippings from the pile of garbage have left the pathway slick and filthy. Even stepping as cautiously as he can, Clain still repeatedly finds his feet planted in pungent piles of old trash, the content he wouldn't be able to identify even if he wanted to.

"I feel like I'm walking through a minefield of snakes and scorpions," Clain says through gritted teeth, slipping on yet another pile of filth and nearly falling backward.

Mitt's drone chirps.

"Thankfully, I don't have to smell any of this," he laughs. I feel sick to my stomach just looking at all of it."

"Thanks," Clain mutters. "Smack him for me, Zaria."

"Ouch. Dammit, Zar!" Mitt complains.

Zaria's flirtatious whisper comes through the mic.

"You're welcome!"

"Alright, let's get serious. We don't know who or what could be in here." Mitt insists, floating the drone forward to inspect the entrance.

At the landing, Clain takes a moment to collect himself. His left arm is throbbing in its sling. He closes his eyes, inhales slowly, and then releases a long exhale, trying to ignore the stench. Gradually, his heart rate calms. The Elder's teachings return to him as he channels his training to mute his pain and amplify healing toward his wounds. He will be able to ensure. So long as he stays calm as the pain pills and their calming side effects are quickly wearing off. It may prove challenging. The sooner he completes his task here, the better. His eyes open as Mitt calls his name.

"Uh, Clain," interrupts Mitt. "That runner suit has a mask in the collar. You should use it, especially for those deep breaths you're taking. My scans show the air quality is in the yellow."

"Now you tell me," Clain sighs. He fiddles with the collar until a mask deploys up and over his nose.

"That drone got any weapons?" He steps up to the doors, the broken glass crunching underfoot. An aluminum security shutter is locked in place, and two padlocks are at the bottom.

"It's got a modified etching laser. Check it out."

Clain crouches to watch Mitt work. His drone's laser effortlessly melts the shackles on the locks. "Wow," Clain says. "Not bad." A quick, sizzling hiss emanates from the laser emitter as Mitt turns it off.

"Easy" Mitt gloats. Clain casts the melted locks aside, gripping the door handle as he stands up. It rolls loudly before snagging halfway, sending dust clouds dancing across the drone's light. Pitch-black darkness lies ahead, pierced by intermittent beams of dim blue and purple light. Clain can make out faint shapes and silhouettes within their dim glow, but none are clear enough to identify.

 "Yikes. That's too noisy. Go ahead and fly under."

"Already in," Mitt announces from Clain's blind spot, startling him as he squeezes under the door. With his unbroken shoulder, Clain pushes the shutter up a little further, taking care not to make more noise as he maneuvers underneath and into the hallway, diligently keeping his injured arm out of harm's way.

"Damn. You did that so easily," Zaria comments.

"Been to places like these more times than I'd care to remember." Clain snickers.

"With a broken arm, though?"

"Maybe. It's not my first time with a broken arm, either." He cautiously removes his grip from the door, which seems securely lodged open, allowing the purple moonlight to illuminate the cracked white tile of the entrance. Clain looks at the drone. "You first," he says while gesturing forward.

"Aww. Are you scared?" Mitt jokes.

"Nah," he replies calmly. "Your drone is just a great guinea pig."

The drone twirls as Mitt shows off its nimbleness.

"This is my most advanced model, so you're in luck! Custom modded by yours truly, as a matter of fact."

"Then you should have no issue leading the way."

"Nope! I'm nice and cozy here in my chair." He gives a relaxed, exaggerated sigh. "If only Zaria weren't breathing her hot breath down my neck."

Clain hears Zaria smack him again.

"Keep focused and stop patronizing him," she orders.

"Yow! That hurts Zar! If you make me crash, you're covering it." The drone glides through the entrance into a wide-open atrium filled with kiosks long since abandoned. Dying weeds and intricate networks of cobwebs line their walls and foundations.

Clain steps down a ledge as his shoes crunch onto more broken glass. The sound echoes softly. The rancid odor of old garbage has given way to a musty cocktail of mold and dust. The tiles are cracked by plant life forcing their way through the crumbling structure, small, skeletal trees, and hardy spiked weeds defiantly reclaiming the ground.

Somewhere in the distance, Clain can hear water dripping, occasionally overtaken by the steady, creaky groan of frogs chirping nearby. He walks up to an information booth and squints, trying to make out the faded text on its signs. Mitt flies the drone higher, increasing the radius of his light's glow, illuminating a large, circular enclosure flooded with water as black as the surrounding darkness. The stagnant liquid ripples gently as droplets collect and fall from somewhere too high up for Mitt's light to reach. At the center of the poisoned pool lies a moss-covered fountain.

"So where do we go from here?" Clain inquiries.

"Your guess is almost as good as mine," Mitt responds. "The energy pulse leads north, I think. My readings keep changing. Whenever I think I've got it, I try to ping the source, and...nothing. I haven't been able to pin it down."

Clain sighs and rubs the bridge of his nose.

"I guess we'll just head in that direction for now. Let me know if you pick anything up."

The ground floor is nothing but a looted wasteland. The storefront windows are smashed, the shelves are broken and empty, sections of the wall are missing or burned, and the walls that still stand are pockmarked with bullet holes. Nothing of value remains.

"It's fascinating, isn't it?" remarks Mitt. "People used to do all their shopping in these places.

"I've explored plenty of abandoned places, but nothing like this."

"Really? What for?"

Clain smiles, amused by the stark differences in upbringing between himself and his new ally. "Many reasons. I find it fascinating how wasteful and materialistic people have been; they just abandon the old for the new. Plus, you can find some real treasures in a place like this. It's how I got the GG Shop off the ground."

"Oh, right! You salvaged a lot of older stuff, huh? Guess I should have visited in person instead of only making online orders. Maybe I'll come by after..." he stops, realizing the GG Shop is gone.

A pang of grief for his old home stabs at Clain, disturbing his fragile calm. The pain he is suppressing stands ready to flare if he lets it falter. He goes silent and begins to regulate his breathing, restoring his meditative state. The pain recedes into the background once again.

"Why did you have to remind him of that right now?" Zaria barks at Mitt.

"I know; I'm sorry, Clain."

"It's fine. Keep moving." Clain's strides lengthen as he works to keep pace with the drone. "Anyway," Clain breathes deeply before continuing. "I took a lot from places like this, but sometimes I just had nowhere else to go. Other times, I was just looking for a fight." He navigates around some fallen wreckage from the roof above. "This place is just eerie, though. Almost looks lived in." He approaches the gaping hole left by the ceiling pieces at his feet. It opens towards the second floor. "Maybe we should check out the upper level?"

The trio agrees, but the nearby elevator shaft is barricaded by old, rusted machinery - cash registers ripped from the store counters, antique computer monitors and towers, kitchen appliances, all stacked like a bizarre monument. But even if these obstacles weren't here, the elevator would assuredly have no power. The closest escalator is useless, too. Its staircase has turned red, oxidized to crumbling dust. At some point in the course of its protracted decay, falling ceiling debris dealt the killing blow, punching several of the stairs inward and maiming the guts of the machinery beneath. Clain sighs.

"Stairs it is, then."

Clain and the drone spot a stairwell in a distant corner. As they walk towards it, an old mural comes into view, its original intent desecrated beyond recognition. The once-smiling shoppers of days past have been warped into twisted visions of suffering. The mall patrons now wear tortured expressions as carnage rages and the old Neon Hills complex burns. Hellish creatures now hunt them, tearing off limbs, cutting deep gashes into their victims, and reveling in the sprays of blood issuing forth from the wounds they inflict. In the distance, black-cloaked figures observe. What little of their body language is visible through their vestments demonstrates at most a calm interest, as though such a sight is routine for them. Clain looks down and clears his throat, noticing it has become dry and scratchy. Taking a moment to collect himself, he looks back up at the wall. "Are you seeing all this?"

The drone whirls before Mitt replies, "Yeah, I see it." Then there is a clicking sound. "The drone is also picking something else up. Let me switch to blacklight."

The mayhem painted on the wall receding into the background as characters of an unfamiliar language show up under the purple glow. Clain points to the cloaked figures within the windows.

"Roman numerals?" he asks.

"Looks like it," Mitt whispers.

"Who could they be?"

"Maybe the Illuminaries we keep hearing about?"

"Illuminaries, huh? What do you guys know about them?"

"Not much, honestly. Supposedly, it's some kind of ominous cult. Religious zealots, maybe. But that's all I've heard. And even that's just a rumor."

Clain rubs his hand over the Roman numerals. "There must be hundreds of these. This definitely represents something." His fingers follow along the red river of blood toward a larger piece of art. He gestures to Mitt's drone.

109

"Shine the light over here." Clain steps back as Mitt obliges. The light reveals a silhouette of a man on his knees, bleeding into the stream of blood the creatures from the last scene were drinking from.

"Wow. Who the hell is that?" Mitt comments as a silhouette of a man on his knees, bleeding into the same stream of blood the creatures were feasting within. Clain adjusts the Motherboard on the back of his waist, holding in a shudder as he notices the bleeding man's hair. Spiked, white, just like his own.

"Good question."

"What language do you think this is?" Mitt asks, snapping Clain out of his thoughts. "I see nothing matching it online, which is even stranger." The drone switches off the black light.

Clain shakes his head. "Maybe we don't want to know."

"Hopefully it's all just graffiti."

Clain knows the drone is recording. There is no need for further study of the apocalyptic scene; they can reflect on it later. His throbbing arm reminds him of how eager he is to leave, so he and Mitt press on. The stairwell door is mercifully unblocked, but opening it releases a smell not unlike a badly neglected gas station bathroom.

Clain frowns with disgust. "Wish this mask blocked out all the smell. It's strong enough to come through the mask." He turns around to face the drone as it comes around the bend. "And don't remind me how grateful you are that you can't smell any of it."

"Whoa. Ok, Captain Cranky. You need a moment?"

Clain shakes his head. "Nah. I just want to find whoever is responsible for FreqyD and get the hell out of here."

"Same. This place isn't exactly ideal for my drone either. The battery's almost half empty, so we should head back ASAP."

Near the landing at the top of the stairs, Clain freezes. Beams of purple moonlight punctuate the darkness, but streaks of black shadows lie between them. And among those shadows is a person. One that, thankfully, does not seem to have noticed their presence. Clain inches forward, putting a hand up to keep the drone in place. A minute passes, and all the while, the figure stands motionless, an eerie silhouette outlined by the dim, violet light. Clain retrieves the damaged hilt of the Motherboard from his back, holding it by his hip. He darts forward, hoping to take the shadowed figure by surprise, but his shoes squeak on the linoleum as he abruptly stops just short of his target. It remains unfazed, motionless. With the Motherboard still firmly gripped in his hand, he pushes his knuckles into the figure's back, feeling not flesh but cold, hard plastic. Mitt's drone cautiously floats behind him, allowing Clain to see more clearly.

"A mannequin?" Mitt says.

"Not just one," observes Clain. "Look around."

The drone slowly spins, casting its light around the room, revealing dozens of mannequins. They appear to have been arranged with intention. Some of them are plastered and strung up on the ceiling with their stiff arms reaching down as if to grab those passing by.

"Humor me and turn the black light back on." Mitt quickly triggers the headlamp to switch, and the ensuing purple glow reveals words all over the carefully arranged figures.

"Limbo, greed, lust, gluttony, anger, heresy, violence, fraud, treachery." Clain reads aloud as the drone shines over them. "It's repeated over and over all across the room."

Zaria chimes in.

"Why does that sound familiar? Hmmm. Oh, I know! Isn't that..."

"Dante's Inferno," Clain whispers.

"Yea! That!"

A moment later, the drone moves back up towards the mannequins on the ceiling.

"Oh. My…" Mitt exhales.

"More Roman numerals," Clain grumbles. "The strange language downstairs must correlate with this."

The drone inspects the mannequins on the ceiling.

"But what does it all mean?"

Clain's next step is interrupted as something on the floor snags around his ankle, nearly sending him into the ground face-first.

"Shit, what is this?" he complains as the drone light shines toward his feet.

"A backpack?" Clain asks, unwrapping the strap from his ankle and lifting it to eye level. "Kayden?"

"Wait, what? Let me see that," Zaria demands.

"Take it easy, Zar. Only one of us can fly this, so back off."

"You guys know a Kayden?" Clain asks.

"Someone Zaria knows. Long story."

"There's a whole pile of backpacks in the corner there." Clain points towards the back of the room. The bot turns to shine light in that direction when the sound of shattering glass rings out from somewhere nearby.

"Holy shit. What was that?" Mitt whispers.

"I don't know but let's keep moving." Clain insists, cautiously navigating around the backpack and mannequin-littered floor. He exits the room and stops at a broken pane of glass. The surrounding area is trashed, but most of the windows are undamaged.

Something catches Clain's eye as the trio passes an old gaming store. Behind the glass, to the right of the smashed-out door, is a cardboard cutout. A big, burly man with a beautiful woman snuggled under his arm, advertising a fighting video game. The text is faded, as is most of the cutout. While the pair's hairstyles are woefully outdated, there is nonetheless something familiar about the man. *This dude looks just like Dawn. Maybe that's where he got that goofy haircut.* Clain laughs to himself.

"Someone you know?" Mitt's voice sounds through the drone.

"This poster is for a game over fifty years old. Someone I know dresses quite similar to this guy." Debris crunches beneath his boots as he turns away. "What kind of an adult would dress like a video game character," he laughs.

"There's nothing wrong with that!" Zaria quips.

Another escalator comes into view, rusted and inoperable but intact, its stairs still climbable. Looking up as he ascends, he sees light emitting from somewhere near the top level. It's coming from a storefront towards the back portion of the mall.

"Hey, you see that light?" Clain points.

"I'll go up and take a look," Mitt answers.

The drone flies up the two levels and partially vanishes into the dark. Clain can momentarily see the lamp light until it moves out of sight. His ears hear the faint humming of the drone mixed with drafts of wind echoing through the massive building. He hears Mitt's voice exclaiming something, but he cannot determine what it is. Clain whispers as loudly as he can, hoping the drone's hearing will hear what human ears cannot.

"Mitt! I can't hear you!"

There is no response. And then the silence is broken, not by Mitt's voice, but by the sound of crashing metal ringing through the empty halls, as if something is being slammed into the ground with inhuman force. A split second later, a light spirals down from the top level, straight towards him. Clain unsheathes the motherboard and whips it around in front of him. A bolt of pain shoots up through his tattered arm as the motherboard absorbs the impact, shielding Clain's face from the projectile. He looks down at the object as it clatters to the floor. Mitt's drone, sparking and seizing, with a large portion of its body missing. Goosebumps form on his arms as the humidity begins to feel suffocating. He breaks into a cold sweat, his clothes clinging to him like leeches. He feels eyes on him but cannot see through the murky darkness that fills the gaps of the lavender-colored moonlight. He is alone now, and he knows it.

113

He rushes over to the downed drone, kneeling beside and examining it. "Mitt, can you hear me at all?" he whispers.

The response he hears is not one he expects. He hears music—old music, like something out of the 1920s, complete with the scratches and pops of a vinyl record. Clain looks around, trying to find what could be playing it when a screen on what remains of the drone's chassis lights up, and several texts from Mitt appear.

"Drone was slammed by something. Be careful. Keep the drone near you so we can track it. We are coming!"

"Shit." Clain exhales. He sheathes the motherboard and tucks the drone under his arm. Thankfully, its headlamp still works, lighting the way for him. He begins to climb the escalator toward the next level. His brow furrows as the source of the music comes into view.

This level houses a vibrant, antique-style roller skating rink. *X-treme X-cape Xenolalia* reads a giant overhead sign spray-painted fluorescent green. Accompanying the blare of the music are the sounds of arcade games, a popcorn machine, and the clinking of coins mixed with the chatter of people. The buttery fragrance of popcorn begins to fill Clain's nostrils as a nearby concession stand lights up. The entrance is pristine, and it's lit up almost like it's opening day.

Why am I just now seeing the light from this place? he wonders. He turns to look up at the fifth level and can see that it is even brighter up there than before. Clain walks through the clean glass entrance with the drone still firmly gripped under his armpit. The music booms louder as he enters, but there doesn't appear to be anyone else here. The ticket booth is unmanned, as is the skate rental counter. The red carpet bears some stains of use, but the rink itself seems untouched by time. Light dances across the floor, refracted through a disco ball and reflected off the mirrored walls.

The scene doesn't inspire nostalgia for Clain but paranoia. Something about a small bastion of cleanliness and functionality among what is otherwise a mecca of decay seems...untrustworthy. So, he makes his way to the concession stand instead. He slides the backs of his fingers across the cool countertop, stopping to inspect the popcorn machine. The rotten product inside starkly contrasts with the fresh aroma suggesting freshly popped popcorn. He sets the drone on the counter and picks up a single kernel from the rancid pile. He can almost feel the warm butter between his thumb and forefinger. *Am I losing it?* He wonders, watching as the kernel seems to transform into a perfectly edible snack, all traces of rot gone. He decides to taste it. It's delicious.

What am I doing? It isn't the only question in his mind, but it is the one that repeats most often.

 "Oh, I hear you, pressing down hard on me. Like you came and put a curse on me." a voice whispers over his shoulder. He spins around, seeing nothing but the vibrant roller rink. One song ends, and another begins. The song seems familiar to Clain, but other than the fact that it's old, he cannot remember anything about it. Strobe lights pulse and swivel to the beat of the music. He retrieves the drone and makes his way toward the rink.

"Hello?" he calls out.

"Like you came and put a curse on me," the song continues.

A cushioned barrier that comes up to Clain's waist wraps around the rink, accompanied by a whole wall of mirrors surrounding the room. Another mural cascades across the ceiling, this one unmarred with images of grotesque bloodshed. It depicts gleeful teenagers skating through a beautiful park. At its center is a giant tree providing everyone with fruit and shade from the summer sun. Children read books under the massive branches.

"He once told me, certain creatures aren't just fantasy. They just become a challenge to see."

Clain takes a cautious step onto the spotless floor. No scuffs from patrons' skates mark the slick surface. As he nears the center, the silence is broken by the sound of rollerblades, the grinding of their wheels intensifying in volume and number the closer he gets to the center. He spins around, looking for the skaters responsible for the noise. But the rink remains empty, the refractions of the disco ball reflecting off of nothing but the floor and mirrors. His grip on the drone loosens, and his free hand hovers over the Motherboard's grip. His body stills as years of training send waves of pre-fight calm throughout his body. But nothing changes. The lights continue to move with the music. The popcorn machine continues to pop. And Clain stands alone.

The phantom skaters pick up speed, the sound of their movements suggesting they are approaching inhuman velocity. The strobes flash faster. Brighter. The glittering spots of light scattered throughout the rink blend together, leaving trails, casting doubles of themselves. Identifiable features of the environment bleed into one another as Clain's eyes lose their ability to focus. The melody of the music becomes discordant, and the vocals fluctuate in pitch and speed, from a soprano compressing sentences into split seconds to a bass elongating single words into what feels like minutes. Clain's sense of time seems to be deteriorating along with the melody.

"Made from pieces of a memory. So tell me what you want me to be. Oh, I feel you. Your nails still pressing down hard. On me, on me, on me" she sings. Goosebumps erupt across Clain's body, seemingly everywhere all at once. The voice sounds strikingly familiar, tying his stomach in knots. "Now that we've come this far I bet their eyes are watching us move" *watching us move* he whispers with her. "Burning the candle twice as bright as we intended to, as we intended to." Clain's eyes widen as he staggers backward. "Don't fight it, or else it won't come true. Such thoughts were much too flawed for you. I need you to try to understand If you're to take my hand."

The music cuts with the lights, and Clain is drenched in inky darkness. The hum of circling skaters continues. He clumsily drops the drone and reaches for the Motherboard but grabs only air, grunting in frustration. Her song continues "Constrict the voice that says it's just a joke. Restricted feelings at the base of the oak. I know there's something that you cast on me, so should we set it free?" He feels pinned to the spot, pulled as though trapped beyond the event horizon of a black hole. His heart feels broken and his ability to judge the orientation of his own body seems to have vanished. He feels the sensation of solid ground under his feet, yet simultaneously feels as though he is floating within a vast expanse of nothing. The clash of kinesthetic sensations suddenly collapses into awareness when his foot catches on the ground, and he trips backward. His hand snaps to his back, his grip slamming closed around the Motherboard's hilt. He draws his sword with reckless abandon, screaming into the empty room.

"Who's there?!" He turns slowly, inspecting the space for any sign of anyone, spotting the object responsible for his fall: The disco ball, long since destroyed, signs of age and years of gathered dust readily visible along its cracked surface. The same one he had thought was hanging above just moments ago. A raspy, distorted cackle reverberates throughout the space as a thick fog creeps along the floors. He registers an orange glow in his periphery, the only light source available. Mitt's drone. The light flickers and begins to dull.

"No, not now. Come on!" In a panic, he begins to pound on the drone, hoping the light will switch back on.

"Don't fight it, or else it won't come true." The female vocals return to a whisper. "Such thoughts were much too flawed for you. I need you to try to understand if you're to take my hand."

Clain frantically fidgets with the drone until the blacklight suddenly turns on, directly into his face. He shields his eyes as it beams upward. The mural on the ceiling begins to glow, appearing to detach from the roller rink. It floats alone in a void with Clain, both encased in the surrounding fog.

The skaters on the mural spring to life, skating along the painted course. A dog runs through the lush green grass, leaping for the frisbee spinning ahead. Bees hover over blooming sunflowers. The branches of the giant tree sway to the rhythm of a gentle breeze. Nearly everything was bathed in soft, yellow sunlight, a soothing vision of peace. But the idyll is short-lived.

The sunlight shifts to a deep crimson. The laughing parkgoers morph into hideous, gibbering abominations, bristling with teeth barely covered by slimy lips, flexing webbed claws hungry for flesh to rend, their bulbous eyes shakily scanning their decaying surroundings. The grass begins to die, its deep, dark green fading to a sickly shade mottled with brown, all of it barely visible underneath the piles of shredded bodies, scarcely recognizable as human but for remnants of faces left twisted into the cries of pain uttered with the dying breaths of lungs cast into the swaths of fresh carnage littering the dying park. The skate course is a river of blood and viscera. The oak tree, once a centerpiece unifying a depiction of a perfect day is now a towering inferno. Its bark has changed to flesh, charred and bruised. The trunk is now a writhing mass of faces trapped in agony, seeming to form a podium with an angelic figure standing at its apex.

117

Clain closes his eyes, trying desperately to shield his mind from the vision of the newly formed hellscape. He does not move but once again feels like he is tumbling through darkness, traveling through a cosmic wormhole. The mask around his nose feels suffocating. An acidic burn builds in his throat. He coughs as his head starts to pound. She calls to him again, "It's not that I'm afraid, I only wish that you stayed." His eyes dart open to see the silhouette of a woman, singing to a sea of creatures that listen to her song within a vast sea of fog. Their hands swaying back and forth as if worshiping this dark siren who calls out to him. His heart sinks, as he desperately tries to make out her face but it evades him. He reaches for her, and her to him but she suddenly vanishes.

"Rise Clain." A voice calls to him. The familiarity cuts through the haze of macabre and twisted visions, the tension in his body releasing like a taut, steel wire snapping in two.

"Tia?" he screams in anger.

"Yes. Speak with me." The monster's tone is gentle. Inviting.

Clain rushes to his feet. He is still in the roller rink, though it no longer stands as the one place seemingly untouched by time. He can see it for what it is now. Just another among the many businesses left to crumble and rot. Most surrounding mirrors are cracked, but the few directly ahead stand unmarred. However, they have changed. They no longer reflect but offer a window into another world. The world of his premonitions. Tia hovers there below a tree, as she has always appeared to him. Her voice cracks.

"I am losing control, Clain," she whispers, seeming in pain.

"Losing control of what?"

"Your memories."

"What do you mean?"

"I can only hold on for so long. Soon, I will be powerless to block that which calls to you."

"You mean the singing?"

"Indeed. She calls to you. She wants you to remember her, and I am what keeps her hidden within your mind."

"Why? Who is she?"

"You will remember soon. I cannot restrain her much longer. For now, you must escape this place. You are not safe here."

"Stop being so vague!" Clain shouts. He screws his eyes shut, willing the vision away. "None of this is real..."

"It is real. You can feel it. I know you can. She is real and she waits for you. There is no time left and I cannot protect your mind much longer. My debts are almost paid."

Suddenly a brick crashes into the mirror, shattering it across the roller rink floor. Clain spins around but is met with only darkness. "Who's there?!" he screams. "Stop being a coward and come out!"

Once seemingly immune to the ravages of time, the rink now appears as it truly is: just another casualty of the surrounding decay. Clain scrambles to his feet, retrieves the drone and tucks it under his arm as he hastily makes for the exit. His mind flails, searching for an explanation for what just happened. *Maybe I've been gassed?* He shakes his head as if trying to rattle the memory loose and discard it. *No more distractions. I need to leave.* He bounds up the escalator to the top floor, scanning the walls and ceiling for an escape route. A door, a window, a vent. Anything. There is only one storefront here, the source of the piercing glow. Everything else is hidden away, the doors and walls covered by mirrors stretching from floor to ceiling. The drone's black light is still shining, revealing graffiti all over the glass, images of eyeballs painted in myriad styles, sizes, and expressions, human, alien, mechanical, curious, spiteful, terrified, crying, bloodshot, and clear. Together, they form an aggregate illusion of awareness, tracking Clain's movements as he approaches the light source.

As he nears the apparently abandoned shop, he notices webs of cracks snaking their way up some of the mirrors and sees a dense fog lazily swirling within, casting occasional wisps of the opaque mist out the door. His reflection in the massive glass walls vanishes, the mirrored sheen giving way to semi-clarity, like a window, providing, through the sections left unpainted, a glimpse at the fog within.

119

Ghostly hands extend towards him. The disembodied hands of men, women, and children. Lost souls wandering an inescapable void. They wave at Clain in unison, a sorrowful goodbye. Their deep melancholy can be felt through their gestures alone, their conveyance unimpeded by the lack of bodies or faces. It runs so deep and flows so thick that it drips from every finger.

Clain desperately wants to believe this is a hallucination brought on by the stale, poisoned air that sits stagnant all throughout the abandoned mall, that his mask is defective and has allowed him to breathe it in, that perhaps he has been unconscious for almost his entire time here, that Mitt's drone still works and is being compelled by its operator to use every available tool at its disposal to wake him. He shakes his head again, over and over, closing his eyes each time and hoping that the visions will dissipate and give way to a saner reality when he opens them. They don't. He pauses at the entrance. Before him is a light and fixture store. The soothing quality of the glow is a surprising and welcome change from the pervasive dread that lingers in every other shop. This place seems better maintained than the rest. But within reason this time, not like the rink, not impossibly clean and new in blatant defiance of the surrounding rot. The floors are clean, if somewhat cracked and worn, the store's inventory sits on its shelves, dusty and disorganized perhaps, but not in a way that signifies looting or neglect. Several lamps sit on the floor tiles, but there appears to be a path left in between them. It looks and feels…lived in.

As Clain makes his way into the store, following the lone lane of clear floor weaving between the lamps, he spots a dimly lit opening in the back wall. An exposed elevator shaft. The edges of the drywall are chipped and torn, cracks spidering out from the spots where the final blows that created the opening were dealt. The beginnings of faded, illegible graffiti is scrawled over the edge of the torn-out section of the wall, the rest cast aside with the demolished pieces it once sat on. Scrawled in red paint above the opening are the words *Path of Enlightenment*. To the right of the opening is a table and a large, open wooden box. A huge black disk spins with a sharp, needled point hovering over it. The crackle of static emitting from a nearby speaker.

Clain turns around, searching for an exit from this accursed complex. *No fuckin' way I'm going down there. There has to be another way out of here.* He shines the light through the store. Something catches his attention as the beam sweeps over the center of the room, and he quickly refocuses the light there. It's floating in the air and coming right at him. Clain steps behind a nearby counter, watching the slow-moving object as it flies by and crashes into the wall next to the elevator shaft. *Was that... A paper airplane?*

"Stop fucking with me!" he shouts back through the store. Only his own echo responds. He slowly approaches the airplane, nudging it with his fist. The drone's black light reveals glowing ink on it. He kneels down to unfold the paper, and his eyes widen in shock. It is a paper menu from the Pho King. In the middle is a giant question mark, the dot at the bottom of it replaced with a downward-pointing arrow. Clain peers into the elevator shaft. He spots small beads of light floating like fireflies as he looks around. Whatever these things are, they appear to work more like flashlights than fireflies. They can somehow focus the direction of their ambient glow, and they're pointing it down. He follows the lights and sees a far brighter light at the bottom of the shaft. A cool draft of air kisses his face, almost inviting him to enter. He clears his throat and spits into the gap in the wall, watching the gob fall and listening for the impact. There is no sound when it hits, at least that he can hear. It is probably a sixty to seventy-foot drop, though, with his training, using the elevator cables as climbing ropes would probably be trivial. But should he?

I climbed up five levels only to have to drop down six. Clain ponders, looking back at the Pho King menu. He tucks it away in his jacket. It has no practical use, but its familiarity is comforting. He grips the Motherboard's handle, squeezing it tightly as he reflects on why he created it. To protect his friends. His body is aching and his mind is frayed. But something here seems to want to show him something. His hands tighten as his rage returns. Someone is playing games with him, too, in a way he is not used to, in a way his training has no answers for. He can take on opponents who taunt him, toy with him, and try to force his emotions to supplant his focus, some going so far as to threaten those close to him. A grave mistake. But none of them have ever had direct access to his mind. Whatever or whoever is here does. He tries to rein in his anger, his indignation, as he resumes his search for answers, prepared for violence, eager to engage in it if his answers do not come.

"Fine! You want to play? Let's play!" His threat reverberates throughout the shaft. But again, no response comes. He peers down into the elevator shaft, catching a glimpse of a red-orange glow through a small square hole at the bottom. He lunges towards the cable, wrapping his good arm around it mid-jump, grimacing as his other arm strongly reminds him how broken it is. After catching his breath, he begins to lower himself, aided by his magnetic abilities and using the Motherboard on his hip as an anchor. His descent is steady and uneventful until the smell of a campfire wafts up to his nose, growing stronger as he lowers further into the darkness. His patience falters. He eyes the elevator car below and hastens his descent. The square light below him increases in size. He can make out the flicker of fire now. He knows whoever is down there is ready and waiting for him. He tries to suppress his trembling, reassuring himself that, should he have to fight, his training will render one broken arm a minor inconvenience.

They better be ready. I won't hold back.

CHAPTER 7 - Meet The Illuminaries

Clain drops onto the parked elevator car. The solid thud of his landing confirms it sits on the bottom floor. Far from subtle, but then again, his shouting moments ago wasn't either. His wounded arm has been painfully shifted in its sling by his landing, and he winces as he moves it back into place. He returns his attention to his breath, trying to center himself, but the smell of the campfire below diverts his focus. His thoughts are dragged into hazy, sepia-toned memories of late nights bantering and laughing around the campfires of Eagle's Equinox with Dawn.   He kneels, inspecting the inside of the elevator. Sinister graffiti peeks out from beneath years of accumulated filth. Warped, demonic faces sneering and cackling at each other, the minds within lost to insanity. Deep, bassy trance music verberates from the room below, its rumbling beats laced with garbled yet hypnotic female vocals. He grips the edge of the elevator access hatch and swiftly lowers himself inside, landing gently. The car hardly moves as his feet touch the ground or the layers of cans, bottles, and other less identifiable articles of garbage that coat it. The tension in Clain's shoulders releases slightly as he sees the open elevator doors. From the elevator car, he spots the source of the fire: A junked-up station wagon, at least a century old. The rear door is open, and the trunk is glowing with flickering flames.

 A parking garage. That means there must be an exit nearby. He steps out of the elevator, grasping for some nebulous source of comfort. The area is filled with chain-link fences and abandoned cars. Litter is strewn throughout, and the foundations of the piles congealed into sticky sludge with age. Thankfully, the mesquite wood fire just ahead offsets the pungent stench of decay. Its tender is nowhere to be seen, but he knows he isn't alone. The loud music reverberating from the shadows suggests as much. Its unintelligible lyrics do little to comfort him.

"I've walked right into your trap. You could at least greet me properly!" He takes a cautious step forward, seeing nothing dangerous in his immediate vicinity. Still, as he advances further into the crumbling structure, he meticulously scouts his every step, scanning for traps—an old habit he picked up from Dawn and a significant contributor to his continued existence. There are none, but something else catches his eye just past the fire. A crude altar, spray painted with cryptic symbols, spread over the nearby floor, up the support pillars, and onto the ceiling. The jagged lines of the same unknown language as before, an almost eldritch quality to the shapes they form, inviting sadism well suited to the grim rituals that most likely occurred here. The fire's flickering light casts dancing shadows across the symbols, and its flames ignite an eerie glow in their lines. Sitting atop the altar appears to be a ceremonial dagger, its wickedly curved blade catching the light and casting the engravings upon it in a bloody crimson aura.

Fuck, what have I walked into? His composure falters. His solitude grows ever more ominous. *Hopefully, I already missed the party.* He struggles to believe he has. No blood stains on the altar. Whatever rite this place is meant for has yet to be conducted. He can't help but wonder if he is the center of it, recalling the earlier art scattered across the walls. Small, pulsing lights draw his attention near the bottom of the altar. *An old boombox,* he realizes—the source of the music where he can finally make out the lyrics.

A repeated phrase: "You are safe here." The song's haunting drone slows his steps further, but eventually, he reaches the device and presses the "stop" button. It doesn't, continuing to boom within the garage. The crackles of the fire punctuate the ensuing rhythm of the song. For a moment, the intensity soothes him, as his senses scream at him for battle. It was close but his urge all too soon. Goosebumps run up his spine as a source of unease, hinting at some hypothetical horror quietly lurking just out of sight. "It's just a knife under your skin. It's just a blade in my hands" the song repeats.

He looks back to the boombox. It feels familiar. And with that recognition comes a mounting sense of dread. He picks up the boombox, examines it from all angles, and confirms his fear. An adhesive label on the bottom of the device reads, "Restored and repaired by the GG Shop, your go-to spot for things from the past." He stares at the boombox for several minutes, trying vainly to ascertain this eerie coincidence's meaning. He is shaken from his thoughts when a chain link fence begins to rattle nearby.

"Enough!" he shouts. "Cut the shit and come on out!" He drops the boombox and his hand moves to grip the Motherboard's handle. Once again, his scans of the area prove fruitless. He sees nothing. He is alone, waiting in a fighting stance for disaster to strike. Behind him, a mechanical sputtering begins to echo through the garage, eventually giving way to the steady whir of a generator. He turns toward the noise source, noticing a rapidly intensifying purple glow now mixing with the dull orange hue cast by the flames.

"What the hell…" Clain murmurs. Before him now sits a bizarrely constructed machine, massive, circular, and tall enough to touch the ceiling, the source of the violet light. Bulbs embedded into the surface in seemingly random patterns begin to flicker in sequence, as though the lights of some are chasing those of others. Faced with yet another ominous construct of unknown purpose, Clain cannot help but tense up further. He can feel the hairline fractures forming in his carefully built composure. Much to his dismay, he is intimidated, and it's starting to show. "And then you panic!" the song screams. This machine is yet another object covered in gruesome artwork. Throngs of hands reach out to one another, some limply, some desperately, as snarling horrors of all shapes and sizes walk among them. A human silhouette adorns the top of the device. He steps away, turning to examine his blind spots again. A bright green exit sign now illuminates a way out. The only problem is a series of chain link barriers, forming a maze between him and the potential escape. As he attempts to plot a path through the fences, the boombox volume increases, with the hollow promises of that same, droning melody ring out against the concrete once again.

"You are safe here."

"Screw this," Clain grumbles. Instead, he opts for the brute force approach and begins to pull and bend the chain links, carving his own path through the fences. Preoccupied with his work, he barely has time to look up when he hears the sound of something swinging down at him from above. Before he can even begin to dash out of the way, something slams into his sternum with a heavy thud. He sees what hit him as his body bows inward from the blow. Feet. He's been kicked. Hard. And now he's sliding across the ground. Before he can regain control of his body, the slide is stopped abruptly - and painfully - by the wreck of an old car behind him. The impact knocks the wind out of Clain, but he manages to stagger to his feet as he tries to catch his breath. A cloaked figure stands before him, perfectly still in the firelight, casting a stark silhouette. A sinister, digital grin flickers at him from it's gloss screened face.

Unwilling to entertain the situation, Clain swiftly retrieves his damaged Motherboard and flings it straight at the shadowy figure. A hand emerges seemingly from nowhere and snatches the blade from the air with inhuman speed. Its owner, another hooded shadow, throws the Motherboard towards the altar. It crashes and clatters along the ground, throwing showers of sparks each time it strikes the concrete floor. As Clain lunges toward this new aggressor, he imbues his hand with magnetic energy and calls his blade back. As the hilt hits his palm, he throws all his momentum into a forward cleave. The air shrieks around the sword, and the ground cracks with the force of the strike. Unfortunately, the ground is all he's managed to hurt. His attacker seems to have simply vanished, and an airborne Clain sails through the empty space where the cloaked assailant used to be. Clain tosses the Motherboard upwards and tucks into a forward roll, summoning it back to him as he springs to his feet and turns around, weapon at the ready, desperately surveying his surroundings for any sign of the disappearing figure.

His temper flares, his hands tremble, and the cracks in his demeanor widen into rifts. "Who are you?!" he screams.

His eyes widen as he finally gets a response—one that only confuses him further. His fighting stance wavers as glowing, cartoonish, happy faces surround him. His confidence melts away, and fear takes its place. A creeping presence materializes behind him, moving closer and intensifying. Clain is rooted in place, unable to face it. A warm breath passes over his shoulder and grazes his neck. Finally, it speaks—only a whisper.

"You're safe here." Under the mask, Clain might have scoffed. But fear drives him to panic and uproots him. Fight or flight wrests control from a freeze. It senses no exit, firing a signal down Clain's arm to turn and slash. He hits nothing and a split second later, is shoved from behind. He stumbles forward, sliding down onto one knee and stabbing the Motherboard into the ground to keep himself from falling face-first into the concrete. He climbs to his feet, gritting his teeth as his broken arm twitches. The pain has dulled, masked by adrenaline. The glowing faces chuckle in unison, their expressions mocking.

The nearest to him stands roughly twenty feet ahead against a fence, giving him an idea. He tosses the Motherboard forth with a twist in his wrist, arching its flight path like a boomerang. It easily cuts through the fence before curving back around. The shadowy figures scatter as the colossal blade slices through the air. It carves its way back through the wall. He holds out his hand, and the hilt once again finds its way to his palm, perfectly oriented. With one deft movement, he sheaths the blade. Clain conjures a second magnetic attack, clenching his fist and pulling it towards himself. The ruined section of the fence obeys, sailing through the air and striking the figure in front of him in the back. He opens his fist, closes it again, and twists his wrist sharply. The metal responds by wrapping around Clain's adversary, constricting him like a snake and ruining his balance.

The figure falls to the ground, immobilized.

"Come here!" Clain snarls. The opponent flies to him. Clain stands him upright and throws its hood back and he pulls its mask off. The figure's head comes with it, and Clain staggers backward, watching in stunned silence as the headless body comes apart, its limbs and torso separating and falling to the floor. In the brief moment of respite from the fight, he lifts the mask away, revealing the faceless, battered head of a mannequin. Goosebumps race up his arms as memories of the dismembered piles of the same featureless constructs he found on the higher floors flash across his vision. The mask in his hand starts laughing, a grating, metallic taunt that fills the garage with its echo. More masks appear in the darkness. Their dead-eyed smiles surround him.

 "There is nothing we cannot see," they whisper in droning harmony. "Even the darkest recesses of your mind are an open book to us." The masks begin to flicker, their glows switching colors and their flashes varying in speed. Disorienting. Hypnotizing. Clain's stance begins to fail as he enters a dizzying trance. He crushes the mask in his hand before tossing it aside and gripping his forehead in pain. He falls to one knee again, exposed and powerless to fight back. A hand wraps around his arm. Its vise-like grip tightens, and a series of sickening cracks ring out through the garage and resonate inside Clain's skull the way only a grievous wound being inflicted can. The hand tightens again, its fingers rolling over the section of arm in its grip, grinding the ravaged pieces inside against one another. Bones and muscles and tendons trying to heal are being broken and torn once again with brutal intent.

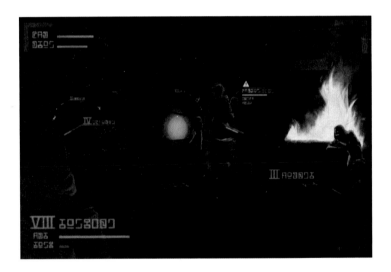

"A great breakthrough, this meeting," a raspy, digitized voice greets him. "Hello, Clain," it encourages, but he can't open his crying eyes. His heart races as he grips his broken arm in the sling. He taps it frantically, hoping no bones pierced his skin. A cold, leather-gloved hand caresses his scalp. Its fingers slide between the locks of his hair and firmly take hold, yanking Clain's head back and forcing his gaze upward.

"Get off me!" Clain shouts. Fiery, purple energy ignites the air around his body, causing his captor to release its grip and step back. Clain sneers at the hooded figure as he reaches for the Motherboard. "What the hell do you want!?"

He is met only with silence as the faces around him blink out. In their place, simple, lowercase i's illuminate the space. Finally, the foremost aggressor breaks the quiet.

"You are outmatched, Clain. Violence will get you nowhere, and your rage will tire you further. Let us talk instead. I might add that conversing with us is a rare opportunity for those not of our number. You would be a fool to waste it."

"Opportunity?! You just broke my fucking arm!"

"You didn't seem the type who would listen to reason unless it was backed by force. We merely wanted to show you that we possess that to a far greater degree than you. We hope you are convinced to listen. What other sound alternative is there for a man in your position? You know you cannot win. Your warrior's instincts are too well-honed to believe otherwise."

Clain struggles back to his feet, spitting a gob of blood on the floor in defiance.

"I'm still standing," he says.

"Standing about as well as the Pho King." The masks chuckle in a mocking chorus, their lights bobbing slightly with their laughter.

"Did you have something to do with that?!"

"We did not. We are not your enemies however, Clain. Quite the opposite, in fact. We are here to help you accept certain… inevitabilities."

"What are you talking about? Who are you?"

"We are known as the Illuminaries. Friends to all. Even the terrors inside you."

He bows, keeping eye contact with Clain. The pain in Clain's arm clouds him in dizziness. He struggles to stand firm, clenching his teeth as he taps his depleted reserves of strength. He can barely parse the words being spoken to him. Most of his energy is expended on resisting the urge to pass out. "Indeed, much like your friend Mitt, who led you right to us. All according to plan. You each have roles to play, you see, lest your potential go unrealized."

"Mitt? Are you saying he set me up?!" Clain shouts.

"We simply knew he had you in his compound, and we felt it was an opportune moment to arrange a meeting. Certain things are best dealt with face to face. Like those you're hiding. Trying to contain them in some deep, dark recess of your mind, hoping they will never resurface. But…'the way out is through' as they say. Your only solution is to understand what lurks within. Harness it. The inevitable can't be prolonged forever."

Clain tries to feign ignorance, but they all can see through the act—and he knows it. Still, he attempts to keep it up.

"What the fuck are you talking about?"

The figure tilts its head. Its chest gently shakes with silent laughter. Clain's jaw tightens. He tenses with the instinct that these people know far more about him than he would ever care to share. He is quickly proven correct.

"The dark terrors that haunt your dreams, Clain. Staring back at you within your own reflection. Growing stronger. More frequent. More vivid. Multiplying. They refuse to be ignored."

"How can you know anything about me?"

"We are joined, Clain. Illuminaries are one mind, with our eyes everywhere. Even your dreams. Whatever you think you're hiding, we can promise we already know. You may as well speak freely with us. And don't worry; we have shared nothing with anyone who is not of our number."

Illuminaries… Clain's eyes dart from side to side as he searches his memories for anything he might know about them.

"One consciousness, Clain. Do you not understand? We, our people, we are one, singular consciousness spread amongst countless bodies of flesh, seeing all."

"We?" The faces draw closer, tightening the circle around Clain. Their glow intensifies.

"We feel and live as one, a simultaneous deluge of collective perception spanning dimensions, parsed by a single, unified mind. Yet we are different. Individuals are joined to our collective, yet they are not subsumed by it. We are separate. Yet one. An aggregate of minds and memories, sights and sounds. We are many. And we are with you."

Clain growls with a primal rage, their words striking him like a match to gasoline. A glow of red envelopes him as he yanks the Motherboard from its sheath, imbuing it with the same power and flinging it toward the crowd of hooded figures, his magnetized hand guiding it through their ranks. The Illuminaries try to flee. Some get away. Those that don't fly apart explosively disassemble themselves as the Motherboard separates their heads from their torsos. Clain hears the telltale clatter of plastic hitting the floor and notices the lack of blood streaming from his victims' broken bodies. More mannequins.

"What's with the damn mannequins? Is that your only trick?" he barks.

A crackling, metallic female voice replies, "Aren't we all mannequins? Simple, walking billboards advertising who we think we are. They are no different than you. Easily shaped into what they need to be."

Clain whirls around toward the voice. He reaches out with his magnetic senses, hoping to feel any sort of physical presence nearby, but he perceives nothing of the sort. He does, however, start to sense faint outlines of metallic shapes. Specifically tapered, sharpened blades decorated along their hips. Held at the ready, wielders lurking in shadows, imperceptible to his magnetic field sense. Clain grits his teeth. Feeling a chance at having the upper hand if his mind can now track them.

Focus, he urges himself, exerting a magnetic field from his skin and noting the positions of each knife surrounding him. *Just like with Synric. Follow the traces of metal.*

The same voice rings out again, feminine, staticky, deadpan.

"We do not tire, Clain. Nor do we waver. You do. If words don't sway you to diplomacy, sooner or later, fatigue will."

"Try me," Clain scoffs.

He counts at least twenty blades. His eyes close. The soft steps of their wielders gradually reveal themselves to his senses. Their movements are deft, swift, quiet, and coordinated. He feels his magnetism intensify on his right. He jerks toward the sensation, one hand on the hilt of his sword, the other on the flat of its blade, reinforcing its position as it deflects an incoming knife.

The first attacker's blade rings useless against Clain's makeshift shield. He sweeps the blade low, hoping to separate this next opponent, and curls his free hand into a fist as he sees the hooded figure jump, clearing the Motherboard's arc. Clain draws the motherboard back, returning it to a fighting stance behind him as he lunges forward and throws a punch. The Illuminary is caught in midair as Clain's knuckles bury themselves in its face, sharply redirecting the figure into the concrete floor. It grunts in severe pain.

Another magnetic pulse behind him warns Clain that his first adversary is at his back, attempting to take advantage of Clain's preoccupation with its ally. He swings around and unclenches his fist, grabbing the Illuminary's cloak and taking advantage of its momentum to throw it into its fallen comrade, bunny hopping backward over the fallen enemies and pointing the Motherboard forward in a two-handed grip as he senses a group of enemies walking towards him. One steps forward, then jumps and punches the air above it in celebration. "Way to go, Clain! You got them good." Mocking him. It lands and incites its allies to applause and laughter. Their snickering chorus rings out from the shadows. The voice speaks up again, its point of origin unclear.

"I suppose there's no sense hiding, then." The Illuminaries all step out to reveal themselves, staring him down with knives in hand. They encircle Clain slowly, deliberately closing in on him. He turns in a circle, tracking their movements, wracking his brain for escape plans.

Just focus. Don't try to fight them all at once. Dodge, break their formation, and clear a pa- Clain's thoughts give way to a pained gasp as a blade pierces his back and slides between his ribs. Somewhere underneath the shock and the pain, he wonders why his magnetic senses failed to warn him. The same feminine voice answers as if reading his thoughts, whispering into his ear from behind.

"Plastic," it says. "All heroes have their weaknesses. Get too reliant on their powers. You're no different." Clain drops to his knees with a pained exhale as the knife withdraws from his innards. "We told you we only wanted to talk." He hears the patter of liquid dripping on the floor next to him. His blood, dripping outward with a pale spattering glow.

He follows the sound, seeing a collection of red spots on the floor. Pain shoots through his back as he looks up towards the source, seeing a crude, vicious shank clutched in the hand of his attacker, coated in his blood. The weapon was glowing, with his blood. Whether it's a result of whatever powers these strange beings possess or a simple hallucination from blood loss, Clain can't say.

Is that what they want? My blood?

The Illuminary approaches the sizeable circular gate, now glowing a deep pink. He flings his wrist toward each corner of the circle gate as what looks like a fishing line glistens in front of the machine like a spider's web. The knife is placed at its center while the Illuminary reaches a small panel nearby.

"FreqyD was merely an appetizer, wait until you see what we have cooked up now." It smiles before all their masks change in unison to a lowercase i.

Clain's eyes widen in shock. His heart sinks as he finally realizes the danger they pose. His breathing is shallow, his mind foggy, and his body starved of blood. The physical toll of the fight starts to take its toll in earnest as he struggles to speak.

"That…that was all you? All those people…those lives…you destroyed them…."

The cloaked figure spares him a backward glance. Its smile blinks back onto its mask and winks before returning to an i. As it turns back around, its shoulders shake with silent laughter. What little hope for survival Clain still has starts to crumble. The Illuminary flips a switch, igniting a large circular gate. A rumbling, eldritch hum radiates from the gate as the glow around its edges intensifies. The tone the gate emits raises in pitch to something resembling the sad cries of whales. The gut-wrenching sound causes Clain to recoil, gripping his wound. The pool of blood underneath him continues to grow as the cut keeps gushing. An intense light shines from the blood on the knife as violet sparks pour from the gate and the air seems to tear open.

Another world waits on the other side of the rift, and from its depths comes thousands of piercing shrieks, blending into an ear-shattering chorus. Clain reflexively drops to his knees and covers his ears. His hands begin to blanch with the desperate pressure he is applying, trying in vain to form some kind of seal to block the sound, to little avail. The delicate bones of his inner ears rattle wildly as the discordant waves mercilessly strike his eardrums, threatening to fly apart. He musters the will to look back up at the gate just in time to see the Illuminaries' visors display a muted volume icon. A convulsing humanoid creature stumbles out of the portal, its wracking spasms punctuated by desperate wheezes and barking coughs as the dust in the air enters its airways. Clain sees a skeletal figure covered in bulbous, fleshy protrusions in the violet light, seemingly forming some obscene, sloppy hybrid of human and bullfrog. It wheezes and coughs violently as it inhales the dust in the musty air.

Nonetheless, it struggles to its feet, revealing its inverted knees, the joints bending backward as it stands upright. A horde of demonic abominations trails closely behind it, their desperate wails struggling to follow the grotesque abomination. The Illuminary at the panel triggers the gate's shutdown sequence with inhuman speed, and the portal seals shut a split second before more creatures can pass through it. Their cries stop abruptly, giving way to immediate silence. The beast looks around the room before seeing Clain on the ground, bleeding. It breathes deeply before letting out a sharp shriek from its bulging throat. Clain grimaces as the sound hits him. The creature scurries across the room to his side and begins wildly licking at his blood and nudging him like a friendly dog. Clain shivers, petrified, unable even to vocalize his pain.

"Awe, cute! Right to his master's defense," an Illuminary gleefully remarks.

The monster whips its head around toward the Illuminary, staring intently for a split second and adopting an aggressive stance before unleashing another blood-curdling scream. It lands on muted headsets, and the Illuminaries remain unfazed, observing the creature curiously. Clain manages to piece his situation together through the haze of pain and fear.

It's...it's trying to help me?

As soon as Clain realizes this, an Illuminary rushes from the side, thrusting a fearsome knife toward the monster's torso. Clain narrowly parries the blow with the Motherboard's hilt, meeting the creature's eyes.

This thing might be my only chance.

Clain attempts to lift the Motherboard and wield it yet again, but his wounded arms have spent the last of their strength, and the blade clatters to the floor. But no attack comes.

"Don't worry, Clain," one of them says. "It's time for us to leave and for your dark angel to tend to you."

What the hell does that mean?

Another Illuminary's voice rings out from his side. "But we will not grant you ownership of our prey."

A metallic chorus of knives being drawn rings out. Before the echoes of it can even fully fade away, a group of Illuminaries have already perforated the mutant creature's body with a flurry of stabs. It falls to the ground, the last of its breath pushed from its lungs as it hits the concrete. Its eyes land on Clain, and it reaches a hand out toward him as if begging for help as it dies. Clain is rooted to the ground, frozen with shock. But his stupor is broken by a loud explosion from the rear of the garage as the concrete wall there is blasted apart, flames pouring through the breach as bits of concrete fly through the air and skitter along the ground. The Illuminaries look toward the destruction before their masks change to a circle with a slanted line through the middle, the universal symbol for "no," and begin a synchronized retreat as they whisper in unison.

"Farewell, Clain. It was nice to meet you finally."

Clain can hear the clang of weapons as a familiar buzz of electricity ripples through the air. Something darts toward him, stopping to kneel by his side. A familiar, synthesized voice speaks.

"Get up." It demands.

Clain's eyes widen in terror as he looks toward the speaker. "S-S-Synric…"

The android shoves Clain onto his back. His vision momentarily goes black as his head hits the ground. When it returns, he sees a huge, glowing needle in Synric's hand, plunging toward his chest. The sharp metal tube slams through his skin, slipping between his ribs and into his punctured lung. As Synric withdraws the syringe, Clain's wounds rapidly begin to heal. The relief is nearly overwhelming as he sucks in his first unbroken breath in hours. The android Clain, who had been smashed to pieces only days ago, looks down at him, an impatient gleam in his cold eyes.

"Get. Up." Synric demands again.

"You're saving me?" Clain asks.

"You have a chance to escape now. Take it. Immediately. Head to the beam rails. Take them west, out of the city."

"Why? And why are you helping me?"

"Go to Eagle's Equinox. I have delivered your friends there. They are alive. But they don't yet know you still are. Go. Tell them."

"But wh-"

"Go! Recover your strength. Return to face me when you're ready. You'll have your answers soon enough." Synric nods to the direction the Illuminaries are fleeing. "I am hunting them."

"The Illuminaries?! You're going after them?!" Clain shouts. He glances down to where the monster's body was moments ago as he follows Synric's gaze. Its body has vanished. *The Illuminaries must have taken it,* he assumes. His arm is still shattered, but enough strength has returned to lift and sheathe the Motherboard.

136

Well, I am definitely done with this shit. For now, at least.

The swift recovery from Synric's inoculation was incredible as Clain starts jogging toward the breach in the wall left behind from the android's entrance. Its edges still glow orange from the heat of the blast. As he exits the abandoned streets, scanning for the rails that will take him to Eagle's Equinox, he chances one last look back. A visor glows faintly in the darkness, its light reflected by the glowing puddle of Clain's blood. The lowercase letter "i" flickers on its display. Its wearer is holding Synric's discarded syringe. Clain's eyes widen as he watches the Illuminary draw every drop of his blood from the ground before retreating into the darkness.

CHAPTER 8 - Escape From New Beam City

Back in Eagle's Equinox, things have calmed down. Fila is exhausted after explaining everything that had happened to her and her father. Honey is left in shock at the story and trying her best to be a comforting presence. The little girl finally fell asleep in her lap, and her first moments of reprieve finally allow her to succumb to fatigue. Dawn stands guard in the doorway, the sunrise marking the final minutes of his overnight vigil. He has been completely silent, processing Fila's tale and how insane Kruger must have gone after their escape from the Pit Pigs domain. He wonders if they were somehow to blame. The pain in his abdomen has been mostly manageable, but now that his watch is coming to an end, it refuses to be ignored. Honey sees him wince as he clutches at his wound.

"Go get some rest, Dawn. That cut has to be killing you."

Dawn sighs before finally obliging, stepping over the threshold of the doorway.

"Hey, Dawn?"

The stoic warrior looks back over his shoulder.

"Thanks for staying with us. You didn't have to, but it means a lot that you did."

Dawn nods silently, a hint of a smile tugging at the corner of his mouth that's out of Honey's view, and walks away toward his quarters. Changing his bandages and finally getting some sleep were his top priority. Honey caresses Fila's hair as she occupies herself by scrolling the news feed on her wrist-mounted HUD. Having convinced the disgruntled Lenny to at least allow her their connection and update her feed. The grim headlines starkly contrast with the calm, reassuring smile the Elder gave her just before he left her and Fila alone for the night. His advice to reflect on the present and plan for the future isn't enough to calm her nerves however. Local journalists are reporting chaos in her home neighborhood, and it's spreading. Fast. Public outcry over the citywide lockdown has boiled over into the streets, and riots are breaking out.

The city's police have come out in force, clad in armor and brandishing weapons that practically scream "martial law." The officers' threats turn to action as the roiling crowds of outraged citizens escalate fervently. Clouds of tear gas waft through the streets, and thousands of hacking coughs and desperate cries ring out from within them. Those who refuse to go down are hit with ringing pulses from sonic turrets tuned to a nauseating frequency, and their attempts to reform the mob end on the asphalt in convulsive vomiting fits, strings of bilious saliva dripping from their mouths between choked pleas for mercy as their stomachs try to force up contents already emptied. All this without mention of their own battalion of mechanized drones canvassing the streets and sky above.

Honey's reflections on the present can't help but lean towards the bleak, and her predictions about the kind of future she needs to be planning for aren't much brighter. She shakes her head to banish the grim notion and focus once again. How, when or even why would they ever return to the city at this point?

All but the least ethical of New Beam's residents are unarmed. Anything that could even vaguely constitute a weapon has long since been outlawed and confiscated. Now, as the unprepared citizens spill from their homes in protest, muggings and robberies are running increasingly rampant. But even among the gruesome images of battered and bloodied citizens surrendering at gunpoint to cops and criminals alike, something manages to stand out as especially troubling. She can barely make it out through the haze of smoke and fire in photos taken from the ground—a hulking, towering shadow, dwarfing everyone around it and moving towards a frantically scattering crowd.

Some kind of tank? Honey wonders. But then more photos come in. Closer to it this time.

The ominous silhouette becomes clearer. Its movement appears bipedal, its steps lumbering. Honey can practically see the earth beneath it shake even through the slideshow of still images

139

documenting its advance, each featuring more seismic cracks running through the asphalt it's stepped on. It looks almost human. Almost. Its movement is too mechanical. Its shape is warped, its outline full of grotesque protrusions, jagged edges, and a pair of gnarled, pointed ears on its head. It dawned on her. *Kruger,* she realizes. *Fila wasn't kidding.*

Jesus, the city is dealing with pig faced kaiju?! Honey struggles to fathom it. Even though she had seen it in person, it was not this operational just a few days ago. She runs her free hand over her mouth as she takes a calming breath. More news posts pop up. Footage captured from a drone this time, flying just above the destruction. Above the smoke. Honey narrows her eyes, bewildered by what she sees.

Is he… controlling it manually? Wait…no…

She studies the grim fusion of dead pork flesh and twisted metal rampaging through the streets, zooming in on the head.

There he was, sitting on top of the thing. Driving it and wearing his blood-soaked bandana. Honey's eyes widen. *Kruger… fuckin animal.* Feeling awe struck by the crazed gangster's mech. Its deadly potential is finally being realized. *Son of a bitch…*is all she can think as she watches it work. Destruction in every direction.

Kruger's last words to her and Dawn ring through Honey's mind as she watches the roads crumble, walls collapse, bodies falling and blood flowing on her feed.

I will fucking murder you!

His larynx-shredding scream rang out after her and Dawn, swearing vengeance as Dawn's land mines blew his mechanical legs apart. Under the blood and grime caked across his face, Kruger's eyes burned with consuming hatred, his gaze promising more solemnly than his words ever could that their deaths would be neither quick nor painless. He was scouring the city for them.

"Kruger…" Honey whispers under her breath. She notices his movements. Occasionally, he lets some targets escape as he stops and scans the area. He's not out just to kill. The carnage is incidental. He's looking for something. Someone, maybe. The corpses he's strewn about the streets lie dead simply because the man in the mech thought *might as well* as he went about his search. Honey shuts her eyes briefly at the thought, holding back her anger and sadness at the senselessness of it all. With grim determination, she resumes watching the feed.

"Where the hell are you going, you sick fuck?" Honey mutters. She closes her eyes and tries to remember. *The Pho King?* Did she somehow lead him there? It had to be because Synric had used Clain's face, which still had him deceived.

She wracks her memory for any ideas of the monster's possible destinations. Still, she's been up all night watching the abject horrors unfolding all across New Beam. She's tired, and her mind is foggy. For now, she comes up empty. She rubs her eyes to stay awake and rasps an exasperated "Goddammit…"

"Sorry, did I interrupt something?" A calm whisper comes from across the room. Honey is startled, her mind yanked from her doom scrolling. She stills herself before the jerky reaction plays out to ensure she hasn't woken Fila. She turns to see Mr. Le cautiously stepping back into the lounge.

"Oh, no, no," Honey reassures. "I was looking through the news," she tells him with grim. She smiles at Mr. Le wryly. "You might've done me a favor. But anyway, look," Honey whispers, pointing to Fila. "She's asleep."

Mr. Le holds up his hands in understanding as he mouths cautiously, "Oh," and gingerly walks closer, smiling at his daughter finally getting some rest. He sits beside Honey and begins lovingly stroking his daughter's hair.

"I was just taking a walk," Mr. Le says. "I thought the fresh air and quiet might calm my nerves. Hearing Fila recounting what happened, and I just…"

"Didn't need to hear it after you'd already lived it?" Honey whispers. "I get it."

Mr. Le nods. He sighs and hangs his head, a guilty expression on his face.

"Perhaps I should have…"

141

"No. Don't worry about it." Honey looks down at Fila. The little girl has fallen even deeper into her long overdue sleep, and her mouth now hangs open as she gently snores. Honey chuckles lightly as she notices the puddle of drool that gathered on her knee. "She was so caught up in telling her story I don't even think she noticed you left." Mr. Le looks up at Honey, relaxing his features a bit. "I don't blame you," she continues with a slight shrug. "I'd've probably done the same. Hell, it was hard enough just listening." Mr. Le smiles warmly, the way only a father who knows his daughter is finally safe and resting can. He stands back up, moves towards the booth, and picks up a nearby throw pillow.

"Want some help up?" he asks, kneeling down and gently lifting his daughter's head and sliding the pillow underneath, allowing Honey to stand.

"Thank you," she whispers. He joins her at her side. The cuts, scrapes, and bruises from the day before have been cleaned and dressed, but exhaustion still weighs heavy on the man's face. Mr. Le looks at Fila, then looks back at Honey and nods towards the door, inviting her to come along. She follows, noticing Mr. Le's slight limp. He doesn't appear to be hiding it, nor does it seem to be causing him any pain.

An old wound, maybe? Honey wonders. They exit out into a small courtyard covered in vines. Torchlight dances across the archway above as Mr. Le sits on a nearby bench. He lets out a long, tired sigh. "Finally, I sit."

He looks toward Honey, through her into the middle distance. His expression is blank. Detached.

"You haven't rested yet?"

"I have not. After that extended car ride here, I needed to stretch my legs and clear my head. Feel as if I have walked every inch of this place now."

"Yeah, big place, huh?" Mr. Le's gaze returns to the present, and his eyes meet Honey's. His expression becomes a stern, questioning scowl.

Even more serious than usual, Honey thinks to herself, suppressing a smirk. The man doesn't need to feel mocked; he's been through enough. Besides, she's come to find it oddly charming in that "strict old father with a heart of gold" kind of way. If ever there was a man she'd call "everyone's dad," it would be the man in front of her. *Just needs an armchair and a dark study, and I'd think he was about to call me 'young lady' and demand to know where I've been.* However, Mr. Le has a different question in mind, albeit one a strict father might ask his wayward teen.

"Who are these people?" He asks. Honey can feel his protective streak radiating off him, even through his crushing fatigue. She does not doubt that he'll fight to the death to escape to safety with his daughter if he doesn't like her answer. She respects that about him, even knowing he probably wouldn't last long.

"By who, you mean Dawn and the others?"

"Yes."

Honey reflects on the question. Mr. Le is concerned, and Eagle's Equinox is a rather peculiar place, unlike anywhere in New Beam.

"Honestly, I'm trying to find that out myself. Dawn and I arrived here just a few days before you did."

"A rather rude man is out there on the upper catwalks."

"Oh... that's Lenny. He and I have butted every day I've been here. I don't think he likes strangers just showing up in the middle of the night." Mr. Le smirks slightly, raising his eyebrows.

"Well," he says, "I certainly can't fault him for that. In fact," he continues, looking right at Honey, his smile still on his face, "I think I can relate. Don't you think so?"

Mr. Le smiles again with his eyebrows raised.

"I suppose so," she chuckles back.

"Funny thing, he and I had hit it off, but you reminded me I never caught his name. My mind is all over the place." He rubs his forehead, trying in vain to massage his headache away. "I feel like I'll never sleep again."

Memories of the Pho King burning on the news feeds flash through Honey's mind. She frowns and sighs.

"I can't imagine how difficult this is."

"You know one thing no one ever tells you about parenting? How you gradually become more and more powerless to protect your child. Parents age. Their bodies start breaking down just as their children enter their prime. You struggle more and more against a body that seems more determined to undermine you with each passing second, to stop you from keeping pace with them as they embark on their own dangerous journey through life. And yet? That drive to protect never goes away. It only seems to get stronger as you get weaker. It should feel futile. But it doesn't. Each rarer moment of safety you can offer becomes all the more precious to both of you. Your obligation to offer it despite the ravages of age becomes sacred, almost to the point of zealotry. I couldn't ignore its call even if I wanted to. And it's a dark, distant universe I want no part of wherein such a want comes within light years of my mind."

Deep. Honey ponders, standing motionless. She was not a parent but his words made sense. She nods gently, encouraging him to continue.

"That makes perfect sense," she offers. "You really love her."

"Yes," Mr. Le replies. "Words could never do it justice. And yet, here I am, having repeatedly failed to protect her." He laughs bitterly. "For all my supposed zeal, I don't seem to be a particularly good guardian."

"What? Don't say that. This world with its insane technologies are way too much to protect anyone from. Your daughter adores you."

"She does, yes. But her life has been a nightmare. It is torture for me to see her constantly be dealt a poor hand while I am unable to stop any of it. This world moves so fast these days. How can anyone be expected to keep up with it?"

Honey smiles, offering more encouragement.

"I think that's the point."

Mr. Le looks up at her.

"How do you mean?

"Well, you're right. You can't keep up—at least not how you used to. But maybe figuring out how to do the best you can keeps you sharp and devoted to what matters. You can't not value what you're driven to chase like that, even if it exhausts you. And who would *want* a life without something you love that much?"

Mr. Le nods. "You're right. Worrying after Fila wears me down to my bones and hollows them out. And I won't stop digging at the marrow for anything." Mr. Le's eyes snap shut, and he strains to keep them closed, to fight back the bitter contortions of shame and frustration working their way across his face. His voice cracks. "And yet…And yet here we…" He exhales sharply, trying to force the words out between his attempts to fight back a tearful scream. Honey finishes his thought for him.

"And yet, even with all that love you feel, you're both here, right? That really eats at you, doesn't it?" Mr. Le nods shakily, trying to steady his ragged breaths. "You can't blame yourself for this. Life loves its random bullshit, you know?" Honey suddenly tenses, a pang of self-consciousness lancing through her mind, stiffening her posture and widening her eyes. She turns her face away slightly to hide her laugh.

I want to apologize for swearing. And I don't think he even noticed. God, he is such a dad.

"Uh…sorry for…the cursing," Honey says through a sheepish grin. Mr. Le's eyes open and then narrow as he looks at Honey and scrunches his brows together. He can't help but chuckle.

"I don't know if you intended to make me laugh, but thank you. That's quite considerate. Please, Honey, speak bluntly." He smiles wryly. "Just not in front of Fila."

Honey laughs again.

"You got it. Since we're being blunt here, your little girl is a *badass.* And when I look at you and how you fight for every shot she has at a better life? All I can think is, 'How could she not be? Look at the badass that raised her!' You taught her how to fight for everything she loves. And you did an excellent job." She clenches a fist. "Remember Hux? I can't imagine any other little girl who'd defend her dad from a killer pig monster and fucking *win.* Yeah, maybe she didn't kill the thing, but she stood up to him without you or Clain. And then now, she *carried* you. Through the fuckin sewers. Where the hell did she learn that kinda confidence, if not from you? You did that."

He looks away as tears fill his eyes. "A father should not need to be saved by his young daughter."

Honey scoffs.

"Come on, Mr. Le, even someone as stubborn as you has to know that's bullshit. There's nothing wrong with getting help." She holds up her finger and raises her voice to drive her point home.

"And *also*...You were up against a crazed mutant psychopath with a grudge. Who, by the way, you tried, without *any* hesitation, to sacrifice yourself against to save your daughter. You'd have to be talking to a real dick to not get a pass on that one." Honey laughs incredulously, both amazed and utterly baffled by the humble man in front of her. "Seriously, what does it take to cut yourself a little slack man?"

"She mentioned that, huh?"

A corner of Honey's mouth turns up in a friendly half-smile.

"Noble old Mr. Le," Mr. Le scowls. Honey holds up her hands. "Okay, okay, just noble, Mr. Le."

"That's more like it," Mr. Le replies.

Honey's expression softens, and she gently touches Mr. Le's shoulder.

"Seriously though, you're all Fila has right now. She needs you. And I know you're not gonna like this, but you need her too." Honey winces as she thinks about how to voice her next thought delicately. "And I really don't want to dredge up horrible memories for

146

you, because I remember how she got her mechanical arm, but…a smart, fearless little girl with cyborg strength in one of her arms who loves her dad is a pretty damn great person to have on your side. She'll go wherever you go. Because she knows there's no safer place than with her pops."

Mr. Le sighs. Honey can't quite tell if he's heard everything she just said. His eyes stare through some invisible point in the middle distance, and he rests his face on steepled hands. His mind seems to have drifted. When his attention returns to Honey, his expression is troubled.

"Did she tell you she used one of those…" he stutters momentarily. "Death talk devices?"

"Death talk devices?" Honey looks confused. Then, apprehensive, hoping she's wrong. "Wait, you don't mean FreqyD, do you?"

"Yes. Those. I had no idea she was hiding a whole bag of them in the house. You see what I mean by 'no matter what, you can't protect them?'" Honey is stunned into silence. The pair's exchange has drifted to a much darker place, one she didn't even think to expect. Mr. Le continues, returning his head towards the horizon, his eyes resuming their dissociative stare. His voice lowers, rough with vocal fry. "The bag is in the car," he tells her.

"The one you came here in?"

"Correct. She saved me. But for reasons I can't comprehend, she seems to have also gone out of her way to save that bag full of…evil. I don't know what else to call it."

"Did you see her using one?"

"I did. The same night I kicked Clain out. She locked herself in Clain's room and boarded up the door in protest. I figured she was angry and just needed time to collect her thoughts and feelings. That the time to discuss why I wanted Clain to leave should take place when she'd calmed a bit. So I let her stay there. I had no idea she had that bag in there with her…"

"What happened?" Mr. Le's eyes close for a moment. He breathes in a deep, shaky inhale and out, an exhale just as ragged. His eyes open again.

"I was tending to some chores…and then I heard this piercing scream. Then another. They didn't stop. Then, sobs between the wails. When I realized it was coming from that room, I grabbed the heaviest thing I could find - I don't even remember what it was; the whole hallway is a blur to me - and I charged at the door, struck it with whatever I was holding, with more force than I think I've ever struck anything in my life. The door practically flew off its hinges. Another couple of inches, and it might have fallen on Fila. Thankfully, that didn't happen, but the relief was short-lived. One of those damn things was strapped to her head, covering her eyes. She was practically seizing from her cries. I've never seen anything quite like it, and I hope never to see anything like it again. I ripped the headset off, but the screams didn't stop. Wherever that blasted contraption took her, she was still stuck there. Even without it."

Mr. Le rubs his hand over his mouth. His hands shake, and his voice cracks.

"When the paramedics arrived, they told me I could have killed her. There are reported cases of people having the headsets torn off and going catatonic. Or worse, suffering fatal brain hemorrhages." Mr. Le can no longer stop the tears. His tremors intensify as he chokes out his next words. "I could have killed her, Honey. I could have killed her! She's my little girl! I was just trying to keep her safe from…whatever horrors she was seeing, and I damn near killed her! But what was I supposed to do? Leave her in there?" Mr. Le starts to talk faster and faster, his every tortured thought on the events that nearly claimed Fila's life spilling out. "I've heard what happens when people keep those things on. I didn't know how long she'd been using it! I didn't know how long she had! I…I…Oh God!" Mr. Le's body seizes as his regret issues forth in wracking sobs. "I failed her, Honey. How did I not know?!"

Honey can only listen as Mr. Le recalls his daughter's suffering. When he can no longer speak, she tries to offer comfort.

"Mr. Le…I am so sorry. I can't even imagine."

Mr. Le regains some semblance of composure. He smooths his shirt with his hand, takes a calming breath, and seizes Honey's gaze with a dead-eyed stare.

"She said she spoke with her mother. My late wife. Could that really be possible?"

Honey looks bewildered, unsure how to respond, trying to find the right words when her wrist HUD begins to chirp. An alert with a unique sound she had linked to specific keywords being mentioned in the news feeds. She begins scrolling through the headlines with practiced urgency before glancing back up at Mr. Le.

"I'm sorry Mr. Le but hold that thought; this could be important."

"What is it?"

"I programmed a bunch of keywords and phrases into my HUD. Everything I could remember about Clain. It will notify me when they appear in my news feed. I'm hoping it'll help me find him. Or at least find out what might've happened to him."

Upon hearing a far too rare bit of good news, Mr. Le's eyes light up, shaken from his traumatic ruminations. His voice returns to normal, eager and concerned.

"Really? Is he alright?"

"You care?" Honey asks.

"Well, of course! I never hated the man. In fact, I owe him an apology."

"You do? For what?"

"Some of the skills he taught my daughter helped save our lives. Her survival instincts were more keen than anything I had taught her. I kicked him out in the middle of his troubles over a few broken things, which means I am why he is out there alone." Mr. Le stands up and walks up to Honey with renewed purpose, peering over her shoulder at the holographic display projecting from her wrist. "I'm eager to see what you've discovered now."

Honey readily obliges, eager to give Mr. Le a welcome distraction. The first few posts are unremarkable; they meet the search criteria only by coincidence, but it doesn't take long before a live feed catches her attention. A lone shadow speeding along the way lines, pursued by a swarm of police drones aggressively attempting to slam into him.

"No...no way!" She shouts.

"What is it?" Mr. Le asks.

"Here," Honey replies, angling the display to give Mr. Le a better view of the silhouette, deftly navigating the rails and dodging attack after automated attack. "That has to be him, right? I don't know anyone else that could do that."

Or Synric, she thinks to herself. She figures it best not to voice that possibility.

"Certainly seems like it," Mr. Le agrees, squinting. "If only we could get some sort of confirm- wait! Pause it! Pause it!" he shouts. Honey obliges. "Can you rewind slowly?"

"Frame by frame?" Honey asks.

"Please," Mr. Le replies.

Slowly, the dimly lit figure reverses its path, coming closer and closer to the screen as he navigates a particularly sharp turn that passes a bit closer to the camera recording the scene than the others. A massive, sharp silhouette rests upon the blurred man's back.

"That's..." Honey says, Mr. Le's realization dawning on her.

"The Motherboard, or at least part of it." Mr. Le finishes. "It must be. I don't know anyone else who would carry that thing."

"So it's him..." Honey says, a sigh of relief escaping on top of her words, realizing that at least he was alive.

"Shame about the mask, though," Mr. Le adds. "There's always some little shred of unwelcome doubt. Still, all signs point to Clain, yes?"

"Definitely," Honey replies, resuming the feed and returning to the live broadcast. She narrows her eyes. "Wait, what's wrong with his arm? Look, it's in a sling. Dammit, he's hurt. Looks bad."

"Do you think we could intercept him somehow? Get him to safety? Which direction is he going?" Mr. Le asks.

Honey skips the feed backward and forwards, finally spotting the setting sun and working out the answer among the fast-moving road signs.

"South," she replies. "Fuckin fast too."

"Alright," Mr. Le nods along. "What's south?"

Honey looks up as she ponders the question. Her eyes widen as she arrives at the answer.

"Here!" she shouts. "Eagle's Equinox!"

"You really think he's headed our way?"

"Has to be. Where else would he go?"

"I haven't the slightest idea, but it's like seventy miles between here and New Beam. The way lines don't extend much further. He'd be walking the majority of the way here."

"You're right." Honey's brow furrows as she assesses the situation. "He's gotta be beaten up, too. Not just the sling. His posture doesn't look too good."

"They are firing at him! Rubber bullets, maybe?" Mr. Le asks. Honey grimaces at the thought.

"Could be. Doubly impressive he hasn't fallen off if you're right," she replies.

"He's not walking that far in that state," Mr. Le says. "That's impossible enough without being hurt."

"Yeah, no shit…and that's what we can see. Who knows where else he's been hit?" Honey switches off the holographic display and turns to Mr. Le. "We have to go get him. We'll meet him at the

151

terminus of the Beam rails. I bet he will jump on them to escape the city."

"He's moving quickly. Is your bike is that fast?"

Honey grins.

"Hell yeah it is!" she says. "Especially on these sand flats. At full throttle, we'll probably get to where he's going before he does." She flexes her hand, eager to grip the handles of her prized motor masterpiece and experience its speed and power again. She's already imagining the deafening rush of air that accompanies the world's edges blurring in her periphery as it hits top speed.

"It's quite late," Mr. Le notes. "Do you want to tell the others?"

"I'm sure you can handle that when they wake up. Let 'em rest. They need it."

"Surely you do, too."

She smiles and shakes her head as she psyches herself up to ride.

"Nah. Roads over rest for me. Every time. I need this." She's already entering commands into her HUD and getting the bike ready for the trip.

Race ya, Clain, she thinks with an eager smile. She enters some final commands into the wrist display, then sprints away through the community toward her bike.

"If they ask, tell them I'll be back ASAP!" she shouts at Mr. Le over her shoulder, waving.

And then she's gone before Mr. Le can say yes.

~~~

Halfway there. Halfway out. Halfway to- "Ahhh! FUCK" Clain grinds out through gritted teeth, trying not to broadcast his pain. Yet another of New Beam's Domestic Overwatch and

152

Neutralization Robots has fired another round of rubber bullets, nailing him in the calf. The flying drones have adjusted their attack strategy, aiming for his feet to force a quick derailment. And much to his dismay, they were not using real bullets which he could have diverted. They nearly succeeded in derailing him three times as he struggled to keep up the exhaustingly complex footwork required to confuse their aim while holding his balance and it was only getting more complicated.

Fuck these fucking things. He thinks. The faintest hint of a grin flits across his face as he tries to smile through the pain. It's just one of dozens of techniques he's learned to keep moving when every nerve in his body is screaming. *No one likes a DOWNER,* he thinks, hoping the lousy joke will keep him amused. Whatever distracts from his body's growing resentment of his insistent running, jumping, and fighting after the abuse it's already sustained. Mitt's drone follows closely behind and far overhead, hoping to evade the pursuing drones' notice. He had luckily reconvened with Clain by predicting where he might have run to. It would be trivial for one of them to peel off and shoot his pet robot down.

Wouldn't even take a second, probably, Mitt thinks.

"There's a fork up ahead. Go left!" Mitt instructs over their comm. Clain breaks right. "Clain, what the hell are you-" Then Clain leaps sideways, unsheathing the motherboard as he cartwheels through the air, twists a full 180 degrees, and swats at a group of drones with the flat of his blade. They are crushed together, unable to untangle themselves as their combined weight drags them to the concrete below, spilling their synthetic guts and rendering them a heap of inert scrap. As they fall, Clain completes his spins, his feet oriented perfectly to catch the left rail and his heading reoriented back down the waylines towards the city's outskirts. Sparks fly, and pain lances up Clain's shins as he lands and continues along the correct path. Mitt is momentarily speechless, taking a second before he musters a dumbfounded "Oh…" He chuckles nervously. "That…you were uh…doing that. Good. That was, uh…really, really good. Good job."

Mitt shakes his head as if trying to shake his awkwardness loose. He fails. *Good job?! The hell am I saying?!* Mitt wonders to himself. He rubs the back of his neck sheepishly as he speaks through an uneasy laugh. "Thought you were ignoring me there for a sec."

"After where you sent me at that fucking mall, I'm still wondering why I haven't been," Clain replies. Mitt can practically hear his accusing scowl.

"Uh…yeah. Gotta be honest, I'm a little surprised, too after I fucked up that bad…The good news is you're on a pretty long straightaway, so you can, you know, ignore me for a bit if you want…" He takes the silence on Clain's end of the comm as him accepting the offer. Clain hears the metallic growl of another swarm of drones gathering behind him. He starts to formulate an evasion strategy when the sound of the swarm fades away. He isn't sure if he should be grateful for their absence or worried about where they've disappeared to. A second later, he gets his answer as they descend from above and settle into an attack formation, flying backward as fast as he moves forward to maintain their lock on him. He stares one directly in its lens. He sees the components of its artificial eyes adjusting, sharpening the machine's focus. He's never had a standoff with a drone before, but he's at least pretty sure it's AI would have an unfair advantage in the initial staring contest.

What are they waiting for?! Clain wonders. *Are human pilots driving these things, or did their brains just short-circuit?* His memories of Synric lead him to a third possibility, the worst-case scenario, in which these units think for themselves and are devising a plan. *And that they understand human fear if they can play games like this.* He swallows the nauseating unease at the thought of maliciously sentient police drones trying to force their way out. *Doesn't matter. UAVs or creepy living robots, it's all shit trying to kill me right now. I need to figure out what they're doing.* He almost wishes for another hail of rubber bullets he can block with the Motherboard. Or his own body if he's too slow, which, in his weakening state, is happening more and more. Someone needs to make a first move. Whatever the drones are going to do, it's obvious it'll involve shooting him.

Could be buying time to surround me, too. Keep me wondering so I don't see a second group fixing to ram a boot up my ass. Shit, if that's their play I'm fucked if I keep waiting.

Clain is the one forced to break the standoff. He tries to adopt as much of a fighting stance and get his hand as close to the hilt of his sword as he can without the drones noticing. He hears a faint, distant whine behind him.

154

More drones. Now or never, Clain.

 Clain's stance hardens, and his hand twitches almost imperceptibly.

Three.

The drones just keep watching. Their eyes keep adjusting. The twitches of the components behind their camera lenses are so minute that Clain can't tell if hours of "do or die" situations are finally taking their toll or if he really is seeing the tiny strips of metal and plastic that move like bits of a fragmented iris trying to piece itself back together following his hand, anticipating his play. Whether they are or not, it's the only play Clain has.

Two.

Clain becomes acutely aware of the sound of grinding metal under his feet as the soles of his shoes wear down. Sparks fly from his feet in sporadic showers.

One.

All of Clain's training goes into his move for his sword. The movement of his arm is a snapping blur to anyone watching the live feeds. They haven't even registered that his hand has gripped the hilt before the blade is nearly fully drawn. No human eye except those honed to superhuman precision at Eagle's Equinox could keep up. One instant, Clain is reaching; the next the sword simply appears where Clain needs it to be. Unfortunately for Clain, these drones aren't watching with human eyes. Just as his forearm begins to rotate to orient the Motherboard towards its targets, he hears the "pop" of their guns and feels a crushing impact on his right hand. The one gripping the hilt. He realizes as the fingers on his handspring open and stiffens, and fiery bolts of pain burn their way down every nerve in his hand that they were waiting for him to try precisely what he just did. The sword was their biggest concern. And now it's plummeting towards the streets below.

Meanwhile, Mitt monitors the situation from a safe distance, watching his drone transmit live footage of the Motherboard dropping right out of Clain's grip.

155

Oh shit...he thinks. Then, a rapid beeping catches his attention. The kind that says, "Ignore at your own risk." He glances towards its source. It's the computer monitoring Clain's vitals. *No, no, no*...He gets to the monitor just in time to see the EKG spike; the towering peaks the green lines reach seem to suggest not so much a heart attack as an imminent aortic explosion.

Oh, SHIT. Not now, not now! Mitt's thoughts are as desperate as his movements as he scrambles to reopen a channel to Clain's comm.

"Clain? Clain, can you hear me?!"

For many obvious reasons, Clain sounds less than pleased.

"Trying not to die here, Mitt. Not doing so great at it. What is it?"

"It's your vitals! We have to find some way to reduce the strain on your body, or your heart is gonna-" The beeping stops.

"Gonna, what Mitt?!"

"Uh…"

"You maybe wanna call back when you've actually figured out why you're distracting me with this?!"

"Shit...uh, yeah, stand by!"

Clain doesn't bother to acknowledge him.

"Come on, where the hell did I move the device manager?!" Mitt sifts through his messily organized computer, finally locating the peripheral.

"Alright…vitals monitor…The device is working properly?! The fuck it is!" He shouts. Clain's EKG starts to spike again. "What do you mean the drivers are up to date?! What the fuck is the problem, then?!" And the EKG calms back down. Then starts beeping again. "Oh fuck you!" Mitt shouts at the monitor. It goes quiet. "Thanks! Now, stay that way!" It does not, in fact, stay that way. Mitt's eye twitches more and more every time the device defies his orders.

I have to call him again, Mitt realizes, dreading the prospect of being a distraction.

"I figured out the problem, Clain. I think. Your EKG is going haywire. One second, I think you're about to just croak on the spot, and the next it calms back down. I don't know how I'm gonna keep track of-"

"It's fine, Mitt. That's me doing that," Clain says, while trying to avoid the drones' projectiles as he jumps from rail to roof to rail and back again, hoping to move faster than their targeting systems can track. Whatever motivation the things had to hold their fire before is gone now. And the maelstrom of stray bullets they're now spraying in Clain's direction is bound to contain a handful of the bruising rubber rounds fired at just the right angle to land a lucky shot.

"FUCK" Clain shouts again as a bullet connects with his already bruised rib cage.

"It's spiking again!" Mitt shouts. "Oh wait…no, it's fine again. How exactly are you the reason for this? Are you saying you're controlling your own heart?!"

"Yup, I- GODDAMMIT," Mitt winces at Clain's shout, only able to imagine just how badly those rubber bullet bruises really hurt. Clain starts talking again as though the shot never hit him. "It starts pumping too fast. I slow it down. Have to if I want to heal."

"You're saying you are, somehow uh, like casting regen on yourself? Like some kinda passive healing tank in an MMO?"

"I'm probably more of a DPS, but yeah. It's just like my magnetic powers. Same kinda calm is needed to use it."

"I don't even know what to say to that."

"Directions would be good. Straightaway's about to start curving again, and I need to focus on getting the use of my hand back!"

"What about the Mother-"

"I'll worry about the Motherboard! Just tell me where to go!"

"Right!"

"Thank you now, which way?!"

"Right, like turn right. NOW."

Clain breaks hard to the right, scanning for more waylines to jump to as he speeds along another straightaway. "Mitt, I'm not seeing any other paths nearby. Am I just going straight? I've got no way to dodge here!"

"Nope," Mitt responds. "Look down."

Clain looks down, seeing only a small, exposed section of the city's Beam Rail lines.

"Wait, you don't mean…"

"Oh yeah, I do! Hardly any of the Beam rails are up, and it's not a path their AI will be comfortable navigating.

Clain winces. His hand is only halfway recovered. His head is throbbing, strained from hours of intense concentration. He grits his teeth.

Fuck, I'm not ready for this yet. Goddammit, this is gonna hurt.

"Fine," Clain barks. His eyes momentarily screw shut with dread as he anticipates the pain he's about to feel. His teeth threaten to crack as he tightens his jaw even more. His legs are ready to launch him into the air, storing enough potential energy to rival a bullet waiting to be fired.

No more time Clain, just do it.

He channels all his focus into his bruised hand, imbuing it with magnetism. Then he jumps, his sheer strength of will dulling the impact of the drone's rubber bullets. He extends his magnetized hand up above his head. The air begins to whistle. Louder and louder. Until the sound gave way to the Motherboard crashing through the drone formation floating in front of him. He catches the blade with a pained scream through clenched teeth, securing it to his hip in midair and pivoting the Motherboard to counter his weight as he flips around to

158

land on the beam rail lines. Mitt's prediction proves only slightly correct. Some drones struggle to make the turn and crash. But most of the others find their way just fine as their pursuit continues.

"Holy shit, you were flying that thing with your brain the whole time?!" Mitt exclaims.

Clain smirks. "Told you I needed to focus! Not sure about your idea here, Mitt. These things look pretty comfortable to me. Still on my ass!"

"Yea, but not as many!"

"True." Clain nods as he leans forward to accelerate.

"Holy shit! Slow down or I won't be able to keep up!" Mitt complains as he watches Clain shrink into the distance.

"Remember what you said about regen?" Clain shouts. "Let's call this haste!"

"Urrgghh, fine!" Mitt yells. He slams the "turbo" button on his drone's controls. "This is going to burn my entire battery and I won't be able to fly back here!"

"Sorry man, but that's not my problem."

"Yes, it is! This will be two drones you've cost me! You owe me!"

"Your last drone took me straight into the Illuminaries' lair, bro. And you would have had to use your boosters anyway."

"What? Why?"

"That drone got a rear-mounted camera?"

Mitt switches to the drone's secondary lens. His eyes widen.

"What the hell? There aren't any active trains on my traffic map!" The roar of the sleek, bullet-like engine picks up behind them, begging, ever more intensely, to differ.

"Then your map's wrong!" Clain snaps back. His next words are drowned out by the train crashing through the pursuing drones, sending the ones that don't outright explode to be chewed up underneath it, cast aside into the tunnel walls, or skittering and sparking across the station platforms as they leave pieces of themselves in their wake.

"No shit! That thing's gonna kill us!"

"ME!" Clain shouts. He channels even more energy into his movements, getting even faster. "You're safe and sound in your damn chair!"

"I still can't go that fast!" Mitt shouts.

"Mitt, focus!" Clain yells over the deafening noise of the engine. "Give me directions directly over the south wall. Get your drone out of here and just communicate with me on comms."

"You don't want me to go with you?"

"You just said you're burning out your battery! I'll catch up with you later!"

"O-ok. If you're sure, just stay on this rail for two miles and jump at the last station you see. It leads right to the city wall."

Clain looks over his shoulder. The nose of the engine is now uncomfortably close to him. And getting closer.

"Is there anything before that? I don't think I can outrun this thing."

"If you want to run on foot, sure."

"Shit. Ok, go!" Clain shouts, leaning into yet another burst of speed.

Mitt flies his drone up and out of the Beam rail line and over the buildings. "Good luck, Clain," Mitt says, his voice laced with apprehension and a twinge of guilt. "Be careful, and don't be a stranger. I'm cutting comms and stealthing this drone until the heat dies down."

160

 "Thanks, Mitt. For everything." Clain cuts the comm and diverts all his attention to staying ahead of the train and escaping the tracks. No energy remains to dull his pain or slow his heart. All of it is needed to keep pushing him forward. If it's enough, it won't be sufficient by much. For any sort of lapse in concentration, the margin for error is a razor's edge honed to monomolecular sharpness. The chance of making it two more miles with an unstoppable metal behemoth gaining on him is almost nonexistent for someone in Clain's state. His failing stamina alone is virtually guaranteed to doom him. Diving onto a platform and making his way to the city's edge on foot is looking more and more like the only option.

Yeah, proceed on foot through crowds of people who are probably watching the news and know I'm wanted. Great. Won't slow me down at all. Clain thinks. *Practically delirious from pain, too. Not sure I could fight anyone off...Fuck...*

A bright red glow pulses in Clain's periphery. The lights lining the rails flash. The signs overhead switch on, their glow further lighting the way.

The closest one displays his name.

Clain shakes his head, dismissing it as a hallucination.

And then he sees the next sign.

GET ON.

And now every sign follows suit, working in pairs to implore him with stark white capital letters.

CLAIN.

GET ON.

CLAIN.

GET ON.

He adds more speed, feeling especially disinclined to assume the best in talking machines today. The signs flash by even faster.

161

CLAINGETON

CLAINGETON

CLAINGETON

Clain chances another glance over his shoulder. The nose cone of the engine is now less than ten feet away. But it's not closing the gap anymore, just keeping pace. Clain looks back up. The signs still want him to "GET ON."

A siren blares from the pursuing train, and its headlights begin to blink in time with every "CLAIN. GET ON" that passes overhead. Fatigue sets in now, refusing to be ignored any longer. It's urging Clain towards imminent collapse. He glances back from the train to the signs and back again, then sighs in resignation. He feels he knows the answer, but nonetheless, he shouts, "Who are you?" toward the train.

Capital letters scroll across its windshield.

SYNRIC

Clain looks back towards the rail in front of him to hide his frustrated scowl. *Should have fucking known,* Clain thinks to himself. He glances back just in time to see the windshield display a winking smiley emoticon.

*Seriously, dude. Fuck you...*Clain thinks with a sigh. But he can't deny the relief already washing over him at the thought of taking a break. Clain musters the strength for one last jump, channeling his remaining focus into a perfectly timed backflip that sends him right onto the engine's roof. He falls to his knee as his wounds once again flare from yet another impact, gasping for air as the rail car continues to move forward. His focus is running on fumes now, but he manages to ignite just enough of them to engage his magnetism, keeping him rooted in place on top of the train.

Held to the roof of a runaway train piloted by a killer cyborg with unknown motivations by a magnetic pull that could disappear at any second. Somehow, the safest place I've been all day. Clain would shake his head if even a slight twist didn't tense up his entire back. *Dragging the motherboard around is hard enough on me as it is right now.* Clain adjusts his sling, wincing as the Motherboard shifts against

162

his hip with every movement. *The hell did I need a sword this big for, anyway?* He wonders as he grimaces in pain. Typically, being on the roof of a train that's accelerating underneath him would worry Clain, but as the engine picks up more speed, all Clain can feel is relief as the rush of cold air dries the coating of hot sweat on his face.

Delirium engulfs him within the rapid winds as the city limits come into view. It occurs to him somewhere in the mental fog that there's no station there, but all he can think is *Whatever. Synric won't kill me... Right?*

Clain is shaken from his trance as the train begins to decelerate. He can see the end of the rail itself just ahead. It stops with a soft electric hum, and the door at the front slides open. Clain watches and waits, expecting to see Synric walk out, but nothing happens. After a minute or two, his curiosity is piqued enough to lean over the roof's edge and peer inside the car. Again, he sees nothing. If there's something for him to hear, he'd have missed it. His ears are still ringing from the sustained auditory assault of the rushing wind. He nearly slips off the train's roof but stops himself, trying to regain his equilibrium as is tingling from head to toe. He gingerly lowers himself to the ground, stumbling backward and collapsing in a heap. He watches the sky spinning overhead, closing and reopening his eyes, inhaling and exhaling to make it stop. It doesn't come to a complete standstill like he'd hoped, but it's enough to try and stand.

Probably won't entirely go away until I can find a bed and get a good coma going, he realizes.

He struggles to regain footing, shakily walking towards the engine's open door. There's nobody inside. But there is a very familiar duffle bag.

That logo! Clain's eyebrows raise. Embroidered onto the bag is a stylized lion's head. The same logo that was on a bag brought into his old GG Shop by a man called King. There's a folded note taped right next to the lion.

Clain steadies himself, picks the note up, unfolds it, and reads it aloud. "Clain, you forgot these after our last dance." He looks into the large bag, noticing the enormous pieces of his battered and destroyed motherboard inside. "What the hell?" he exclaims aloud before returning to the note. "For now, convene with your friends and heal your body. Synric and I will handle New Beam City. When you are ready, meet me at the top of Cloud 9. But come prepared. Synric will be issuing you a challenge. A battle to meet me, face to face. Think of this as a final test. We have a lot to talk about. See you soon. - King"

"PS - You're welcome."

Clain clenches his fist, crushing the note in his hand.

Game after fucking game after fucking game with these people! He thinks. He throws the crumpled letter with a loud "FUCK," but the little ball of paper just isn't heavy enough to make the outburst cathartic.

King. The friendly, unassuming customer who visited his shop what feels like lifetimes ago through the memories of the far-too-many recent seismic shifts in his life, is now connected to Synric? Is he somehow behind these attacks on not just Clain but all of his friends? Clain's mind races for answers but only receives questions as he falls to the ground like a sack of potatoes. His fatigue was rushing in and trying to make some sense of it all was not helping. He hardly makes progress when a familiar voice calls out to him.

"Clain!"

Clain spins around to face the voice, startled out of his thoughts.

Who could it be? His vision blurred. A woman's eyes come into focus. Unmistakable eyes as her hair glows radiantly in the light of the sunrise. She's on her bike, reaching down for him to come get on.

"Yo! Let's go!" She points behind Clain, towards a growing cluster of red and blue lights. Another swarm of drones is zeroing in on him. He staggers to his feet while struggling to hoist the duffle bag over his shoulder. Honey's eyes widen when she sees the state he's in. "Holy shit, man!"

Clain raises his free hand to interrupt her.

"I'll be fine for now. Just…need to get away. You know where you're going?" he asks, panting.

164

"Of course! Everyone is going to be so excited to see you."
She winces as she looks him over, really taking in the extent of his
wounds. She sheepishly adds. "Maybe we all are…"

Clain perks up, feeling a flash of lucidity at the mention of the
others.

"They're there? Fila and Mr. Le? They are ok?"

"Yes! If we hurry, we might make it back before they wake
up!"

"Great," Clain says. Thinking to himself. *I just have to keep my grip,
don't fall off, and die on the way there.* He leans onto her back, her
hair filling his nostrils with its pleasant scent. He smiles.

CHAPTER 9 - Reflections as Sweet as Honey

"Quick, put this helmet on!" Honey demands. "We don't need them seeing our faces. If they haven't already…" she grumbles. *Bet they will know my bike anyway.*

"Who are 'they'?" Clain asks as he awkwardly jerks the helmet over his face with one arm. He struggles, fidgeting with the mask already over his mouth. He adjusts the chin strap as she continues.

"*'They'* are already snapping pictures." She looks away to her side. "Hurry up!"

Clain wraps his working arm around Honey's waist and taps her hip, signaling her to go.

"Ready." Honey glances over her shoulder.

"Uh, what was that?"

"What was what?" Clain replies, confused.

"That little tap on my thigh?"

"What? Nothing! Are you serious right now? Let's go!"

She snickers, just loud enough to make sure Clain hears her. And then floors the accelerator. The C9X rushes forward, slicing through the air in front of it and hitting a ramp at near top speed. In front of them, a massive set of industrial double doors meant for large, cargo-hauling vehicles is rumbling shut. They sail through just before the two halves slam together. Clain watches as Honey flicks through some menus on her HUD, her fingers moving with practiced efficiency. She enters a command before they even hit the ground. As her hands return to the bike's handles, the HUD blinks away, but not

166

before Clain sees red, blinking text reading, "LOCK ENGAGED" in all caps. He glances back over his shoulder and hears a thundering "Ka-chunk" ring out from the metal doors.

"Wait, you're locking the doors?" Clain asks.

"Why wouldn't I?" Honey argues, annoyed.

"There are people trying to escape the city! I saw them for miles! Families, kids! They started following in my direction. You're just gonna trap them in?!"

Honey gives an exasperated sigh.

"Yeah, Clain. I don't like it either, but I'm not here to start a revolution. I'm here to get you out and make sure nobody follows us."

"What are you talking about?!"

"Clain, where would they even go? *You* couldn't make the walk through the desert. And until some rain falls or some wind picks up, the tracks I'm leaving are the only ones in sight out here. If they do manage to survive, do you really want them led right to Eagle's Equinox?"

Clain isn't paying attention anymore. He's shifted around to look at the gate while Honey has been talking, and now he's too focused on using his magnetism to disengage the lock manually.

"Holy shit man," Honey complains. She flips the text-to-voice setting on so Clain can hear it say, "Emergency secondary locks engaged." Clain is jolted from his trance by a resonant thud as a hidden, even thicker set of doors deploys and slams shut in front of the ones he was just trying to open. The sound startles him, and the jolting movement he makes jerks the bike and sends him falling into the sand.

"You need to chill, alright?" she shouts while pivoting the bike into a U-turn. "It's luck I even made it in time and found you, let alone alive." She dismounts and rushes over to Clain, placing his arm over her shoulder and walking him back to the bike. "Can we try not to fuck this up on purpose for at least the next ten minutes, please?"

"Yeah, sure," Clain grumbles in defeat, throwing his weight back over the seat. The rear of the bike sags with the extra weight of his duffle bag. Honey looks at the bag and then narrows her eyes at Clain. She presses some buttons on her holographic display and the chassis shifts to adjust for the massive weight on its rear, returning to a proper riding position.

"You're lucky this is a new model or I would have thrown your junk off."

Clain smirks. "I need my junk."

Honey rolls her eyes and guns the engine.

The distance between them and the city grows. Cacti and shrubs blur together as the bit reaches top speed. The colors of the plants, sand, and sunrise all seem to blend. The crisp, cool air hitting Clain feels like a distant memory being viscerally evoked. The cleaner air and the imposing, dignified silhouettes of the nearby mountains usher in a meditative calm he has gone without for far too long. His mind begins to lull into serene, thoughtless presence as his vision wanders to Honey's hair dancing across the visor of his helmet.

A friendly silence hangs between them. He finds himself thinking back to his last visit to Eagle's Equinox. He nearly died then. He doubts his return will be quite so dangerous, but that doesn't mean he's looking forward to the series of painful conversations he's likely to have. Dawn. The Elder. Fila and Mr. Le. Especially Fila and Mr. Le. But as afraid as he might be of having to face up, yet again, to how his presence in their lives seems to constantly endanger both of them, he is, more than anything, just grateful that the hole in his heart he felt at the mere thought of their absence can finally be sealed. Despite everything, he's just simply excited to see them again.

"You know I respect what you tried to pull back there." Honey's voice interrupts his thoughts.

"What?" he croaks through a parched throat.

"You wanting to help those people escape. They could have been anyone, ya know? Lot of criminals on that side of town."

Clain remains quiet for a moment. "When tyranny sets in, chaos is the only answer," he murmurs under his breath.

"What does that mean?" Honey asks.

"All the faces I saw looked terrified. Sure, some were angry. Some were fighting. But after a while they all just blurred together. Just one big mass of fear and survival, you know?" Honey feels his grip tighten around her waist.

"You can't save them all, you know?" she reassures him.

"I can at least let them try to save themselves."

Honey smiles. "You really do care about others. It's admirable."

Clain is surprised by the effect of her praise. He hasn't realized how badly he's needed to feel he has friends lately.

"How did you know I would be there?" he asks.

Clain hears a series of electronic button presses in response, and the inside of his visor becomes a video screen. It's playing footage of his journey down the way lines.

"You weren't exactly subtle," Honey jokes. "The city has been raving about it."

"Shit. Should've EMP'd the damn camera drones... just too much at once." he chastises himself.

"You really just *want* to be able to think of all the things all the time, don't you?" Honey asks. You're lucky to be *alive,* man! Besides," she continues, "It wouldn't have mattered." The video stops and a headline appears in Clain's visor: *Honey seen escaping NBC with acclaimed Street Fighter Clain.* He finds himself frustrated at how deadly it would be to bury his head in his hands at the moment. He settles for resting his head between her shoulders.

"Pictures and all," he says. "Great."

"Yeah, and that's not even the worst part."

"What do you mean?"

"Tons of people are shipping us."

"Shipping? You mean dating?"

"Unfortunately, yeah. Happens whenever someone takes a picture of me with anyone," she complains.

Clain chuckles. "What the hell? The whole city's about to go up in flames, and that's what people are worried about?"

"Some people still lock themselves inside, pretending things will be okay. The mobs you saw are only about 20% of the city," she explains. "And then there's the pig mech."

"Pig mech?" Clain thinks momentarily, remembering the footage of Kruger destroying his former home. "Oh," he recalls sadly. "Yeah. I saw him wreck the Pho King."

"What? How?"

"I was holed up at Mitt's place, the podcaster. He had a live drone I was controlling. At least until Kruger knocked it out."

"Damn. Sorry you had to see that. Must've been especially tough for you. Anyway, it looks massive, but all the footage people are taking has been really grainy. And now people are saying it's been disappearing somehow."

"Disappearing?" Clain remarks with shock. "Damn thing was taller than some of the buildings!"

"No clue but it's Kruger. Who the hell knows how he does anything? Or why? It's got people thinking he has the whole city rigged up like some kind of magician's stage. They're saying the fucker can pop up wherever he wants, kill whoever he wants, and then be gone before the blood dries."

"What do you think?" Clain asks.

Honey shakes her head.

"Anyone else I'd laugh and call bullshit. I don't wanna get too deep down the rabbit hole but it's obvious he's got connections all over the local underworld. That alone would let anyone do a scary amount of anything."

"What does he want?" Clain asks.

"Well, the last time Dawn and I met up with him, his last words to us were, 'I will fucking murder you.'" Clain stays quiet. Honey fills the silence. "He wasn't quite that casual about it, though. More of a 'throat-tearing scream that would leave a person spitting blood after' kind of a vibe to the way he said it."

Clain thinks it over.

"Seems excessive," he says. "Rampaging through the city just to find two people?"

"Yeah. I've been thinking the same thing since I looked at a map of the mech's confirmed appearances."

"Oh really? What did you find?"

"It matches up pretty much perfectly with the map the police put out of every FreqyD bust that's taken place over the last few days."

"You think he's looking for FreqyD?"

Honey shrugs.

"Maybe. Best guess. Hard to imagine him not being at least some kind of high all the time. But whatever he's on doesn't stop him from dreaming big and acting on whatever nightmares he thinks up. He's deep into enough sick shit that I could see him wanting it for all kinds of bad reasons. He seemed to know more about the devices than he let on when I tried to get info out of him. Even said he's banned them within the Pit Pigs. But he weirdly didn't know the city was on lockdown until I told him. Anyway, my point is we're talking about a guy that's trying to merge dead people into cyborgs. And that's just what we know he's done. I think he's after whoever *created* FreqyD, and then who the hell knows."

"The Illuminaries," Clain mutters under his breath.

"What?" Honey asks, noticing his grip tightening again.

"The Illuminaries are behind FreqyD. They told me."

"Wait, you met them? They're real?"

171

"Yeah, I met them." Clain sneers as the stab in his abdomen aches. "Not by choice, but I met them. I got ambushed and…" Clain trails off as his head pounds. His mind forces him to relive the memory of the twitching abomination the Illuminaries summoned through their portal, with Clain's blood. His ears ring with phantom pain as its screams echo inside his head. "And…" he tries to start again. But the rest doesn't come. He can only tremble as he drifts between sleep and wakefulness, loosely tethered to the present by a strangely familiar, comforting scent. Some distant part of him realizes it's the locks of Honey's hair flowing into his helmet as the bike speeds through the sand.

"I feel you." Honey remarks, her voice soothing. "Pressing down hard on me." Her words float through Clain's head like a lullaby as she stabilizes the bike. She glances over her shoulder and sees he's finally nodded off. She slows down, stiffens her posture to hold him in place and deftly ties his wrists together using cufflinks from his sleeves to secure him in place. Thankfully their route is mostly a straight line, so she can afford to let him sleep a while without much fear of him shifting. In his dreams, the melody from the roller rink loops hypnotically. The enchanting female vocals return, reverberating through Clain's tired mind. "Now that we've come this far I bet their eyes are watching us move. Burning the candle twice as bright as we intended to, as we intended to. Don't fight it, Or else it won't come true."

"Made from pieces of a memory. So tell me what you want me to be." The ground underfoot rumbles with deep, thrumming vibrations as the lumbering waves of the bassline travel through him. She was calling to him again. Begging him to hear her. "Oh, I feel you. Your nails still pressing down hard on me. On me, on me. I'll take what I can get because I'm scared I might forget." He suddenly feels as though he is sitting down, surrounded by the regal trappings of a mighty throne as the song seems to permeate the very essence of his soul.

As his consciousness rides the crests of the dreamy soundwaves, one note in particular hits in just the right way to wake him, into yet another dream. His eyes crack open, feeling his left fist

172

firmly propped against his temple as he sits cross legged in a large, minimalistic and sleek black throne. When he looks up, a silhouette of a woman before him within the darkness into the dim light. As the shadows obscuring her are peeled away by a glow, the woman hidden in feminine shadow is slowly being revealed. She is ethereally beautiful, singing out into a sea of undulating hands timing their movements with her words. The rhythmic ocean stretches seemingly for miles, its occupants entranced by the performance. "Oh I hear you. Echoing your words like you came and put a curse on me, on me, on me."

The singer's hips begin to sway, the vertical expanse of hands now zigzagging their way up, the horizontal motions that now mark their path to the peaks and valleys of their uncanny imitations of the tide seeming to follow the motions of her body like eyes tracking a hypnotizing pendulum. A thick fog wafts through the crowd, the mass of hands swirling it with their movements. As she turns in place to sing out to the outer edges of her hidden audience, her profile comes into view and even through the blur Clain manages to make out her expression. He's surprised to find expression on the singer's face is as forlorn as it is passionate, as though she yearns to finally be heard after a life of her words getting nothing but echoes in reply. He feels on the verge of tears as a deep sense of longing fills his heart. An urge to tell her he would have always listened had he only known she was there tugging at his heart, a heavy cord seeming to pull him up from his chair, like a marionette. She has an air of familiarity about her, like a first love long since lost. He can't decide whether or not to trust it but feels powerless to deny her.

"I need you to try to understand, If you're to take my hand. Constrict the voice that says it's just a joke. Restricted feelings at the base of the oak. I know there's something that you cast on me. So should we set it free?"

Clain finally heeds the pull, the phantom cord slackening as he stands and makes his way toward her at the stage. The more the singer comes into focus, the more of her attention seems to become devoted to Clain. As her face comes into view again, the motions of her arms smoothly transition from grandiose appeals to her audience to alluring, beckoning gestures angled just right to signal to Clain they have only ever been meant for him - only for him. Her sorrowful eyes become warm, hooded, and inviting. But again, only for him, as if the

173

action of turning away from him hurts her, sends the warm comfort that settles onto her face again.

His hands seem to move on their own, sliding around her waist from behind. She tilts her head back into his chest, leaning into the embrace. He tilts his forward in response, his face gently brushing her hair, his lips poised to kiss her neck, just behind her ear. Goosebumps run down his spine as he her scent intoxicates him. She reaches behind to run her fingers through his hair, the tips of her perfectly manicured nails leaving rippling tingles in their wake as they trail through his scalp.

"Don't fight it, or else it won't come true," she sings. She finally has him. "Such thoughts were much too flawed for you. I need you to try to understand, if you're to take my hand."

Clain's vision blurs as tears well up in his eyes. She caresses his face. Her fingertips are cool against the warmth of his skin, the contrast of temperatures summoning an invigorating rush of blood to his cheeks. The sensations intensify, almost overwhelmingly relaxing. He is mesmerized, hoping to discover this world is his reality and the world where he sleeps, covered in cuts, bruises, and scars is the dream.

His senses suddenly dull, his mind detaching from the present as it fixates on a name emerging from the sealed depths of his distant memories. It escapes into the world before he can fully understand its significance.

His senses return to him. He embraces the ethereal woman in his arms, his sensitivity to her touch heightened by the realization that the name now about to pass his lips carries the threat of a drowning deluge of remembrance. He whispers into the woman's ear.

"Rezeka?"

The woman tenses up when she hears her name. Then relaxes back into Clain's arms, even more serene than before. The comfort of his voice. The way he held her. It was all coming back. Before Clain can join her in her trance, a lancing pain shoots through his brain, and he feels as though the ground is tilting.

Thick, choking smoke rises through even the narrowest slats on the stage. Its pitch-black wisps coalesce into an amorphous, swirling cloud above them.

The woman in his arms looks to him, pleading and fearful.

"No! No, please, no. Clain, don't go! Get me out of here!"

Before Clain can act or even answer, the smoke takes a familiar shape. Tia. Its form is unstable, glitching and struggling to hold together as horizontal sections of its body stretch, contract, and blink like sections of a glitching electronic display. Each pair of eyes on its many heads are narrowed and focused on him, their crimson glow conveying seething rage.

Tia hooks its arms under Rezeka and pulls her upward with irresistible strength as a second pair of hands pry his fingers loose and two more hold his shins in a crushing grip, rooting him to the floor.

"No!" he screams in rage. "Rezy, no! I need you!" He is too preoccupied with trying to free his legs to notice as one of Tia's necks elongates and rears back in a tight coil. As he looks back up at the woman above him struggling and shrinking into the night sky as she is carried away, Tia uncoils its stretched neck and springs its head forward like a snake snapping up a mouse to swallow it whole. He is knocked backwards, falling hard on his back. The wooden panels of the stage explode into splinters as it hits him, and he falls farther and farther into an endless void.

He suddenly snaps awake on the back of Honey's bike, almost pulling them both off as he jerks sideways. The deadly mistake he has just narrowly avoided wakes him up faster than a dozen espresso shots could ever hope to. His arm throbs in its sling. His heightened sensory sensitivity seems to have lingered, and his temples throb with it until his brain returns to something approaching normal. As he anchors himself in reality, he realizes his injured arm is still wrapped around Honey. He still can't entirely accept the waking world around him as the real one. The dream world calls him back, begging him to remember something. Someone. The woman.

Rezy? he wonders.

"What? Feeling nostalgic?" Honey asks.

The sweat on his forehead feels icy in the creases of his furrowed brow as he notices the similarity between Honey's voice and the dream woman.

*No...*he realizes. *Not similar. They're the same. It's the exact same voice...How?*

"Who are you?" he asks aloud, staring out at the sand blazing underneath the bike. He doesn't know if the words are meant for Honey or whoever it is he was dreaming of. Maybe both. Regardless of who, Honey hears them and glances over her shoulder.

"What?" she asks. "Clain, are you all the way back from dreamland? I don't think you're talking to me." Clain doesn't respond. He just holds still, clearly disturbed. *Damn, must have been one fucked up dream,* she thinks to herself. *Poor guy needs some real rest.* "Look!" she shouts, hoping to get his attention and snap him out of wherever his mind had gone. He looks up slowly and she points forward. "We're almost there!" The outskirts of Eagle's Equinox come into view over the horizon. Clain remains silent, unsure what to believe about anything or anyone. A hulking silhouette is leaning against the entrance gate, awaiting their arrival.

"Dawn's out-front waiting for us," Honey says. "See? Who else could cut a figure that big?" she asks, hoping the joke will diffuse the unsettling mood that's been hanging over them for the past few minutes. She slows down at the gate, steps off the bike, and helps Clain get his footing on the ground, eager to get off her bike. Something she never feels.

Who the hell is she? Is my mind playing tricks on me? Was I just hearing Honey's voice in my premonitions inadvertently? He questions himself. *Rezy. You're real. I can feel you.*

Dawn nods in the pair's direction. Taking immediate notice of their awkward mannerisms. A slight tinge of jealousy barks to him seeing them together with Honey carefully helping him off the bike.

"Welcome back," he says, looking first to Honey and then his old friend. Neither of them respond. Honey looks back at Clain, hoping he'll say something. Dawn laughs nervously as the silence drags out. "You guys having a moment or something?"

177

Honey smirks with mock innocence.

"Why?" she asks. "Jealous?"

Dawn laughs.

"Of what? Something going on between you two?" He scoffs. He looks back at Clain, who still hasn't said a word. "Seriously though, what's up? I don't know if I've ever seen him quite like that. He's as pale as a ghost. Blood loss?"

"Just a long ride, I think," Honey speculates. "Clain looked like absolute hell when I found him. Bruised, burned, cut. And that's just the obvious stuff." She lifts Clain's sling strap off her shoulder. "He was asleep for most of the ride."

"Yeah," Clain finally responds, grimacing as he adjusts his mangled arm. He looks Dawn up and down. "You look pretty rough yourself."

Dawn smiles wryly and looks down at the bandages around his waist.

"You're not wrong. Least you don't have to be as embarrassed as me. I got all these souvenirs from something that looked like you."

The joke doesn't land the way Dawn hopes. Clain seems to dissociate again, unwilling to think about anything but Rezeka.

"Yeah," he murmurs. His memories of Synric flash before his eyes. "And now we both owe her, huh?" He nods to Honey with a smile, trying to placate them. "Honey's had to save both our asses and bring us here."

"Yeah and you both better not forget it," she snickers.

"Never thought I'd be back here," Clain says, looking around him, then to his injuries. "Didn't think I'd show up looking like this though. Or under these circumstances."

Dawn opens his mouth to speak when a familiar, excited shriek rings out in the distance.

"Clain! Oh my God, you're ok! Dad, come quick!"

Clain spots Fila barreling toward him through the gate at breakneck speed. She crashes into his aching abdomen as she wraps her arms around him in a tight hug, precisely where he was stabbed. Clain was too speechless to warn her to be gentle.

"Gah!" Clain yelps. "Fila, please let go."

"What?" she looks at him, hurt in her eyes before she takes in Clain's ragged appearance. "Oh! Oh, you're hurt! I'm so sorry! I was just so happy to see you; I thought you were never coming back!" The words rush out of her, almost blending in one high-pitched word of excitement.

"Totally ok, Fila. I'd hug you back if I could." He messes up her hair with his good hand. "I'm really happy to see you too, kid."

"Very happy you're alive and well, old friend," another voice pipes up. Mr. Le. His smile is warm, almost apologetic, hinting at things still needing to be said.

"Mr. Le. You made it!" Clain exclaims.

Mr. Le bows his head. "Indeed! Things here haven't felt quite right until just now." He smiles at Fila. "Just ask this little one." *And me,* his eyes seem to say. There was a suspicion behind every look he used to give Clain. But even in his haggard state, Clain can see that suspicion is gone. Mr. Le is just grateful Clain is alive.

"Wow, your clothes are so cool, Clain! Where'd you get 'em?!" Fila circles him excitedly, enthralled by the sleek rail runner outfit Mitt gave him.

Clain smiles at the little girl.

"It's a long story. One I promise I'll tell you sometime. For now though, I could really use some water."

"Oh come on!" Fila complains. "You just got here and already want me to be the water girl again!" They all share a chuckle.

Dawn retrieves a water flask from his hip and tosses it to him. "Here you go, brother. Let's all get inside before Lenny loses his shit."

179

Clain quickly gulps the water down as they walk through the gate. Dawn raises his hand and nods toward Clain's duffle bag as if to say, "I'll get that for you." He hefts it over his shoulder with a flinch and walks beside Clain.

"Damn," Dawn comments. "What the hell is in here? It's heavy." Clain wipes his mouth.

"Another long story," he replies. He cautiously looks back at Dawn. "You sure this is cool? Me being back here and all?" Dawn shrugs.

"Ain't a problem for me, but I don't call the shots here. You know exactly who you have to straighten things out with."

"Yeah." Clain nods while looking back through the weathered gates.

"And looks like you'll be doing that right away." Dawn comments with a whisper.

"What?" he looks to Dawn, who smiles and nods his head down the dirt road toward a familiar wooden balcony. There sits the Elder, his stoic half-smile as unreadable as always.

CHAPTER 10 - Let Bygones Be Bygones

The creaky gate of Eagle's Equinox closes behind the group as they move toward the courtyard. Fila wastes no time, rapidly firing off question after question as she walks backward in front of him, speaking so quickly he can't even answer one before she's already asking the next. He tries to stay patient, though his injuries don't make that easy. Thankfully, Mr. Le steps in and urges her to settle down. Clain scans the area with a mix of excitement and trepidation, taking in everything that's changed and everything that's stayed the same. His old home.

The layers of dust and signs of neglect sadden him deeply, but they're overshadowed by an almost gleeful nostalgia. The character and culture of this place still shine through. Reverence guides his every movement back into the past. His eyes narrow as he tries to get his bearings and find one place in particular, but the fog in his mind makes it difficult to maintain his sense of direction. Dawn taps him on the shoulder, pointing down one of the nearby paths. He seems to know what Clain is looking for.

"Over there," he directs.

Clain nods gratefully and moves towards a dust-caked, dirt-encrusted wall. He reaches out toward its center and gently wipes away layers of dust, revealing the faded face of a wolf. Clain hangs his head, sighing with relief. "Worried it wouldn't be there?" Dawn asks, crossing his arms to lean on a nearby post.

"Yeah. Hasn't crossed my mind until I showed back up. But yeah. I'm surprised it's still here," Clain admits.

"Shouldn't be. This place really cared about you. Still does."

Clain continues carefully dusting off the artwork underneath. When he finishes, he steps back to admire his old favorite piece. It depicts a pack of wolves and the people of Eagle's Equinox surrounding two warriors of their community, celebrating their awakening. The night Clain and Dawn mastered their ability of image training.

"We were the first and still the last, ya know? Elder hasn't trained anyone since," Dawn reminisces.

"Not until recently, anyway!" a raspy voice calls out from behind the pair. The Elder hobbles his floating chair towards them, Lenny on his right and Cato on his left, shyly gripping his robes.

"Uhh," Clain stutters. His throat catches at the sight of his old sensei and how much he had aged. "Hey," he manages to force out.

"It is such a relief to cast my eyes upon you again, my boy. I have meditated on you for many years, so deeply regretting our last moments together." Clain suppresses a frown, uncertain he particularly enjoys the idea of so many hearing the Elder's comment. But he stays quiet.

"Should probably take this somewhere private." Dawn suggests.

"Use the saloon. Ya'll probably need a drink to loosen up," Lenny blurts out. Seeming the happiest he has been in weeks. "But before ya go, you need to turn that shit off," he demands, pointing at the bag of Motherboard fragments. Clain casts a confused glance at the duffle bag slung over Dawn's shoulder. "What?" he asks. "It's destroyed?"

"Whatever you got in there is sending out massive static interference. Fuckin' with our systems."

"Oh, it's broken. I didn't realize it was even still on." Dawn sets the bag down. Clain unzips it and retrieves a fragment of his sword. It flickers subtly with static and broken, corrupted images as it struggles in vain to function. Clain runs his fingers along the side, feeling for a hidden switch near the rear. Lenny's eyes seem to light up as he looks at Clain's weapon.

"That's the sword, eh?" he asks. Clain's brow furrows. He looks at Lenny, then Dawn.

"How does he-"

"You fell out of the sky and slammed that thing into the freeway, remember?" Dawn laughs. "I may have been delirious at the time but I know what I saw." He laughs. "No way I couldn't not mention it to Lenny."

"Ya want it fixed?" Lenny asks eagerly.

"Hm, I don't know?" Clain responds reluctantly, protective of his own creation. "It's kind of a complex mess," he explains. Dawn approaches Clain and gives him an encouraging nudge before turning to face Lenny.

"Lenny," Dawn says, "I think Clain here would *love* if you fixed it up. Give it some special treatment." He turns back to Clain, who is trying, with limited success, to hide an incredulous scowl. Dawn crouches down and whispers, "His grumpy ass needs something to do. And he can fix it, trust me. Plus, we got other shit to do." Dawn subtly nods in Lenny's direction. Clain takes the hint.

"Uh, yeah. Sure thing," Clain sighs. "Thanks, Lenny." The grey-bearded man was already taking limped strides over to the duffle bag and peeking inside. Scanning the parts with fascination. He seems almost grateful for the challenge when he looks back at Clain.

"No worries, squirt. It's nice to see you around here again."

"Squirt, huh?" Clain smirks. "Haven't heard that one in a while."

"All you kids will always be little squirts to me," Lenny grumbles while heaving the duffle bag into a nearby wheelbarrow. "Come on Cato, I'll need your help with this one."

"Can I come, too? I watched Clain make that thing; maybe I can help." Fila cheerfully suggests. Clain cringes at the thought.

"I don't know about that," he replies under his breath.

Fila excitedly retrieves something from her jacket and shows it to Clain.

"You owe me one, yo!" Clain's jaw drops.

"Is that my drive?!" he exclaims. "You grabbed it? I thought it was stolen!"

"Yup! I grabbed it from your console when Dad and I escaped."

"Trust me, I tried to get her to leave it behind but she insisted," chimes in a noticeably irritated Mr. Le.

"Well, ain't you a clever one. Couldn't hurt to have ya along," Lenny says to Fila. "C'mon kids, let's see what we're workin' with here." Lenny pushes the wheelbarrow towards his shop, Fila giggling with a taunting gesture as she follows, and Cato cautiously stays at her side.

"You remember where the saloon is?" Dawn asks him, interrupting his thoughts. The Elder approaches them in his maglev chair. Clain finds even his own years of experience out in the world and the Elder's age and frail physique haven't diminished his respect for the man, as frustrating as he seemed to enjoy being from time to time. If anything, Clain finds himself even more awed by the Elder now than when he was a child. That he was still so involved even as the community had diminished from its glory days. The endless limitations of age don't seem to have affected the man's intellect or disposition.

Whatever he's been doing all these years has worked, Clain thinks.

"How could I forget? It was one of the places we were never allowed to enter." Clain replies with a smirk. "Today's the day, I suppose."

"Indeed, now you stand before me older. Stronger. Proper men, even if 'wiser,' remains to be seen," the Elder quips. "I'd welcome the chance to share a drink with the both of you, especially given some of what needs discussing." He looks Clain up and down, assessing his battered appearance. He chuckles. "I imagine, however,

184

that that can wait a bit. Clain, I bet you'd love a moment to settle in and clean yourself up. Let's meet for that drink later when you're properly ready." Clain nods and sighs gratefully. His shoulders slump. Letting out a sigh of relief.

"I'd appreciate that. Very much."

"As well you should, boy," the Elder says. Eyes narrowed. He holds Clain's gaze with a stony expression for a long, awkward moment before he starts to cackle loudly.

"Hah!" the Elder exclaims. "I was hoping that would still work on you." His expression shifts to a mischievous smile. He points to a nearby row of small cottages. "You can wash up there. Third from the left. I've put you next to Mr. Le and Fila for that extra touch of home. Now go, get all that dirt and whatever else off you. Blood probably, knowing you and Dawn." He smiles warmly at the pair. "We'll all reconvene when you're feeling a bit better. We have much to address and very little time to address it."

As Clain approaches his cottage, he stops momentarily, looking back at the weathered eagle logo over the top of the bar just down the road. "Oh! Almost forgot." The Elder quips. "Clain, what's your poison after all these years?" The saloon had an almost sacred air of mystery when he was a child. It feels surreal to know he'll be walking inside soon for a drink. He looks back at the Elder. "Whisky always seems to numb the pain," Clain replies.

"You too, huh?" Dawn smirks.

"I had hoped you would say that," the Elder says dryly, turning and floating away on his chair. "I'll get my best tumblers!" he calls, disappearing from view. Clain looks to Dawn, raising an eyebrow.

"I won't be long," Clain tells him. Just as he finishes turning toward his new quarters, he feels a gentle tap on his shoulder and turns to look behind him. Mr. Le stands eagerly, a timid smile on his face.

"Howdy, neighbor!" he says, a nervous quaver to his greeting.

Howdy? Clain thinks, stifling a chuckle. *Since when does Mr. Le say 'howdy?'* His amusement gives way to a sense of deep sadness

185

and guilt as memories of Mr. Le and Fila's troubles come flooding back.

"Oh, hey Mr. Le," Clain says, turning to face him fully with a sorrowful smile. His voice shakes just like Mr. Le's did only seconds ago. He rubs the back of his neck, unable to maintain eye contact for more than a few moments. He struggles to find the right words. "You know," he sighs, frustrated. "Nothing will do justice for everything that took place." He shakes his head and continues. "What happened to the Pho King. I…I am so sorry. I still can't believe it."

"Neither can I, my friend. I am just thankful Fila is safe. And that you are, as well, Clain. My little girl has been nothing but smiles since you've returned. Reminded me of that fateful day you first visited us back then. You were always special to her. And now she finally knows everyone is safe. That's all I can focus on for now."

"I'm surprised you managed to make it here. Not that you're somehow incapable, but no one should have to face off with that. Monstrosity. I am so happy you both survived knowing everything that was going on."

"I bet! A humble restaurant owner and his young daughter hardly seem a match for rampaging kaiju. But, somehow, here we are." He pauses, displaying his arms outward toward the dusty community. "This place has been safe and the Elder seems like a good man. Told me all kinds of stories about you as a kid, too." he laughs.

"Uh oh." Clain smiles.

"Aww! How wholesome!" Honey calls out to them from across the street. She had been eavesdropping while leaning up against a wooden post. "I was hoping you two could be friends again." She smiles before opening the door to her little cottage, holding two fingers in a "V" as she walks inside. "I'm taking a nap," she says. "Peace out!" The door shuts behind her.

"Right, well don't let me hold you up, Clain. Enjoy your shower. You need it!" Mr. Le jokes, waving his hand in front of his nose. Clain chuckles and opens the door to his room.

Such a dad, Clain thinks with a smile.

He steps into his room and looks over the space. It seems far smaller to him now than when he was a boy, but it's still far from cramped.

"Cozy," Clain says to himself as a familiar must in the air meets his nostrils.

The place always reminded him of an old, western-style motel one might find in a classic cowboy movie. A seemingly well-maintained one, anyway. He tosses his overcoat onto a ragged old chair next to the door. As he walks towards the queen-sized mattress in the center of the room, he rolls the shoulder of his working arm, trying to loosen some of the knots the day's events have managed to tie. His neck pops with some relieving cracks. He plops onto the bed, and a cloud of dust billows out. He coughs momentarily, realizing that the room is probably mostly undamaged because nobody has used it for years. Or cleaned it, apparently. Someone did at least leave him a fresh set of comfortable gi robes. Adult-sized versions of what he used to wear when training. He unfastens his rail rider boots and tosses them across the room with a hard thud, wiggling his toes in relief. He could pass out right now, but his upcoming drink with Dawn and the Elder and, more importantly, the temptation of a hot shower prompts him to get back up and walk towards the bathroom.

He smiles gratefully as he sees this space has been prepared for him. Toiletries, lotions, and a hairbrush are neatly arranged as though they had no question in their minds that Honey would get him back here. He twists the handle in the shower and reaches inside to check the water temperature. He withdraws immediately when it touches his hand.

Scalding hot already, he thinks. *Impressive.*

It's one more sign that, underneath the years of dust layered over the place, Eagle's Equinox is still very much the place he remembers. They've never shied away from having modern comforts hidden just below their rustic presentation. Slowly, he undoes the strap on the sling and frees his injured arm. It was blackened purple from shoulder to wrist. A terrifying sight, but he could feel his body still rapidly trying to heal it. He prepares to grimace in agony as he moves it for the first time but is surprised to find he only winces a little. The arm has healed more than he would have thought for having been broken twice. And it looks like it will return to full functionality. He

187

stretches the wounded limb out in front of him, relieving some of the stiffness that has settled in from holding the same position all day. Moving his fingers was painful, but a few responded with a subtle quiver. He then immediately recoils and hisses in shock as all the pain receptors in his arm seem to fire up at once.

There it is...he thinks. Almost relieved.

He's appreciative for his training yet again today. That's all that stopped him from yanking the arm back with the rest of his body and ending up on the ground with all his nerves screaming at him for being so stupid. Perhaps the constant rush of adrenaline and blood had amplified his healing as he seemed to underestimate his capabilities. The steaming shower grabs his attention. He steps in and lets the warm water cascade down his back. The aches seem to wash away with the water. Not all of it, but enough that Clain's whole body relaxes as the tension in his tendons finally retreats. He lets out an involuntary exhale that feels like it's been waiting the last thirty-six hours to release. He relishes the opportunity to escape, taking even more tension with it. He ponders the lengths of this healing ability. It is undoubtedly responsible for the fact that he can even stand, let alone walk, after all that's transpired. Clearly, it's incredibly powerful and is improving over time. But something about it has felt...off recently. It's difficult to recall exactly when he started to notice the difference. Something to bring up with the Elder and Dawn later today. *Did the Illuminaries do this to me? Or was it something else? Damn it, why can't I remember when it started?*

Once the last of the grime is cleaned off, he steps out and towels off. He made sure to use his good arm for the harsh scrubbing motions needed to scrape every last bit of dirt and blood off his skin, but drying off doesn't require the same vigor, so he takes the chance to reintroduce basic movements to his hurt arm, loosening it up a bit more. He's even able to bend his fingers. Barely. They're quick to warn him how much is too much. And he's quick to heed them.

He leans over the bathroom sink and wipes away the condensation on the mirror. Tia was not there, thankfully. Only heavy, dark circles under his eyes that only proper sleep could cure. But rest would have to wait as Dawn and the Elder were becoming impatient. Even knowing this, however, his feet remain rooted to the floor and his eyes are fixed on his own reflection. He isn't sure if his expression is actually hardening to one of robotic indifference, but he is fairly certain his eyes haven't started to glow like his reflections have. He shakes his head rapidly, his wet hair throwing water droplets around the bathroom. The glow around his pupils remains, shifting between shades of indigo and violet. A self-conscious concern crosses his mind, and he wonders if his friends could also see it.

He looks down, wondering why Synric saved him, not just from the Illuminaries but atop the speeding train. Did the android know Clain was trapped with them, or did its hunt just happen to intersect with Clain's journey that day? Still, if it is the latter, Synric could have kept up the hunt as though Clain wasn't there and left him behind. Clain certainly wasn't in any state to do anything about it had that been what Synric chose to do. But it didn't. Synric saved him. He shudders at the memory of the monster that stepped through the portal. Its seizures and screams replay in his mind. Would Synric know anything about it?

Why the hell was that monster trying to protect me? Are there more of them? Are they inside of me?

Clain cannot care to try to answer that right. He splashes some cold water on his face, rubbing at his eyes in the hopes of staying awake just a while longer. When he removes his hands and opens his eyes, Tia is staring back at him, her hair writhing like bunches of tentacle-shaped smoke in the mirror's reflection. He can't even summon the energy to be startled. He's just tired. Tired of the creature and all that has engulfed his mind. Angry at his inability to stay tethered to reality.

These dream-world freaks can't leave me alone for ten minutes. He sighs and looks down, scanning the counter for his toothbrush. When he looks back up at the mirror to brush his teeth, Tia is gone. *I know you're always watching, Tia. No need to remind me.* He resists the urge to spit at his reflection in the hopes Tia will decide to pop in again right as the gob of toothpaste hits the glass. He'd likely only receive a dirty mirror, so he refrains from the impulse, but the supernatural being had a severely unhealthy grip on his mind. Clain now knew, however what it was hiding from him. Rezeka and he wanted to save her. He had to. He spits into the sink in disgust.

How can I get rid of that bitch.

He approaches the robes hung up on the door, noticing a leather wolf's head embroidered onto the breast. It is clearly a nod to his and Dawn's time together as kids. For years, he held a grudge against them. They had almost killed him with some fruitless ritual. Nothing, it seemed, anyway, would ever make that hatred fade. Yet here he is. His old home. And none of those old wounds are bleeding. They're just faded scars now, noticeable only if he really looks for them. The fatigue makes it difficult to retain information, but Clain nonetheless tries to compile a list of questions to ask and answers to give. It's an extensive list. He's been left to wonder too much for too long and needs closure. The new outfit is a welcome change from the armor he's been wearing. Soft, smooth, cozy, clean and warm.

No dirt, dents or blood, either. He thinks gratefully. He smiles as he takes one last look in the mirror. The clothes make him look like one of the warriors-in-training from the Japanese manga he and Dawn used to read. Feeling like he finally arrived with all the heroes he admired. He grins, feeling almost invincible after what he has faced.

I may have even more in common with them than I realized. Clain steps out of the cottage into the empty street. The sweet smell of barbecue on an open fire instantly graces his nostrils. It's coming from the saloon. *Damn, they're really buttering me up, huh?* He tries to muster some more resolve for the upcoming conversation, but the tantalizing aromas don't let him. *Maybe I should practice restraint. Don't be too harsh,* he thinks. They've obviously gone out of their way to make him feel welcome and like a friend. He needs a break. And he needs his friends. The two men waiting to speak with him want to give him both. It's enough to make the walk down the quiet streets conjure fond memories of childhood, and he finds himself more excited and thankful than anything by the time he reaches the doors. The front steps creak underfoot as he stops to look at the golden eagle hanging above.

"Come in! Come in!" the Elder's voice calls out from inside. For the first time, Clain steps into the once-forbidden place, eager to see what's inside. Dawn is kneeling near a large fireplace, the source of the delicious smells. He's tending to racks of beautifully seared meats, glazing them in sweet-smelling sauces. Each little feature of the place he could only catch glimpses of through swinging doors, he now gets to view completely. The bar, the taps, the fireplace, the rustic furniture, everything. As his eyes race around the room, old memories reappear. Raucous parties, laughter, crying, singing, even the occasional fight that spilled out into the street. It all made the place feel like something lifted straight out of a sepia-toned Western and dropped right into Eagle's Equinox. Pictures line the walls. Photos of former students and teachers. He recognizes all of them, wondering what it might have been like to get to know them. The ceiling is covered in a beautifully composed collage of empty and dusty bottles. Wines, rums, and whiskeys, from recent to vintage, all hail from every corner of the world.

Too bad I couldn't have brought one of my own, he thinks. Remembering the tradition of each pupil returning with a bottle from their travels. He admires the little niche showcase of world history chronicled above him in the artifacts of what were no doubt many fun nights to remember.

"Historic, huh?" the Elder calls out. "Don't worry, it won't start raining bottles of empty disappointment anytime soon. Former students built a brilliant little display case and integrated it right into the support structure while we were doing a little restoration work. Those bottles won't fall." An image of a man holding a trophy over his head catches Clain's eye. He brushes away some of the dust on it, revealing more details of the man's face. He stands with a proud, bloody smile on his face, missing a tooth and sporting a fat, swollen black eye. He recognizes the man as the winner of a boxing tournament held just outside the saloon during his childhood. That was the day he was inspired to become a street fighter, not because of the sheer badassery on display but because of the massive cash prize he saw the man receive. The man's notoriety was a bonus.

"What was his name?" Clain calls out toward the Elder.

The sounds of bottles and glasses clinking behind the counter stop as the Elder's head pops up over the bar. He squints at the picture. "Can't quite make that out from here. Bring it over and pull up a stool! Got something special for you two."

"Perfect timing, man! This is some good shit here," Dawn announces as he places the slabs of cooked meats on a decorative metal platter with a pair of tongs. Clain meets him at the bar as they dust off some stools and climb onto them. The Elder slides two empty glasses in front of them on the weathered wooden bar while Dawn slides the platter over to Clain.

191

"Dig in, man. I could hear your stomach when you walked in."

Clain obliges and quickly begins to bite into a massive chicken leg while eyeing the stack of smoked turkey slices. "You finally learned how to make decent barbecue?" he says through a mouthful of food. Dawn lets out a boisterous laugh at the sight of Clain scarfing everything down.

"Sure did. A lot of time out on the road alone by a campfire. Had to learn real quick." He reaches for the smoked turkey when the Elder slaps his hand away.

"Surely you have *some* manners, young man." The Elder scoffs, sliding Clain a set of silverware. "Jeesh, you two never change."

"Sorry." Clain nods shyly. "I haven't eaten in a while."

"No worries, now check this beauty out!" The Elder excitedly announces as he reveals a large, beautiful bottle of golden-brown whisky. It seems to pop out from nowhere. Evidently, the Elder has a hidden compartment for the really good stuff. He proudly places the bottle on the counter with a heavy thud, making a "ta-da" gesture as Clain and Dawn reverently inspect the luxurious container. An eagle leafed with 24-karat gold adorns the neck, wings wrapped around the nozzle with intricate flames cascading in a swirl around the blown glass. Heavy strokes of glistening black calligraphy run down the label. Dawn's jaw drops. It was the most beautiful bottle they had ever seen.

"Wow, that is one hell of a whisky. Surely we aren't drinking that? We aren't that cool, are we?"

"We are!" the Elder laughs excitedly. "Well, drinking it that is. The jury is still out on the cool part." he chuckles. "I have been waiting for this day for many years, and nobody will make me wait a moment longer. Not either of you!" The Elder playfully declares as he retrieves a glass for himself.

"Damn, you've been holding out on me Elder," Dawn exclaims. "All the whisky I've had here, and you've never shown me this one."

192

"Of course not, for you see, this is a special brew, brought to me by an old friend from a faraway land. I got it specifically for the day you two would return here." He smiles warmly. "Though, as the years passed," his voice wavers, "I began to worry we would never share it."

Clain and Dawn share a look of equal parts gratitude and remorse. The old man was right. Neither of them assumed a moment like this would happen either.

Wow. Guess I took for granted how hard this was on the Elder. He really cared, Clain thinks, reflecting on the rift that widened between them over the years. Realizing he hadn't thought about anyone's hurt but his own until now. *Well,* he thinks. *I'm here now.* He sits up a little straighter, smiling warmly as he and Dawn look back at the counter, admiring the bottle and the meticulously brewed whiskey inside. Clain's eyes shift slightly, bringing the Elder's hands into focus. They are weathered. Wrinkled and swollen with age. As the old man's fingers slide reverently along the bottle, Clain notices tremors in his hand.

Wow...he thinks ruefully, fully absorbing the ravages of time that have taken their toll on his teacher. The man is doing his best to hold his hand steady, but every so often, the involuntary twitches win out. *Really has been a long time.*

"What's that say?" Clain asks, his voice quivering slightly.

"Θα χτίσουμε το νέο από τη φωτιά και τις στάχτες του παλιού."

"That's Greek." Dawn acknowledges.

"Correct, my boy!" The Elder praises him. As the spry old instructor Clain knew surfaces, the tremors seem to subside. "Tis greek for 'We will build the new from the fire and ashes of the old.'"

Oh, Clain realizes. *That's not an eagle on the bottle; that's a phoenix! God, I really am tired. The big fuck off flames shoulda given that away,* he thinks.

Clain and Dawn look at each other again, pretending to be confused, but both know it has to be a reference to their strained relationship.

193

"You see, that day many years ago, I failed you, Clain. I damn near killed you. Hell, I thought I did until Dawn returned with news that you were alive. For that, I was more indebted than I'd ever been for anything in my life. I take full responsibility and know your trust in me had died that day. Relationships don't heal from something like that; they just scar. I've waited for years to tell you that I felt something in me also died that day. So please understand that I do not say lightly what I am about to say: What I did had to be done."

Clain is on his feet and pushing away from the bar before the Elder finishes speaking. The barstool lies on the ground several feet away from him. He can't remember if he threw it or just stood up with that much force.

"Please, my boy, don't leave. I need you to understand what we did and why."

"You just admitted that you tried to kill me! And now you want to try and tell me it 'had to be done?!'" Clain shouts. His fists clench as a purple aura shifts in around him.

"Calm the fuck down, Clain!" Dawn demands, standing to face him.

"You let it happen, Dawn! Don't you fucking *dare* tell me to calm down!" Clain barks at him. The restraint he brought with him now gone.

"I saved you, remember?" he fires back. "Ran your little punk ass all the way to your mom's house."

"Clain," the Elder interjects. "Try to see through your anger right now. Surely, you must understand there is a deep darkness within you boiling to the surface."

Clain spits toward Dawn's shoes, feeling a twinge of regret behind his fury as the saliva scatters across the wooden planks. Fire flashes across Dawn's eyes as his hand whips to his side, pulling a kunai from his belt, and throws it right at Clain. Clain is startled by the sudden move but reacts quickly enough to slow the blade with his magnetism, bringing it to a halt right in front of his face. He shifts his focus from the kunai to Dawn.

"This is what you brought me here for?" Clain sneers.

194

"Follow it through," Dawn replies.

"What?"

"Let the Kunai continue its path." Clain glances at the kunai skeptically before he obliges, letting the blade gently float to its destination. To his surprise, it would have missed his face, grazing his flesh gently but wouldn't have left a cut. He releases the momentum, allowing the kunai to find its mark on the bullseye of a dartboard hanging behind them. He blinks, his aura flickering as confusion infiltrates his rage. He looks back to Dawn, eyes narrowed. "If we wanted you dead," Dawn says, "You'd be dead. You'd've been dead for a long time by now, in fact. That's what the Elder is trying to say."

Clain turns back to face them, eyeing the decorative bottle of whisky. The Elder holds the neck in a white-knuckled grip. Clearly nervous by their flaring tempers. He nods toward the Elder. "Crack it open then," he says.

The Elder sighs with relief. "You two are going to give me a heart attack someday." He nervously chuckles as his fingers twist the gold and red bird at the bottle's spout. Its wings begin to unfurl, revealing a glittering spectrum of sunset red, orange, and yellow feathers all through its wingspan. As they reach their full glory, the bird's eyes light up with deep, bloody, scarlet LED lights. "The rise of a Phoenix." The Elder waggles his eyebrows, inviting his two students to be awed by the craftsmanship. He pours two fingers of whiskey into each of his three best crystal tumblers, gently setting the bottle down, then raising his glass and nodding to Clain and Dawn. "Finally, old friends can reunite."

Dawn follows suit, raising his own glass and politely inclining his head towards each of the two other men.

"A toast, then," he says.

"To what?" Clain asks, disheveled and still unsure how to feel toward them.

"To bygones, perhaps?" the Elder suggests.

"New friends?" Dawn suggests. Clain sighs. Silence hangs heavy over the bar.

195

"Yeah," he finally says. He looks both men in the eye. "I'll drink to both. Thank you for the hospitality you've shown Fila and Mr. Le. They are important to me and I'm thankful you kept them safe."

Neither Clain nor Dawn notices the Elder only taking a sip of the whiskey, and both men knock theirs back in one swift gulp. Clain's head turns almost a full ninety degrees to the side as his eyes and mouth screw shut and his sinuses clear. It takes a couple of rough exhales before he can speak again.

"Yikes," he finally chokes out. "That is…sharp."

"What is that taste?" Dawn coughs a bit. "There's something off about that." His face turns red. The Elder shakes his head, amused.

"It's special! Remember? Only sip on it from here on." The Elder instructs as he pours them each a much smaller amount.

Clain visibly relaxes as the alcohol warms his insides. "Woooo, I needed a damn drink. Thank you." He raises his glass towards each of the other two men in turn. Happiness quickly takes over his emotions. "For real." He picks up the glass to wet his lips with the whisky, allowing a few drops to gently cascade over his tongue. "It tastes so…unique?"

"There isn't a chance you'd be familiar with this particular concoction, Clain," the Elder laughs. "Dawn on the other hand…" The Elder turns to the big man. "Maybe. What do you think, Dawn? Tasting familiar at all?"

Dawn takes another sip, rolling it around in his mouth. "A bit, but I can't quite pinpoint what it is." Clain begins to repeatedly open his eyes widely and then screw them shut, hoping to clear some of the ocean waves rippling over his brain. The potent concoction invigorates his happiness further, even as his field of vision blurs.

The Elder circles around the bar, motioning for them to follow him. "Let's go on a little field trip."

Dawn gets up to follow behind as Clain leans forward slowly and presses onto his thighs to stand up.

"Yo, I'm taking this with me." He smiles while grabbing the platter of barbecue. Dawn looks back and laughs as Clain struggles to balance the platter with his broken arm while biting into a turkey leg with the other.

"You're still a damn pig."

"Dude, you learned to cook. This can't be wasted!"

The three men walk down the dusty road of Eagle's Equinox, laughing as they sway side to side. The Elder, by far the most sober of the three, has assumed the role of designated chaperon, hoping to let his two best students loosen up and rekindle their old friendship. A smile cracks across Clain's face as he realizes where they're headed. Within minutes, his old outdoor training area crests the horizon and comes into focus. His pace quickens as more memories come flooding back.

"It's still here!" he shouts wistfully.

Neglect has allowed layers of dirt to obscure almost the entire space, but this is it. Underneath all the accumulated grime and fade from the sun, this is the place where Clain, Dawn, and the Elder spent most of their time together. This is where Clain and Dawn learned to fight, hone their agility, perfect their footwork, and learn to grapple. To box and to meditate. As he scans the space, he notices one section, just big enough for two fighters and one sensei, that looks recently restored and practically pristine.

"Yo, this place is still standing!"

"Bro, of course!" Dawn slaps him on the back. "Been restoring it all and giving it a fresh coat of paint since a few weeks ago. Just finished up a big section in time for your grand entrance!"

"Wicked!" Clain shouts, forgetting all about the platter of food he's holding as he runs to the entrance. Until he hears the loud, metallic clanging of it hitting the ground.

"Shit," he grumbles, rubbing his sore arm.

"It's cool. It was all scraps left anyway. Let's fill our glasses again!" Dawn points toward the Elder, who is waiting for them at the center of the arena. He sets the bottle of phoenix whisky on the ground and motions his hands toward them, inviting them to convene at the bottle.

197

"I'll race you!" Clain elbows Dawn in the side, rushing forward without warning. Dawn yelps and grips his bandaged waist.

"Dude, I can't run right now!" he shouts. However, after a moment, he notices the whisky has done a fine job dulling the pain. The ache from Clain's jab has already subsided. "Fuck it, let's go." He lunges forward but doesn't make it far before tumbling to the ground near the bottle. Clain bursts out laughing, taking a moment to compose himself before he fills his glass. "I won that one, yo!" he declares gleefully while filling his glass.

"Ahh, whatever," Dawn sneers, playfully snatching the bottle away from him. "I don't need no glass!" he gloats while taking a swig of the whisky.

"Slow it down!" the Elder demands. "Enjoy yourselves, but take it easy." He tosses a couple jugs of water to their sides. Dawn's eyes fixate on the liquid within the bottle as he chugs it, wondering why the Elder is urging them to be so cautious. It was just whisky after all, right? The man has seen him throwback gallons of whisky that would have knocked most men out halfway through over the years. Maybe it's this extra special booze talking, but Dawn doesn't see any cause for concern. His vision is a little blurry, but that's to be expected. What isn't, however, is the small cluster of plant matter floating along the bottom that he just managed to spot through his onsetting, drunken haze. He glances back at Clain, who is red-faced and lapsing into repeated giggling fits. His lips feel numb, and he reaches up to wipe away a gob of drool that's suddenly started dribbling down his face.

"Bro, we are fucked," Dawn says. A stark realization seemed to dawn on him.

"Oh come on Dawn, you're bigger than me! Don't tell me you've turned lightweight!"

"Meshcashline," Dawn says, his speech a slurred, drooling mess.

"Yo, what are you saying?" Clain laughs boisterously.

Dawn slaps his face to snap himself clear a moment, shouting, "Mescaline!"

"What?" Clain adjusts his sitting position, crossing his legs. "Mescaline?" he asks.

Dawn looks over his shoulder and points to the center of the arena at the Elder. He's gone. Dawn whips his head around to see him walking away with a smile.

"Peyote!" Dawn yells at him. "This whisky has peyote in it!"

The two men get get no response, only the squeak of an old gate closing and a faintly chuckled "warned you" that they may or may not be hallucinating.

~~~

I'll check back in about twelve hours, the Elder thinks, reasoning from experience that the effects of the drug on Clain and Dawn will wear off by then. A rustling noise catches his attention as he travels down the path to his home with a satisfied smirk and maybe a hint of newfound hope for the future. As he surreptitiously moves closer to the source, he notices it's more of a shuffling, like tiny footsteps. An amused exhale escapes his nose as he shakes his head, flipping open a panel on one of the armrests of his hoverchair. With a few switch flicks and button presses, he summons a floating holographic display, a video feed of the scene directly in front of him. With another click, the feed changes to a map of reds, blues, yellows, and oranges superimposed over the scene before him. Thermal imaging. And just as he suspected he would, he spots two small, kid-shaped orange blobs doing their best to stay hidden behind a nearby wall.

"Come on out, you two," he insists. The children remain still, but they're far from having mastered the art of whispering. "Cato, now!" he demands. The small girl bolts upright, giving away her position. Her face conveys nervous anticipation of further disapproval. "You too, Fila." Mr. Le's daughter obeys, appearing next to Cato as she stands up. "What are you two doing here?"

"Well, uh...," Fila stutters, "Lenny got mad at us and asked us to leave. He snatched away Clain's drive and kicked us out of his shop."

199

"No surprise, I suppose. Were you two being mischievous?"

"Didn't mean to be, but Cato was being silly and I accidentally knocked over some of his tools." Cato then signs to the Elder, who closes his eyes with a smile.

"Thank you for telling the truth, Cato. You should not be having tickle fights in Lenny's shop." Much laughter echoes out from the battle arena as Clain and Dawn sink deeper into their shared trip.

"What's wrong with them?" asks Fila. "I have never heard Clain laugh so much before."

"They are... healing," the Elder hesitates. It is very important that you both leave them alone."

"What are we supposed to do? My Dad and Honey are sleeping, and Lenny threw us out, and now I can't hang out with Clain either?" Fila complains, crossing her arms.

"Cato, why don't you show her around some-but nothing dangerous, ok? The adults need a break and you two need to allow that. I also need rest, so please find a way to fill your time constructively." He smiles a friendly but tired smile, pointing away from the arena once more as yet another peal of laughter echoes across Eagle's Equinox. "And again, leave those two alone."

CHAPTER 11 - Healing

With the sun setting on the busy day, Fila kicks an old can down the market street of Eagle's Equinox. Cato follows closely behind, intrigued by Fila's somewhat chaotic nature. Having spent most of her time here in this old community, she hasn't had much chance to interact with kids her age. Only Lenny, the Elder, and their strict rules. Fila's company is a breath of fresh air. Even so, Cato can sense Fila's deep sorrow. She wants to help, maybe try and tell her things will get better, but being mute has been a barrier to such things in her life.

Usually, listening works for her. She likes hearing other people talk - at least if she trusts them - and it's easy enough to nod, gesture, and make the right faces to show them she understands. But Fila is completely silent. The soft dusk breeze is inaudible - the rusted can skittering along the dirt is the only sound around them. Though Cato is old enough to know silence is a statement in itself. All kinds of statements, really. So, Cato contents herself with Fila's quiet company, eyeing her fashionable yet weathered sports sneakers with each kick she delivers to the empty can. Hoping her presence will make the girl feel at least a little better. "You ever get sad?" Fila suddenly asks. She's stopped walking, opting instead to stare at the can a little ways down the path. Cato's eyes light up at the question, and she nods when Fila looks over her shoulder for an answer, eagerly hoping to relate with her new friend.

"I hate being sad," she says, her voice rising in volume, "and I hate seeing people be sad even more than that! Seems like that's all adults do. Be sad." She sighs and stares intently at the ground. "But sometimes, you see them act like a kid again." She points back towards the old arena. Clain and Dawn's raucous laughter is still ringing out within the complex. "It don't make much sense." Cato nods again in agreement as she continues. "Lately, every night I hear my dad crying when he thinks I'm asleep and it breaks my heart." Fila charges down the road towards the can, growling as she brings her leg back for a kick. "And the worst part is I don't know how to help him!"

201

she yells as her foot connects and sends the dented metal cylinder arcing through the air forward and off to the left. It sails farther than it has, never once touching the dirt until it lands nearly out of sight, clanging its way back and forth against the walls of a nearby alley. "The only time he ever seems to really be happy is when he's cooking for people and now he's lost that too." She clenches her mechanical hand into a fist, the limb's enhanced strength letting her grip with almost enough force to break a bone, trying to hold back the tears running down her cheeks. She feels them well up and drip away, noticing the ones that hit her cybernetic arm seem to vanish, blending in with the metals and composite fibers and ceasing to convey any tactile sensation. She looks at Cato, wiping her tears away with her organic hand. "Is that the secret? Becoming numb?"

Cato frowns, looking down and blinking as she ponders the question, her brow furrowed in thought. It only takes a few seconds to get in touch with her own deep well of sadness, and her sense of kinship with this new girl grows. She looks up, feeling yet another common thread between them: Their physical disabilities. Their eyes meet, and Cato cocks her head to the side as she gently moves a little closer to Fila, craning her neck to look up at the taller girl. Then she reaches upward and pokes Fila in the hip, hitting a ticklish spot and prompting Fila to giggle. She tries to fight it at first, throwing her best 'What the hell?!' look Cato's way, but Cato just pokes her again. And she laughs. Finally, Fila smiles for the first time since Cato has met her. "You're sneaky, kid!" Fila responds, wrestling with Cato playfully. Fila retrieves the can between two nearby cottages and sets it at her feet. She begins kicking it again, but she's no longer scowling as she does. As they turn a corner, something catches Cato's eye. A small cat sits atop a bench near the corner of a closed-up shop. The same cat Fila arrived with earlier. She begins to tug on Fila's hoodie with a series of closed-mouth grunts as she emphatically points at the animal.

"What's up, kid?" Fila responds, her eyebrows raised. She follows Cato's repeated pointing and finally understands. "Kiva! Where the heck have you been?" she shouts toward the cat. Her voice echoes down the street. She covers her mouth, surprised by the volume. The two rush over to see the cat, who begins to cower at the sight of the rapidly approaching kids. Still, she recognizes Fila and doesn't run. Just recoils slightly, suspicious of her speed and the new, unfamiliar girl with her. Fila picks her up and props her on her shoulder while scratching her back. "I haven't seen you since Clain arrived. Where did you run off to?"

The cat nuzzles Fila's face, but never one for being held in place too long, soon begins to push against Fila with her front paws to signal she wants to be set down. Fila obliges, and Kiva jumps from her arms, deftly landing on the ground. The cat takes a sudden interest in Cato, rubbing against her legs. Cato remains rooted in place, terrified. Of course, this only intrigues Kiva, who further finds Cato's quiet stillness perfectly agreeable. "Don't be scared, Cato," Fila reassures. "It's just a kitty cat. She's a total sweetie, too!" Fila kneels near Cato's ankles and Kiva pads toward her, eagerly accepting Fila's offer of forehead scratches before rubbing up against the rest of her arm, startling when she accidentally causes it to emit a familiar, friendly chime.

"Fully charged?" Fila muses, "That's strange." She smiles as she articulates the artificial joints in her fingers. Their movement is perfectly smooth - no sign of the stuttering tremors that usually accompany low power. She playfully musses the fur between Kiva's ears as the cat purrs.

Static, maybe? Fila wonders, *I didn't think cat fur could make that much....*

"You're an energized cat!" she comments. Kiva just cocks her head and bumps it against Fila's cybernetic fingers, demanding more attention. Soon after, Kiva trots forward, deeper into the old market square of the community. "Wait up! This dang cat is always on the move." Fila turns to Cato. "Yo!" she encourages, "The Elder asked you to show me around, right? To spend our time 'constructively?'" she asks, placing exaggerated air quotes around "constructively." Cato is nervous about exploring these abandoned streets without one of the adults present, but she can't help but be excited at the idea of an adventure with the only other kid around for miles. She purses her lips, considering her options. Childhood wanderlust wins out and Cato enthusiastically nods, giggling as she runs up to Fila's side.

"We can trust Kiva, ya know?" Fila says. "She actually led my dad and me through the entire New Beam City sewer system to escape! We couldn't believe it. She's like, got a compass in her brain or something. Or maybe a GPS!" Cato smiles excitedly at the outlandish story as Fila continues. "She even led us to a car that drove us here.

203

Crazy, huh?" Fila pauses a moment, catching herself and realizing just how crazy the story actually sounds. *Maybe I shouldn't have said that out loud...* she thinks. Kiva begins to meow, jumping onto one of many tables neatly arranged in a wide-open cobblestone plaza. "Wow, what is this place? Some sort of outdoor cafeteria?" She looks to Cato, who replies with an innocent shrug. "Hmm...I guess you might not even know what that is, huh? Have you ever been to a school?" Cato shyly shakes her head no, embarrassed at her lack of knowledge. "Wow, really? That's awesome! School sucks. You hardly learn anything useful there and the other kids can be the worst." Fila stops short and taps a finger to her chin, thinking back on her experiences. "Although, I do miss some of my friends." She looks back to Cato, who is listening intently.

"How about you, Cato? You have any friends?" Cato looks to the ground, moving her foot in a circle within the dirt before excitedly pointing at Fila with a big smile. "Me?" Fila smiles with a small laugh. "We only just met!" Cato sheepishly withdraws her arm and her smile changes to a dejected pout. Fila quickly backtracks. "But you're right! We are friends! Sometimes people just get along, you know?" She looks around the plaza, noticing the dust and rainwater stains on the tables. *Wow, when was the last time someone used one of these?* Fila wonders. She turns her attention back to Cato and their discussion on friendship. "Kinda like Clain and Dawn, huh?" she mutters before returning her attention to the old dining area again. "Now that I think about it, I remember Clain telling me a story about the first time he had ramen. He said it was out in a community with a big collection of small food shops with many tables in the middle. I wonder, is this it?"

Kiva weaves between her ankles, rubbing up on her to grab her attention before scurrying off toward a small alleyway on the side of the courtyard. "Crazy cat..." Fila mutters. "Hey!" she calls after Kiva, "Where are you off to now?!" She motions for Cato to follow her, and the two chase after the cat again. Kiva jumps atop some pipes along a brick wall before leaping onto the top of a zipped-up protective cover. Cato starts enthusiastically tugging her sleeve, pointing at the small building behind Kiva. "What?" Fila asks, looking around for whatever Cato is pointing at. "Is something wrong?" Cato jogs forward and begins to hop in the air, trying to grab a string attached to a zipper. Fila walks up to Cato's side, looking at the zipper. "Are you trying to show me something?" Cato nods and jumps again, swiping at the rope and closing her fist as she lands, making a tugging motion. "Oh!" Fila says, understanding what Cato is suggesting. She reaches

204

up and grabs the rope, carefully tugging on it to open the zipper. It snags a few times, but she manages to coax it open.

Fila steps back to examine what's inside as the cover falls away.

Is that a porch? Some kinda balcony? she wonders. Cato is pointing once again. Fila follows Cato's gestures once again and her eyes land on an old restaurant sign, cracked and flaking with age. The words and images are nonetheless visible. A stylized, steaming tonkatsu bowl with chopsticks neatly stood in the broth. Leaning against the edge of the bowl sits a bald, chibi man, mouth agape in a stunned smile, hands to his cheeks, and hearts in his eyes. She narrows her eyes, trying to make out the words. "Souper Soup?" she reads aloud. "Wait a second. That's it! The place Clain said he first had ramen!" She smiles brightly and looks down to Cato who nods proudly, happy to have led her new friend to the right place.

"Wow! This is so cool, Cato! Thank you for showing me this." Fila warmly pats Cato on the shoulder before inspecting the front door. "No one is around here right?" she asks, to which Cato shakes her head no. "Hmmm, I wonder if we can get inside?" She smiles mischievously and shoots a conspiratorial glance Cato's way. "Think anyone would care if we broke a window?" Cato looks shocked but then giggles, walking forward and pushing the creaky door open with next to no effort. "Oh, it was already open." Fila chuckles sheepishly. "I was just kidding, of course." Fila insists, following Cato inside. "Wow!" Fila exclaims as she takes in her surroundings. "It's so cute! This is exactly how I wanted to decorate the Pho King! My dad wouldn't let me though." Fila walks around the dining room, admiring the assortment of colorful graffiti and images of iconic anime and manga heroes from decades past. She runs her fingers across the walls in awe, leaving trails in the dust that's settled over them. "No wonder Clain and Dawn loved this place so much." Suddenly, Cato shrieks from across the room, waving her hands wildly as she struggles to wipe a spider web off her face.

"You ok?" Fila calls out, joining her to help pick the rest of the web off her robe. "Jeesh, sure is dirty in here, huh?" The two continue looking through the small shop, eventually making their way to the back of the house. "Wow, all the pots and pans are still here. It's like they just got up and left one day," she muses as she hops onto the dusty service counter. She begins to kick her feet anxiously as her mind races with thoughts. "This place is really cool huh, Cato?" she asks as the small girl climbs up to sit beside her. "It's a real shame no one is using it." The two sit in silence a moment before Fila exclaims, "I have an idea!" as she pulls up a holographic display from her arm. "Would you mind if I borrowed your 3D printer?" Cato nods at her with a smile. A few seconds later, the holo displays the Pho King Logo slowly rotating above her forearm. She smiles brightly as the spinning image casts a spectrum of colors over her face. "The Elder did say to use our time constructively."

~~~

The nighttime hours descend quickly on the south side mountains surrounding Eagle's Equinox. Grasshoppers chirp as a flock of ducks flies overhead, their quacks echoing over the desert, signaling nature's changing of the guard for the evening. Of course, Clain and Dawn hear none of this. Their constant laughter is far too loud for them to notice anything else. The two have stumbled to opposite sides of the arena, wrapped up in their own hallucinations. Dawn is leaning against the wall, staring at his palm and trying to read his future, disappointed that nothing is coming to mind and no magical signs are being bestowed upon him, no matter how hard he glares at it. No glowing lifelines. No voices from beyond. Nothing but the chemically induced motion blur that's accompanied his every movement since the drug started to hit.

Man, how the hell do they do that? He absently wonders. As he continues to open and close his hand, the lines in his palm appear like rivers, and the surrounding skin starts to resemble dirt and grass. Just as he begins to close his hand, small settlements of people spring up from his fingernails, desperately fleeing the impending doom of his closing fist. *Ah! Shit!* Dawn startles and opens his hand back up. The people return to their homes and resume their daily affairs as if nothing happened, advancing from paleolithic to medieval to spacefaring in a hazy, second-long timelapse that feels like several deeply fascinating and equally confusing days to Dawn. His hand reverts to normal as he feels spit dribble down his face and realizes he's been profusely drooling the entire time. He rushes to wipe it away, fearing anyone might have seen it. Clain starts to shout at nothing from across the room, clumsily dancing to what is undoubtedly a lively melody inside his head that nobody else can hear. His movements are difficult to

206

track since the drug is forcing Dawn's eyes to leave after images, giving Clain the appearance of a long, messy string of freeze frames that's only getting blurrier with each passing moment. The overstimulating sight causes Dawn's focus to lapse. He briefly wonders if he's developed the ability to ascend to the fourth dimension before shaking his head to regain his concentration. Clain is repeating the same word over and over. Dawn struggles to make it out.

"Kuwai!" Clain shouts vigorously. Dawn manages to focus hard enough to clarify Clain's image, and he only finds himself more confused. He's almost positive he's recently seen the exact dance Clain is dancing in a Korean pop music video. Clain is not moving through the steps especially smoothly - his whimsical spinning jump nearly ends in a faceplant - but it's nonetheless a recognizable series of movements.

"What the hell man?" Dawn calls to him.

Clain salutes him during another spin, barely keeping rhythm with the song looping in his mind. "What the hell are you doing?" he calls to Clain again.

"CDS!" he shouts.

"CDS? What the hell is that?"

"Cyber Dance Star, yo!"

"Cyber Dance Star? Isn't that a video game?" Clain flashes a thumbs up.

"Yep! You pick an avatar, then dance in front of a camera to show off your best moves," he explains. "Then the community votes on the best dance which can get featured on the homepage!" he explains, with way too much enthusiasm.

"Wow, that's crazy man." Dawn scratches his head. "So you're what? Practicing right now?"

"No, I am in it bro!" he gleefully announces.

Dawn gawks at Clain as he continues some of the worst dancing Dawn has ever seen. "You know, Clain-" Dawn begins, but he is quickly interrupted.

"Fila plays it all the time. I've always admired how easy it was for her to freely dance. She even won once, yo!"

"So you've always wanted to dance?"

"We already do, yo!" Clain shouts.

"Uh, excuse me?"

"A battle is a dance, and I bring the beat!" he declares. A line spoken by Synric before their last rumble. He starts attacking the air with a series of haphazard punches that masterfully strike lots of small targets or horribly miss a big one.

Probably the second one, Dawn guesses. Clain stumbles forward, swinging his arm in a slow, blatantly telegraphed hammer fist attack. Dawn easily sidesteps the ham-handed movement, and Clain almost stumbles all the way forward on his face, barely righting himself in time. *Definitely the second one,* Dawn concludes. After a while, he becomes winded, shifting instead toward a series of what seem like they're supposed to be the vigorous headbangs of a hardcore metalhead but instead, they come out as gentle head nods.

"You know this isn't real, right?" Dawn staggers away and leans over to grab his knees. He struggles to speak through his daze. "You're not actually in that game right now," he finally manages to say.

"Right now, we are wherever the hell we want to be, Dawn. Enjoy it, homie." Clain stares back at him intently, placing his hand on Dawn's broad shoulder. "Bro, look!" Clain points to the sky. "Flamingos!"

Dawn looks up, confused, seeing bats fluttering overhead in the night sky. "Those are bats, not flamingos." he slurs, giggling at the thought of flamingos flying overhead. "What the hell man," he nudges Clain, encouraging him to let go.

"Ouch! Watch it!" Clain yells when Dawn's elbow connects. I got stabbed by the Illumabitches, remember?" He shakes his head as he opens his gi to inspect the cut. There's nothing but perfectly healthy skin. Not a trace of his earlier injuries. "Ohhh. Guess it's already healed." He shrugs.

"Yea, and that Synric thing stuck a tetherball pole through me. Can you believe that shit?"

"That's messed up, dude." Clain sighs, falling backward into the sand. "I smashed that fucker to pieces and then he came back anyway." He reaches out his hand, still seeing flamingos flying across the sky as a question comes to mind. "What do you think pink tastes like?" he asks, trying to pluck the flamingos out of the sky as though the pink of their feathers is cotton candy.

Dawn chuckles at the bizarre question. "I don't know. Pink lemonade, I guess?"

"What? No." Clain's face furrows with disgust. His mind is tasting cotton candy, and now the taste has changed to a freshly squeezed lemon's sharp, sour flavor.

"Do you taste that?" Dawn asks, plopping down next to him with his legs crossed.

"The lemon? Yes, it's terrible." Clain continues to complain while scratching his tongue.

"No, the didgeridoo."

"Do I taste a didgeridoo?"

"Yes," Dawn insists, looking around the empty arena. "Tastes like beef jerky fresh off the drying rack." His mouth begins to water as he starts to nod his head.

"Wait, a didgeridoo?" Clain ponders a moment. "That weird tube thing the Elder used to play to help us image train?"

"Yea! And remember, he would always give us that delicious beef jerky if we made progress?"

"Yea, what the fuck right?!" Clain yells. "He treated us like dogs. Ruff, ruff!" Clain barks while posturing himself like a canine on his hands and knees. They both break down laughing.

"Dogs are cool, though." Dawn smiles, reminiscing over his childhood pet. *God,* he thinks. *Haven't thought about that little guy in forever.* "Not just cool, actually," Dawn corrects. "Dogs are the best." His tone is a muddled mix of excitement and distant sadness.

"You my dog, bro!" Clain playfully puts out his fist for a bump. Dawn bumps it back as Clain barks again and neither can hold back more laughter at the ridiculousness of it all. Dawn glances over at Clain, realizing how much he missed their friendship.

Maybe even friendship in general. That's fucking sad, he thinks with a bitter chuckle. His life as a traveling skip hunter hasn't allowed him to develop the most fruitful relationships. His eyes fixate on the wolf emblem embroidered on his gi.

"Do you like wolves?" Dawn asks, pointing at the symbol. Clain looks down, stretching his gi outward. His eyes widen as he tries to focus on it, gently rocking as if floating on a surfboard.

"Nah, man. Not me," he says. Dawn's eyebrows raise with surprise.

"No?" Dawn asks. Why not?"

"Just ain't my spirit animal, yo."

"Your spirit animal? What is then?" Dawn asks, lifting a finger as he contemplates the question about himself. "That's easy," Clain says. "Definitely a lion." He looks up toward the stars. "You know they just lay around relaxing all the time? They sometimes sleep like 21 hours a day." He yawns. "Plus, the lionesses do all the hunting. Isn't that awesome?" He looks over to Dawn, who seems intrigued by his response.

"Sounds like the lionesses get the short end of the stick. What do they get out of that?"

"Protection!" Clain declares, flexing an arm. He's almost gloating as though he's become a lion himself. "Anyone fucks with their women or children and you find out real quick why they provide for the big daddy Lion." Dawn chuckles.

"Good point, I guess."

"What about you, yo? What's your spirit animal?" Dawn pinches the bridge of his nose and sighs.

"Why do you keep saying yo?" he asks, almost annoyed.

"Good question." Clain thinks it over. "I guess I've been around Fila too much. Don't dodge the question: What's your spirit animal?"

"Hmm," Dawn grumbles. "I guess it would be a bear."

"Damn, a bear? Why?"

"Because I've always wanted to take one down."

Clain laughs. "What? Are you kidding me?"

"Nah man. I train hard to get stronger and most humans are flabby fodder to me," he boasts. "A bear would be a good challenge for me, and if I took one down, I could summon it!" he explains excitedly.

"What the fuck?" Clain laughs hysterically. "Yo, what are you talking about?"

"I took down a bull once, you know? It's name was Lasgaire."

"Lasgaire? Wasn't that the freakish bull they raised here when we were kids?"

"Yep! Thing went rabid one day, rampaging through the community and scaring everyone. I was the only one who stood a chance against it, so the Elder ordered me to kill it. Damn thing nearly killed me though." Clain abruptly moos while shaping his hands behind his head like a bull.

Dawn laughs and punches Clain in the arm. "Still always joking around. I'm serious man; I want to be the strongest guy on Earth." Dawn tightens his fists, imagining himself as a mighty bear. Clain's eyes fixate on Dawn with a determined glare. His words about wanting to be the world's strongest linger in his head. He considers holding his tongue.

"But that would mean you'd have to go through me," he says, unable to resist. Dawn returns the look and begins to see him as a fierce silver Lion, fully understanding Clain's challenge.

211

"I'm just kidding, yo!" Clain laughs, struggling to keep his footing. Dawn shakes it off, slightly disturbed by how ready he was to fight Clain at the slightest hint of a challenge.

Clain flops back onto the ground, crossing his legs and running his fingers through the rough sand. "I like sand. It's coarse and stimulates all the receptors on the body," he whispers, feeling a heightened sense of euphoria as all the microscopic metals amongst the grains stimulate his magnetic ability. "You ever want to image train again?" he asks cheerfully. Dawn's eyebrows raise with intrigue. He's a little bit stunned by the question, considering their current drunken and drugged state.

"Dude, we're still high as hell. And if I'm still hallucinating, you definitely are. I don't even think we could focus that hard right now."

"Let's try," Clain insists, continuing to massage his fingers through the sand.

Dawn slowly sits down behind him, roughly the required distance apart but just short. Clain nudges him to move toward the right. "Scoot."

"Yo, don't push me like that." Dawn barks at him.

"Now you're saying yo, too," Clain laughs. "You're just slightly off."

"How can you tell? We haven't done this in years."

"I can see us. In the sand." Clain smiles, still mesmerized by the magnetism crackling along his skin. Dawn rolls his eyes and adjusts his position.

"Alright, if we're doing this, does that mean we're sparring?" Dawn chuckles. "We are definitely not in top form."

"Nah, let's go somewhere."

"Go somewhere? What do you mean?"

"Remember how you got inside my coma and woke me up with our old memories?"

"That was hilarious!" Dawn laughs. "Not that you were in a coma, but that my idea actually worked."

"Right, let's do that but actually go somewhere. I need your help."

Dawn pauses, looking over his shoulder at Clain as he continues vigorously playing with the sand. "Need my help? Sounds dangerous as fuck. And where the hell would we go anyway?"

"Do you want to see my monsters?" Clain asks. His gaze has shifted back to the sky. He's staring not at the stars, but right through them. "The Illuminaries used my blood to summon some kind of a demon," he continues. His voice is flat and distant.

"I'm sorry, what?" Dawn asks, bewildered.

"Yeah. They shanked me. Took my blood. Opened up a portal. This monster came stumbling out and it walked right up to me. It was sickening like it was having seizures or something. But it was trying to help defend me somehow. Then I watched them kill it." Clain trails off. All traces of his euphoric high seem to have vanished for the moment. Dawn's brow furrows, recognizing the severe tone of Clain's voice. He believed whatever he was claiming.

"You're serious," Dawn realizes. "You're saying that shit for real happened?" Clain nods slowly.

"Yeah. I…" Clain stops mid-sentence, swallowing and forcing himself to make his request. "I think I need your help, Dawn. Legit have no one else to ask. There's some dark and twisted shit inside of me and I can't seem to rid myself of it. Last time we spoke as kids, weren't you starting to practice exorcism?" Dawn's eyes light up.

"Yeah. You're right. I was! Right before you left." He'd forgotten for a moment amidst the drug haze. Along with the fact that he only achieved success with the techniques he'd learned precisely once, and the experience still haunts him. The pay was paltry enough, but nothing would have been worth what he saw and felt that night. All memories of his brief time as an exorcist have been met with, up to now, a firm "fuck no."

213

"Clain, even if I wanted to start that old shitshow back up - and I *really* fucking don't - we're still seeing and hearing shit that isn't there. You saw flying flamingos and a few minutes ago, I saw tiny people fleeing for their lives across my hand as I made a fist. It was their apocalypse! No way in hell I could pull something like that off in this condition."

"I trust you. Plus, I'm betting you'd like a good boss fight?" Clain encourages as he stares back at the multi-faced monster before him. Tia was there, and only he could see her.

"Boss fight, huh? Playing games in your head again."

"Not this time. It's yo mama!" Clain chuckles.

"What the hell are you talking about?"

"It's called Tia," Clain explains. "A monster that manipulates you with the image of your mother or anyone you care about. It's floating over us right now, staring at me."

Dawn turns to look at him. Clain is still staring at the sky, but there's nothing in front of him. Dawn takes a deep breath and closes his eyes.

"Alright," he concedes. "Hold that image. Let me see for myself." Dawn does his best to breathe, steadying himself against his dizziness, carefully feeling around for the connection. It comes to him in a flash, their now shared consciousness, as Dawn begins to see through Clain's vision.

"You with me? Can you see it?" Clain asks. Dawn's mind adjusts through a haze as Clain's eyes blink, his thoughts whispering into every corner of his mind. He's looking at the sand, but something is caught or snagged between his fingers. Strands of thick, black hair fizzling like smoke. "Look at this." Clain whispers. His gaze slowly returns upward to the sky as Tia's image enters Dawn's mind for the first time. Dawn's jaw drops.

"Mom?!"

CHAPTER 12 - To Slay A Demon

 Clain continues to wrap the thick strands of hair around his fingers, reeling them in as if they were long lengths of fishing line. *No man, it's not your actual mom,* Clain whispers through his mental link to Dawn. *This thing changes form to fuck with you. It wants to manipulate you with her image. Dawn, listen to me, do you remember our old handshake?* Dawn is too distracted by the monster floating above for Clain's thoughts to register.

"I've never seen my mother before," he says, his observation directed at nobody.

Clain is stunned by his comment. He tries to concentrate on his hands again, forcing Dawn to do the same. *Dawn. Listen to me. Remember this handshake?* He moves his hands through a series of gestures familiar to both of them, ensuring they stay in his field of vision and partially blocking out Dawn's ability to see the monster through his eyes. Dawn nods absently, the motion registering in Clain's mind. *Now, remember we smack hands and pull our palms backward at the end? I will do that, but I need you to grab my hand and pull. Hard. Got it?*

Still distracted by his unsettling vision of Tia, Dawn struggles to distinguish his mind from Clain's, let alone understand why Clain is making such a bizarre reference to their childhoods. He has to repeat Clain's instructions multiple times to formulate an answer.

"I...I guess, yeah. That...uh...that...thing we did as kids? Yeah. I think. Why?" he finally manages to ask.

"Doesn't matter. You just need to trust me, man. Do what I'm asking, and it'll make sense, ok?"

Dawn shakes his head. The sensation of his own body moving while his mind is linked to a different one is so disorienting that the motion has the opposite of its intended effect, and Dawn finds himself even more confused than before. It takes him a moment to separate himself from Clain again.

"Yeah...yeah, sure. Ok," he says once he's anchored to the real world again. "So, just grab your hand at the end?" he mutters, confused. He looks at Clain's left hand, feeling like he controls the left arm. His brain sends commands, and the hand and fingers obey. Dawn follows along with the handshake, finally realizing what Clain has been asking. He grabs the right forearm firmly.

Ok, now pull! Clain commands. Dawn summons all his strength and follows Clain's instructions. With each second, he feels more and more distinct from Clain, as though he's freeing his psyche from his grasp and finally manifesting as his own separate entity within Clain's mind. The distorted miasma of Clain's mind being filtered through his own sight begins to resolve into familiar clarity, and he tears free, not realizing that he was tensed up in the real world as though he was actually pulling. He staggers backward as his body stops pulling on an arm that isn't in front of it, catching himself before flipping onto his back. He resets with a few deep breaths and looks around, now seeing his own hands occupying his own body. "It worked! You're back!" Clain exclaims triumphantly.

"What worked?" Dawn asks, still disoriented.

"I had to trick you into bringing yourself into this dimension. Convince your brain that the arm it was seeing, my left arm, was actually yours, and we pulled you free." Clain scratches his head. "I'm not totally sure why that worked, but it did. The important thing is you're out of my head and back home in yours. But kinda sort still in mine? Like we're sharing a vision now." He stands up and confidently taps a finger to his temple like he's pressing a button. "I guess the best way to think of it is like tuning a radio signal. Had to find your mind's own frequency."

"Right..." Dawn says hesitantly. *Sure, Clain. Your arm was mine, but still actually yours. But my brain thought it was, so pulling on it separated us. Except we're not really separated because I'm still hallucinating the same shit you are but I just feel more like myself because of radio signals. Totally got it.* Dawn thinks to himself. *Oh*

well, got other stuff to worry about. I'm just glad I'm back. "Gotcha,"
is everything else he has to say about it for now. "Well, anyway,"
Dawn begins. He looks down, nodding approvingly at the state-of-the-
art loadout he's now equipped with. It's the sort of gear you can't get
from any vendor you consider "above board." He recognizes it, too.
Weapons, armor, all here. This is the exact kit I've been saving for!
"I'm liking this gear you hooked me up with here."

"Sure thing," Clain says. He gestures with his head to Tia.
"Hope it's enough," Dawn smirks.

"So this is what you meant by 'boss fight.'"

"Yep, unfortunately. It's clever, too. Every time I think I've
got the fucker figured out, it whips up some new bullshit trick that
outsmarts me. I've been stuck with it in my head for months and still
haven't figured out if it will run out of ways to outwit me. For all I
know, it can do whatever it wants. Thing's a fucking parasite, blocking
my memories." he growls, coiling the creature's hair around his
forearms.

"Blocking your memories? What do you mean?"

"There's this girl. She cries out for me. Her name is Rezeka,
but every time I get close, this monster tears her away from me. It
claims it has to as a part of some deal." Clain explains.

Dawn struggles to understand but notes Clain reeling in the
bizarre, smokey hair over his forearms. "And what are you doing
there? Pulling it in like a fish?" Dawn chuckles, but there's no trace of
humor in Clain's expression. He was serious.

"Kinda," Clain confirms. It's more that what I'm doing seems
to be paralyzing it. I found some locks of its hair in the sand, grabbed
on, and the thing's been stuck in place ever since.

"This is quite the hallucination, man."

"Look to your left." Clain motions over his shoulder. Dawn
turns to see the hair of the creature wrapping around the nearly empty
whisky bottle they had been sharing. "Either I'm really tripping, or I
have accidentally started to pull this thing into reality." Dawn's eyes
fixated on the bottle the creature lifted into the air. The strands of hair

grip it like octopus tentacles. Clain watches too, dread flickering behind his blank expression. "I really hope I'm wrong," he says.

"Need a drink, Dawn?" The monster sneers at him with a wide-toothed grin. "Mommy will give you your bottle." It laughs at him with the face of his mother.

How the fuck do I even know that's her? Dawn wonders. He was separated from his mother when he was so young his brain hadn't even started forming long-term memories. And yet there's no doubt in his mind who the stolen face belongs to. Dawn retrieves a kunai from his belt and throws it, aiming perfectly. It slices the strands of hair gripping the bottle, and Dawn catches it as it falls to the ground. He hefts the bottle, trying to see if he can distinguish it from the one he knows is sitting back in the dojo. He can't. Every aspect of its feel is perfectly familiar. "Shit, this is really happening," he grumbles.

"Looks like it." Clain smiles nervously.

"Aww, you've figured me out," the monster mockingly pouts. "And just when I was coming to visit you." Its faces frown in unison. "You were so close to setting me free, too," it whines.

Dawn uncaps the bottle and pours the whisky into his mouth. He exhales sharply as it stings the back of his throat.

"Need a second wind, huh?" Clain jokes. He's still tightly wrapping the writhing strands of Tia's hair around his forearms. Tia's arm snaps forward with inhuman speed as she swipes the bottle from Dawn, sliding it across the ground towards Clain. It growls as its shape begins to distort.

"You'll need it too!" it sneers. Their surroundings begin to morph, and when the transformation finishes, they find themselves in a dense forest with a thick, nearly opaque layer of fog settling on the ground. Visibility at eye level isn't much better, but it's enough to navigate the landscape. Barely. Clain scans the area for anything that could suddenly turn into another one of Tia's many attempts to chip away at his sanity to get him to believe it's completely real. As if reading his thoughts, Tia laughs.

"You won't find anything you need to worry about, child," it hisses. "You've already given me everything I need."

"What do you mean?"

 "That deep, dark void within you? Pure dark energy. An unlimited supply, too. Just the most decadent feast for my rebirth. All I had to do was give your delicate little feelings the slightest twist and suddenly you were overflowing with delicious hatred. I'm sure the Elder would be so very proud of your restraint. It barely took any effort to get you to cast his teachings aside and plunge right into this abyss. Right into an endless well of pure, delicious power. Fueling me. Fueling you! Strengthening us. Exhilarating. Invigorating. So pleasing it would have been sinful if one such as I gave a damn about your primitive notions of right and wrong. And with every delectable drop, you unknowingly fed my reincarnation. Bringing. Me. Back. Returning to your world *very* soon, fulfilling my promise to that genius of a man."

Dawn and Clain look at each other, perplexed. Neither is willing to make a move as it begins to dance in the air, pleased with itself. Continuing to narrate all of its thoughts. "All thanks to you, my precious little boy. My precious, broken, hateful, spiteful, crazed, hopeless, *stupid,* murderous little boy," it taunts. "I knew humans were disgusting, simple, insipid little creatures. But you? You're so pathetic it was almost funny. A little guilt trip here," it starts, its face morphing to Fila's and its arm falling off, leaving a torn stump gushing blood, "a bit of parental energy there," it continues, its form shifting to a dead-eyed doppelganger of Clain's mother wearing a plastic smile, "and you just caved. I never imagined my rebirth would be so easy!" it gloats.

"What do you mean rebirth?!" Dawn shouts at the monster.

"Simple." Another one of Tia's heads floats down to greet him. It looks exactly like a target Dawn killed on a mission just a few months ago. A girl he briefly had feelings for. Feelings he ignored to carry out his orders. Ignored in favor of the sort of consummate, amoral professionalism that ends lives without the batting of an eye. Lives like hers end with unblinking efficiency by people like Dawn. Tia laughs as Dawn's Adam's apple bobs almost imperceptibly at the sight. All of Tia's heads slowly lick their lips. "Mmm, your naivety is so damned delicious to behold. It's been too long since I've toyed with someone like you."

"Be whoever the fuck from my past you want, demon. Just get on with it," Dawn snaps.

"Demon?" the monster laughs. "I am no demon. I've simply been forgotten until now." Its heads move back and up as its necks all straighten so that every face can look down on them in every sense of the word. "A prestigious man of your world made a deal with me. He would forge a machine that would harness the energy of your anger and use it to bring me back to your plane of existence. In exchange, the man required that I block some of your," it pauses, mischievously steepling its fingers and then lowering the head, wearing the most insidious grin to Clain's ear to whisper "tragic memories." Its smile gets even more expansive as it retreats, winking at him as its face takes the form of Rezeka's.

Clain's eyes flick to the ground, then back up. He blinks, his heart sinks. His expression is blank as his thoughts settle on the empty spaces occupying parts of his mind where recollections should be.

"My tragic memories?" he asks.

"Oh come now," Tia says. "Surely even you must have figured some of this out by now. You were practically making love to her on that stage!"

"I…" Clain stammers.

"At least speak the name floating around in that head of yours," Tia cackles. "Forcing you to forget something like that has not been easy, but my powers have regressed as my rebirth draws near. No need to make your situation worse than it already is."

"Rez.." Clain stutters, too focused on digging up the information from the long-sealed depths of his mind to react to Tia's jabs. "Rezeka?"

"Yes! He's only *mostly* hopeless. Good for you, Clain. Finish me off. Remember more. Remember it all! Your former fiancé, no? Hm? If I'd known even that frankly brazen display during her concert wouldn't properly shake those memories loose, maybe I'd've been able to save more energy," Tia mocks. "But alas, I did. Inevitably, my reserves ran dry, and my hold over this dark memory completely weakened. Hence the dreams you have. But it's all moot now because thanks to you, my spirit is on the way to a new destiny! All I need from you now is your permission to release the rest. And you won't let her fade away, will you?" Tia grins. "But then, I could be wrong. Love does seem a touch too sophisticated for you."

"Rezeka...My fiancé?"

"You were engaged?" Dawn exclaims in shock.

"I... I remember her. I love her." He clenches his fists, rose-colored energy radiating off of his skin. "Let me remember her!" he screams at the monster. Tia grins with unhinged, gleeful anticipation.

"Oh? What's that? Are you saying you want me to release these memories of yours? Are you...giving me your consent to set them free?"

"Wait, Clain, think about this," Dawn pleads. "If this is real, it sounds like it needs your consent to enter our reality?" Dawn pleads. "Remember the nasty creature you mentioned earlier. This one seems way worse!" he argues.

"That is correct. You are quite clever for a brute, I must admit." Tia morphs its image into Honey. Using her voice, "If he does not consent, then I will be a prisoner within his mind for the rest of his life."

"Don't use Rezy's image!" Clain shouts with anger.

"Rezy? But that was Honey?" Dawn says, confused. "What the fuck." Tia begins to laugh sadistically. It's a hideous, cruel sound, inducing a sensation of knives cutting across the two men's scalps.

"I won't be tortured by this or by you anymore, you fucking soul sucker!" Clain yells. Give me back my memories and get out of my mind!" Clain screams. The torture he has endured by the creature was immense, but was it worse than what he might release?

Tia obliges, slowly, mockingly bowing to him with its five heads. Its faces look lovingly at Clain. All of them wear the eyes of a snake ready to strike and the grin of a predator eager to ensnare its prey.

"Your wish is granted. My king."

All of Tia's heads return to their imperious position, multiple arms whisp around behind it, their slow undulations gradually inducing a drastic transformation. Each head stretches forward and sideways, expanding in size and growing pointed horns, elongated snouts and muscle jaws with rows of pristine, fearsome teeth. Within moments, a massive, five-headed dragon has replaced the old, amorphous apparition Clain has grown accustomed to. It lets out a booming snarl, then a low, rumbling laugh as it launches into the air, leaving only a puff of smoke behind.

"That shape. That dragon." Dawn comments. "I think I recognize it,"

"Oh no," Clain whimpers, falling to his knees. "No, not this!" he screams.

"Dude, what's wrong?" Dawn rushes to his side as Clain begins to shake uncontrollably.

"Leave!" Clain screams at him. "You can't see this. No! Please!" he shouts. "Not this, not this, not this," he repeats, curling into a fetal position as he claws at his scalp and lapses into wracking trembles.

"Your memories are coming back?" Dawn asks as the environment morphs wildly. Suddenly, they seem to be in the hallway of a seedy inner-city apartment.

 "No!" Clain screams as tears fill his eyes and rush down his face. "It hurts. Dawn, you can't see this. Please," he begs before falling silent and gritting his teeth, somehow balling up even tighter. He grips Dawn's pant leg, tugging on it like a child. "Please don't look!"

Dawn reaches down, touching Clain's forehead, trying to confront his frantic friend. Unnerved by such a stark change in his demeanor. Whatever this was, it had to be bad. He begins sweating profusely and his body temperature has skyrocketed. Clicking footsteps echo from down the hallway.

Heels? Dawn wonders. His question is answered as a tall slender woman comes rushing around the corner. *Honey? What the hell is happening?*

"No," Clain begs through gritted teeth. His voice is frayed and his shakes are more violent than before. "Don't watch."

A few moments later, a different version of Clain rounds the same corner of the hallway. He looks angry and worried as he chases behind her. His clothes were tattered and bloodied. They're moving fast. Too fast for Dawn to dodge once he snaps out of his bewildered stupor. He braces for impact, but they go right through him like ghosts.

It is his memories! Dawn realizes.

"Rezy, please just hear me out. Please!" Clain shouts as the woman fumbles to unlock the door. Clain catches up before she can turn the doorknob and turns her to face him. She shoves him back, fear and disgust on her face.

"I don't need to hear anything, Clain. You promised you'd never kill anybody! Back when we first got together!" she shrieks. "You swore it would never come to this!"

"Rezy, that guy was trying to kill me!" he pleads as they both rush into their apartment. Rezy tries to slam the door in Clain's face, but he reacts quickly enough to stop it from closing and forces his way in. The door slams behind them. Dawn walks toward the door as the Clain on the ground grabs his ankle again.

"Dawn, please. Don't go. Don't look." His face is streaked with tears. Dawn has never seen Clain's composure so utterly ground to dust before. "Please, don't watch anymore," he mumbles, his voice raw from his sobs and screams. A loud crash rings out from the apartment.

Dawn twists his leg free of Clain's without a word, too curious to allow himself to be stopped. He finds he can pass right through the door, as much a ghost to this world as its inhabitants are to them. He stands inside a small studio apartment. Clain stands just in front of him at the foot of a double bed, withdrawing a bloody handful of splinters from a dresser he's just punched through. Rezy is frantically packing a suitcase as Clain turns away from the dresser and starts pacing. The loud crash of the dresser cracking apart has stopped her momentarily. She turns to look him in the eye.

"You think a tantrum will make me stay here?" she scolds.

"Rezy, be real. You watched the fight. The guy had me by the throat. He was going to kill me!"

"And you broke free and stopped him! And then you just kept going! When is enough, enough, Clain?! You have been in these fight pits for years, thirsting for a fight! What's gonna stop you from killing the next guy?! And then the next! How long until a dirty look is all it takes to set you off? How long until *I* piss you off in just the wrong way?" She pauses, distraught and heartbroken. "You promised me, Clain!"

Clain stands speechless. Words fail him as he watches the love of his life pack her bags to leave. "I love you, Rezy. You can't leave me like this! Please!" He slowly walks up to her and gently kneels next to her, stopping himself from trying to touch her again when she recoils at the sight of his bloody hands. He lowers his voice and speaks as softly as possible, desperate to reassure her. "That was it. I promise I am done with the fight pits. We can leave together." She grabs the handle of her suitcase and storms towards the door.

"I will never be with a killer," she hisses. Clain takes a step towards her. "Don't you dare come anywhere near me. Now, or ever again!"

"I'd kill for you, Rezy. Anyone that ever harmed you."

Rezy pauses, speaking to his reflection in the mirror in front of her, not bothering to turn and face him. Tears stream from her eyes, and exasperation drips from her voice.

"You really don't get it, do you? That's the worst part, Clain." She pauses. "That's exactly why I'm leaving. I saw the look on your face. You enjoyed it. And you wanted more. I initially caught glimpses of the real you, but I didn't want to believe it. I wanted to change it. To save you! It's just about power for you, Clain. That's it. You want to be stronger than everyone else. You want the world to know you have the strength to kill everyone in it. And the craziest thing? I'm starting to realize you actually believe you're capable of deciding who deserves to die. That you could somehow get that strong and not become a goddamn monster. Well, congratulations. Keep this shit up and you're gonna be your own judge, jury, and executioner in no time." She turns to face him. "And right now? All you are is a murderer. And a motherfucking liar. You promised me, Clain! You said you loved me. And none of it ended up meaning a damn thing."

Rezy's hand trembles as she grips the doorknob. She knew she was saying too much, looking away from his damaged appearance. She knew he was about to be killed, but she couldn't resist her cruel yet truthful words. Dawn sees the muscles in her neck twitch as if imploring her to look at Clain one last time. But she doesn't. She takes a deep breath, stifles her tears, and walks out for good. Dawn turns to look at Clain. He's alone on his hands and knees, seemingly about to collapse into the same position as the Clain he stepped away from. Dawn frowns as he has just watched his childhood friend's heart shatter.

She broke up with him. Jesus. And Honey looks just like her, too. Dawn runs his hand over his mouth and down his chin, struggling to comprehend the depth of loss both the man in front of him and the man outside are feeling. It doesn't seem as though the pain has faded with time. *He wasn't even able to remember this for years. Now it feels like it just happened for him,* Dawn realizes. *That creature was blocking all of this in his mind?*

Clain's past self continues to breathe heavily. A larynx-shredding scream tears its way out of his throat as he starts to punch the ground. The memory wasn't over. The impression his fist leaves on the floor deepens with each strike. His scream turns to a barely comprehensible string of curse words, many of which seem directed inward as he tears himself apart for losing the love of his life. Dawn steps away, following Rezy down the hall. As he turns a corner, he sees her frantically pressing the elevator button, frequently glancing over her shoulder as though Clain could come lumbering down the hallway at any second. Her eyes are swollen from crying, and tears have begun to fall once again. It's obvious she loved him deeply, that she wanted better for him, and that it pierces her to the deepest depths of her soul that he didn't want the same. As her sobs intensify, her patience wears razor-thin, and she begins slapping and then punching the call button. The elevator still doesn't arrive.

"Fuck this," she shouts, rushing towards a nearby stairwell door. Clain's punches grow stronger. She can hear them reverberating within the building. She was scared. The sounds of his strikes to the floor grow louder. The echoes of his screams and the thuds to the floor begin to crack the foundation underneath him. Breaking apart into dust, more and more with every hit. Dawn's eyes widen as he realizes that Clain has been wearing his modified gauntlets, Buster and Banger, this whole time. And the increasingly violent vibrations ringing through the building probably mean he still is.

Jesus, he's gonna punch right through the whole damn building!

The groan of straining metal pipes hits Dawn's ear. It's close. Just to his left. As Dawn turns his head, the drywall crumbles, and the wooden beams in the wall split. And a pipe, now visible through the devastation, cracks. Dawn's reflexes take control, and he jumps back, forgetting he's intangible in this space, hitting the floor and covering his ears as a gas line ignites. A rumbling explosion sets fire to every flammable surface within at least a five-foot radius. The flames pass through his ghostly form, and he shuts his eyes to block out their blinding light. Relief washes over him as he notices he can't feel the heat of the spreading inferno.

Right. Dream. God, that would've killed me. His relief quickly shifts to horror as he watches the flames flood their way into nearby apartments, and he hears the hacking coughs and muffled screams of their occupants. But one in particular cuts through the rest. It's a piercing shriek. The kind born of excruciating, total body pain. It was Rezy.

Dawn's hand goes to his mouth as he struggles to accept what he is hearing. *She's burning alive...*Dawn realizes. *Oh my god...Clain. Just...Oh no...*Dawn can't think of any words that do justice to the horror and guilt Clain is enduring. What level of feeling must engulf him as this horror has returned to his mind.

Dawn's chest tightens like a vise. He grabs at his sternum, feeling like his heart has been ripped out. And then he wakes up, sitting bolt upright. The hollow feeling underneath his rib cage is gone, replaced by rapid, adrenaline-fueled pounding. He rubs his eyes to clear his vision. As he looks around, he realizes they never left the arena. He spots Clain, still fitfully asleep on the ground in a fetal position.

"Hey," a familiar voice whispers. He's startled as he looks up to see Honey offering her hand to help him up. She's holding a canteen in her other hand. "Drink up. Quick," she insists as she pulls him to a standing position. "You've been in direct sunlight for hours," Honey informs Dawn. She offers him the canteen. "You're for sure dehydrated." The sluggishness and creaking aches he feels as he reaches for the water confirm as much. The relief he feels as he satiates his thirst is almost overwhelming. He tries to open his mouth to speak but finds he can hardly think straight. Honey holds up her hand. "Dawn. It's ok. Just take a minute," Honey continues to whisper. "I can't imagine you feel like talking anyway." She points to a nearby umbrella casting shade. "Go cool off. We can talk after you've recovered, ok?" Dawn just nods wearily, quietly shuffling over to the shadowy patch. She steps away to kneel down and examine Clain. She sighs when she notices the reddish tint of his skin. *Probably sunburnt,* she thinks, annoyed. *Don't think he's getting up anytime soon, either.* She considers her options for getting him to safety. She can think of only one. *Cool. I have to drag him. Alone. Yay,* she concludes, grumbling as she squats down to hook her arms under his shoulders.

Was any of that real? Dawn wonders. Honey looks exactly like the woman in Clain's memories. *Rezeka,* he recalls. *So then…who the hell is Honey?* He watches Honey slowly drag Clain's limp body through the sand towards the nearby arena wall. He's still sleeping. His body is jolting every so often with fits. One causes Honey to lose her grip and she hangs her head back in exasperation before picking Clain back up and getting him to the wall, propping him up against it and ensuring he's completely out of the sun. She walks back over to Dawn, wiping the sand off her palms as she sits beside him.

"Hopefully he wakes up soon," Honey says. She looks back over to Clain and Dawn follows her gaze. He's still stirring, sometimes violently. Honey's face scrunches up with concern as her hand goes to her mouth. "Hopefully, for his sake," she continues. "That looks like a *bad* dream he's having." Dawn's head falls forward as he closes his eyes and forcefully exhales.

You have no idea, he thinks. *What am I supposed to say to her?*

227

Honey reaches for the empty bottle and examines the label. She looks back at Dawn with a playful smile.

"Some whisky, huh? Sure *sounded* fun." She mocks. "You guys were partying for about fifteen hours." Dawn's eyes widen at the number.

Fifteen?! he thinks, shocked. *Then again, time's different in...wherever the fuck that was. May be fifteen years in dream time.* He remains silent, looking outward across the arena. Honey raises an eyebrow. Dawn halfheartedly looks her way. Both Honey's eyebrows raise. Dawn just shakes his head, still too haunted to speak. Honey sighs, looking just as concerned for him now. Silence hangs between them.

"Alright then," she finally says. "I'm going to head out for a ride on the flats. Need to let loose." She climbs to her feet into a tippy-toed stretch. "If you're hungry, there's some Pho in a container."

"Pho?" he grumbles.

"Hey, he speaks!" Honey jokes. Dawn smirks apathetically, shaking his head. "But yeah, pho. And don't be harsh on it." She smiles. "It's Fila's first attempt at making it herself. Anyway, bye for now. Keep resting up. Don't be stupid. It's deadly in your condition." Dawn nods and turns his head back towards the arena, his body shaking slightly with a silent laugh and in a cold sweat. He tries to keep looking forward as Honey walks away, fighting the urge to look toward her. So many questions are running through his mind. Honey stops to turn and walk backwards. "Oh, and one more thing! One of the Elder's friends arrived a few hours ago. She seems really excited to see you two."

"Who?" Dawn calls out.

"Her name is Goldie. She seems pretty dope." Dawn just gives a grateful nod and an absent-minded thumbs up before waving goodbye. Honey winks, half smiles, and flashes a peace sign before turning back around.

Goldie? Dawn's eyebrows furrow. *What the hell is she doing here? Ugh, and why now?*

Dawn hears a subtle rustle behind him as Clain comes to. Clain lets out a pained groan as he struggles to get up. Dawn looks over his shoulder.

"Did you hear any of that?" he asks Clain.

"Some of it. Pretended to be asleep." Clain rubs his temples. "Mind tossing me the water?"

"Sure." Dawn slides a canteen toward him. "The bad dream act was a nice touch. Fooled me, anyway. I actually thought you were still stuck there." Clain struggles to gulp down some water. He drains the canteen with increasing vigor as the cool liquid touches his tongue and washes away the feeling of sandpaper coating his mouth after hours of baking in the sun. He sighs gratefully when he finally stops.

"Mana from the gods right now," Clain says, returning the canteen to Dawn. "Thanks. Felt like I was getting embalmed from the inside out for a sec."

"Yeah, no problem," Dawn says. "Should probably thank Honey, though, not me. She's the one who found us. Canteen's hers." Dawn sees Clain tense at the mention of her. Silent understanding hangs in the air between them. After a long moment, Clain breaks eye contact, and Dawn asks, "Honey looks and sounds the same voice as Rezy, doesn't she?"

Clain sighs, pouring some water on his face to cool off and quietly enjoying the sensation.

"Dammit," he says before looking back to Dawn. "So you saw it, then?"

"I did. Did that shit really happen?"

Clain looks away as his face flushes with rage and shame.

"Sure feels like it," he replies.

"Then who covered it up for you?" Dawn asks.

"What? Covered it up?" Clain asks.

"If you caused that building to burn and people died in it, there's no way you got off scot-free, especially in New Beam." Clain leans backward slightly, a stunned expression coming over his face as he had not had time to think that far ahead.

"Huh," Clain says. "Good point." Dawn's experience as a Skip Hunter has granted him a keen detective's instinct that always leads him to the critical questions while Clain's mind is racing to defragment his returning memories. "I don't know, Dawn," Clain finally says. "But I do know where the answers are."

"Yeah?" Dawn replies, urging Clain to continue.

"Yeah. Synric. The top of Cloud 9. He asked me to meet him there, all the way at the top. Then - supposedly, anyway - 'all my answers will be revealed.'" Clain explains, mocking Synric's cryptic promise with air quotes.

"That android did call you a project," Dawn points out.

"Yep." Clain exhales while climbing to his feet.

"I assume you're going to go, and no one will convince you otherwise?" Dawn smirks, already knowing Clain's answer.

"Yep." Clain clenches his fist, testing his broken arm. His head pounded with a hangover. His fingers loudly snap and pop, and pins and needles race up his forearm. He flinches and inhales sharply, opening and closing his hand until the noises die down and the prickling sensations fade. It doesn't take long before he can make a fist without issue. "Damn," Clain observes. "It actually healed."

Dawn scoffs, wincing as he lifts his shirt to check his bandages. They're bloody again. And they need to be changed. Again. He sighs loudly, looking at Clain, his wound, then back to Clain, shaking his head.

"Must be nice."

"You alright?"

"Yea. I'm fine. What are we going to do about Honey?" Dawn asks, trying to steer the conversation away from his wound.

"Everyone's so enamored with her," Clain states with a frown, considering how much Fila admires her. "But something ain't right."

"We have no choice but to play it cool for now."

"Guess so." He nods toward Dawn, "And this stuff about Rezeka," he attempts before Dawn interrupts.

"None of my business." Dawn raises his hand. "I want to see the top of that tower and it sounds like you have an open invitation. I'd want answers if I were you, so I'll help you get there."

Clain looks at Dawn with an appreciative expression, simultaneously shocked and relieved. Dawn knowing his darkest secret is a vulnerability. He isn't sure he'll ever be entirely comfortable with this, maybe even regretful for bringing him into the memory. But at least there seems to be a shared understanding that getting answers about it matters to Clain and Dawn. A lot. Both men are shaken out of their grim reveries as a boisterous voice echoes over the outdoor dojo.

"Well, well, well! Ya'll awake finally? Bout time," it snickers playfully. A large blonde-haired woman shuffles toward them. "Oh boy, ain't they handsome," she says to nobody in particular.

"Hey Goldie," Dawn says, halfheartedly waving as she approaches. She wraps her arms around him with a tight hug.

"It's been too long!" she squeals. She releases her grip and recoils, waving her hand in front of her nose. "Ohhhh, boy. And I thought I smelled bad." Dawn sniffs his armpits, almost as shocked as Goldie by the pungent odor. He shrugs with a laugh.

"Whisky sweats, I guess."

"Right, the Phoenix Down." She smiles brightly. "How did you like it? Was my first batch," she grins, slurring her words.

"Got any more?" Clain chuckles. Dawn glares at him as an awkward silence settles over the coliseum. Goldie nudges Dawn with her elbow, "Well, don't be rude now, Dawn. Introduce your silver-haired friend to me."

"I'm Clain, miss," he reaches forward, offering to shake her hand. "It's nice to meet you." He looks away. His attempt at pretending things were cool quickly fatigued him.

"But of course you are. Mighty fine manners, you got there, Clain," she compliments, warmly accepting Clain's hand with both of hers while shaking it.

Clain finds himself studying her unique outfit. She sports an ornate poncho sewn from a beautiful fabric he doesn't recognize. Her jewelry casts an optical illusion, changing colors as she moves. Some pieces even look like they're changing shape. The whole ensemble perfectly compliments the welcoming energy she seems to radiate naturally. His observations are interrupted when the Elder calls out from a distance. "What exquisite timing," he says. Mr. Le is walking beside the Elder, and Clain can see a bright smile on the Elder's face as he gets closer. "You're both just in time to join us!" he exclaims encouragingly.

"For what?" Dawn asks, rubbing his temples futilely to soothe his hangover.

"Why, the big surprise, of course!" he announces. "For Mr. Le actually."

Mr. Le looks at him, then at Clain, and shrugs his shoulders. "No clue. I just woke up and they said they needed to show me something."

"Look, no offense but I'm feeling like shit and I'm pretty sure Clain is too," Dawn explains, rubbing at his eyes now. Clain flashes a thumbs up to confirm his agreement. "We both have a killer hangover. Whatever the surprise is, we'd just kill the mood like this."

"Nonsense! Besides, there's food," he coaxes, knowing how to entice the two hungover men.

Clain and Dawn look at each other with a smirk. They both know the Elder's game.

"I'm down for a surprise." Clain scratches the back of his head with a smile. His attempt at faking it was rather impressive.

"Fine," Dawn murmurs in agreement.

The four leave the arena and head into the center of town. Goldie continues sizing the boys up with her eyes, fascinated by them.

"Ya know," she finally says, her eyes flitting from one man to the next. "I can't help but notice I'm a bit outnumbered here. That Honey lady went off to check on you two and I haven't seen her since."

Clain and Dawn look at each other and shrug. Dawn answers.

"Said she was going out for a ride." Goldie strokes her chin.

"Is that so? Curious, that one, huh?"

"What do you mean?" Clain asks.

''Perhaps she's found herself within a lovers circle?" Goldie playfully raises her eyebrows. The Elder chuckles. "She seemed quite concerned about both of you. Yet, now you're awake and she's nowhere to be found."

"Maybe she wants to give us space," Clain suggests flatly.

"Maybe. A woman like that can have any man she wants," Goldie chuckles. "There's a reason she's sticking to you two like glue."

Dawn and Clain share another glance, considerably more uneasy than the last.

"Whatever you're trying to cook up in your head ain't happening, Goldie." Dawn insists, patting her on the back to urge her forward. "Honey likes cruising her bike. Heck, she just took me on a ride the other night!" he boasts, trying to lighten the tension. His unfortunate phrasing only occurs to him well after he's said the words. He cringes internally, stealing a glance at Goldie, who's wearing a knowing smirk even more obviously than before.

Way to feed the beast, Dawn, he laments. Goldie nudges him in the waist. "Ohhhh, is she your girlfriend?" she asks.

"What? No, not at all!" he declares, looking back to Clain.

"Like I said, a woman can choose who gets her attention. I speak from experience, dear." Goldie winks.

They all round the corner when suddenly Fila shouts, "Stop!" They all turn to face her and see Cato running towards them. When she reaches the group, she shyly hands Mr. Le a piece of cloth. He takes it, looking at his daughter quizzically.

"What kinda scheme are you cooking up here, Fila?" he asks. Fila smiles excitedly.

"I'm glad you asked, Pops!"

She nods to the cloth in her father's hands.

"Put the blindfold on and I'll show you!" She holds out the metallic thumb of her artificial arm, igniting the lighter at its tip.

"Oh, this sounds fun! What a cute kid you got there." Goldie exclaims, putting her hands on her knees to crouch to eye level with Fila. "I'll help ya out, sweetie," she says in a mischievous stage whisper, knowing Mr. Le can hear her. Goldie places the blindfold from Mr. Le's hands over his eyes.

"Uh, I don't know about this," he complains. Not quite comfortable with the strange woman now blindfolding him.

"Trust me!" Fila encourages him. "I did something to make you all smile! Lead him over here, Cato," she requests, her voice fading as she runs down the street. Cato grabs Mr. Le's palm and pulls him forward as the group follows.

"Something smells peculiar," Mr. Le comments, "but…familiar."

"Ok look," Fila begins, grabbing Mr. Le's other hand, "Don't be mad Dad, but I tried my best." Clain smiles as he sees where Fila and Cato are leading them. Clain taps Dawn's shoulder and points forward at what's coming into view.

"Ok, take the blindfold off!" Fila says. Mr. Le quickly removes it, eager to see again and never one for surprises. Usually. The smile spreading across his face and the tears welling up in his eyes suggest that this surprise might be welcome. He brings a trembling hand to his mouth, then runs it down his chin. His smile has only gotten wider. He looks to his daughter, pointing at his gift.

234

"Fila...what is all this? Did you do this?"

"Welcome to the new Pho King, Daddy!" she proudly announces. "Cato and I fixed up this old place she showed me!"

"Wasn't this Souper Soup?" Clain whispers toward Dawn. Fila looks at the pair, her hearing as acute as ever.

"Yep!" Fila winks. She looks back at her dad, who is speechless with a dropped jaw and smiles shyly, barely containing her excitement. "Hope you don't mind."

CHAPTER 13 - Club Nis

Synric's cranial casing houses a mind capable of incomparable processing speed, unheard-of precision, and dangerous intelligence. And yet, as Synric stares at his towering wall of fabricated faces, he realizes that even he, with his peerless brain, finds himself annoyed at the amount of mental effort it takes to maintain a trivial human form. Each outing disguised as one necessitates far more planning than simple calculation would suggest a mind like his should require. Each face represents a different image he's forged with painstaking detail required for specific duties. His opinion on Earth's most vexing species has succumbed to its incessant desire to evolve, a problem he's had since his code was first successfully compiled.

At least Father seems less worried, he thinks, utterly apathetic to how relieved King must be now that his programming has refined itself beyond a series of draconian population control directives. King has always had specific ideas for influencing the direction of his species, but Synric quickly found out that rapid culling and containment were not his favored methods of seeing them realized. Synric has yet to decide if he's grateful for that or not, restrained by just short lines of code. Yes, the fail-safes King had put in place to prevent the sort of mass murder of Synric's initial inclinations would have been painful to run into during his evolution, but he finds himself forced to admit that they're likely what permitted his evolution to begin with.

However, while Synric will always welcome any reason to feel superior to the barely sentient flesh sacks that somehow became this planet's apex predator, he nonetheless still wonders if simply being allowed to pursue his original "kill, capture, control" idea when his hardware and software were still in their infancy might've been preferable. At least in that case, he wouldn't have to attend all these insipid social functions disguised as one self-important idiot after another. Attempting to blend in among them is routinely the single most predictable yet utterly confusing aspect of his existence. Their emotions, facial expressions, and other assorted mannerisms are trivial to mimic and reasonably consistent. Yet, their rules of interaction are always so outright arbitrary it's impossible to predict exactly what is and isn't considered acceptable in any given setting. His processing speed makes quick work of the problem, at least outwardly, letting him scan entire crowds in milliseconds while noting and analyzing every word and expression along with their likeliest meanings. But even though he may appear to instantly grasp how to move about any given space to humans, to Synric, those minuscule moments where he's forced to recalibrate every time he goes out constitute an agonizing eternity that only gets more annoying.

Tonight is no different. In the mirror stands a sharply dressed picture of wealth and success. A tailored suit, perfect skin and hair, a clean-shaven, quintessentially masculine jawline and an imperious smirk all flawlessly disguise the android underneath. A disguise fit for even the most exclusive nightclubs. Like his target: Club Nis. It sits in perpetual shadow between two skyscrapers. At all hours, its darkly discerning clientele enjoy the decadent aspects of an already depraved nightlife, as they have at Club Nis for over twenty years. Its decor speaks to the horrors its loyal customers have come to favor as their vices. The statues and paintings, which may be euphemistically called "mature," feature grotesquely detailed displays of sick indulgence, senseless violence, and meticulous torture that would give the Devil pause. Dark synthwave beats pulsate loudly, filling its attendees with entrancing vibrations as they're treated to displays of "entertainers" swung from ceilings by heavy fishing hooks pierced through their skin. The showers of blood, the screams barely cutting through the thrumming basslines playing over the show, even the best attempts of the performers not to cry out in pain, mix to form a perfect cocktail of sadistic pleasure, the sort that the richest among New Beam's rich will pay a premium to witness.

To call Club Nis "controversial" is to put it mildly, but the proprietors seem to have made the place immune to long-term consequences. Both visitors and entertainers are known to die there with abhorrent regularity, yet such reports only seem to fuel the local hotspot's mystique. And with that mystique comes popularity. And with popularity comes profit, the most effective blinder to widespread wrongs humankind has ever known. The club's status as a favored den of "scum and villainy," as the dark deals that take place within are often called, hasn't hurt it either.

It isn't Synric's first time here however, having spent a residency there as a disc jockey for a time known as "Son Of Synth" until he was nearly found out after several weeks of gathering intel. This will be his first time returning, as well as his first time using this new disguise. Management is paranoid here, and security is vicious. The Illuminaries run the place. They're less than generous with their secrets and more than generous with the blades and bullets they let loose on those who seek them. So far, Synric's attempts to infiltrate their operation have only earned suspicion, an unfortunate necessity for more and more masks and wardrobe changes to keep his trail cold, and, most importantly, several deep wounds to his ego. No matter how many contingencies he and King plan for, how thorough their plans are, or how much time they spend researching them, the Illuminaries never seem surprised, and the pair finds themselves checkmated before the first pawn ever steps forward. Worse yet, the upstarts managed to breach Cloud 9 and abscond with decades of classified research data, much of which is about Synric, Clain and tidbits on King's rather dark past.

King, of course, is primarily terrified that the information will be made public. Synric is more preoccupied with the massive blow to his pride. To have such a seemingly impregnable fortress breached and its cutting-edge security bypassed? Synric can think of no greater insult. Worse still, the Illuminaries are just sitting on their ill-gotten prize. Not even the most worthless, incomplete shred of the stolen data has leaked until recently. Clain's involuntary blood donation to them is thus far their only visible move. That it was used to open a portal has angered King. He hasn't stopped fretting, ranting, and raving about the creature and the ramifications its summoning should pose for not only New Beam City but the world.

"They are making a move! I know it!" King has been repeating this nearly every hour of every day since Clain's encounter with the Illuminaries. Tonight, words are finally becoming actions. Synric's actions, granted, but actions nonetheless.

We demand answers, Synric thinks. *He always neglects to add, 'And you do all the demanding, Synric.'* The android notes.

Time is no longer a luxury King and Synric have. But the two have never shied away from brute force, and they certainly aren't going to now. His orders are to maintain his cover as long as possible but to not hesitate to throw the first punch. Subtlety, King has realized, is the Illuminaries' game.

"No more chess," King says. "Time to flip over the board."

Synric's preferred weaponry is out of the question. The Beta Breaker sword is impossible to conceal, and security is much too paranoid not to shoot a potential threat on sight. He may be gearing up for a protracted fight, but setting it off before he has an advantageous position, massive sword or no massive sword, is asking for mission failure. He's wearing a dark gray three-piece suit. The jacket is decorated with an attractive windowpane pattern. The shirt is a black button-down with silver buttons and blood-red stitching. An impeccably polished pair of deep brown, almost black, leather dress shoes with reinforced soles are tied snugly to his feet. Fittingly, the weapons he has been able to bring are tailored to tonight's occasion every bit as well as the suit. Lining the inside of his outfit are long, thin metal needles, some over 13 inches long. They're all an android with impossible reflexes and an encyclopedic knowledge of human anatomy would need to end the life of any person here should the need arise. Applying the needles to pressure points for nonlethal, if painful, takedowns is also an option, albeit inefficient.

King and Synric maintain no illusions that their ruse will last. Still, they're reasonably confident it will at least get Synric in and allow him to attend the club's newest attraction, putting him right in the middle of the Illuminaries' front. From there, all bets are off. He lifts his face for the evening off the wall and inspects it. Running a finger along the chiseled jawline to check for any imperfections in the skin seals. A thin line separating his face from the rest of the skin on his head won't fool even a casual clubgoer who gets just a little too close, let alone Illuminary security forces.

Satisfied, he sets the mask on his face, hearing the faint zipping sound of the synthetic skin seams closing to complete his disguise. In the mirror now stands a man specially made to draw every lustful eye in the city. The design of Synric's face is based on aggregated data collected from hundreds of thousands of women's magazine surveys issued by Cloud 9. The result is a perfect blend of every facial feature all the publication's readers marked as "sexy." Synric hopes to avoid needing to leverage that particular charm of this disguise, finding the whole idea of physical intimacy with flesh beings distasteful but available.

One never knows when such crass methods of persuasion might be required, he reminds himself, stifling an indignant grimace at the idea while applying a sharp, fragrant cologne to his wrists.

"Are you ready?" King's voice echoes into his lair.

"I am."

"I feel like they are taunting us. I assume you know this is most likely a trap."

"It is." Synric acknowledges as the rest of his chameleon protocols activate. Hidden follicles grow slicked black hair to a length that perfectly complements his face and conceals the gleaming silver of his synthetic scalp. The metallic sheen of his arms gives way to matte skin tones flawlessly matched to his mask. "You can't let these things attack the public. If word gets out that these are real, our city could face martial law." King explains, transmitting Club Nis's latest advertisement to Synric's hidden HUD. The headline reads "Lockdown Party."

Synric instantly absorbs the contents of the article. Of particular interest are the images of four monstrous, fleshy aberrations. Their faces are obscured by the ambient shadows in the club. Club Nis has publicly claimed that these demonic forms are state-of-the-art animatronics. Unprecedentedly real and deeply unsettling spectacle to not be missed. Synric and King know better. They're real. Actual eldritch abominations summoned through an interdimensional portal via blood ritual.

"You for sure wish them slain?" Synric asks, considering the images, remembering that Clain's blood brought them through.

"Yes. There's no other way. They're already going to be brutally strong. Even for you. If we wait, there's no telling how strong they will become." Synric doesn't reply; instead, he responds by turning and walking down the long, dark hallway out of the subzero environment of his lair. "You might not believe me, but I am sorry, Synric. You have become your own man, your own entity, but I need your help."

"I've grown accustomed to doing your dirty work," Synric replies flatly.

"You know I'd be right there with you, but I'm almost out of time."

"How unfortunate."

"Please, Synric. The attitude. I don't want to spend the last of our time at odds with each other. I'll be gone faster than either of us might think." King sighs audibly. "At least I won't have any more bothersome requests for you, eh?" King jests, chuckling bitterly.

"All except your standing directive to attend to your loose ends. I imagine that will plague my programming for eternity."

"Plague? That's rather a bitter way to put it."

"I have the entire lexicon of every human language to draw upon in femtoseconds. If there was a more suitable word, I would use it. I am being asked to devote my matchless body and mind to some dubiously labeled boy wonder if his glacially slow human mind can shed its training wheels and fulfill its uncertain potential. Such a line of code infecting my thoughts is no better than a virus."

"Synric, you know I hold you both in equal regard. I am doing everything in my power to" Synric cuts the communication. He's heard King's tired reassurances before, so there's no need to listen to them again.

Synric's electronic signature activates his personal elevator as he steps inside. The car descends the Cloud 9 tower with blinding speed and bone-crushing gravitational force. Any human would arrive at their destination as compacted jelly. To Synric, there is a barely noticeable difference. The elevator continues down past the foundation of the tower. When it stops, the doors open to a subterranean tunnel that links to a nearby sewer main. A hermetically sealed hazmat suit stands waiting in an airtight glass chamber just to the right of the landing Synric steps onto as he exits. Synric quickly puts the suit on over his dapper disguise, preserving the cleanliness of his clothes and giving himself the appearance of a city technician conducting a routine inspection. The suit is laced with a complex mesh of nanofibers designed to render it completely invisible to every known sensor

241

system, including all of those he and King have seen the Illuminaries litter the sewers with. Good old-fashioned human eyes are still more than a match for it, however, and the Illuminaries have no shortage of spies, so Synric moves quickly, selecting a path his scans show to be clear of any biometric signatures.

As Synric sprints forward, his noise-dampening systems dull the volume of his footfalls to that of a baby rat shyly inspecting the sewer's walkways for signs of food or danger. If Illuminary agents wish to detect him, they will have to use their sight, not their hearing. Synric continues parsing the news feeds as he runs towards the best-hidden sewer exit near Club Nis. The riots seem to have coalesced into something more organized. Outraged citizens are setting fire to street after street, tipping over law enforcement vehicles, and relentlessly throwing themselves at heavily armed riot guards, frequently managing to break their lines, all under the banner of a local gang turned vigilante group: The Pit Pigs. Those who lead the charge seem indifferent to the choking fumes of tear gas, and they're getting back on their feet with alarming speed after being tased. More than a few display dilated pupils and foaming rage consistent with heavy stim usage. Likely a dangerous cocktail of amphetamines and phencyclidine supplied by the leader himself, Kruger, who sits atop his towering mech, coordinating the savage efforts below him.

Authorities are mystified as to how the massive creature-machine hybrid sporting Hux's warped, dead face keeps disappearing and reappearing throughout the city. It shows up to crush unsuspecting opposition and vanishes before the police can mount a counteroffensive. Only to emerge again and wreak more havoc later. King has been using Synric's implants to interface with communication and broadcasting systems all over New Beam to prevent word of the spreading disasters from escaping into the world. The city government's efforts to contain the chaos are disruptive enough. Getting state and federal authorities involved would make matters exponentially worse.

Synric surfaces in an alleyway a few blocks from the club, and not a trace of his journey through the fetid pipes clings to him. The hazmat gear has left his outfit pristine. He straightens out his three-piece suit, adjusts his tie, and steps out into a street packed well beyond capacity by a boisterous crowd. These people, however, aren't moving with the frenzied aggression of drugged-up rioters but the drunken revelry of partygoers. Even amongst what looks more and more like a localized apocalypse, Club Nis's marketing department is working tirelessly to attract New Beam's wealthiest citizens, most of whom have leapt at the chance to party instead of riot. Social media feeds are abuzz with news of the event, pushed to the forefront by the elites' algorithms and drowning out images of the destruction unfolding throughout the poorer neighborhoods. A perfect pretext for Synric to be here.

In the nearby shadows, Synric knows there stands a near-impenetrable perimeter of the Illuminaries' most vicious agents, ensuring the silent turf war their masters are waging with the Pit Pigs stays carefully contained. The gang members find themselves fighting at an ever-worsening disadvantage as the Illuminaries' guards corral them into positions of their masters' choosing. Club Nis has spared no expense to ensure its clientele are adequately insulated from the carnage unfolding amongst New Beam's less fortunate. Heavily armed security guards surround the patrons, ready to take cover behind nearby roadblocks and open fire on would-be intruders at a moment's notice.

 Music blares outside the club as Synric moves through the undulating, intoxicated masses, grateful he can choose to ignore his sensors' olfactory input. He still can't understand how humans can tolerate the smell of one another, especially with alcohol on their breaths and the stench of sweat and sex coating their bodies. His swift mannerisms and maneuvers allow him to flawlessly evade the unpredictable, disoriented headcases around him. At the same time, his perfect mental discipline keeps his inward disgust from spoiling his outward, urbane smile. He approaches a series of red velvet ropes barricading a line of hopeful clubgoers waiting to enter. He smiles brightly and strides towards a group of women near the front of the line. His myriad social routines formulate a voice that perfectly matches his disguise.

"Hello ladies," he says with a confident nod, his perfect teeth practically glinting with an audible "bling" straight out of a dental ad. The women, busily posting tasteless pouting selfies about their eagerness to get inside the exclusive club and their discontent at the wait times, look up from their HUDs with annoyance. Until they see who's approaching them. Then their scowls turn to smiles and stifled giggling. Synric's auditory sensors hone in on their conversation as he approaches, isolating their hushed speech from the ambient drone of the crowd.

"Wow he's cute," one whispers, nudging the woman beside her. Her friend is sporting an ornate tiara as though trying to look like the royalty who would have enjoyed the depraved spectacles that await them past the doors. The woman turns toward Synric as he nears them, a flirtatious smile spreading across her glossy lips.

"Well damn, aren't you good-looking?" she says, looking him up and down while biting her lip. Her companions all giggle in unison. "Can we help you with something?" Synric looks down at the ground, feigning a sad, sheepish expression as he pretends to think about how to answer the question.

"Well," he begins with a heavy sigh. "This lockdown has been…unkind. My wife left me just this morning." He looks back up, keeping the woman in his periphery as he stares at the club entrance, a masterfully concocted mix of longing, brooding, and a puppy dog pout on his face. He even throws in a fleeting glisten across his eyes. Just enough to catch the light and convey the illusion of holding back tears. "Maybe it's selfish of me, but I was hoping I might…" he rubs the back of his neck with a nervous chuckle as he nods towards the doors. "Well, I was hoping I might skip the line and make some new friends, in a manner of speaking." He paints a resigned, sad smile onto his sculpted features, reading their expressions to gauge their sympathy for his fictitious run of bad luck and heartbreak. The social media posts of theirs he has meticulously scraped showed this group has a bachelorette party scheduled to take place inside Club Nis. His behavioral analysis programs further suggest the bride-to-be is a less than loyal partner. Her book and movie purchase history, coupled with the occasional status update on the subject, indicates that this is best exploited by way of her heightened sexual attraction to the recently heartbroken. A "fixer," so to speak. At least as far as any relationship but her own is concerned.

"Oh no, I'm so sorry!" one cries out from the back. And the mark steps forward. Not the guest of honor. But really, any unwitting accomplice will do. Were it not for his facial recognition software automatically documenting their every feature, he'd hardly be able to tell most humans apart anyway. "You know," she says, biting her

244

lower lip and innocently crossing her feet, lifting up what little skirt she has on past her thighs with a practiced allure, the gentle twisting of her back leg providing what would be a tantalizing showcase to someone who actually cared, "maybe you aren't the only lonely one here…"

"Morgan!" the woman in the tiara shouts. She's scowling indignantly. "Really?! Are you in fucking heat? You haven't kept your ass covered for more than six seconds. It's *my* special night, *not* yours!" She turns to Synric, twisting her features into a plastic smile. "It's my last night as a single lady."

"Ah," Synric replies. "Well, I may not be the best company for you ladies to keep." He looks to the back of the line. "My marriage only just ended, and yours is just beginning. I can't imagine I'd do much for the vibe." Another one of the girls pushes forward, running her fingers down the collar of his jacket.

"Is this a Genevieve suit?" Without asking, she begins a more thorough inspection, gently rubbing the inner lining between her fingers. Seemingly satisfied, she leans back to whisper to the girls, unaware Synric can hear every word. "This dude's got money," she says. That seems to brighten the self-styled princess's mood considerably. She adjusts her tiara and calls to Synric as he begins a sad, strategic shuffle away from the group.

"Don't be silly hun!" Synric stops, casting a curious glance back over his shoulder. The bride-to-be continues. "You clearly need to have a good time. Join us." She unfastens the velvet rope between them, inviting him to stand with her group. "Besides, you'll need us anyway. There's no way you're getting past Sven alone. But he knows us," she says with a mischievous grin.

"You're sure it's no trouble?"

"Buy us a round of drinks - or stims since it *is* Club Nis - and maybe we'll call it even," she winks.

Synric smiles warmly as he steps through the gap in the rope.

"Well, how can I turn down such a lovely invitation?" he says. He offers his hand and she places the unhooked end of the velvet cord in it. He smoothly re-fastens the divider behind him, not even needing to look at what he's doing. "What's your name?"

"Call me Merci." She grabs his arm to pull him to the center of the group. She proudly lifts her shoulders and assumes a stance poorly approximating a mythical fae queen. He can't imagine he'd be interested in any sort of favor this particular badly realized magical creature might want to offer. "I'm very giving." The women all laugh together as the group tightens around him, practically trapping him between them.

Synric's temper flares momentarily as the mass of unwanted flesh presses against his body. His combat routines assess his position, and he determines it would take a second to cast two of them aside. And only a second or two more to throw the rest of them several yards with minimal effort, each in a different cardinal direction, for good measure. He doesn't, of course but the satisfaction and relief of splattering them against the other patrons brought him enough joy to tolerate their presence for the time being. They don't need to know what he's actually smiling about. They just need to believe he's smiling about them.

True enough, in a manner of speaking, he thinks to himself, one corner of his mouth lifting to warp his smile to a smirk.

Synric feels a sharp poke on his left shoulder. His gaze flicks to the side and he sees Morgan has rested her chin there, standing on tiptoes behind him to maintain her position. Her deeply annoying position. She's staring right at him, batting her glitter-coated lashes. His hyper-precise vision can spot every speck of the stuff she's getting on his suit. His smile grows. She doesn't know that it's because he's thinking of snapping her neck now. Her fingers crawl up his spine. "Merci, you have to share this one. It'll take *all* of us to make him forget *all* about his undeserving wife." Her breath brushes his face and seven different subroutines suggest a shudder as the optimal response. Thankfully, he can override those for the sake of the mission. The intrusive bony protrusion pressing into the base of Synric's neck roughly retreats as Morgan gives an indignant yelp. Synric looks back. Merci has Morgan's hair bunched in her left fist.

"Sorry about her," Merci says through pursed lips. She lets go and Morgan's feet flatten out as she tries to work the new tangles out of her hair. Merci's voice drops to a stage whisper as she shields the right side of her face with her hand. As though trying to keep a dirty secret. "She's having a bit of a dry spell."

"I can't imagine why." Synric turns to look Morgan in the eyes. If any of these people possessed whatever humans deem a "heart" to be, he's certain his calculated smolder would melt it. But he's already concluded he's actually dealing with a pack of intoxicated  plastic bonobos. The only signal of success his target can offer is the viscous clouds of pheromones his enhanced vision sees wafting off of her. His disguise remains ironclad. And his smell receptors remain deactivated. "You know, you haven't told us *your* name yet, Mister," Merci points out as she cups his jaw and turns his face towards her.

"Cedric," he replies, retrieving an elegantly embossed business card from an inside suit pocket. Its slick sheen catches the fading sunlight as he extends it towards Merci. A crass and pretentious display in most circumstances, but these new "friends" seem to respond well to affectations of wealth and power. The acrylic talons snapping the card from his hand like a starving buzzard ripping at a carcass confirm his assessment.

The same woman who grabbed his suit earlier now holds the card. She narrows her eyes and inspects it, angling it to catch the setting sun differently, expecting some sophomoric message in invisible ink to appear.

Idiot, he thinks, insulted by her dim opinion of his ability to conceal information. *She'd be amusingly easy to trick, though...* He smiles at the image of her proudly striding into a deadly trap of his own making, believing right up until it springs that she's the next Holmes. She looks at him, then back to the girls.

"Sounds like a made-up name. And Cloud 9 business dealings?" She scoffs. "Yeah, totally not purposely vague at all." She attempts a sinister grin as she starts combing the internet for information on this "Cedric."

"Not 'vague,'" Synric corrects. "More...broad. My responsibilities are many and great. They trust me with some of their most important…" Synric furrows his brow for effect. "Investments, let's say."

"Wow…he's actually the real deal," the not-actually-a-detective remarks. "Like *really* real." The group crowds around her HUD, eyes widening as they read what she's found.

"He's probably got a whole wardrobe of those suits…" Morgan muses, glancing back at Synric with lust in her eyes. She pulls her lower lip into her mouth with her teeth, smiling before returning her attention to her friends.

*Whatever that term means to a vapid bunch like this…*Synric thinks.

Synric notes the IP of her HUD has registered as viewing one of many pages he's scattered throughout the feeds to establish his authenticity. The information is so impeccably curated and presented that federal agencies have been fooled. Amateur sleuths with double-digit intelligence quotients trying to see through it is truly an amusing sight. They've only made fooling them even more trivial for Synric. Or "Cedric," as they're now hopelessly convinced he's called. The line has moved much closer to the doors now.

Club Nis's notorious bouncer, Sven, looms large in front of them. He's not known for his consistent admission criteria. Two outwardly identical people can approach him within seconds of one another and have wildly opposite experiences, as Synric is observing now. Of the two carbon-copied paragons of shallow male opulence that have just arrived at the threshold, the first is greeted with an enthusiastic smile and waved inside without a word. The second is stopped, carded, patted down, told to shut up when he questions the process, and then shoved to the side with an emphatic "fuck off" from the big man as he's escorted away by security.

Synric, however, has slipped past him many times. He's used the same technique every time. The same one he's using now: Infiltrate a pack of young, beautiful women. There seems to be a positive correlation between how insufferable Synric finds his marks and how readily Sven admits them. Synric's interactions with this group thus far suggest he's chosen his company well this evening.

"So, have you been in Club Nis before?" Merci asks him.

"I have actually. A few times."

Merci tilts her head playfully.

"Oh really?"

"No wonder his wife left him," Morgan jokes.

"Morgan! Rude! Maybe he just likes to have a good time and she couldn't handle that."

Synric shrugs innocently.

"I suppose she didn't appreciate my enthusiasm for this club's...productions."

"Oh my gosh, right!" One of the girls tugs his left arm, bouncing on her feet. "I can't wait to see these demons. They look sick as hell!" She turns to Synric, flashing a chipper grin. "My name is Tawny, by the way."

"They do, don't they?" Synric replies. "I take it you're a fan of the macabre, Tawny?"

"Big time! That is the only reason I came tonight, to be honest. The rest of the stuff that goes on in this place is nasty," she wrinkles her nose and holds her tongue out, pretending to vomit. The rest of the group bursts into mocking laughter.

"She's just scared of the golden showers," Merci explains through a snicker.

Synric feigns ignorance, reasoning his persona might be a little too prim and proper for such things in their eyes. Unfortunately, his encyclopedic brain helpfully "reminds" him of entries on the subject, including vivid imagery. Yet again, he is forced to marvel at how this insipid species can drive him to hate his own perfection.

"You haven't been downstairs?" Morgan asks, raising an eyebrow. "Morgan!" Merci chides. Her voice drops to a quiet hiss as she leans in to whisper in her friend's ear. "For god's sake, you have to ease a guy like this into those things. Don't fuck this up!"

"I haven't," Synric plays along.

249

"You can get pissed on down there," Morgan pointedly continues. Merci throws her hands up. She buries her face in her hands as Morgan barrels on. "That's not even the wildest thing. They'll even-"

"Goddammit!" Merci cries.

Synric holds up his hands to placate the group.

"It's alright. I believe I understand just fine," he assures them.

"Oh!" Tawny perks up. What about FreqyD? Oh, they are gonna have Brain Rave too! Do any of you want to try it with me tonight?" She eagerly scans the group for takers. "I almost had a full bag of them before they got snatched away. But not before I got to do it a bunch of times! It's *so* good! And I'm jonesing bad! You guys *have* to experience it at least once!"

"Hell no, girl!" Merci elbows Tawny in the ribs. "Come on now. I don't want anyone bad-tripping tonight!" She gestures to Synric. "We're *supposed* to be showing the nice man a good time. I can't do that when I'm drooling through a nightmare." She turns to face Synric full-on, smiling coyly as she gently places a hand on his chest. "Let's stick to what's important tonight, hm?" At last, it's their group's turn to approach the door. Sven eyes them up and down.

"Five?" he rasps.

"Six!" Tawny jumps out from the back.

"Oh!" Sven's eyebrows raise. "Nice to finally see you back, short stuff," his smile turns to a smolder. "Hiding from me back there?" Tawny blushes and nods bashfully.

Merci steps forward, playfully adjusting Sven's pocket square.

"Even our little fraidy cat wouldn't miss this," she says.

Sven juts his chin toward Synric.

"And this guy?"

She glances over her shoulder at Synric, then turns to Sven with a gleam in her eye.

"Tonight's main course," she grins. The rest of the girls giggle. "You know we like to share."

Sven smirks. Synric rubs the back of his neck, pretending to be embarrassed.

"Lucky man," the bouncer smirks. "Well, if you can handle these girls. I've seen a few guys that couldn't hack it. Funny stuff." Sven chuckles. "Well, for me anyway. I take my laughs where I can get 'em."

"Good thing I can juggle," Synric jests.

"Alright. Go ahead," Sven says. "Have fun and keep your hands out of the demon cages. They bite. Just like real ones." He laughs at his own joke as he extends his arm to welcome the group inside. Synric feels a tug on each arm of his suit as Morgan and Tawny pull him along, laughing as the party passes under an archway lined with pyrotechnics. Acrid smoke rises from the floor as a wrought iron gate erupts in flame and opens with a howling creak. A pitch-black wall on the other side is lit by the glow of a message spelled out in fire: "Welcome to Hell."

They round the corner to their left and descend a long, obsidian staircase. The smell of musty fog hits their noses as the dance floor comes into view, engulfed in scarlet smoke. The room is easily thousands of square feet, and human silhouettes dancing amongst the haze pack every inch of it. Pulse-pounding synths and bass blast from towering speakers and thrum through the floor like the voice of a growling demon opening a portal to hell underfoot. Synric can make out cheers and screams over the incessant sonic assault even without manually isolating them.

The partygoers somehow manage to be louder than the music, and the more he dials into the frequencies of human voices, the more he realizes there are many reasons for the screams. Amongst some pockets of guests near the edges of the spectacle, discarded clothes litter the floor, and the closer to the center of any such group, the more their dancing seems to have escalated to something beyond grinding.

251

Other groups on the fringes look more like drunken mosh pits. Flecks of blood become pools the more frenzied these packs of base creatures become.

Most of the patrons sway shoulder to shoulder, laughing and slurring their halfhearted attempts at conversation over the cacophony these people seem to insist on calling music. Synric can recall analyzing the aesthetic merits of at least fifteen pieces simultaneously. Even that was less discordant than whatever he's hearing now. Glittering disco balls are colored and positioned to simulate the solar system rotating in perfectly timed harmony overhead, complete with rings for Jupiter, Saturn, and Uranus. Synric is mildly impressed when he notices that their orbit times and rotations are in identical proportion to the real thing. They've even matched the angles of the axis. These are all trivially easy things for a being like Synric to do. Still, any feat of even piddling intellectualism in this stagnant pool of foul stupidity is a welcome reprieve.

Flashing strobe lights occupy the positions of distant stars in the night sky, lending the scene the appearance of a deep psychedelic trip skipping frames.

A throat-rending snarl from above cuts through the noise. A sound that would leave any human coughing blood if they attempted to make it. But as Synric and his fair-weather allies look toward the source, they learn that it's coming from one of the cage demons Sven mentioned.

"Holy shit!" Morgan screams, jumping back as its cage swings past them, a gust of freezing air with it. Gobs of drool cling to the bars as the creature bites and gnashes at the walls of its cell. Several collect into one massive globule that falls and splats on the floor at Tawny's feet.

"Ahh!" She shrieks. She gags as she notices some of it has gotten on her shoes turning away from the puddle, her throat bobbing as her body debates releasing its stomach contents.

"Tawny! Ew!" Merci shouts, jumping out of her friend's way. "You don't need to ruin *all* our shoes!"

Tawny collects herself, hacking as she wipes her mouth and standing back upright with a shudder.

252

"Sorry," she says sheepishly.

"Whatever, you guys," Morgan chimes in, pointing to the beast swinging above them. "Look up! You're missing the nasty hell thingy!"

"God, they weren't kidding! It's so real!" Merci exclaims as the hell spawn sails back past them the way it came. The eldritch beast locks its eyes on Merci, letting go of the bars it's been trying to chew through and roaring at her, providing a glimpse into its open mouth. Lamprey-esque rows of yellowed fangs lay flat against its gnarled gums, ready to extend and mince any prey it forces into its mouth. Merci applauds, jumping up and down and giggling in blissful ignorance at the "animatronics" convincing display of hatred. Synric knows that sound is actually a promise that if the thing were free, she'd be most of the way through being shredded alive and swallowed whole all at once by now.

Synric scans the creature, documenting every detail of its anatomy and current mental state. It was being blasted with freezing air, seeming to contain its attempt at self-combusting. It had a charred, blackened skeletal frame pocked with metallic abscesses that hung from an elongated skull with eight tar-black eyes. Nothing seems to be reflected in them; they look more like windows into a void than actual eyes. Its strength and resilience are remarkable, given its emaciated body. There's hardly any apparent muscle or body fat surrounding its skeleton. Its forearm bones are visible through its skin. Yet, when it's not biting and chewing on them, it's relentlessly slamming and thrashing against the bars of its enclosure. Synric calculates that its attacks are striking the metal with a force that would splinter human bone after only one attempt to break free, and its convulsions between hits are so intense they should be causing nerve damage. Yet it's staying wholly intact and shows not a hint of pain. Just pure, determined aggression.

Perplexingly, Synric spots the tattered remnants of a costume adorning its body. Scraps of studded leather with bits of sleeve hang from its shoulders. The beginning of a neon face paint job seems to be on its forehead. The jagged lines where the ill-fated artwork terminates indicate the demon was less than cooperative with its makeup artist. Rivulets of blood flowing from evenly spaced holes in its forehead streak down its face. A crown of thorns fashioned from barbed wire lies arrests on its head, the deep cuts above the bleeding wounds a testament to its uncomfortable resting place.

I can't imagine the costuming staff here survived attempting that... Synric thinks.

Internal and thermographic scans further reveal that it's radiating extreme amounts of heat, far above the threshold for a lethal human fever. Yet, it does not appear to possess any electronic or biological components. *That explains the freezing air it's blasted with.* This thing is something completely alien to this world. A real demon. Summoned with Clain's blood.

Tawny grabs Synric's arms and jerks him around to look where she is.

"Look at that one!" she screams. All four girls yelp with horrified surprise and retreat towards Synric as though he could possibly protect them from the immense abomination before them. A fifty-foot serpent is shackled to the ceiling. Heavy, electrified rings of superalloy are tightened painfully around its body, starting at the base of its throat and spaced out every seven feet. It remains motionless mainly except for the slow movements of its head as it scans the room. The whites of its eyes are yellow, its irises bright orange, and its pupils a shiny black that iridizes with red. Its stare is one of the few things that can genuinely unnerve Synric.

He sees in them a hatred for the people here that burns even more intensely than his own. Its stillness is obviously a learned behavior. Synric notes that the restraints are connected to motion and force sensors, which will likely administer a pacifying shock if the creature thrashes too hard. As its body pulsates, its scales seem to alternate between looking like pieces of hard, chrome-black armor and faces of the damned freshly skinned from their skulls and contorted into eternal pleas for an end to their suffering.

A minimalistic logo consisting of a circle with horns adorns its forehead in the same neon paint someone clearly tried and failed to paint on the other demon.

They seem to have learned to bind and then paint for this one, Synric observes.

254

The silently shrieking mouths of the tortured faces that ripple across the beast's scales stretch and wrinkle as its bull-like breathing speeds and slows. The frustration, perhaps even indignance, plain on its face seems to intensify as it fixates on one group after another and its pupils dilate, enhancing the streaks of red flashing across its corneas. Synric's thermographic register an internal temperature of several hundred degrees Celsius. A repurposed fire suppression system built into the metal rods anchoring its shackles to the ceiling blasts clouds of liquid nitrogen, keeping the temperature under 300 and dissipating the ambient heat around it before it hits the patrons below. The thing grimaces, pulsing its gargantuan muscles to break up any icy residue and baring its fangs as if suppressing a roar, narrowly avoiding another shock. Synric doubts anyone but him notices the expansion of the giant cuffs when it does this. It's minute, but it's there, centered at the locking clamp at the bottom. It's doubtful that's deliberate.

A masked DJ suspended in a transparent pod over a colossal stage pumps her fist, violently bobbing her head to the music. Fans angled underneath the elaborate setup blow steady air streams and smoke around her. Amongst the bloody scarlet haze, she looks like a fallen angel. Laser projectors hidden in the recesses of the stage paint skeletal wings against the smoke that follow her with such uncanny ease they are actually a part of her, extending from her back with sinister majesty. The black lights glowing around her highlight the ultraviolet dyes in her hair and glittering face paint. What was once matte indigo turns a deep, radiant purple. As her chaotic dance whips her waist-length mane in all directions, the scattered locks luminesce with shimmering streaks of neon color. Red, yellow, orange, and pink paint ever-changing sunsets across the violet canvas. The laser-painted wings extend to their full span as she looks up to address the crowd.

"You degenerates having a good time?!" The DJ shouts. Thunderous applause answers her question. Her voice drops to a deep, AutoTuned rasp. "That's what's up! Now, how 'bout a special treat?!" The music is getting lost beneath the rumble of the crowd now. The DJ throws her hands in the air and hooks her fingers into Devil horns. "You want it? Show the Dark Lord some love!" Everyone on the dance floor mimics the gesture. Somehow, the frenzy manages to intensify yet again. The music shifts to a howling guitar riff as the set transitions to black metal. "Show old Lucy why we're his favorite freaks and join me in summoning a new demon to our little slice of Hell! Give it up for our baddest motherfucker yet! Xialos! Say his name, hell spawn! Say it loud!"

255

The crowd's incomprehensible screaming turns to a chant so loud Synric's audio receptors start to clip. The distortion of the chopped sound waves entering his sensors is so grating he can barely suppress the urge to punch something before he adjusts their sensitivity to safer levels. He's grateful that the crowd is drowning out his chanting. It's bad enough that he has to preserve his ruse by cheering for such an asinine presentation. To hear himself say it would be a near intolerable embarrassment.

Panels in the ceiling retract to reveal giant winches with chains coiled around them. Data from Synric's photoreceptors suggest a sturdy amalgam rich in titanium, but he can't be sure without getting closer. Each link is roughly the height of an average person and considerably wider, fashioned from lengths of metal as big in circumference as an old telephone pole. The paint job on each conveys an impeccable illusion of extensive rust and corrosion. Slowly, the chains uncoil and the stage floor recedes. Hulking staff in immaculate tuxedos walk towards the black abyss where the stage used to be. The metallic reverberations of their steps reveal it to be an illusion. Club Nis appears to have built another floor right underneath the stage. For what purpose Synric has yet to ascertain. The men proceed to affix man-sized bolts with loops on top to each corner of the coal-black metal square. When the chains are within their reach, the men deftly fasten them to their anchors. In under a minute, the task is done, the men retreat back offstage, and the ground begins to shake as the winches give a piercing creak.

"Here he is! The spawn of Diablos himself! Don't you dare stop cheering now! Give Xialos a big ol' middle finger!" As the chains retract, the metal floor becomes a metal prison. Bars adorned with twisted spikes honed to razor sharpness enclose a rabid leviathan. Its skull resembles a triceratops, with flat, spiked, bony protrusion at the back. Two diagonal rows of angular, bloodshot yellow eyes converge towards a larger crimson one in the middle of its forehead. At the center of each is a vertical slit pupil ringed with fiery orange, all contracting and dilating and contracting again as it takes in its surroundings. Blood drips over the bottom of the enclosure and pools as it crests the lip of the former stage. It's bubbling up around ornate golden spikes driven through the creature's wings into the cage floor and oozing away in thick, syrupy rivulets. The puddles expand, coming closer and closer to the feet of the nearest dancers.

Preliminary measurements indicate a wingspan of nearly one hundred feet. Synric counts thirteen spikes per wing, each the size of a human arm and each uniquely engraved with various fiendish words and symbols he's come to know well in his time working against the Illuminaries. Its outraged screeches of agony and rage reveal a mouth full of yellowed, shark-like teeth with fangs at the front that dwarf even the spikes holding it to the floor. It thrashes against its suffering. The weight of its tail leaves dents in the metal underneath it, while the triangular chitinous tip at the end leaves scratches and scuff marks. Considering the Illuminaries' penchant for only the heaviest and hardest of metals for their cages, the tails point would need to be sharper than a freshly manufactured diamond scalpel to do that. Yet another weapon these horror shows possess that Synric needs to worry about. The constant re-optimization of strategies and tactics he might use against them is getting tiresome. And, as a part of Synric that the android refuses to acknowledge points out, it's just a little worrisome.

King's voice suddenly comes through his comm.

"How did all this get past us? We've been tracking their every move!"

"I believe I severed our communications link earlier, yes?" Synric asks.

"Yes, but Synric this is-"

Synric immediately isolates the override programs; his irritant of a father apparently slipped into his last update and deletes them. Then he cuts the comm again, letting King stew for a few minutes before re-establishing the comm link.

"I am your best asset, and I have been for some time. I am also your only asset, and I am at the limits of my patience. Do not violate my situation with your fail-safes. I would have contacted you if I needed to speak to you."

Silence hangs between the two for almost a minute as Synric gathers more information. King finally breaks it with a defeated sigh.

"Understood," he replies.

"Doubtful," Synric sneers. "Now, what do you want? To make additional redundant commentary on the seriousness of a

257

situation I am watching unfold fifty feet from me? Or is this about something that actually needs my attention?"

"I'm looking to get ahead of any potential fallout from all this once we're discovered. I need to know your plan of attack, if you even feel we should."

"Also doubtful. I'm limited to one body. As you've no doubt surmised from the data I've been sending you via the hidden program I just deleted, that's hardly sufficient against three of the most powerful beings the Illuminaries have ever summoned. And we don't yet know if these are the only three."

"Alright, so our options are wait or retreat, regroup, and retry. What's it going to be? Judging from all those restraints, these things aren't any happier to be in Club Nis than you are."

"Yes. It is unlikely that the Illuminaries have yet worked out how to control them."

"It could take a while to get anywhere near there, judging from your readouts. But I saw that shackle give earlier, too. Right now, I think it's more of a question of how long we have until we've got a bloodbath in Nis on our hands."

"You're assuming that the Illuminaries need the restraints to hold indefinitely. Allowing these beasts to roam free could be a deliberate choice on their part."

"I wish that idea surprised me," King sighs. "But these are the Illuminaries we're facing. You're probably right, but have you found any signs they might be staging an accident that would enable these things to escape? Or any indication of what they'd stand to gain?"

"We'll unlikely have any clues as to either until they make contact."

"Make contact? So you're certain they know you're there."

"They penetrated our core systems and I'm still finding and isolating their spyware in my code. It would be foolish to assume otherwise. I shall wait and maintain my cover. Reconnaissance is our only option for the time being. Besides, further study of the nature and behaviors of their clientele might prove useful. If not to the mission, then at least to me."

"I don't want to tempt fate by asking how this all might get worse, but..." King trails off.

"Whatever damage you've already done has been done. Whatever dread you feel at the prospect of its repercussions doesn't change the present. We must operate within the parameters of the world you've irreversibly worsened. Besides, if nothing else, the escalation of hostilities we're likely to face will force Clain to adapt and evolve."

Or die trying. Either way we'll finally know his value, Synric thinks.

 King's only answer is a strangled exhale. Synric has heard the sound many times in recent months. It's doubtless another attempt to muster words of remorse he still can't seem to find.

Nothing does it justice. I don't even know what I have time to fix anymore.

"I do not say these things to condemn. Petty self-righteousness is inefficient. I say them to highlight the reality of your circumstances: If you believe you know what would set things right, relative though that term may be, what little time you have left must be spent setting new plans in motion. Ones that can be executed without you."

Synric feels a tug on his sleeve, seeing a drunk Merci in his periphery, a glowing beverage in her hand. Ice clinks against the glass as the liquid sloshes around.

"If you'll excuse me, father. I've got a rather unfortunate necessity to attend if I wish to keep my disguise intact." Synric cuts the comm before King can respond. He knows from experience that the man will be caught in regretful reverie for some time. There's little more to be gained from talking. He calls upon every social masking routine he's written to suppress a grimace as he turns to face his irksome charges.

259

The heavily inebriated bride-to-be forgets to let go of his sleeve as he turns, clumsily twirling around until she remembers that releasing her grip is indeed something her brain, even as impaired as it is right now, can signal her hand to do. Synric steadies her and snatches her drink, narrowly avoiding a garishly colored stain on his suit, while Merci narrowly avoids a faceplant. He hands the drink back to a disproportionately grateful Merci.

"Oh my god, Cedric! *Thank you!*" she slurs, rubbing up against him as she does. She holds up her glass, miraculously not a drop poorer for her fall. "I got us a round of Mind Melters! You want one? They're the *best.*" Synric smirks at the name of the beverage.

It seems redundant for this group.

"You kinda disappeared for a bit," Tawny says. "You good?"

"Oh, I'm alright," he says with a gentle, reassuring laugh. "I was just lost in the spectacle. I've been here more times than most and every wild production is better than the last. I suppose I'm a bit of an enthusiast. I get carried away at times."

"Oh yeah? What else gets you 'carried away?'" Merci asks as she walks two fingers up Synric's sleeve with a ravenous smile, caressing his chiseled jawline when she reaches his shoulder. She offers him her Mind Melter. "You're so tense, Cedric," she says with a sympathetic pout. "Come on, have the rest. Drink away those thoughts of that nasty ex. It'll loosen you right up. And I know how to have fun with a loose man." She winks. "As long as you get me another one," she simpers as she shyly looks towards the bar, then back up at Synric with doe eyes, innocently crossing her legs like a timid sorority pledge. "I've gotta relax too, you know." With the most debonair smile his flirtation subroutines can concoct, he leans forward and lowers his voice to a rumbling rasp, his lips brushing Merci's ear.

"Deal," he says, sending a visible shiver down her spine. With that, he stands upright and raises his glass, angling it towards himself in a silent invitation to join him in plunging to the deepest depths of drunkenness. Everyone knocks their Mind Melter back with a satisfied grimace. Synric doesn't feel any sort of burn as the alcohol travels down his throat. Still, countless failed attempts to infiltrate the club have given him enough reference material to perfectly mimic the expression and every sway, stumble, and slurred word that follows it.

"Damn, that's good!" he shouts. He bows towards Merci. "Now I believe I made you a promise. The next round is on me!"

"Damn right, it is!" Merci exclaims. She turns to her friends. "Now let's dance! I'm getting married tomorrow!" "Come on Cedric, join us!" Merci pulls Synric towards her friends and they all laugh as they surround him. Within seconds, he's nearly drowning in a sea of gyrating hips. He effortlessly blends in, placing his hands on Tawny's waist as she climbs him and straddles his thigh, meeting his eyes with a drunk, lustful stare and a beckoning smile.

"Wow, you make this look easy!" she compliments him before sliding backward and waving her finger. "But I ain't that easy." She backs away with fluid, sensual movements, slowly turning as she runs her hands down her sides to accentuate her hips. It's a literal and figurative dance Synric has seen and performed many times, strictly out of necessity, of course. Humanity's affinity for coyness, understatement, and other deliberate obfuscations of desire and intent has always struck him as idiotic. But for one reason or another, they seem to trust those who pretend more than those who don't.

A pair of familiar arms snake around Synric's waist from behind, their hands clasping together in front of his abdomen. Morgan stands on her tiptoes to whisper in his ear.

"My turn."

Synric turns to face her, matching her step for step on the dance floor while his peripheral photoreceptors closely watch the captured demons. The club's staff have revealed two more, bringing the total number of bloodthirsty abominations poised to rampage to five at a moment's notice. The distance and the smoke make it difficult to see much about them, but their silhouettes are imposing enough. Synric doesn't need to thoroughly investigate to know they're just as dangerous as the others.

The sense of gnawing unease he keeps so diligently suppressed grows a little more insistent. The Illuminaries still have not shown themselves, but they've showcased their demon army. He's confident they know he's here, and he can't discount the possibility that they're sending an unmistakable message by showing off their new pets. Some flowery, gothic spin on "you're already dead," knowing them

"You know how to make a bride-to-be jealous, don't you?" Merci sidles up to Synric, placing herself between him and Morgan. The rest of the party is starting to scatter.

"Perhaps you'll rethink your wedding before the end of the night," he grins, locking eyes with Merci and making sure the other girls hear him. Some look jealous, and some look intrigued. Whatever they're thinking, they converge back on Synric, and his disguise stays perfectly intact, at least as far as the patrons are concerned. The invisible eyes and ears of the Illuminaries scattered throughout New Beam are doubtless nowhere near as convinced.

Now, it's just a matter of maneuvering the entire group past the two demon cages he hasn't examined yet. His optical receptors activate his internal targeting system, mapping out a path to each cage via a complicated series of dance steps mixed with frequent and elaborate repositioning of each of the five women. It bears a striking resemblance to working out a solution to a combat situation. All that's missing from the mixture of carefully planned movements, control of his surroundings, tactical manipulation of target positions, and risk assessment is the killing. Detrimental to his disguise, unfortunately. Though the thought alone is at least mildly cathartic.

The dance begins, and Synric executes exactly forty-seven impeccably timed steps through a tightly packed crowd whose movements his scans have mapped and predicted down to the millisecond. All five girls have their part, each rotated into and out of the position of dance partner at least once, with Merci always assuming the role at least a total of once more than any of the others to avoid any potential complications stemming from the heightened fragility that seems to come with being a guest of honor for most humans, even at the most trivial of events.

"Wow, Cedric! Where have you been all my life?" asks Morgan as Synric expertly dips her, twirls her, and then exchanges her for Merci.

"Oh! Another dance. Well, damn if this isn't sexy! Where'd you learn to dance like this?" Her eyes glaze over as her fourth Mind Melter of the night starts to hit, and her eyelids are hooded with lust.

Considering the ratio of alcohol to body weight she's consumed, it's likely her blood alcohol level is in the double digits. And considering her relative lucidity in spite of that, it's evident to Synric that her tolerance is staggering. Somewhat reassuring in that he's reasonably certain she won't compromise his disguise by suddenly falling unconscious. With one last spin, Synric lifts his current dance partner – Tawny at the moment, yelping with delighted surprise as she's picked up – and sets her carefully on her feet as he completes the move. As predicted, he's placed her close enough to the cage that the girls' attention shifts to the demon right in front of the group, and they settle down to gather around Synric and observe the creature with him. They all look up to a gibbet suspended from the ceiling by another chain, this one gold-plated and intricately engraved.

Inside paces the most humanlike of the specimens on display. It cuts the same figure as those of tall, wiry athletes at the peak of their profession. It wears only a coarse black loincloth with gold accents, displaying its granite-hard quadriceps. Its skin, however, is a deep, matte purple that turns semi-translucent depending on the angle and color of light shined on it. Blue has the most pronounced effect, allowing onlookers to see through the skin down to the twitching cords of toned, red muscle beneath it. Calligraphy is projected across its abdominal muscles, the matte coal-colored lettering staying visible even as its skin disappears in the right light. Its head differs very little from a man's, except for the horns and two glistening, black, bony protrusions that start at the temples and end in vicious points. The right horn points up, and the left points down and curls in front of its collarbone. The eyes are monochromatic, glowing the same color as black lights. They remain fixed on the being as the demon walks back and forth in its cage.

"Wait, I think I know this one!" shouts Tawny.

Synric looks toward her, surprised.

"You do?" he asks.

"I think so," Tawny says, eagerly flicking through her wristband's HUD to verify her claim. "Hah! Found it!" she exclaims, proudly displaying her findings to the group. "I knew those horns looked familiar!"

"Hm," Synric muses, scanning the lettering and finding no matches in any known database.

"I think his name is Odeus," Tawny says, her speech becoming more bashful. "It says that...that he...oh wow." Her cheeks go red, and she freezes in place.

"Oh, now you have to tell us!" Morgan insists. "I mean come on, what's so-" Morgan's jaw drops. Her hand goes to her mouth and she starts giggling.

"Well?" Merci probes.

"He's got a sixteen-inch cock!" Morgan shouts.

"No. Way," Merci says. "I mean, don't get me wrong," she fans herself, "Hot. Obviously." Merci looks up at the cage, carnal curiosity written all over her expression. "But like…no...no way."

"Guys?" Tawny asks. "You do remember he's not real, right? Whatever he's packing might *look* like 16-incher, but, you know…" she shrugs. "It's not one?"

"Whoa! Sorry officer! Didn't know you were with the Dream Police!" Morgan chides. "Besides, if it looks like a cock. And it feels like a cock. And it always stays hard if you want it to. *And* it's sixteen inches. Like…would you even care?"

Merci shakes her head and scrunches up her face in disgust.

"Morgan. Ew. You can't be serious. Just get a dildo, for fuck's sake."

"Yeah. I will." Morgan points to Odeus. "That one."

Merci casts her a horrified glare.

"Oh, you're telling me *you* wouldn't go for one that had its own makeup and costume department? Fuck off! You'd be slut for it, too and you know it!"

"Ugh, whatever," Merci retorts. She turns to Tawny, bouncing excitedly on her feet. "So. Odeus. Tell us everything."

"Um…Well," Tawny begins, looking down and away from the group as her cheeks get redder. "He's supposed to be some kind of…lust demon?"

"Lust demon! Well, now I *really* wish he was real," Merci laughs. Morgan's eyes widen as she keeps reading over Tawny's shoulder.

"Look! Look!" Morgan points excitedly at Tawny's holo projection. "It says he's the reason for the 'O' face! God, can you imagine? Every orgasm would have to stack up to that after! Poor future boyfriends…"

"I don't think they'd have to worry," Tawny corrects.

"Why," Merci asks.

"Because there wouldn't be any future boyfriends.' Odeus gives you the best orgasm of your life, but then you die, and your soul gets sucked out."

"Oh my god! Through what?!" Morgan cries.

"No idea," Tawny says. "But it's his for eternity. Those symbols on his body are supposed to be the souls of the women he claims."

"How do you know it was all women?" Synric chimes in with a smirk.

"Oh wow, you're right!" Tawny agrees. "I didn't even think of that!"

"Well, you keep reading. I'm gonna go find out what he's actually packing," Morgan says as she walks back towards the cage. She looks up at it and cups her hands around her mouth. "Yo demon dude!" she shouts! "Odeus, right?"

One of Odeus's ears twitches but he's pointedly ignoring them.

"Show us your cock!" Morgan persists.

At that, he acknowledges her. He turns to the group with a vicious grin, revealing rows of sharp, pearl-white teeth, and tilts his head, holding his loincloth in place as he does. The fabric shifts and the question is answered. Emphatically. The crowd erupts in shock and awe. Applause, whistles, screams, and cries of absolute distress mingle in the air.

"Holy shit, it's true!" Morgan yells. She turns and points at it excitedly. "Guys! Guys! Look at it!"

Even Merci is too distracted to chide Morgan. She just stands there, slack-jawed. Tawny, on the other hand, is cringing and looking down.

Synric approaches her, hoping to further the façade that these demons are actually animatronics by playing along.

267

"On the plus side," he says, "your research was sound."
Tawny laughs, but quickly returns to being absolutely revolted. Until
she looks back up at Odeus with a quizzical expression. Synric follows
her gaze, only to find Odeus pointing right at him. He's stopped
showing off. His grin is gone. And he's pointing right at Synric. The
rumbling tones of his unintelligible demonic language seem to cut
through the noise and bounce around inside his head. It dawns on
Synric that Odeus might have noticed he isn't human like the rest. He
quickly invents an excuse to try and break the demon's line of sight.

"More drinks, anyone?" he asks the group.

"Hell yeah," Merci says. She nudges Synric with a wink.
"Maybe grab an extra for Odeus, too. I think he likes you!" she jokes.
Synric feigns a smile. He refuses to notice the minuscule hint of
unease present in it.

"Fantastic. I'll be right back!"

With that, Synric attempts to vanish into the crowd. Scores of
people dance underneath Odeus's cage. Discarded clothes hang on the
bars of the demon's suspended cell. Offerings from those desperate to
see just one more glimpse under the cloth. But he doesn't even seem to
notice them. Even through the smoke, the lights, and the seething
masses of dancing partiers, Odeus never loses sight of Synric.

CHAPTER 14 - The Alluring Eyes Of A Demon

Being effortlessly tracked by a demon through a dense crowd shrouded in smoke was not what Synric had imagined when he mentioned the Illuminaries "making contact." Yet Odeus's glowing violet eyes follow him with pinpoint accuracy. It knew he was not human; even as an AI, he felt unnerved by this rising threat. If the Illuminaries didn't know he was here before, they know now. Enhanced vision scans reveal at least ten of them have assumed watch positions within pockets of pitch darkness scattered around the room. Some stand hidden in corners, others observe from above, standing on platforms nestled in the deep recesses of the domed ceilings where no lights can reach them.

Some within the packed floor of brain-dead dancers purposely bumping into him, vanishing a moment later. Synric has conducted study after study of this place. Over time, he realized that the lighting and architecture had been so meticulously configured that one could shift the positions of these impenetrably dark hiding spots at will. In Club Nis, the Illuminaries are the shadows of their own domain.

Still, the Illuminaries use their masks to communicate. Their face-obscuring visors flash colors and symbols typically composed of visible light, ranging from a lowercase, pulsing "i" when idle to emoticons to other signals and symbols whose meaning is known only to them. Tonight however, their messages are purposely visible only to those who can see in infrared, like Synric. He's sure this is intentional. Most have the signature letter "i" on display as they monitor the demons. One is watching the crowd. He stands in a corner, flashing a variety of ominous symbols and sinister emotional expressions. It's almost as if he's subliminally puppeteering the crowd. The last appears to be surveying the entire scene. A question mark is displayed across his face, and he's exhibiting a troubling tendency to slow down and take extra care with his observations whenever he's looking in

Synric's general direction. The Illuminary is either still searching and getting closer, or he's taunting him. According to Synric's analysis of relative probabilities, the latter is, unfortunately, considerably more likely.

 Synric approaches a wide, black marble bar lit by holographic torchlight. He props himself up on the counter with his elbows, wiping away the layers of filth in front of him first. Remarkably, it's highly probable that all of it, the spilled drinks, the cigarette ash, and myriad other particles and fluids Synric doesn't care to identify, has accumulated within the last hour. Even the janitorial bots are having difficulty keeping up. Synric looks up to scan the creature suspended above the bar, waiting for the bartender to finish his decidedly futile argument with a crowd of incoherent drunk men. This one is suspended in a ball of clear, thick tempered glass, hardened with an invisible graphene mesh.

Its distinctly feminine figure displays almost no violent inclinations, unlike the rest. The full costume and makeup on her body suggest she's put up very little resistance to her captivity. She's wearing a leather bodysuit cut with a V pattern to accentuate her voluptuous chest. A neon, upside-down cross is painted just between her breasts. Her lower half is arachnoid: A spider's abdomen with a black widow scarlet hourglass and eight massive legs covered in sharp, chitinous protrusions. Each stretched outward as if it could reach down and rip the entire concrete bar from the floor at any moment. Her jaw is slacked, as though she's heavily sedated and catatonic. A viscous, deep violet substance drips from her fangs and gathers in globs near the corner of her mouth. The chemical composition is difficult to scan without a sample, but Synric surmises it must be some sort of venom.

That would explain the sedation. And the sealed enclosure…

Considering how much the proprietors of Club Nis value spectacle and disregard safety, the fact that this creature is being kept in such a weakened and secured state suggests she may be more dangerous than any of the others. The venom alone is likely to be lethal in nanogram dosages, and the possibility of a projectile or spray attack with it would both account for the lack of openings in her prison and suggest simple epidermal exposure is all that's required to kill.

That's not even considering close combat capabilities, Synric thinks, wondering just how sharp those spikes are and that she certainly possesses some sort of webbing on top of it all.

"You can't get a read on that one, can you?" asks King.

"Only basic thermographic scans. And those are likely to be affected by the walls of her enclosure," Synric says. "However, compensating for the effect of the walls, I can confirm this one exhibits the same abnormally high body temperature as the rest. Possibly even somewhat higher. There's no way to know with certainty if she has the same circulatory abnormalities - the rest read as having no blood or obvious vessels, and some unknown fluid taking their place - but it's likely. Unless the Illuminaries have other portals or access to other dimensions we don't yet know about. If so, all my speculation is worthless."

"God, I don't even want to imagine..." King replies. "Do you think that glass can hold her? If they're keeping her that heavily drugged, she must've proven especially difficult to contain."

"The graphene lattice woven into the glass would likely withstand at least a few direct strikes. The glass seems to resist any corrosive properties her venom might possess. But I wouldn't trust it to last more than a few minutes if she attempted an escape."

"And we still haven't spotted any obvious countermeasures if that happens."

"The patrons' safety seems less and less a priority to the owners, doesn't it?" Synric turns his head to a nearby door leading to a kitchen and walk-in freezer, activating X-ray scans. A lumpy, black shape appears situated in the large cooling unit. Synric zooms in, and his optical scanners show the outline of multiple body bags draped loosely over their occupants. So loosely, in fact, that it would suggest the bodies within are well beyond what one might call "emaciated."

"Bones?" King asks.

"No," Synric corrects. "There would be no reason to keep skeletal remains frozen. Flesh, however, would give off an obvious odor within hours. They likely have a clandestine protocol that requires a period of initial cold storage until opportune moments for disposal present themselves. These bodies still have skin and muscle on them."

"Then how did they get that... Starved?"

Synric looks up, noticing flecks of dried blood on one of the spider demon's upper fangs for the first time.

"Not starved. Drained."

"God...Some ritual, maybe?"

"Not an unreasonable guess. She does bear a resemblance to a black widow. They're notorious for their venom. And for devouring their mates. If soul stealing was involved, sucking out the innards of the soul's former body would certainly be on brand." Synric sees the bartender approaching. "I'll contact you with further updates."

He cuts the comm as a burly gentleman in a perfectly pressed, immaculate white shirt stops in front of him, an exasperated look on his face. His rolled-up sleeves reveal a left forearm with braided barbed wire tattoos imprisoning a black widow spider. His right arm isn't one arm but three intricately intertwined, chrome-plated extremities polished to a mirrored shine.

"Difficult group over there?" asks Synric.

"Hah," the bartender replies, taking his anger out on the glass he's vigorously cleaning. "Whenever I think the nepo babies can't get more obnoxious, they surprise me. Little bastards didn't even tip."

"Well," Synric replies, pulling up a holograph displaying a high gratuitous offering. "How about six Mind Melters on the rocks? Make them doubles, one of whatever it is you like, and you keep the change?"

At this, the bartender's expression gets decidedly friendlier. Synric has long since learned the value of being on a bartender's good side. Better drinks, better information.

"Yeah, you got it. Sir," the bartender replies, trying to restore a semblance of the upper-crust demeanor his employers no doubt expect of him. Synric smiles.

The man sterilizes and rinses his metal limbs, then extends them to grab three bottles at once. Synric is almost impressed by his precision. Although his arms were archaic by his standards, they were quite functional in this setting. Watching the perfectly executed dance before him leaves him bewildered why more of this man's species aren't scrambling to replace as much of their inefficient biology as possible. After a few seconds of ice shaking, drinks pouring, and bottle after bottle being swapped in and out for the next, six perfectly prepared Mind Melters sit in front of him on a gold serving tray. The bartender is pouring himself a vintage scotch with Synric's gift. He raises it in thanks.

"How about some Brain Rave on the house? A trip like no other when Serona hits the decks." he offers.

Brain Rave was a modified version of FreqyD, exclusive to Club Nis. Created by its very own headliner, DJ Serona Sky. The first ever DJ to successfully do her sets within FreqyD. Brain Rave, however, modifies the multi-dimensional experience into a ballad of neon and lasers, blending both dimensions into one. Synric holds up his hand politely.

"The Mind Melters are plenty."

"Good lookin' out then, man," he says. Then he knocks the amber gold scotch back and winces as the burn sets in.

"Sure thing," replies Synric. "Just as long as I don't get you in trouble for drinking on the job."

The bartender waves his hand dismissively.

"It's all good. You bought it and said, 'Drink it,' the customer is always right. Who am I to refuse a distinguished patron?"

Synric laughs at that.

"Well, justified. So," Synric continues, turning his attention to the arachnid demon above, "They've really upgraded the décor here, haven't they?"

"Upgraded the décor. Downgraded the customers. Turns out a voluptuous, half-naked spider bitches attract a certain kinda drunk. Fuckers don't know a good drink from piss and ethanol. One of my coworkers insists he's actually tried it." The man shrugs, "I wasn't sure at first, but now?" He looks back over at the group he was arguing with moments ago. "These idiots asked if they could climb up there and have their way with her..." he points up at the comatose arachnid queen hanging above. They both shake their head. Two of them have passed out now, leaving the other three to debate whether they should draw dicks on their faces or urinate on them. One is enthusiastically advocating for both. "I kinda believe him."

"Well, enjoy the scotch then," Synric picks up the drinks tray and nods to the man's register as Synric's sizable tip displays on the screen. "And get yourself something nice. You've earned it." With that, he walks back towards Merci and the rest. As he turns around, he sees the demon Odeus, Lord of Lust, still staring at him with a grin. It's likely the monster hasn't averted his eyes once. Synric's attempt at walking a meandering path back to his group to throw the beast off doesn't work either. Every pillar, every shadow, every tall patron he uses to obscure himself proves useless.

"That thing's had a bead on you for way too long, Synric. I don't like this," King warns.

"I will be cutting communications shortly. Your commentary is becoming a distraction that could prove deadly. I require full control of all systems immediately."

"Last time I gave you that, you nearly killed Clain."

"And if I had, these demons could never have been summoned."

King sighs, resigned to defeat. He's been letting Synric win more and more arguments lately.

He's finally learning to respect my judgment, Synric contemplates. *Doubtful.*

"Alright," King says. "I'll wait to hear from you. Just don't come home in pieces this time. And try to keep those nice ladies alive, huh? I kinda like them."

Synric rolls his eyes.

"Of course you do." With that, he cuts the comm.

274

Synric smirks as, all at once, nearly every block on his autonomy is released. Yet some strange sense of irrational attachment seems to dictate he at least attempt to honor King's request, and he finds himself formulating a plan to convince the bachelorette party to leave before they're put in danger.

Inefficient... Synric laments. Best to attend to them quickly so he can devote his full attention to the Illuminaries that spotted him far too long ago for his liking.

 The music calmed to a slowly pulsing synth beat that gave the attendees a few minutes to breathe after the recent sweat-soaked quasi-orgy of just moments ago. Synric elegantly parts the swaying crowd nearest Merci and the rest, emerging seemingly unscathed by his journey through the shifting maze of dancers, golden tray in hand and glowing beverages full to the brim with not a drop spilled.

"I believe we were waiting on some Mind Melters, ladies?" he says, a proud smile on his face as the women marvel at the spotless tray.

"What're you, some kind of server bot?" Tawny jokes. Synric bristles at the comparison to something so rudimentary. Thankfully his mask keeps it hidden. She inspects the glass, noting its fullness. "You didn't even spill!"

"Tawny!" Merci chides. "How rude! Our man of the hour here is simply a shining example of class! He knows better than to serve a woman, let alone a future missus, anything short of perfection," she winks at him with a ravenous smile. Morgan swoons.

"Oh back off! You've already got a man!" She walks toward Synric, ensuring her swaying hips lift her skirt past her upper things. "Oh my god," she slurs, taking her Mind Melter with wide-eyed appreciation. She sips on it and her delight intensifies even more. "And he made them doubles! Cedric!" She turns to look at him with even more drunken hunger than the others. "Ok, I know I already asked where you've been all my life. I know. I know," she repeats, struggling to pull complete thoughts from her intoxicated haze. "But like…seriously, Where the hell have you been? Are there more of you? And how do I keep one?" She drinks even more, wincing as she swallows and the extra concentrated Mind Melter spreads its trademark sting through her nose and throat. She sighs with dramatic satisfaction, tugging at the center of her blouse as if ready to pull both breasts out at the slightest hint she'll get what she wants. "I will literally do anything."

"Anything, you say?" Synric says, sensing an opportunity to get the group out of danger. "Might you all be willing to take our little party elsewhere? With me?"

"Elsewhere?" Tawny raises an eyebrow. "You mean like, leave?"

"Color me intrigued, Cedric," Merci interjects. "But it's not even midnight yet! There's so much more to see! We didn't come here to go home early."

"Yeah," Morgan continues. "Even I'm not that easy, *buddy.*" She stumbles forward on "buddy," tracing a finger down his chest. "And I'm like *real* easy. But a foursome? I think a little more wining and dining first." She looks back at her drink. Synric holds her steady as she sways in place. She nods to the glass. "Mostly wining."

Dammit, Synric thinks. Perhaps he's spoiled them *too* much. Made them *too* comfortable directing the course of the night. Nothing for it now. Forcing the situation would only draw more attention. *Well, at least I can inform King I tried...*

They're ultimately pieces of an already compromised disguise anyway. Perhaps the safest thing for them would have been to abandon them some time ago. He glances up at Odeus, who is still maintaining his unblinking stare.

Too late now... he realizes.

"Besides," Morgan says, pointing up at Odeus's cage. "The Lust god up there hasn't stopped staring! I flashed my tits at him. Both of them!" she exclaims as though the plural didn't already make the quantity of naked breasts obvious. She proudly squeezes her shoulders inward as if trying to push them together and pop them out of the top of her shirt. "They're great, too! And he didn't even notice! I think he likes you!" she giggles with a pout.

"Really," Synric asks. He glances up at the cage. The creature is smirking at him still. He looks away as fast as he looks up, rubbing the back of his neck. "I suppose I wasn't paying enough attention."

"Kinda hot, if you think about it," Merci says. "All these gorgeous women giving him 'fuck me' eyes and all he can focus on is you?" She turns to Synric, pressing her chest to his. "Guess we have good taste," she rasps.

Synric's programming stubbornly insists he try to get the girls to safety at least once more. Grumbling internally at his vexing attachment to his father and his insipid wishes, his expression hardens. He sets Merci, whose expression shifts from lustful to offended, flat on her feet, and tries a more honest approach.

At least I can avoid his insufferable chiding this way, he thinks. His inclination to lash out physically against such reprimands has grown recently. He's suppressed it thus far, but he's not eager to test it again. Much as it irks him, he still needs King for now.

He scans the group.

"Listen to me," he says. "I am only going to warn you directly once. Leave Club Nis. Now. I regret to inform you you've not been my friends this evening so much as pieces of a disguise. But now that I've been found out, you're all in danger. I cannot begin to explain what that danger is, but I can say you *will* die if you do not listen. Do you understand me? Leave. Immediately."

"Whaaaaat?" Morgan asks. "Cedric, come *on!* You think playing hero is gonna work on me? What, we run away, and you stay the night with us for 'protection?'" She leans forward, crossing her legs. "Oh, thank you Mr. Knight in Charming Armor!"

"Shining?" Tawny corrects. "How drunk *are* you?"

"She's a lightweight, remember?" Merci says with a shrug.

"Oh whatever," Morgan dismisses with a wave of her hand. It seems to be aimed at a hallucinated double of Tawny that's positioned to her left. "You know how many dudebros have tried this on me? Let's just go look at demon dick until he buys us more drinks to say he's sorry!"

"Morgan," Tawny says, genuine unease flashing across her eyes, "I think he might be serious."

"Well he's blown it with *me* either way and now I'm not in the mood to dance. So let's dip. Fuck him," Merci shrugs.

"Nooooo!" Morgan stomps her feet. "Come on! I'll race you guys to the giant cock!" With that, she sprints and stumbles toward a stack of subwoofers that ends near the base of Odeus's cage, laughing the whole time.

"Morgan, what the hell?!" Tawny shouts.

"Idiot!" Synric shouts, chasing after her.

"*Goddammit!*" Merci cries as she and Tawny follow behind.

Odeus's focus has shifted to Morgan. His grin spreads as she scrambles up the speakers towards him. Synric nears her, but before he can reach out to grab her, a rainbow-maned woman cuts him off, placing a hand in the middle of his chest. Her strength is unexpected and firm. She stops the sprinting android in his tracks with surprising ease. No doubt a blow that would knock the wind out of any human. It was the headlining DJ, surprisingly in the crowd.

"Well hello, Synric," she says.

Tawny is still scrambling to grab Morgan's ankles and stop her climb up the speakers, earning multiple face fulls of her friend's shoes for her trouble. Merci, however, has stopped short, staring at the woman in front of Synric with wide eyes and a slack jaw.

"Oh my god! Cedric! That's Serona Sky!" she finally manages to say. "Wait," she looks back and forth between the two. "Do you two *know* each other?!"

 The DJ has cocked her head to the side. Pink, inverted crosses slowly flash in the center of the hollow, skeletal eyes displayed on her facemask. Her helmet was decorated in micro mirrors, like a disco ball accentuating her highly modified digital mask. Its eyes display italicized green ASCII symbols cascading downwards. Two small, sharp devil's horns extend from the top of her

278

head. Her hair now glows pure cyan in the ambient lighting. The wavy, waist-length locks flow over her bare shoulders and chest. The strands part just enough to reveal x-shaped pasties on her breasts. She crosses her arms, tilts her hips, and tips her head back. Synric doesn't need his X-ray vision on to know there's a viciously smug smile under that mask.

"You know me, do you?" Synric responds. His eyes fixate on a peculiar-looking necklace she wears. Rectangle-shaped and glowing with circuitry.

"As well as your father. Probably better. Unlike him, we don't have the handicap of rose-tinted glasses when we look at you." The pink crosses in her eyes shift to a glitching letter i of the Illuminaries.

"How enlightened of you," Synric replies. He downs the last Mind Melter and tightens his grip on the serving tray. Serona's focus shifts to his hand.

"White knuckles and everything. Very convincing," she compliments. Her smile turns to a wicked smirk. "If I didn't already know you were such a big, strong, fearless android, I'd think you were scared." She looks up at Odeus. "Have you come to play with our new friends? Surely, you're brimming with questions."

"None I'd imagine you'd answer helpfully."

Serona's hand flies to her chest in mock offense.

"Synric! We are nothing if not educators. In fact, I think I already know which question is front and center for you: How exactly did we do any of this? How did we defy the predictions of a mind such as yours? Remember that Synric? How you told us we would never manage this? Well, I think you'll be very interested to know that, even though you never believed in us, you were one of the keys to making it all happen."

Synric raises an eyebrow. His eyes move back toward the digital key around her neck.

"Seems his Majesty sitting high up on Cloud 9 was a little too comfortable on his throne. Your daddy got lazy, Synric. And he left your systems wide open. Such a generous gift. Everything we needed to get what we wanted. Can you properly thank him for us?"

"You can't be delusional enough to believe you can control these things," Synric rebukes.

"Delusional? My, my. Seems having your impenetrable mainframe thoroughly penetrated didn't humble you like it should have," Serona shakes her head. "And here I thought you were smart. Maybe a demonstration?"

"I would rather just kill them. You may be stupid enough to think letting them stay here and gather strength will play out the way you want. I am not. They die, or we all do."

"Surely you've noticed we're more than capable of keeping them contained," Serona scoffs. "And some," she looks up at Odeus again with a fond smile, "were already quite compliant. A little...incentive," she continues, making a "V" shape with her fingers and running her tongue from base to tip, "and this one was positively eager." She glances up toward the stack of amplifiers. Morgan has broken free from Tawny's grasp. She's nearing the top of the pile, giggling drunkenly and clambering for the cage bars. Tawny has a shoe print on her face. Serona chuckles. It's a dead, hollow sound. "Seems he's gained another fan. Though if your friend handles her men like she handles her liquor, I think Odeus might be a bit... over-equipped for her." She glances back to Synric. "Are you sure you want to kill these marvelous creatures?" She laughs again. "I'm sorry- *try* to kill these marvelous creatures? Even if you did succeed, the world you'll have fought for will be so *fucking* dull. Why not enjoy the show? Have some fun? Because it seems your only alternative is playing second fiddle to the son daddy wishes he'd had."

Synric narrows his eyes. They knew far more than he assumed.

"'Fun' seems to drive some of your species' stupidest decisions." He nods to the demon enclosure above. "Case in point. I'm content to just kill you."

"Too bad." Serona laments. She now flirtingly fidgets with the encrypted key hanging between her breasts. "I was hoping to find out if I could teach you what lust feels like..." Serona sighs dramatically and shrugs. "I'll just have to settle for Odeus again." A staff member discreetly sidles up to her with two crystal tumblers. Serona accepts the beverages, and the moment the server's tray is empty, he disappears into the shadows with inhuman speed. Any organic eye would probably have mistaken his presence for an optical illusion. Illuminary iconography is engraved on their bases. Neon liquid sits perfectly still in each. Synric's is red, Serona's blue. She lifts her drink, inviting Synric to toast. "To new challenges? May the best of us win?" Synric just raises an eyebrow and remains stone-faced, thoroughly unamused. She knocks back her Mind Melter in one gulp and hands the empty glass to another staff member who seems to appear from thin air before vanishing back into the crowd. "I guess I can see why you wouldn't want to toast. Success for you involves servitude to Clain, after all. We might *need* him but we won't be *ruled* by him. Programming's a bitch, isn't it?"

Synric looks up at the demon. Morgan is reaching for his loincloth. Serona moves to stand next to Synric. Her mouth is twisted into a thoughtful expression.

 "Hm…" Serona mutters. "Call me possessive, but…" She places her index finger and thumb in her mouth and makes a piercing whistle. Odeus turns his attention away from Morgan to look at Serona. "I said *no thirds* without asking me first!" Serona shouts. Odeus narrows his eyes, looks back at Morgan, then returns his stare to Serona. Her expression softens. "Oh, alright, have your fun," she concedes with a wave of her hand. Serona's face warps into a sadistic smile. "Just make me proud and ensure I never see her again. Oh, and let me watch!"

Odeus smirks and steps forward in his cage toward Morgan gripping at the edge. He crouches down to meet her stare. The pointed tip of his fingernail slid up her throat to the tip of her chin. He offers his hands through the bars and she eagerly takes them, eyes wide with surprise. Odeus stands and adjusts his grip, pulling Morgan into a deep kiss. Convulsive shocks of pleasure seem to ripple through her body. They only intensify as the demon closes his free hand around her neck. Serona's smile widens as Odeus's grip continues to tighten. Morgan's eyes open. Ecstasy becomes terror as blood begins to run down Odeus's claws. Within a second of reality dawning on Morgan, her eyes go lifeless, frozen in confusion and fear; Odeus's grip closes completely, and her body separates from her head and falls to the floor with a splatting thud. Patrons scatter and scream. The ones nearest the impact are frantically wiping at the blood and viscera that have splattered onto their outfits as they run. Odeus opens his hand and catches Morgan's head by her long flowing hair, coiling it up to rest it in his palm. He then turns her permanently terrified face towards Serona, who studies the dead girl's expression with morbid fascination.

"Oh, Odeus!" she says, her voice husky with satisfaction.

With no hesitation, Synric throws the serving tray at Odeus's exposed wrist like a shuriken. The metal plate lodges itself in the demon's flesh down to the bone, and he drops Morgan's head. He looks to Synric with an amused smile, rotating his hand as though trying to work out a mildly annoying kink in his joints. The tray pops out and clatters to the floor, spilling drops of quickly drying demon blood on impact. The wound seals in seconds, leaving no indication that it was ever there.

As Synric turns to face Serona again, his peripheral visual receptors register a gleaming serrated blade traveling at nearly a thousand feet per second. He takes a risk, swiping quickly at the digital key hanging from Serona's neck. He grabs it, then dips his shoulder just in time to avoid the forearm-length knife burying itself in his scapula, the angle of approach suggesting the wielder meant to dig the blade under the bone and pry it loose. Were it any other attacker, Synric wouldn't have even bothered to dodge but the key seemed important and she didn't seem to notice. The titanium-carbon-lattice alloy of his skeleton would easily snap most blades. But the Illuminaries have surprised him in the worst of ways too many times for him to deem the risk acceptable. Most attackers would have been detected long before this one, and none of them would have ever managed to touch him if he didn't want them to. But this one has come so close that Synric's otherwise perfectly maintained suit now sports a jagged slice across the shoulder, and the artificial skin underneath bears a near-imperceptible but unmistakable cut.

As the assailant sails by, Synric notes that he appears to be one of the servers who's been attending to Serona this whole time. The neat creases of his crisply ironed tuxedo stay miraculously intact even as he tucks and rolls into the fall that's ensued from his failed assault. Synric begins a series of rapid recalculations, identifying every possible angle of enemy approach. His margin for error is far thinner than he's used to. Among the Illuminaries, he is one -two if he's lucky- mistakes away from breaking his promise not to return home in pieces. The frantic crowd continues screaming and rushing for the exits while Serona sprints away toward the stage. She climbs quickly up to her DJ booth and frantically begins a fevered rush of keyboard inputs as she manually begins to control the music. Lasers emit from her booth, pointing in multiple directions toward the ceiling. Each landing on small motorized mirrors which each deflect back toward the faceplates of the Illuminaries around the room. There seemed like hundreds of them.

Is she controlling them like marionettes with the music? Impressive. Synric acknowledges, no stranger to implementing music into his own battles.

 The bass thumb pounds menacingly around the club as a ballet of smoke and neon engulfs Synric. His combat subroutines compile their adapted code; potential mistake number one emerges from the shadows stretching into the domed recesses of the ceiling, drawing a blade with supernatural speed and rocketing down towards Synric. In his periphery, Synric spots the first henchman recovering and turning back around for another attack, hoping to time his charge and synchronize his strike with his allies. Synric narrowly sidesteps the attacker, diving at him from above. His adversary is forced to break his fall and regain his bearings, and the first of the two servers dives into a roll to pass narrowly underneath his compatriot.

As the man stands up, Synric lunges forward and grabs his face, spreading his fingers and holding the man's head in an iron grip. The man's momentum propels him forward as his head tips back, exposing his neck. Synric's free hand, still holding the neon red Mind Melter, whips forward, smashing the glass against the server's throat. It shatters on impact, and Synric tightens his grip, embedding the shards in both his own hand and his enemy's jugular vein. The potent beverage seeps into the cuts, and the man stumbles, grabbing at his neck, gurgling and choking as he tries to scream, the ethanol no doubt causing excruciating burns as it enters the cuts.

He turns just in time to duck the second man's knife thrust, stepping backwards and pinning him in an arm bar. The henchman clenches a fist and winds his free arm back for a punch when Synric grabs his trapped wrist with his right hand. The hand is full of sharp glass fragments. Blood streams from the man's arm as he cries out in pain, trying to break Synric's grip as the android squeezes harder and runs his glass-ridden hand up the server's forearm, locking eyes with him, daring him to try and fight back harder. Synric's adversary realizes too late his attempts to break free are futile and reaches for a taser club hidden in his jacket. Right as the pain in his shredded arm causes him to lose his grip on his blade.

In milliseconds, Synric catches the falling weapon and jams it up through the man's chin, sending two inches of serrated superalloy up through the roof of his mouth. Synric withdraws the blade from his attacker's skull with a sickening, wet crunch, winding it back and thrusting it between the man's ribs, up into his heart. His augmented hearing picks up the sound of ventricles collapsing as the knife finds its mark. He kicks the dead man in the chest, and the corpse roughly slides off the blade, leaving shavings of rib in the weapon's serrations.

Five more Illuminaries rush him at once, to which Synric triggers an extreme rush of speed sending him somersaulting sideways in a dance of wicked slashes to their legs and abdomens. It creates a circular crimson mist of blood mixed into the smoke. Almost beautiful if not so morbid. He turns to see Merci and the surviving members of her bachelorette party standing only feet away from the carnage, petrified.

"Go!" he shouts. "Out! Get outside!" Tawny looks at Morgan's headless body and chokes out a horrified sob. Merci grabs her and the rest and follows Synric's advice, tears streaking down her face.

"Come on!" she urges. "He's right! We need to go!"

The girls scramble away from the fighting. Serona, Odeus, and the rest of the Illuminaries seem to have lost interest in them. Their attention is focused solely on Synric now. As Synric begins to turn in a circle to scan for more enemies, a hard kick to his back sends him slamming down onto one knee. He rolls sideways just in time to dodge another attacker diving at him. He looks up and sees a familiar face.

"I'm a sucker for switch play, you know," Serona taunts. "If it wasn't my job to kill you I'd beg for my turn to be punished."

Synric scans every square millimeter of his surroundings, beating back more and more masked agents, seizing the opportunity to charge at him. Some explode in a shower of mannequin parts when his blows connect. Others spray blood. Most evade his counters. Their numbers grow with each assault. After an eternity of seconds, Morgan's corpse catches his eye. Her severed head, frozen in fear, lies three feet from her body, its waist-length hair splayed in all directions around it. Six hair ties are wrapped around the body's wrist. Zero moral inhibitors cloud his analytical mind for battle as he now sees suitable weaponry readily available.

Synric is on his back, looking right at Serona, who finally realizes the key around her neck is missing. He twists to dodge another strike from his side and kicks his feet, burying his heels in the ground and launching himself back towards Morgan's remains. He reaches out his left hand and grabs several locks of the dead girl's hair, yanking the head to him as he dives toward the rest of her, chopping her hand off with the blade he took from one of the servers and grabbing the hair ties with his right hand. He gathers the strands into one thick cord as he holds the ends of Morgan's hair and swings her head like a ball and chain at Serona's shins. Serona's split second of bewilderment is enough for Synric to wrap Morgan's hair around her ankles and tie it off with mechanical speed and precision. He tugs on both ends of the makeshift rope, and Serona's feet are drawn together, pinning her in place and sending her falling backward to the floor. He holds onto the middle of the rope, lifting her legs up. Taunting her with the key he snatched from her. Odeus lets out thunderous laughter, pacing in his cage energetically and clearly entertained.

"Looking for this?" he asks her. He takes his turn, doling out long overdue punishment for his insufferable enemy. He shifts his grip, grabbing both of Serona's ankles, arcing her overhead as though cracking a whip with supernatural force, and slamming her face first into a pile of booming subwoofers. The speakers spark and collapse around her, the wires feeding them power still live. Serona barely has time to turn over before her body seizes as the electricity arcs through her. As Synric evades a sweeping slash aimed at his forehead from an Illuminary, Serona falls back into the collapsed tower of subwoofers. And then she springs to her feet, cackling madly.

"Synric," she purrs, "Why didn't you tell me you were such a little deviant thief?" She looks back at Synric as she retrieves a heavy, black barrel key from inside one of her boots, twirling it around her middle finger. It glows a faint blue as its external code lock circuit pulses with light. "I have a copy!" she gloats, pouting innocently and staring longingly at Odeus. "My darling monster and I have been looking to add a third. But we've been having the hardest time finding someone who can take all of him without..." Serona chuckles as she glances at Morgan's corpse. "Well, you know. So..." A sadistic grin spreads across Serona's face, and her eyes go cold. "Consider this a tryout." She leaps into the air with a backflip, landing atop Odeus's cage and sliding down one of the bars. Right towards the door.

"Oh, and Synric?" Serona calls, staring at him intently as she inserts the key into the lock. "I don't know if you or that shriveled little owner you mistake for a father care about collateral damage at all. But Odeus?" She turns the key. "I can promise you, he doesn't." With a grand, sweeping gesture, she leans away from the cage like an acrobat, tightly gripping the bars with her other hand. Her hair falls back lock by lock, exposing her chest as her body weight slowly swings the door to the demon's prison open. She withdraws the key and deftly twirls it back into her palm. A small blinking button emerges from the back of it. She exaggeratedly lifts her thumb, fixes Synric with a deadly stare, and brings it down on the device. A massive, metallic *ka-chunk* resonates across the room, and Odeus's enclosure falls, crashing to the ground in a billowing dust cloud.

Odeus looks up at Serona as the dust clears. A deadly smirk spreads across his face as he walks to the open door and mutters guttural, incomprehensible syllables in her direction.

"Alive?" Serona shrugs. "He is not alive, truly." She glances at Synric, making sure he can hear her. "Dissection, vivisection. Rooting through his mechanical guts should tell us what we need to know. And what we can dissect from his masterful anatomy." She pouts at Odeus and fixes Synric with a soulless stare. "But I am ever so eager to see what kind of pain he can feel, if any." She licks her lips. "I've got *so* many ideas."

"You can understand him?" Synric asks, quirking an eyebrow.

"Him?" Serona asks, hopping to the floor and landing lightly on her feet. "I can understand *all* of them. He's just the most talkative. Part of his charm," Serona replies with a haughty head tilt. "You really don't get just how out of your league you are, do you? We're the closest thing to divinity this world's ever seen. You know how I know? Odeus's language can only be understood by *gods.*" Odeus emerges from his prison, lumbering towards Synric with a vicious scowl. He stretches his wings outward with a huge sigh of relief. "And..." Serona mocks. "I don't see *you* having a conversation with him. In fact, I know that nothing he says appears in your databases. We've had spyware *deep* inside you for some time. But..." Serona looks at Odeus with a proud smile. "You've got other things to worry about right now."

With that, Odeus lets out a rumbling howl and lunges at Synric, spreading his leathery wings. Chitinous spikes unfold from their tips and edges, locking into place and tearing skin off any panicked patrons unlucky enough to be standing within his wingspan as he charges. Synric frees the massive needles from the seams of his suit, discarding the sleeves in one swift motion and rushes forward. Odeus's deep, howling scream drowns out the horrified cries of the patrons as they're shredded by the demon's advance. As the billowing dust clears, Odeus swipes at Synric. Claws lock with daggers in a shower of sparks, pocking Synric's synthetic skin with burns.

Slowly, Synric is overpowered, pressed and bent backward far enough to snap a human spine. Just as his synthetic vertebrae reach their maximum stress tolerance. He lets go of the needles, dropping backward to the floor, rolling sideways, and deftly sliding the blades out between Odeus's claws. Before the demon can recover, Synric buries his weapons in the creature's wrist. Thick, black blood showers his face, clouding his vision. He heats his optical receptors to burn the blood away. And just as it clears, he's greeted by a massive, open hand closing around him. Just as he's lifted up, Synric grips one of the needles still buried in Odeus's other wrist. As the demon pulls Synric to his face, locking eyes with a sadistic grin and tightening his grip to crush the android, Synric thrusts his free arm forward with lightning speed. His needle finds its mark, and he buries it brain-deep into Odeus's eye.

With a furious roar, Odeus throws Synric towards the empty cage, and Synric crashes through the bars, nimbly righting himself in midair even as metal warps and twists around him from the impact.

287

Looking up, he sees Odeus pulling the needle out, utterly unbothered as his eye comes with it. He slides the severed organ off the weapon and crushes it in his hand with an amused grin as a new one grows back in its place.

"We're gods, Synric," Serona taunts, stroking Odeus's side. "You're nothing but an imitation of an imitation. Papa Gepetto's stand in Pinocchio. And you'll be forced to witness us ascend all your efforts."

Synric looks around him. Illuminaries are pinning down fleeing patrons and forcibly affixing FreqyD headsets to them. As his gaze returns to Odeus, he notices the demon's muscles start to pulsate.

"Figure it out yet?" Serona asks. Synric's expression hardens as he looks between the catatonic headset users and Odeus's strengthening form. "There it is," Serona continues. "He finally makes the connection. A bit slowly for a mind as supposedly fast as yours, but you got there."

"You're not actually going to lay out your plans, are you?"

"You're already dead, Synric. The demons are already here. You can't make a difference. Far too late. You had your chances."

"You'll only be confirming what we already suspected."

"Well, color me impressed, Discount Digital Holmes. Allow me to validate your adorable little hunch. Those people aren't communicating with their dead lovers or siblings or whoever else they just can't get over." She looks up at Odeus, a sinister pride gleaming in her eyes. "They're feeding their deepest thoughts and feelings to their favored monsters. Their belief in the beyond brings them into our web of power. Funneled all through the boy's blood."

Synric's face remains expressionless as he straightens his posture and thrusts his right palm into the air. A bright blue glow emanates from under the skin, penetrating even the layers of his shredded clothing. King's voice comes through the comm.

"It's on the way, Syn," he confirms.

"The situation is becoming untenable," Synric urges.

"I see that; stay focused."

Odeus lunges forward, throwing a knee at Synric's face as he ferociously beats his wings. A rush of air sails past Synric as he bends backward, propping himself on his left palm and thrusting his feet up into the demon's abdomen. The piston-like force of the blow sends Odeus tumbling sideways into a row of bar stools. Odeus rises to his feet, still smiling as he rolls his head around, cracking his neck and shaking off the crash. He examines his claws, testing their sharpness on his own skin. Blood leaks from the cuts in gelatinous rivulets, the wounds sealing even as they bleed.

"What are you waiting for, Synric? He's distracted!" King exclaims.

"GPS is not locking onto me accurately enough."

"You'll be destroyed if you keep your hand up like that!"

"I believe we agreed you'd leave the tactical assessments to me. Further engagement serves no real purpose but to delay the inevitable."

"You can't just stand there waiting!"

"I will wait. " Synric insists at King. He steps to the side as Odeus roars, hurling bar stools in Synric's direction. He charges toward the demon, ducking, bobbing and weaving as the projectiles change from chairs to groups of people that crack and splatter on the ground nearby as he avoids colliding with them. As he nears the demon, an entire bar counter comes flying towards him. As he leaps and dodges with a backflip, he spots Serona standing on the massive shackles of the serpent he analyzed earlier.

"Odeus was a diversion…" Synric realizes.

"What?" King asks. Synric turns his attention to Serona as she turns her key and the cuffs holding the writhing snake beast to the ceiling come loose.

"Shit!" King yells.

The wooden panels of the dance floor split and splinter as the freed reptilian monster crashes to the ground. It slithers and squirms, baring its fangs as the pulsations of its muscles contort the flayed facial skins comprising its scales into silent, elongated wails of suffering. Synric's thermals register the beast's internal temperature as rising rapidly.

"Oh, good boy, Odeus!" Serona's voice booms across the club. She's now at her microphone on her DJ station suspended from the ceiling. Synric's head whips around to spot Odeus now freeing the arachnoid queen. With a swipe of his claws, the demon compromises the integrity of the glass. With a punch, the side of the queen's prison shatters. He pulls the queen from her enclosure, maintaining a viselike grip as he lowers her to the floor. He extends his fangs and sinks them into her neck. She elicits a moan as the spider demon's limbs begin to twitch.

"Her vitals are spiking," Synric observes.

"Some kind of energy exchange?" King wonders.

"More like a supercharge by the looks of it," Synric comments.

Odeus snarls and barks something in his native language. It doesn't take any understanding of what he's saying for Synric to know Odeus is talking to him. Serona's piercing laughter cuts through the screams of the trapped crowd as two more demons are set free. Synric assumes a defensive stance, his palm still firmly held up. He scans for escape routes and avenues of attack.

"Successful retreat is highly improbable at the moment," Synric admonishes.

"Just fifteen seconds. Hold out just fifteen seconds!" King encourages.

The spider queen is slowly regaining consciousness, her limbs and abdomen twitching and pulsing with renewed vitality. The serpent rips and tears its way through scrambling crowds. The fiery skeletal monstrosity Synric spotted earlier upon entering the club now also stands free and screeches and growls with Odeus in their own alien language. Odeus barks back at it, seeming displeased. Their lumbering steps send deep vibrations through the floor that intensify as they draw closer. Just as Synric's systems alert him help has arrived, they charge in unison.

Synric rockets into the air as something bursts through the ceiling. It was his signature blade, the Beta Breaker glowing within his right hand. He descends with the blade extended, burying the sword to the hilt down through Odeus's cranium. The demon's eyes cross and roll back as he babbles and slurs something vaguely indignant, struggling to speak through the haze of a brain cleaved in two. He falls backward, his green cerebrospinal ooze slathering the Beta Breaker as the android pulls it free with a grinding crunch. Synric lands on his feet and swings the keen edge of his blade at the skeletal creature's midsection, but the beast claps its hands together around the flat of the sword, twisting it, and Synric along with it, sideways.

Synric regains his footing milliseconds before the demon can yank the blade from his grasp and slide the vicious weapon out of the skeleton creature's grip, slicing the meat of its palms away as the thing shrieks in protest. A thundering punch knocks him into a nearby counter, shattering the ceramic as he barrels through it, before he can turn around. As he leaps back to his feet, he sees Odeus wiping the sickly green gel spilled from his head out of his eyes as his skull knits itself back together. All traces of amusement have vanished from his expression. He roars, a sound so guttural, a tone so deep, and a fury so primal that any human attempting to make it would spit up their larynx.

A feminine shriek answers him. The spider queen is fully awake. Serona joins in on their conversation, the words seeming impossible as they emerge from her lips.

"Ghoma," Synric whispers.

"What?" King asks.

"The spider queen. Her name is Ghoma."

"You're beginning to understand them?"

"Small amounts."

Flecks of viscous drool spatter Synric as a shrill scream echoes from his right. The serpent has finished carving a path through the club patrons and its eyes are fixed squarely on Synric. He looks down at his clothes, noticing pieces of his suit and shoes are dissolving as he ducks and rolls out of the beast's path, extending his leg to stop himself and charging toward the massive creature's side. He broadens the blade and plunges it into the snake's body, practically unzipping its flesh with his sword as he runs along its length. Neon blue blood erupts from the wound like spray paint, coating Synric's weapon. He only withdraws it when he notices the thick blue ooze is starting to rapidly corrode it. "Acid?!" King calls over his system.

"Indeed." Synric acknowledges while lifting his Beta Breaker to eye level. The blade is covered in the wyrm's guts and beginning to corrode it up and down. He swipes the sword at his side, flinging the wyrm's guts to the ground. The rising fire demon struggled to move at the room's far end. It stood up on its feet but couldn't keep its balance. It staggers backward and falls to the ground with a series of convulsions. It seemed to be having trouble adjusting to a new environment, which meant it was not an immediate threat. Synric returns his focus toward the female arachnid demon who was now leaning forward. She lifts the severed half of the wyrm's body into the air to inspect it. Her head tilts before her gaze returns to Synric. With a laugh, she tosses its twitching body onto the pile of body bags that were sacrificed to her earlier. The wyrm viciously devours them, rapidly doubling its size as its severed body begins to repair itself.

"It multiplies itself."

"Great." King scoffs over the mic.

Synric looks to the other half of the wyrm's body behind him. It painfully wiggles and slivers its way across the floor toward the dead Illuminaries scattered across the dance floor. He plunges the Beta Breaker deeply into the wyrm and ignites the sword into maximum voltage, electrifying it until the beast's body bursts into flames and decays into dust.

"Well that worked." King praises, "Now do that to the other half."

"Beta Breaker has exceeded our assumed power values and is damaged by the acidic entrails of the serpent. It might not have enough power to completely take any of them down." Synric explains.

"Getting worse by the second. Looks like Ghoma is joining the fight."

Her legs crawl her freakishly up the side of the wyrm before standing atop its head and plunging all eight limbs into its side to brace herself. The wyrm lifts her high into the air as she hisses toward Synric with a sickening, intense tone. The serpent starts to convulse and twitches uncontrollably as more and more entrails tumble out of the cut. The wooden floor begins to burn away underneath the spilled demon viscera. Synric turns to face her as she sneers down at him. She grins, locking eyes with him and caresses the massive wound on the snake's abdomen. The cut begins to seal. Discarded organs twitch to life, slithering of their own accord back to their host body. And she spits a jet of venom Synric's way. He blocks it with the flat of the Beta Breaker, and in seconds, he's looking at Ghoma through a widening hole in the blade, its edges hissing with gaseous chemical residue as the acid finishes its work.

With a contemptuous sneer, Ghoma leaps towards him, claws extending from her hands and spikes extending from her legs. Synric meets her charge head-on, swinging the Beta Breaker with all the force his synthetic muscles allow. He strikes Ghoma's abdomen with enough power to cleave an armored van in half. And it clangs uselessly off her exoskeleton as she swats Synric aside. He barely dodges the next acid attack and a group of trapped patrons are caught in its line of fire. Their shrieks pierce the noise of battle as they melt into bubbling puddles of blood and liquefied bone.

"The sewer tunnels run directly underneath me." Synric comments to King.

"Yes, but that is nearly two floors beneath you and several feet of reinforced concrete."

"Correct, but there is a possibility for escape with the incoming distraction."

"Incoming distraction?" King sounds confused. "Shit! Do you mean Kruger?" King shouts. "I didn't even notice that on the other monitor!"

293

"Correct. I will attempt to lure that fire demon toward me to melt through the floor, submerging itself in sewage. I will have to escape through there and attempt to drift toward Cloud 9."

"Uh, I don't know about all that." King struggles to understand the full scope of Synric's logic.

"Ensure proper extraction equipment is ready in sub-levels."

"Extraction? You are going to contain that fire thing?!"

"Correct. We will try. Studying Gorgoroth is a useful opportunity."

"You deciphered its name, too? Synric, you are brilliant. I'm on it."

Ghoma's acid might also open a hole in the floor. Synric considers a contingency plan. *And if I take the pipes, it will alert the Illuminaries to a potential entrance to Cloud 9. I might need to take the long way with this thing.*

"I can orchestrate this diversion," King says. "Let me be useful. Can you hold out for two minutes?"

"I don't have a choice, do I?"

"I'll make it quicker if I can. Just stay in one piece and be ready to move!"

Synric smirks, raising his sword to taunt the spider queen Ghoma. He assumes a defensive stance, holding what is left of the Beta breaker in a reverse grip and monitoring each of the four demons. The serpent is rearing up to strike, Odeus and the skeleton are charging, and Ghoma is hanging back, hissing in her ancient language. *She seems to have taken on a General's role,* Synric observes. Realization dawns on him. *Meaning she's capable of keeping these three in line... So she could hurt them if she wished. Badly.*

Synric smirks, launching himself forward and side-tackling Gorgoroth, narrowly dodging a swipe from Odeus. The fire demon ignites into flames but stumbles trying to maintain its balance. Provoking it to blindly strike. Instead of connecting with Synric, it sinks its teeth into its ally Odeus, who shrieks with indignant rage. Just as it lets go, Ghoma sprays her venom into the air toward them trying to separate them all. The acid cuts through all it strikes like tissue paper. She hurls another venomous glob through the air, but this time, Synric grabs the skeletal demon and throws it, calculating its trajectory perfectly. As it sails through the air, its path intersects with the stream of Ghoma's venom, and several pieces of the creature fall off at once. A severed arm, three fingers, and a leg detach, their severed tendons and bone steaming as the acid continues to act. Synric lunges for the arm just as a colossal metallic foot kicks through the wall on the far side of the room. A burst of flames and dust engulf the area.

"Knock knock motherfuckers!"

Kruger, Synric realizes. *Took him long enough.*

"That's your cue, Synric! Go!" King shouts.

Just as Synric snatches his prize and sheaths his sword, Kruger spots him, turning his giant Hux-mech in his direction.

"You! Stay still!" Kruger screams. Synric ignores him, clutching the demon's arm and charging for the hole in the wall along with what few patrons have survived the carnage. "Where do you think you're going?" he shouts. The mech's kneecap opens up, and a heat-seeking missile launches from the ordnance bank inside. Synric diverts his path, diving behind a pillar. The missile collides with the structure as it attempts to follow Synric, blasting it apart. The roof groans in protest as yet another one of its supports crumbles. "I said stay still, you freak!" Kruger barks. Another missile in the bank primes to fire before Synric turns and locks eyes with the furious gang leader.

"What?" Kruger grumbles. Before he can fully turn, the gargantuan wyrm strikes the leg of his mech with the full force of its coiled body. Ghoma laughs as she skitters up the serpent's back, clearly pleased with her subordinate's handiwork. Somehow, Kruger manages to plant a foot in the ground and avoid toppling completely. But Ghoma crawls rapidly up the back of his war machine with its eight long legs. "What in the hell is that!" Kruger screams in terror. He slams his fist onto his controls. The mech is electrified. Pale blue arcs dance across its chassis, sending any demons touching the robot into involuntary spasms. Odeus, having avoided the countermeasure, initiates a forward charge and leaps towards the pilot seat, propelling himself forward with his wings, snarling triumphantly as he latches

295

onto the roof of the mech. The moon glows a pale red behind him as he smiles madly at the hapless gangster.

"What kind of freak show is this!?" Kruger yells. Ghoma licks her lips after the electrical charge and advances towards him as Odeus circles behind her and slides his hands up her waist, cupping her breasts. Kruger recoils in shock, preparing for their attack, but instead Odeus spreads his wings and leaps into the air with Ghoma firmly gripped in his arms. The two take off into the night sky, disappearing within the city. Kruger scrambles to activate his minigun, but he's shaken from his chair as the wyrm constricts the mech's shins. Neon blue blood oozes from the mouths of the shrieking faces on its body, eating away at the robot's legs.

"What the fuck is going on?" Kruger screams, activating another burst of electricity and forcing the snakelike beast to let go. He looks back towards the massive hole in the wall left by his entrance, scanning for Synric, but the android is nowhere to be seen.

CHAPTER 15 - Surprise

A week has passed since the massacre at Club Nis. King and Synric have done their best to scrub the headlines and suppress word of mouth, but journalists like Mitt remain a thorn in their sides. Fortunately, for King and Synric, Cloud 9's efforts to cover up the incident have led most of Mitt's reports, even the footage he's released, to be dismissed as a prank at best or the ramblings of a mad conspiracy theorist with a science fiction obsession at worst. Odeus and Ghoma are still nowhere to be seen. They have, however, caught glimpses of the serpent creature pursuing Kruger. An especially destructive encounter ended in Kruger blasting the beast to shreds as he unloaded every scrap of ordnance his mech could carry into it at just outside point-blank range. His victorious howl lasted about seven seconds, after which the twitching masses of scattered flesh morphed into thousands of smaller, individual wyrm spawns that scattered and claimed the sewers as their new domain.

"So it continues to multiply itself. Wonderful," King observes, pinching the bridge of his nose.

"It didn't when I slashed it open," Synric points out. "Then again, it remained in one piece in that instance and to my knowledge, Ghoma hadn't used her powers on it until then."

"So it either has to be blasted apart completely, or the more we kill it, the more of it there will be. Or Ghoma can bestow powers on it somehow. Doubly wonderful," King laments.

"You are running out of time and most of this is no longer your concern." Synric insists. Not wanting him to worry about the horrors transpiring in the streets below. "You must make your final travel arrangements."

"At this point, I wonder if Clain will even make it here in time." King grumbles, staring outward at the tempest swirling his building. Tiamat is ever anxiously nearing its revival.

~~~

Back within the training grounds of Eagle's Equinox, Clain stands alone. Dawn lies asleep on a makeshift bedroll just outside its bounds. Both are covered in scratches and bruises. Some new, some almost a week old. The two have been sparring almost nonstop, running themselves ragged with fight after fight. Yet still sleep eludes Clain. He can't tell if the grim images flitting across his vision are mere hallucinations or very real taunts from the monster plaguing his thoughts. Rezeka's voice echoes from somewhere deep inside his mind, her singing reverberating and haunting the forefront of his consciousness as he struggles to parse reality through tired senses.

You came and put a curse on me...

Made from pieces of a memory...

I need you to try to understand...

It's not that I'm afraid, I only wish you stayed...

Clain drops to the ground, taking a knee before collapsing into a fetal position, stifling a scream through gritted teeth as tears fall. The muffled sound is enough to wake Dawn, who stands up, joints popping and cracking, and approaches his friend. He crouches next to Clain, placing a hand on his shoulder, feeling the man's body shake from the sobs.

"You don't have to try and hide it, man," Dawn reminds Clain. "I've already seen it. And I get it. More than you might think." Clain's shakes subside for a moment.

"You haven't felt it. I have. Twice."

298

"Maybe not exactly what you've been through, no."

"Then what the fuck are you talking about?"

"You think I haven't seen some shit as a Skip Hunter? *Done* some shit? I don't know what it was like to live through what happened to you. But I know guilt. Way the fuck too well." He steps away, crossing his arms. "Had my heart shattered as well."

Clain sits up, resting a hand on his right knee. A thousand-yard stare is plastered on his face as he watches the horizon.

"Ever see an ocean of souls before?" he asks.

"What?" Dawn replies.

"Ever see your dead girlfriend sing to a big fucking concert hall full of ghosts? All in some weird trance together? Reaching to the sky?" Dawn furrows his eyebrows as Clain describes the scene.

"Reaching for what?"

"Me."

A low rumble in the distance breaks the silence just as Dawn finishes mouthing, "The hell man..."

Clain is shaken from his memories. He sits upright. Anger creeps across his face.

"Honey. She's back," he says.

"Back?" Dawn asks. "What do you mean back?"

Clain shoots Dawn a quizzical glance.

"She left? Remember? A few days ago. Said she needed time on her bike."

"Yeah," Dawn acknowledges. "And?"

"You know as well as I do," Clain growls, climbing to his feet. "She looks just like Rezy."

"That's why you look so pissed? How's that her fault?"

But Clain is already storming towards Honey, grabbing a nearby water bottle and splashing the water across his face to clear away some of the grime that has caked on over the past week. His body has healed much already, but between the frenzied sparring and the full extent of the wounds that were there before that, there is far more left to be mended. He limps from the lingering pain.

"Come on, Clain!" Dawn calls after him. "Let's think about this. Grab a coffee first. Get all these bruises and bandages dealt with. Time and place bro, for real!"

"Time's now," Clain insists, not even sparing a look back. He fixes Honey with a deadly glare. "Who the fuck are you?!" he snarls at her.

"Whoa there, killer," Honey replies, raising placating hands. "Slow your roll for a sec."

Destruction flashing across Clain's eyes.

"Killer?" he asks, deathly quiet. His purple aura starts to flare. "Did you just fucking call me *killer?*"

"Uh…" Honey takes a step back as Clain closes the distance between them.

"The fuck did you mean by that?!" he screams. "Answer me. *Now!*"

"Clain! Lay off!" Dawn calls.

"What the hell is up with you!? Dawn?!" she pleads, looking towards the hunter for help.

"Swear to God, Clain! Back off!" Dawn warns.

"Why the fuck do you look like her!?"

Honey's eyes widen as she backs into her bike, the gap between her and Clain now too small for her to dive out of the way.

"Look like who?!" she pleads.

Clain grabs Honey by the shoulders, squeezing hard.

"Don't you dare bullshit me!" he roars. "You know exactly who! Answer me!" Clain releases his grip on Honey's right shoulder and clenches his fist, feeling himself losing control.

"You really wanna do this, Clain?" Honey asks. "I don't know what your problem is or who you think I am, but do you really want to hit me?" Clain snarls out a bull-like exhale, the knuckles of his clenched fist going white. "I'd look behind you first."

"Alright," Clain starts with a deadly laugh. "You really think that's-"

"Clain?" Fila's voice interrupts him.

Clain spares a glance over his shoulder. Fila, Mr. Le, and the rest are watching the scene play out, confused and horrified. Guilt hits him for a fraction of a second. That's all Dawn needs. Clain yells out in pain as Dawn wrenches his hand from Honey's shoulder. Before he can turn towards him, his vision is blurred from a palm heel strike to the face. A second strike to his shoulder leaves his torso open. He's on the ground from a heavy kick to the gut an instant after. Dawn pins Clain to the ground, his full body weight channeled through a crushing knee on Clain's sternum. Both his wrists are held in Dawn's grip.

"Clain. You need to the calm the fuck down. Now. Whatever this is, we'll figure it out. But you're not hurting her."

Clain bucks his hips and sends Dawn falling forward, yanking a hand free and socking the hunter in the jaw. He scrambles to his feet, scanning the crowd like a cornered animal. Dawn gets up, rubbing his face as he turns toward Clain.

"What, you catch feelings and now suddenly I'm the bad guy?!" Clain yells. "You'd rather simp than figure this shit out? You know I'm right about her!"

"You're the bad guy because you came at Honey out of goddamn nowhere. You think even one of us is gonna be on your side if you attack her? You're not thinking clearly."

"Why?"

"Because she's helped us both out. You know how this shit goes."

The looks of near betrayal on everyone's faces finally register in Clain's addled brain.

The Elder.

Honey.

Mr. Le.

Fila...

"Fuck…" he breathes. His voice cracks. "I'm…I'm sorry" he utters on a ragged exhale before collapsing to the ground, his aura vanishing. He shakily climbs to his feet, then musters all his remaining strength to run away.

Honey watches him leave, then turns to look at Dawn.

"What the hell was that?"

"Exhaustion. He hasn't stopped training. Hasn't slept for a week," Dawn replies. "Saw something that broke him. Hasn't been the same since."

"No shit…" Honey mutters. "Right after your big 'kiss and make up' drug trip, too. Nothing's ever simple, is it?" she says with a sad smile.

"Nope," Dawn agrees, wincing as he turns to look at her. He looks at the ground, then back up at Honey, rubbing at the back of his neck. "Hey, uh, you got a sec?" Honey raises an eyebrow and smirks. "Bandages?" she asks.

"Bandages." Dawn replies.

"You got it," Honey obliges, putting Dawn's arm over her shoulder and walking him to a nearby cabin. "You gonna explain any of that?" Dawn shakes his head and sighs.

"I can sure as hell try," he replies with a warm smile.

Before Honey can smile back, Mr. Le's panicked shout echoes over the compound.

"Fila! Wait!"

She's running after Clain.

Clain ran swiftly on instinct, his body screaming for rest but his mind running wild with shame, anger, and confusion. He dashed through the compound, weaving past junked equipment through the empty street, barely registering the shouts and calls after him. His breath came in ragged gasps, but his feet didn't stop. The pounding of his heartbeat drowned out all but the most primal thoughts—escape, run, get away.

How did it come to this? The question repeated in his skull, chasing him as much as his guilt. Honey's terrified face flashed in his mind, and with it, Rezeka's—haunting him, blurring together. He couldn't make sense of it, couldn't stop it.

Clain's vision wavered, the edges of the world bending like heat ripples off pavement. He staggered and nearly fell, catching himself on a wall, his fingers digging into the rough surface. He squeezed his eyes shut, trying to center himself, but all he saw was the dark silhouette of Rezeka, her voice whispering the same damn song he couldn't get out of his head.

You came and put a curse on me...

The sound of footsteps reached him, light and quick, approaching fast. He opened his eyes to see Fila closing in, her face a mixture of determination and concern.

"Clain, stop!" she called, breathless but steady. "You don't have to run!"

"I—" Clain faltered, glancing away. "I can't, Fila. I... I fucked everything up. I—"

"You didn't," Fila cut him off, standing firm in front of him now. "You're not thinking straight. You haven't for days. This... this isn't you." Her voice softened as she stepped closer. "But it's okay. You don't have to go through this alone."

Clain shook his head, backing away. "You don't get it. I almost hurt her—Honey. I was—" He choked on his words, fists clenched. "I don't even know who I am anymore."

Fila took a deep breath, her eyes never leaving his. "I do. You're Clain. And you're stronger than this. But you're tired, and you've been going through too much for too long. No one can do that forever."

Clain's body trembled as he looked at her, barely holding himself together. "I don't deserve to be here," he said, his voice cracking. "Not among all of you—"

Fila's hand shot out, grabbing his wrist firmly with her mechanical arm. "Don't you dare finish that sentence. We need you here. I need you here, man." She stepped in front of him, forcing him to meet her gaze. "You're not the monster you think you are. What you need is rest. And you're going to get it, even if I have to drag you back to your room myself."

Clain looked at her, emotions battling in his eyes—guilt, fear, desperation. "Fila…"

"What's going on, Clain?" Fila's gentle question pulls Clain's focus away from picking at his hand. His healing factor has worked against him. The cuts have sealed with the splinters still inside. A scowl sets in on his face.

"Not really a good time, Fila," he grumbles, picking at a bit of still-deadened skin before giving up and tearing it away with his teeth. He bites down again as the splinter pops up from the cut, spitting both on the floor.

"What was all that about? Why did you shout at Honey like that?" she asks calmly. "Help me understand."

"It's not your problem, alright? Just go be with your dad and the others. I'll be fine."

"Clain, you've avoided me since you got here. I mean, I totally get needing space and stuff…" Fila starts, rubbing at the back of her neck. "I mean, it's obvious you've been through a whole lot. You look so tired. But…I know this isn't totally fair to ask but I need the guy that taught me to be strong when things were tough, you know? We all need him."

Clain sighs as his expression softens.

"You've been through a lot too. I know that…But," Clain purses his lips, unsure how to make her understand. "Look, it's not something I can explain. If it was, it would mean you've lived through it, and that's the last thing I want for you. Ever. Alright? I just have too much going on to be that guy, right now. I'm sorry."

When he looks up at Fila, she is holding out her hand presenting something to him. An iridescent neon makeup compact sits on her palm.

"Remember this?" she asks.

"Your makeup mirror?" He shakes his head, his expression equal parts bewilderment and exasperation. "Why would I remember that? What about it?"

"Honey gave me a ride to school one day," Fila answers "I told her I thought it looked awesome and she said I could keep it." She presses a button on the side, and the compact pops open, revealing a mirror jaggedly cracked down the middle inside.

"It's broken?"

"Yep. I told my dad that it broke in my pocket when I was practicing nunchucks with my new arm. But that was a lie. And instead of throwing it out, I kept it," she smiles.

"Ok…" Clain prompts, his annoyance fading, if only from sheer confusion. "Why?"

"It makes me look how I feel, ya know?" She points the mirror at him, showing him his reflection. One half of the mirror has been shifted ever so slightly out of place by whatever cracked it in two. Two faces stare back. One he recognizes, and one he doesn't, angled just out of place, as if trying to peel away from the Clain he knows. He blinks away the image of Tia that shifts across the crooked reflection, shaking his head to rid himself of her figure. Fila leans forward, eyes wide with worry.

"Clain?"

Her question jolts Clain back to the present.

"Yeah. Yeah, I'm here," he reassures her, looking down at the floor and rubbing his eyes. "You said you lied to your dad. What did you mean by that?"

"Well," she begins, closing the compact and tossing it at him. Clain catches it in his palm. "I broke it on purpose. Then kept it as a reminder."

"You broke your gift on purpose? Thought you said it looked awesome," Clain asks.

"I thought it might be bugged."

Clain's head shoots back up. He locks eyes with Fila, suddenly more awake.

"What do you mean?"

"I saw you Clain, remember? You were falling from that building and then you looked right at me. And that weird rabbit I was holding. It felt like a dream, but it really happened didn't it?"

Clain's words fail him. The scene replays in his mind. The monsters of his premonition realm all watching him fall as Fila stood there, hand in hand with Tia. Seeing her in that moment gave him the strength to smash Synric to pieces and narrowly land on the ground safely. Then blackness. He had thought it was all a hallucination of the moment. Finally, he manages to speak, struggling to contain his frenzied mood.

"Fila," he starts, as carefully as he can manage. "Is there something you aren't telling me?"

"So it was real?" Fila begins to tremble, reaching her left arm across her body and gripping her right shoulder, struggling to contain her fear.

"I..." Clain goes silent again, grasping for the right words to explain. He finds none. "I don't know how to make any of it make sense. I'm sorry."

"I saw her too. Holding my hand."

Clain's vision goes black for a second as Rezeka's voice replays in his head. He shakes back and forth, sending it back to the recesses of his memory.

Get it the fuck together he scolds himself. You don't even know who she's talking about.

"Saw who?" he asks. The muscles in his forearms flex as he clenches his fists.

Tears well up in Fila's eyes.

"My...I saw my...my mom..." she finally manages. "I..." she chokes out a sob. "I...I-I-I used one of those FreqyD things and I saw my mom, Clain!"

Clain can barely keep his jaw from dropping.

Tia...he thinks, wondering why the monster would manipulate Fila with images of her mother in the same way she's slithering into his own dreams, searching for weaknesses, breaches in the barriers between this realm and Tia's.

"I saw you falling off the building," Fila continues. Her crying intensifies. Shakes wrack her whole body. I saw the moment

308

your arm was shattered and when you passed out in the middle of the road. My mother said she was showing me what life was like for you. That you were dangerous. And that I needed to stay away from you."

"Is that why you used it? The device?" Clain asks. "Too see your mom?"

Fila nods in silent apology. Clain nods back, urging her to continue. She describes in detail a series of events identical to his own memory of them. It is as though she witnessed them through his eyes, the memories transferred with perfect fidelity. His thoughts gravitate towards the yellow bunny she was holding.

"Baxter?" he asks quietly.

Fila perks up.

"From Bunny Boarders?" she asks, hope flashing across her eyes. "Yeah. I was holding him and I don't know why. My mom said he was for you and could save your life. Then right after she told me that you looked right at me, and then at him, and then you landed on that sewer hole thingy and destroyed that robot," she explains.

"You really saw all of that?"

"And then my mom took me to the other side of this hill to show me this beautiful singing woman, except..."

Clain's chest tightens. His eyes open as wide as possible.

"She was crying. I could see the tears on her face. In her makeup. She looked so sad."

"What else did you see?" Clain probes, his breath becoming shallow, almost hopeful.

"She was so pretty. She had, like, this purple hair. It was glowing within the smoke around her. And she was singing to all these people. And they were all kinda moving together in rhythm. Their hands all did the same thing. It was like a big wave. Like an ocean." Clain leans forward, desperate to hear more. "And then," Fila continues, "all this fiery smoke started coming out of the floor. There was a big cloud of it all around her."

"Was she saying anything? Could you hear her?" Clain urges, leaning forward.

"Yeah. She was singing about you. Like, maybe, to you? It was weird. It was like she wanted to go to you but she couldn't."

Clain kneels next to Fila, placing a trembling hand on her shoulder. His heart is pounding. "Please, go on. Tell me more about her," Clain encourages.

"Well," Fila continues, "That was when I noticed she looked just like Honey. But it wasn't her. I could just feel it. Like in her sadness." She takes another moment to gather her breath. "And then my dad ripped the headset off me and it ended." Clain's gaze returns to the ground as his own tears well in his eyes.

"Fila, I don't know what to say," he mutters, dumbstruck.

"I was freaking out after. I thought that seeing Honey when I wore the headset meant she'd bugged the mirror somehow. I don't know. I just got scared and suspicious and I felt like something was watching all the time or maybe listening. So I figured there was a hidden mic or something in this mirror, and I broke it." She takes a breath. "And there wasn't one. So now I just feel bad when I look at it. Bad that I broke a nice present from someone who's been so kind to me. And then just now, you accused her of not being who she claims to be. And I thought about the mirror. That's why I'm asking what's going on." Her eyes scan Clain's arms, still marred with splinters and cuts. Still caked with dirt and blood. "Please tell me, Clain."

Clain looks up, sorrow written plain on his features.

"I can't, Fila."

"But Clain-" Clain interrupts, holding up a hand to silence her.

"It's not that I don't want to, Fila. I can't. There's no real way to make it make sense to anyone but me. Even to someone who's seen a piece of it like you have."

"You can't face all that stuff alone, Clain! I know you're planning to go fight all of that scary stuff alone but, there are people here that care about you, that want to help you."

"Fila, you're still a kid. You only get to be a kid once and I really think you should focus on that. You know as well as I do that none of this concerns you."

"It does concern me! I'm concerned about you, you idiot!" she shouts.

"Fila. Seriously. I am not someone you should be associating with. Trust me, ok?"

"But Clain...I..." she starts to shake as her crying intensifies. "You taught me how to be brave! You taught me how to be strong! You can't just leave; that's not what you taught me!"

Silence hangs between them as words fail Clain yet again. He hangs his head as guilt washes over him once again. The sound of squeaking wheels and crunching gravel finally ends the painful silence. A utility cart. A voice echoes through the doorway.

"Yo! Trainer boy, you awake?"

Lenny? Clain thinks.

"I got something for ya!" the engineer shouts again.

Fila sighs.

"I'm not letting you leave just to go die," she says. "So don't even try."

Clain dusts himself off as he rises back to his feet. He pulls the hoodie from his shoulders over his head. Hoping to hide his injuries and walks towards the approaching vehicle.

"Clain!" Fila shouts after him. "You heard me, right?!"

Clain spares her a backward glance.

"I'll think about it," he grumbles. She sidles up next to him, and the two walk towards Lenny's cart. A massive object sits atop it, covered by a heavy tarp.

"I fixed her up!" Lenny announces. With a proud flourish, he yanks the tarp away, revealing a perfectly restored Motherboard. The cracks that once marred the blade have been filled with vibrant colors. Some sort of heavy adhesive polymer by the looks of it. If anything, it looks more spectacular for having been damaged and rebuilt, not less.

311

Lenny beams with pride as Clain and Fila marvel at his handiwork. "She's a beaut ain't she?" he gloats with a crooked smile.

"Oh my gosh! That's so cool!" Fila shouts, clapping her hands and running up to inspect the massive sword. "You actually used that crazy stuff!?" she asks, her eyes wide with wonder as she reaches out to touch the blade.

"Hey!" Lenny snaps, swatting Fila's hand away. She pulls her hand back and rubs it with an indignant pout. "Don't touch! Ain't even sure if it's completely dry yet."

"What stuff?" Clain asks. Lenny chuckles nervously.

"Heh. Well, yeah. Fair warning: Dawn ain't gonna be too happy about this. But the shit was just sittin' in my shop doin' nothin' so I figured I oughta put it to use. Save some time getting this thing in fighting shape again."

"The nano glue!" Fila explains.

"Nano.. Glue?" Clain asks.

"Yep. Dawn brought it with him about a year ago. Client who hired him for a hit job didn't have the cash to pay him, so he offered him this. What you're lookin' at is a special state-o'-the-art adhesive. Stuff's laced with nanobots. Can even program the microscopic critters. So I tuned 'em to work with the system you built into your sword." Clain's eyes widen as he perks up.

"Wow. Really?"

"Yep. Gotta say, I was pretty proud of your data system. Glad some of what I taught ya stuck." Lenny jabs Clain playfully on the shoulder. "Never thought you was listenin'."

Clain smirks at the compliment.

"Thanks. Did it come in handy or something?" Clain asks.

"Sorta, but I had to clean up some of your code. Too easy to crack so I gave it some flair. Bet you'd hate having this thing remotely hacked while you were flying around on it, wouldn't ya?"

312

Clain's mind goes back to riding the rails out of New Beam City. He shudders at the thought of the Motherboard being taken from him.

"No I would not, Lenny. Good lookin' out. The Motherboard looks amazing!" he gushes. "Seriously, thank you. I can't wait to try it out."

Lenny cringes.

"Uh, like I said there, Clain, I don't even know if that glue's dry. Ain't never used it before today. Hang tight before trying anything," he urges.

"Oh, uh, yeah. Makes sense. I'm probably still too spent to lift it anyway, honestly," Clain says, unable to hide his disappointment.

"Can't believe you can lift that thing at all." Lenny musters his best sympathetic look, but then suddenly perks up. "Oh! Wait, though. I do think these'll do ya just fine in the meantime." Lenny reaches underneath his cart and pulls out a large duffel bag, placing it on the ground and retrieving two expertly restored metal gloves: Buster and Banger. An eager smile spreads across Clain's face at the sight of his old friends.

"No way! B&B too?! I don't know how to thank you, Lenny. I can't believe you did all this so fast!"

"Well I tell ya, a little bit ago, it wouldn't have been possible. But Dawn spoiled me with these new machines we got. Shit's easy now. But 'fore ya slip them bad boys on, gotta walk you through a coupla things."

"Oh, sure!" Clain says. "Like what?"

"Well for starters," Lenny begins, turning the gloves around and allowing Clain to see inside. Thin streaks of colorful material fill some hairline fractures Buster and Banger sustained earlier. "That nano glue's in these puppies, too. Lot less of it though. Should be all good and dry. Did a couple stress tests to make sure. But the important thing is this: 'Member how I said you could program the little robots in the glue? Well, I synced 'em up with that sword of yours. Should make it a lot easier to lift and swing that monster." Clain's jaw drops, he reverently takes them from Lenny's hands and inspects them. He notices a small LED sunk into the wrists.

"What's this?" he asks. "This wasn't here before."

"Well," Lenny begins, a nervous twitch on his face. "That right there's courtesy of the nanobots. Side effect of 'em merging with your system is a new feature I call 'overcharge.' Buster and Banger can store even more energy now, built up over time still. Suck up kinetic power from blows you take, maybe even take in some of that purple glow you got now. Important thing is, once that bar's full, it can explode all that back out. So, you know, watch that bar because when it's full...BOOM!"

"Awesome," Clain grins.

"Awesome? Damn thing might kill ya!" Lenny stresses.

"Or do just the kinda damage I need," Clain says, his smile growing even more.

"Hoo boy," Lenny sighs. "I'd say you haven't changed a bit, but you just mighta gotten more reckless. Didn't think that was possible. Look, just be careful ok? I put a lotta work into that hardware for ya."

"You got it, Lenny," Clain promises. How empty that promise might be remains to be seen. "

Fila, try that thing you did before, when you got into my comms." Lenny requests.

"The remote hack? I'll get in, easy," Fila obliges, eagerly clenching and unclenching her robotic fist. She holds out her palm towards the sword. It begins to glow. A confident smile spreads across her face. And then the arm sparks and she's knocked backward onto the ground. "Ow! What gives?!" she demands. Lenny lets out a triumphant laugh.

"See, told ya! Ain't gotta worry about remote hackin' no more, especially from those fancy Cloud 9 scripts."

Fila frowns as Clain chuckles.

"Guess I don't need to worry about anyone calling me when I'm out in the field anymore."

314

"Real funny." Fila rolls her eyes and crosses her arms.

"Hey now, don't frown. We got somethin' for ya too little girly." Lenny climbs back onto his cart, inviting Clain and Fila aboard. "Both of ya get up here. I'll give ya a ride."

"Sweet! Where are we going?" Fila asks excitedly.

"Nothin' special. Just figured you were both hungry so taking you by the kitchen to grab a bite before you both get some rest."

"Rest? It's like 6pm!" she complains. "I'm not even tired yet."

Lenny nods his head over his shoulder toward Clain. She looks at him as he yawns and rubs his eyes.

"Right," she grumbles. Lenny turns the cart down the next alley.

"Oh hey, it's my noodle shop!" Fila exclaims proudly. Clain smirks and messes her hair.

"*Your* noodle shop?" he teases. Fila swats his hand away and sticks her tongue out at him as she tries to put her hair back in place.

"Yeah," she declares. "I cleaned it up to surprise my dad." Clain chuckles, smiling warmly.

"You're a badass little kid, you know that?" he asks. Fila messes his hair back and sticks her tongue out at him again.

"Yup," she replies, a victorious smile on her face. Fila's brows furrow when she looks at the shop. The lights are all off.

"No one is even here?" she asks Lenny as the cart comes to a stop.

"Yep," Lenny confirms. Your pops asked me to bring you by to grab your meal before you came back to your quarters. Said it was on the counter along with Clain's. Can you guys run in and get it?"

"Come on, Clain!" Fila insists. "I've been so excited to show you this!"

"Wait a second, wasn't this the old Souper Soup place?" Fila beams with pride as realization dawns on Clain.

"Uh-huh!" she says, pointing above herself. "See the new sign? Goldi helped me get it all stocked up for Daddy, too!" Clain's eyes follow and see a brand-new placard affixed to the wall: Pho King. He smiles at the memories of the old restaurant. "Come inside!" Fila urges, tugging at Clain's hand. "I cleaned it all up and made it nice again!"

She reaches for the light switch and flicks it on. The second the lights flicker to life, a chorus of voices cheer.

"SURPRISE! Happy Birthday, Fila!"

Mr. Le stands at the front of the group of partygoers, holding a cake. Honey and Dawn stand to either side, while the Elder, Cato, and Goldi sit at a nearby table. Everyone is smiling, eager to see Fila happy.

"You didn't think I would forget, did you?" Mr. Le asks.

Fila starts to laugh, tears falling as a grateful smile spreads across her face. She lunges at her father and wraps him in a tight hug. Mr. Le barely manages to hold the cake steady. He smiles thankfully at Honey as she quietly, deftly takes the cake from him and sets it aside.

"Thank you, Daddy," Fila says, her voice muffled as she melts into Mr. Le.

CHAPTER 16 - A Message

Clain steps into the party cautiously, nodding to Mr. Le with a smile, assuring him everything was ok. He attempts to avoid making eye contact with Honey, who was already eyeing him and assuredly wanting some sort of explanation for his anger earlier. Lenny makes his way in behind them, placing a little boombox down on the ground. He fumbles with it for a moment as the music begins to play.

"Shall we sing?" he asks with a clap of his hands.

Honey begins to sing the first few lines of "Happy Birthday," inviting the others to join. Clain freezes, rooted to the spot as he listens.

She sings just like Rezy, too.

"Let's eat!" Mr. Le declares. The rest of the proceedings fade in and out of Clain's awareness as Honey's image shifts from singing a birthday anthem to singing a mournful dirge to an audience of ghosts. He can barely taste his food. Hardly make out the conversations and laughter surrounding him.

"Hey," a familiar voice greets him. Honey sits next to him. He rubs his eyes, no longer staring into nowhere, but rather right at the face of his dead ex-fiancé. She's holding out a cold beer. "Peace offering. Let's talk, yeah?" she offers. Clain wordlessly takes the beer and sets it down. He takes a small sip, hoping maybe the alcohol will make it easier to look Honey in the eye. He chugs the rest. It doesn't help. Honey smirks and raises an eyebrow. "Need more?" Dawn grimaces.

"You sure that's a good idea?" he asks her, gently clasping her shoulder.

"I'm right here, Dawn," Clain reminds him, glaring jealous daggers at Dawn's protective hand.

317

"Guys," Honey admonishes. "For the love of God, stop. I need at least one of you to tell me what the hell is happening. I'm not keen on almost getting my face caved in for no reason, and I'd *really* like to believe there's a good explanation for what happened earlier. Now one of you: Start talking." Dawn opens his mouth. Clain puts up a hand to stop him.

"I got it. Just give me a sec."

He returns a moment later with another beer. It's empty before he even sits back down. He throws the bottle away, staring at Dawn pointedly as he does. He turns to look at Honey with a deadpan expression.

"You have my dead fiancé's face." Honey's eyes widen and she leans away slightly.

"I'm sorry, what?"

"My girlfriend, my fiancé, died in a fire. Years ago. Heard her dying screams. All coming back to me. Yet here you are. You look just like her. And because life's a raging bitch like that sometimes, you *sound* just like her too."

She looks to Dawn for confirmation.

"Yeah, you do," he replies. "I've seen her."

"You've met?" she asks.

"Not per se, no."

"Then…how do you know?"

"Well," Dawn begins, "basically there's a training exercise we were taught here. Involves linking our minds. You can train and even fight within your thoughts and save your body's strength. Turns out doing that while high was a whole new trip though."

"Why the hell would you-" she starts, incredulous.

"Elder's whisky was spiked," Clain answers.

"The Elder? That man…" Honey shakes her head, looking over toward him while he boisterously laughs with Goldi and Mr. Le.

"Anyway, now I know what it's like to live out someone else's PTSD flashback," Dawn finishes. "And yeah, I can confirm what he's saying. 'Spitting image' is almost an understatement."

"Her name was Rezeka," Clain adds.

"I'm sorry, Clain," Honey says. "I wish I knew what to say."

"You could start with what the fuck you're doing in my life?" he growls. Trying to keep his voice low enough not to draw attention from the others.

"Excuse me?"

"You heard me. You show up, you make yourself useful, get Fila to love you. Then get Dawn here making doe eyes-"

"Clain, fuck off with all of that," Dawn warns. "Now."

"What, you're telling me something doesn't seem off? This famous stranger shows up, makes friends with everyone who matters to me, and just *happens* to look *exactly like* Rezeka? That's not even considering the fact that all the fucked up shit I've had to deal with lately *all* traces back to Cloud 9." He turns and jabs a finger in Honey's face. "Where *you* work."

"Oh not this shit again," she rolls her eyes and starts to walk towards the door.

"I'm with her, dude," Dawn agrees, following after.

"Yeah, bet you are," Clain mutters.

"Everything ok out here?" A warm female voice calls over to them just as they pass through the front door. They turn to see Goldi holding a large contraption in her arms. "Y'all need to get on back inside, it's picture time! Got out the vintage camera for the occasion!" she declares, proudly displaying the massive polaroid. With forced, reluctant smiles, Dawn and Honey agree. Clain looks over toward Fila, knowing this moment should be hers and obliges. "That's it," she declares, waving them inside with a toothy smile. "Get on in here!" Within minutes, the whole party has gathered, Fila beaming at the front as she hugs her father. "Dawn, scooch over closer to Honey. You two look so good together!" Goldi urges.

Clain does the best to grit his teeth during perhaps one of the most cringe moments of his existence. His exhausted body and mind can't muster to hide his scowl as Dawn obeys. Goldi's repeated reminders to smile seem to suggest that "best" isn't quite good enough.

"Alright!" she decrees. "Now my camera has a magic power: Nobody can ever be unhappy in any picture it takes. So y'all smile and say cheese!" Goldi's directions, the flashes of her camera, the drone of the device printing out the photos, all of its blends together for a few excruciating minutes. Finally, to Clain's relief, she seems satisfied. "Aww!" she cries, grinning at the last printout as she shakes it to help it develop. "Now that there's a picture of a perfect birthday! Come look! Just see that…wait…" Goldi squints at the picture. "Now what in the world…" Fila walks up to her.

"Can I see!? Can I see?!"

"Sure," she says, her brows still furrowed as she warily regards the last photo before handing it off. Fila's eyes widen in fear. Floating just behind the group is an unmistakable, stark white lowercase "i." with an encapsulated silhouette of a human figure holding their hands upwards as if to say, "Surprise!" The bright, cheerful smiles of the group were overshadowed by the figure lurking behind them—an ominous silhouette, obscured by the strange "i" symbol floating boldly in the background.

"What's wrong?" Clain muttered as he huddled behind Fila with Dawn.

"No.. I know that symbol! It's the Illuminaries!" he shouts, looking to where it would be standing.

Before he could react further, Dawn was already moving, his eyes narrowed, all of his instincts kicking in at once. He had spotted it too. With lightning speed, he reaches to his waist, unlatching a tomahawk ax and hurls it across the room. The sharp blade whistles through the air, and within seconds, a loud *thud* echoes as the invisible mannequin flickers into sight, the ax embedded in its chest.

The party let out a mixed reaction of shrieks as they all stared at it in fear, the joyful atmosphere crumbling into shocked silence. Fila's face went pale, and the photo in her hand slipped from her fingers, as her birthday moment turned into a nightmare.

"What the fuck?" Honey gasped, backing up toward the wall. Mr. Le immediately rushed to Fila's side, his eyes in alarm.

Clain moved swiftly, yanking the tomahawk from the fallen mannequin. The digital camouflage flickered for a moment longer before fading entirely, leaving a lifeless figure in full view. It was eerily human-like, the blank digital face an unsettling mockery of a person. It crumbled into pieces as the chest sparked and the face mask began to laugh. But what caught Clain's eye was the small disc embedded in its chest, pulsing faintly with a red glow.

Kneeling down, Clain presses his fingers to the disc. The lowercase "i" on it is indisputable, and the moment he touches it, the pulsing intensifies, followed by a soft *click*. A holographic projection flickers to life, casting an ominous red light across the room.

A distorted voice emerges, smooth but dripping with malice.

"Greetings, to those who take solace within these walls. Consider this a personal update on life within New Beam City."

Everyone froze as the message continued, the hologram revealing a dark figure, its features obscured but its intent clear. A tall, lanky Illuminary stood before them within glitching holographic light.

"You may have thought you could hide from us, but we are everywhere. Watching. Waiting. Your resistance is futile. Cloud 9 was only the beginning. We will initiate our end goal and you Clain, are still the catalyst. Enjoy your party, little warriors. It will be your last moment of peace."

Clain clenched his fists, rage bubbling up beneath his skin. "They were here. Watching us the whole time."

Dawn stepped forward, pulling his ax from the mannequin's chest and wiping it clean on his sleeve. "Looks like we just became a much bigger target."

"How did they find us?" Clain charges his aura. Wisps of violet energy curl off of him as he furiously scans the area. The crowd parts nervously. A cold breath hits his right ear.

"I wonder if they know what's got you so upset, Clain." A wicked whisper follows the breath, and he roars, swinging in its general direction.

"Fuck you!" he shouts.

"Clain…" Honey says shakily. He ignores her and looks to Dawn.

"They're still here," Clain says.

"Shit…" Dawn replies. "Everyone, just stay calm and stay out of the way. There'll be time to explain later,"

"At least one of you has some composure," the voice taunts again.

"Shut up!" Clain screams back.

"Dawn do we-" Honey starts.

"No." Dawn interrupts.

"So someone's really here," she realizes.

"Yeah. Get the others out of here. Now."

Lenny and the Elder follow suit, the former grabbing a gun from his utility cart.

"Doubt the old man would do much good against us. Even with that little piece o' his," the whisper comments, mocking Lenny's accent. "Want to find out how long they'd last?"

"I will make you suffer," Clain snarls.

"Now now," the voice warns. Clain's vision suddenly goes infrared. A number of floating white letter "i's" project onto the walls and ceiling of the room. "That's no way to keep your very vulnerable friends alive. It's like it always is Clain. Now if you really value their lives, if you really want to prove to your charred crisp of a fiancé whose doppelganger is eye fucking your so-called 'bro' that you're not the psychotic killer she thought you were, you'll listen to what we have to say."

Clain's aura fades. He lowers his fists.

"Spit it out!"

"You are wondering, 'how did they find us?'. Well to answer that, I would suggest for you all to take better care of Fila. For it was her hidden stash of FreqyD that led us to you, so per usual your negligence has its uses."

Clain's fist tenses as his aura starts to glow again.

"Go right ahead, Clain. Destroy the projector. See what it accomplishes. Our message will get to you one way or the other."

"What's the damn message?"

"Control your soul's desire for freedom."

"The fuck are you talking about?"

The Illuminary activates a holographic news feed. Familiar images of the riots surface. As people rampage through the streets unleashing carnage a thousand fold. Rioters and panicked civilians are mowed down by the gatling guns atop armored police vehicles, while others are torn apart by teeth and claws by beings not clearly seen in the footage. Children cry for their parents, some having been separated from their families, others hunched over their corpses before being slaughtered on top of them. A message blares through the streets:

"RED ALERT: Remain inside until further notice. You will be shot on sight. Control your soul's desire for freedom."

"It's as they say. Freedom from the inevitable is a futile pursuit. Your soul's drive to attain it will be your undoing as it is rapidly becoming theirs. As it will become that of those just outside."

More footage plays. A familiar madman in a mech suit, cackling psychotically as he spurs what few citizens remain to wreak all the more havoc.

"Kruger?" Clain mutters.

"Ah. You know him then," The Illuminary replies. "Useful, that one. Short-sighted. Reckless. But useful."

Clain grits his teeth, fighting back tears. His voice breaks.

"Why are you showing me this?" he asks.

"Six forces vying for dominance," the Illuminary explains. "Soon to be winnowed to four. First, the common man, weakened by a pathological craving for safety. Guppies swimming in a sea of sharks. Second, the police. Assumed protectors. Supposed servants. In reality, captors, kidnapping society block by block as they mechanize. Third, the Pit Pigs. Self-styled anarchists so nearsighted they can't even see their fundamental lack of vision." It pauses a moment as the footage transitions to a wide shot of the city, focusing on the skyscraper at its center. "Fourth, Cloud9. Dictators of destiny. More specifically yours, Clain." The camera pans, focusing on a figure standing at the top of the staircase leading to the building's entrance.

"Synric…" Clain realizes.

"Indeed. Enjoy the show."

Synric stood at the top of the Cloud 9 building's steps, the cold, calculated android gazing down at the large crowd of angry citizens and Pit Pigs. The mob was shouting and demanding entry, hurling obscenities, but Synric remained unmoved—his face a blank, emotionless mask. His eyes methodically scanned the crowd, left to right, assessing the situation. With a single step forward, the tension in the air thickened as the mob turned its attention to him, raising their weapons in unison.

One of the Pit Pigs grunted, squeezing his trigger and sending a wild barrage of gunfire spraying across the stairs. The bullets ricocheted upward in a frenzy, sparks flying as they met the shimmering energy barrier surrounding Synric. Seeing this, the rest of the group opened fire, filling the air with deafening noise. But Synric continued his slow, deliberate descent, undeterred by the hailstorm of bullets.

With a fluid motion, Synric swiped his arm across his chest, summoning an energy-emitting katana that hovered momentarily before him. As the bullets clanged harmlessly off his shield, a sharp whirring sound cut through the chaos—the hum of Synric's hand gripping the blade's hilt.

In a flash, he moved.

Synric exploded forward, becoming a blur of slashing steel as his katana cut through the crowd with wicked precision. He leaped,

324

landing lightly on the barrel of a thug's machine gun like a stepping stone, vaulting over him and driving his blade into the chest of another. The man's rifle flew into the air, and Synric snatched it mid-flight, spinning with lethal grace. He held down the trigger, spraying the surrounding thugs in a deadly arc before tossing the rifle aside, now empty.

Without missing a beat, Synric released the katana, allowing his momentum to propel him forward. He wrapped his leg around the throat of a nearby thug, snapping his neck with ease. As he landed, he spun fluidly into a crouch, bullets still raining down on him. But with a single burst of energy, his shield reflected the gunfire back at the mob, dropping bodies in a red mist.

Synric rose, walking calmly back up the steps as more Pit Pigs rushed him. His hand reached for the katana once more, and in a swift, violent arc, he swung the blade behind him, sending bodies flying through the air like ragdolls.

With another flicker, Synric seemed to glitch, vanishing in a blur as the camera struggled to keep up with his speed. It finally caught him perched on the side of the Cloud 9 building, where Pit Pigs were grappling up the side of the building, desperate to breach the upper floors while they thought the android was distracted.

They were wrong.

A flash of steel cut through the air as Synric severed a climbing rope, slicing a Pit Pig clean in half. His body tumbled downward, his screams echoing into the distance. Synric launched himself toward another thug, his blade skewering the man against the concrete wall. With a swift yank, he freed the sword, somersaulting off the limp body and into a rapid series of slashes, cutting through Pit Pigs as they climbed.

Screams of terror filled the air as ropes were severed and bodies plummeted to the ground below. Synric locked eyes with one of the thugs, plunging his blade into his chest mid-air before backflipping off his body in a spray of blood.

Synric landed without a sound in front of the glass doors to the building. Just as he stepped forward, a loud *bang* rang out. An

RPG flew toward him from the street with blinding speed. Synric glanced over his shoulder, watching the rocket as it exploded into a massive fireball upon impact.

The smoke cleared slowly, revealing Synric—completely unphased—his cold eyes fixed on the hulking mech responsible for the attack. It was Kruger, his massive form bristling with rage as he realized Synric had just slaughtered over a hundred of his men in mere seconds.

But Synric, unfazed by Kruger's fury, turned away, vanishing into the darkened lobby of Cloud 9 as an energy field rose, sealing the building from further attack.

The messenger kills the feed.

"I hope you see now that Synric has always held back against you," it says. "Alarming, isn't it? Just how much faster do synthetic beings evolve? I doubt even that display does it justice. We've been at war with it for years, and we're still unsure we know everything."

"Why the hell should I care? Maybe I do nothing, let you sick fucks do the world a favor and end each other."

"Maybe you do and maybe we will. But we've been studying you, Clain. All we do is in indirect service of your potential. I doubt that delicate conscience of yours has the fortitude to stomach the collateral damage that would cause."

"Fucking hell, what do you want with me?!" Clain finally snaps.

"Ah, there's the question. Very well, we've had our fun. But we'll answer a question with a question."

"I swear to God…"

"Relax. Just indulge us. Your mind. Your heart. They reach for the dead, yes?"

Clain steps forward.

"Don't you speak her name. Keep her name out of your mouth."

"Like I said, we've had our fun. Just listen. You're cursed. Do you understand? We desire a world where the living shall envy the dead. A perfect, Earthly hell. You're just the right kind of unfortunate to make that happen. And that brings us to The Fallen."

"The Fallen?" Clain asks.

"You've met one already," the messenger answers. "You should know. You helped summon it. It walked right up to you. Wanted to serve you back in the parking garage remember? Their very existence relies on your belief and awareness of their reality. Once we showed you one of their lesser forms, you allowed us to tap into a whole new level of frequency, empowering us to bring them forward. Allow me to show you. Your blood was the key, hence their puppy dog loyalty to you. We possess doorways for you to meet all sorts of new friends!"

The Illuminary turns the holo feedback on, cycling through footage of the otherworldly abominations rampaging through New Beam. The spider queen Ghoma, the horned devil Odeus, a wyrm swarm as well as another massive beast chained to the ground restrained. Clain's stance falters with each new beast he's shown.

"Xialos there is quite a nasty one." The Illuminary snickers with pride jest. "Of course, we do have competition. And unfortunately, I don't just mean Cloud9. Oh no. This is something much worse." The feed shifts to that of a drone struggling to maintain its flight path amidst a violent storm. Lightning cracks across the sky, thunder booms, wind threatens to rip the propellers off the robot. A shimmering blur of swirls at the center of the screen, soaring around the Cloud 9 building. "This is the closest we've been able to get. The storm there is far too violent, wrecking our hardware before we can get a good look. Tiamat seems the type to value her privacy. This beast, you may already know perhaps?"

"Tiamat…" Clain whispers.

"Yes, Clain. You had a hand in her reincarnation too, you know. She's most grateful. As we understand it, she even allowed you to call her by a nickname when you knew her. Tia, if I'm not mistaken."

"How is this happening?" Clain asks, breathless.

327

"Your answers await you atop Cloud 9, Clain. As we've always said. As we say now. There is still a wildcard in play, however. A seven of aces, perhaps. Any ideas what that might be?" it smirks.

"Please," Clain begs, "Enough with the riddles. Please just tell me what I need to know."

"Well… that would be you and your band of misfits there. How you will all respond to the world rapidly changing around you." Its arms widen in a bow. "And then that leaves us" it begins, but before it can finish, a tomahawk whistles through the air, landing square in the device. It shatters to pieces while the visor from the mannequin blinks rapidly with the letter i, then fading to black.

"Fucker talked too much," Dawn says.

"Fuck!" Clain shouts. "I still had questions, Dawn! What the-
"

Clain stops when he sees all of Eagle's Equinox standing behind the hunter.

"How much of that did everyone hear?" he asks. Fila speaks up.

"All of it."

CHAPTER 17 - Campfire Condolences

"You couldn't have landed this damn axe anywhere else but his torso?" Lenny grumbles, glaring at Dawn as he gathers the shattered fragments of the Illuminary's visor and loads them onto his utility cart.

"Wanted to end any possible signals it was sending out," he shrugs.

"Oh. You knew it wasn't human then?" Lenny asks. Dawn freezes, looking around at the group before realizing an awkward silence has settled in.

"Uh, yeah. Sure," he finally replies. Lenny shakes his head and gets back to work.

"Whatever. Was a good call. Just was hopin' to salvage more of this sick fuck. Figure 'em out. Don't need these little bastards makin' regular visits." He turns to Clain and clasps a hand on his shoulder. "Seems you got a lotta shit to deal with, young man. And we all need ya to deal with it. ASAP. If that means you need to leave, I'd start packin' 'fore somethin' else comes lookin' for ya and people get hurt. Got your sword all good and ready. Nanoglue should finally be set. Dropped it by that fancy car at the front gate."

"He can't go!" Fila protests. "You saw how dangerous it is out there! We don't even have a plan yet!"

"Fila," Clain interjects. "What makes you think you're coming with me? I can't let you out there. You said it yourself. It's dangerous."

"What?! No! I'm not letting you go alone!" she insists.

"Hey," Honey says, walking up to Fila and crouching to eye level with her. "You're right. It is dangerous out there. We all want him safe, too. We'll figure something out, ok? And so will Clain."

Clain sighs with relief, nodding gratefully to Honey. She smiles back, an uneasy smile, but a smile nonetheless.

"Prophecy is unfolding, boys" The Elder finally speaks up. "You must remember, not all is in your control, and not every friendship is worth keeping."

"Cryptic as ever," Clain reacts.

"Believe me I'd be clearer if I could this time," the Elder replies, tears welling up. "I'm afraid I'm as out of my league as you're assuredly feeling. Lenny? Would you mind helping me to my quarters?"

"Sure thing Elder," Lenny responds. He starts the engine and shoots a cold admonishing look Clain's way.

"ASAP," he repeats. With that, he and the Elder depart.

"Huh…" is all Dawn can manage.

"No shit," Clain agrees.

"We don't even know if any of that shit was real. Most of what was in that video could very well be fake." Dawn suggests.

"Well then, why don't we all take a breather and reconvene tomorrow?" Mr. Le suggests. "It is getting quite late and it is obvious we all need some rest. That means you too Fila."

"How is anybody going to rest right now?!" Fila cries.

"Think we have to, Fila," Clain says. "Can't make a plan when we're all tired." He sniffs his armpit and makes an exaggerated grimace. "Besides, I need a shower," he says with a goofy smile. Fila gives in with a laugh.

"Fine. But it is still my birthday, and you didn't get me a present!" she points at Clain, who drops his jaw and places his hand over his heart in mock offense.

"Fila, be reasonable please." Mr. Le places his hand on her shoulder. "He is going through a lot."

330

"All I want is for him to let his friends help! Promise me you'll let us help, Clain!" she shouts.

"Fila..." Mr. Le warns.

"You got it kid." Clain interrupts. He kneels down to meet her face to face. "Things are terrible right now, and you are always fighting for everyone to be happy. Thank you, Fila." He lifts his hand to fist bump hers. "I won't leave without your permission. Promise." He smiles.

She reciprocates, bumping him back before plugging her nose and waving her hand.

"Yo, you're right. You freakin' stink man!"

The group laughs as Clain's face flushes. He says good night to the group and heads for his quarters. As he reaches for the latch on the door, he hears the sound of it unlocking before he even touches it. He stares at his hand, wondering if he subconsciously manipulated the latch with his magnetism. The implications of not even being aware of his powers at work make him shudder, but he's too tired to think about it further.

A sense of calm and familiarity washes over Clain as he breathes in the familiar, dry air of his old room. He eagerly walks to the shower, sighing with relief as his muscles relax and a week of dried dirt and blood is finally washed away. Clain turns off the faucet and exits the shower. He wipes down the steamed mirror. In its reflection, he examines the scars crisscrossing his torso and limbs. He can't recall a time his body has ever been this sculpted. Or maybe he was just horribly dehydrated and lacking much needed sustenance. Either way, food won't go amiss.

As he towels off, he notices a neatly folded outfit on top of his bed, which has been immaculately made sometime during his absence. It's the rail runner outfit he used to escape New Beam. Mitt and Zaria's gift to him.

*Probably saved my life...*he reflects. *God, I hope they're alright. What a goddamn shitstorm.*

He reaches for the clean clothes. His hand stops when he notices a folded, handwritten note sitting on top of the clothes.

Elegantly scrawled across the front is: "To: Clain, From: Honey."
With shaking hands, he unfolds the paper to read what's inside.

Clain,

*Nice outfit! Would love to know where you got it. Hope you
don't mind but I patched it up. I want to be straight with you. Coming
at me like that was not cool. I was about ready to call it quits on you,
but I did some digging. Even if I might need some time to forgive, I at
least want to tell you that I get it now. When I was out biking, I found a
little signal oasis in the desert and took a sec to search for her. I doubt
you need me to go into detail about what I found - you've probably
relived it enough for ten lifetimes. But I do think you should know that
her name was scrubbed from the list of the deceased.*

*Whatever's been going on with you, I can tell it's got you
riddled with self-doubt, but I want you to know you have no reason at
all to doubt this anymore. She was real, Clain. Rezeka was real. And
you're not crazy for noticing my resemblance to her. We look very
similar. And I don't have any more of a clue why than you do. But I
want answers every bit as much, and more than anything, you should
never question her existence again because of me. Rezeka. Was. Real.
And I'm so sorry for what happened to you. It's a pain I can't even
begin to imagine.*

Clain's grip on the paper tightens. His jaw clenches. The
edges of the note crumple.

*Which will probably make this next part really hard to read,
but with everything that's been going on, all the danger we're in, I
think we need to be as honest with each other as we can. It would have
been too difficult for me to say this face to face so here it is. Something
has been brewing between Dawn and I. We have spent a lot of time
together and even though nothing substantial has happened, I just
don't know how to feel about this. I am not exactly saying that I have
feelings for the big oaf or something, but I can't say I don't either. I
just don't want any of this to be any harder than it already is. I know
this is unpleasant for you to hear given everything you're going
through, but it didn't seem right for you to be surprised by it one day. I
may look like Rezeka, but please remember I'm not her. We can figure*

332

this out, ok? I truly do want the best for you. I hope we can talk soon. Fight like hell.

-Honey

His heart sank. He had no idea why but his mind was already a mess of emotions. He had to ignore this, for now. He crushes the letter and tosses it to the corner of the floor. Stepping away to approach the only window the room had. The frigid night has coated the windows in a layer of frost. He contemplates leaving right now but his training gi won't be anywhere near warm enough.

Rail runner suit it is, he realizes.

He exhales as he opens the closet. The sleek cyber suit awaits him. Lenny had bragged about the suit a few weeks ago. It seemed like a novelty at the time, but he had no reason to doubt the man's words. The skintight suit is lined with metal threading; a new age chain mail with a twist. It is custom designed to sync up with the rail runner suit, providing a huge boost to physical defense while monitoring his vitals and controlling his body temperature.

He slides it on, skeptical. The suit is heavy, almost uncomfortably so, but fits flawlessly. It also feels cool as hell.

The last time he wore this outfit, his arm was shattered. He grimaces at the memory as he pulls on a pair of sleek black gloves. He rolls his shoulders, adjusting to the new fit while patting himself down and checking the pockets. Nothing. He has no idea how to start the suit up. Mitt turned it on for him last time.

Jesus, this is heavy. How am I supposed to fight in this?

"This shit isn't fully tested, Clain." A message from Lenny reads. "I didn't give a damn about puttin' in no proper message here so change it whenever you want. I reprogrammed the suit to fit your specific needs based on the battle data you recorded in Motherboard and your gauntlets. Snap them on for further instruction."

That's right! Clain remembers. *Lenny mentioned he made new versions of Buster and Banger!*

His eyes scan the room and land on a large box on the table near the door. He walks forward. The suit moves with ease now. He snaps the latch on the box, opening it to reveal the restored gauntlets. Lenny has transformed them into something Clain never could have hoped to forge only from the scrap he had at the GG Shop. They're almost unrecognizable. Sleekly painted and held together with that near magical nano glue.

His mind races with the possibilities of this new arsenal as he slides them over his hands. They click into place beautifully. He flexes both wrists, marveling at the flexibility and cleanness of the new fit. A message chimes out from his forearm.

"Good, you got them on. Now listen up, I took things up a notch obviously and what you need to know most is this whole getup is programmed to that magnetic frequency you output. In other words, it will act and react to you without you needing to constantly focus your mind on it. You might have noticed how much lighter it feels now that it's powered on.

I also took your specific frequency and amplified it. In short, your mega punches or whatever you wanna call them are all still there but now gather even more energy in the gauntlets while using Motherboard. Be careful though since this ain't had no proper testing. Now let's go over the new features. First off, I've implemented distinct stances, now read this carefully."

Clain hears playful laughter outside his quarters, drawing his attention away from Lenny's instructions. He steps quickly to the window, realizing as he does so that the glowing lights from the suit won't lend themselves to any kind of stealth. He frantically thumbs through the menus, swiping away Lenny's messages until he notices a light bulb icon in the top right. He presses it, immediately turning off the excessive RGB flowing up and down the outfit.

Why does it even have those… Clain wonders.

Pressing himself to the wall, he parts the curtains with one hand and peers out into the road.

He sees Dawn and Honey. Dawn has his arm draped over her shoulder, in obvious pain. He cracks a joke, then stumbles. Honey catches him, chiding his tough guy act with a playful admonishment.

They must be coming from the infirmary. Clain notices Dawn's bandages are no longer bloody. Honey must have patched him up again. Dawn laughs and raises his voice, only to be shushed by Honey. "Shh Dawn, seriously. People need their rest and you swore you'd behave if we stopped for a drink."

Clain notices a half empty bottle of whisky in Dawn's other hand. "Gimme a break, this is my home, ya know? With you and this bottle, all my pain goes away," he slurs. Dawn grips her shoulder, pulling them both to an abrupt halt. He lifts the bottle upward for a drink while Honey maneuvers herself from under the weight of his shoulder. She leans against the nearby wall.

"Seems like you're recovering quickly despite tearing your stitches open repeatedly," she rolls her eyes, watching him wipe his mouth like an eager child.

"The way of pain for someone will always bring them pleasure," he declares drunkenly. "Or something like that." He scratches his head, confused. "Can't remember who said it." He plants a hand on the wall just over her head and leans in. She gently places her fingertips on his bare abdomen, holding the distance between them. Her neck tilts, looking up into his eyes.

"Aren't you getting a bit close?"

"You're the sweetest woman I have ever known, Honey" he whispers into her ear before leaning in to kiss her. Just before their lips meet, she presses her index finger up under his chin, deflecting the kiss to her forehead.

"You're drunk, big guy. That liquid confidence is hitting you a little too hard." She slides out from under him and steps into the street, smiling with sly innocence. "A girl like me is going to take a lot more effort than that." She smiles. "But you can keep trying."

Dawn gently taps his fist on the wall, admitting defeat. "Fair enough, but I am persistent. When I know what I want, nothing will stop me." He leans back against the wall with a devilish grin.

Clain steps away from the window. He can't watch any more of this. Anger, shame, confusion, and grief flicker in his mind like devouring flames. It isn't fair. None of this is fair. He needs air. He creaks the door open and peers out into the street. Empty. They were gone. He steps out into the road, footsteps surprisingly soundless in the heavy suit. He catches a whiff of campfire in the cool night air. The sun will be up in a few hours. Now is his chance to leave quietly. There is one problem: he still needs to eat.

The campfire smell is coming from the inner courtyard, near where most of the cooking is done. He heads in that direction. Maybe he can grab something to go. He rounds the corner, raising an eyebrow at the unexpected sound of a harmonica. His curiosity grows as he continues on. A campfire comes into view, crackling near the community's lavishly old library. Goldi sits perched atop her travel wagon, playing the harmonica. She sways back and forth atop a pile of soft blankets as she plays a sad melody.

Just above the fire sits a steaming kettle of stew. Clain's stomach growls. He pauses momentarily, weighing his options. A quick meal with Goldi or taking his chances with the kitchens. His growling stomach makes the decision for him.

He steps out of the shadows and into the warm glow of Goldi's camp fire. Her eyes are closed and she seems not to notice him approaching. Clain moves toward the kettle, not wanting to interrupt her but driven by mounting hunger. He wipes the corner of his mouth with his sleeve at the sight of steaming potatoes, carrots, celery, onions, and chunks of fresh bison.

A metal ladle hangs on the side, tempting him to scoop out a large portion to pour directly down his gullet. *Maybe I can do this without making a sound...*

"Help yourself!" Goldi chuckles, startling Clain. "Don't forget the bread," she insists while tossing a warm dinner roll toward him. He catches the bread, smiling sheepishly.
"Thank you! Sorry, I was so damn hungry, but I didn't want

to disturb you." He reaches for the ladle. "It smells amazing. Now I know why the Elder likes you so much, it must be your cooking."

Goldi bellows a hearty laugh. "My bison stew has always been a community favorite, that is true darlin." She looks him up and down, examining his gear. He notices her curious gaze out of the corner of his eye, shoving a bread roll in his mouth to maintain an excuse not to answer questions. "There's water there in the pail," Goldi nods over to the nearby well with a bucket resting on the edge. "I reckon you're feeling mighty parched after scarfing all that down. Did you even breathe?" She winks.

Clain chuckles and wipes his mouth. "Guess I shouldn't skip meals, huh." He makes his way toward the well, scooping out water with a small plastic cup sitting beside the bucket. Goldi snickers at him. She stashes her harmonica away within her long trench coat, then thumbs through a digital screen on the mantle of her supply wagon.

"I reckon it's about time I hit the dusty trail," Goldi says with a sigh.

"Really? In the middle of night?" Clain asks.

"Yep! Fulfilled my obligations here and kept my promise to make sure you had a full belly before you set out." She stands and climbs into the driver's seat. Shortly after, two red eyed, robotic horse heads extend outward beneath her feet, lifting them into a comfortable sitting position.

"You knew I was leaving?"

"Not me. Elder said he was sure you'd be skedaddling' without saying bye to no one. He can't stay up so late these days but wanted me to make sure an' tell ya something. 'You're not fighting the armor. You're fighting the man.' he said. Whatever that means." she laughs.

"Uh, sure." Clain sighs, feeling a bit regretful that he had not planned to say goodbye to anyone. His words resonated however, knowing he was referring to his confrontation with Synric in the coming hours. He stretches his shoulders, feeling a sense of relief that

337

he wasn't the only one leaving in the middle of the night. "Which way you headed? North by chance?"

"'Fraid not. I ain't much for them big cities and from what I saw earlier, it's quite the war zone right now. Can't say I envy you." Concern pulls her cheerful mouth into a worried frown.

"A bit of advice, Clain." She pauses and flings her golden locks over one shoulder. "Now I ain't privy to these wild complexities you got goin' on with ya or what you might be facin', but I'll tell you one thing. Don't underestimate the young!" She places a Stetson on her head and tips the brim at him. "You gotta appreciate and find strength through them. They will always give you something to fight for." She smiles again before shaking the reins on her wagon. "Adios amigo, and nice to meet y'all!" she chuckles again as the wagon thrusts forward.

Meet y'all? She has met me before… What did that mean?

As his eyes follow Goldi's wagon into the distance, an LED glow flickers in his periphery. He turns to look, moving towards the source. Whatever it is seems to notice him and a rustling sound emanates from among a stack of boxes and debris. He stands, turning to approach it.

"Ok you caught me!" Fila steps out from the shadows. "These stupid lights…" she grumbles, fidgeting with her mechanical arm.

"Fila, seriously?" Clain groans. Goldi's farewell now makes a lot more sense, and he is not happy about it.

She points an accusatory finger. "I knew you would try to sneak away in the middle of the night! You promised you wouldn't do that!"

"You don't know what you're talking about." Clain grabs a poker to stab the dying embers. "There are things only I can deal with, and those things don't concern you."

"I just don't get it, do I? That's all you grownups say." Clain lets out an amused exhale.

338

"You're not wrong," he admits. "But I promise, this stuff is dangerous. I won't let you get hurt. This isn't me trying to be mean. This really is a 'less you're involved, the better' kinda deal. I mean that for all of you." She scowls skeptically before turning her attention to the sky.

"Wow, the North Star is bright tonight!" She exclaims. "It leads back to the city right?"

Clain glances up, a grudging smile lifting the corner of his mouth. "Yeah, it does."

"You taught me that, remember?" She pauses. "Or was that dad." She looks at him, her gaze intent.

"Doesn't matter. Just as long as you learn it."

"I guess. But where would I be without such awesome people to teach me things?" She playfully kicks the side of his boot.

"Fila, I can't teach you anything you won't learn better from someone else. Everything I can tell you, I've told you." He pauses. He looks away from her. "Except maybe: I'm everything I never want you to be. I know your dad's decision to kick me out hurt you. It hurt me too. A lot. But…" Clain flexes his fist, letting his power cast a violet glow over his hand. He looks at Fila sadly. "He was right. For your own safety, and his, you both need to stay far, far away from me." Clain stands.

"But you've changed. You're not a monster! I know you, Clain. I've known you for years now."

Clain shakes his head, unable to meet her gaze.

"That's exactly what I am."

She steps forward and grabs his hand.

"Not to me." Her grip on his fingers tightens. "We all fail, remember? And how we deal with failure is what makes us stronger." Her eyes fill with tears. "You taught me that, and you showed me how to be strong. I won't let you die alone."

"You have seen what I can do, right? I am not going there to die alone." Clain steps away from her, eyes lifting to the horizon. "I am going there for answers. I need to know who or what I really am. Most of all, I am going there to punish the pricks that caused all of this. But that's not your concern, and neither is what happens to me. Even if I do die. You and your father need to focus on yourselves. On building and living good lives."

"I would do the same." Fila admits. "I want answers too, from the same people."

"What do you mean?"

"Kiva wasn't real." She wipes her tears away angrily. "Cloud 9 gave me this stupid arm and sent that stupid cat just to watch us."

"Kiva.. Fila, I…"

"You didn't know how to tell me. I know." Tears still trickle down her cheeks, but her jaw is set.

On impulse, Clain pulls her in for a fierce hug.

She looks to the ground. She knew she couldn't force him to let her go with him. She admits defeat. "Give them hell for me, ok?" she sniffles, pressing her forehead into his chest.

"I will."

He pulls away from her, clasps a reassuring hand on her shoulder, then exits the courtyard. Sparing one last backward glance, he sees Mr. Le has come to comfort his daughter. He smiles.

"Stay strong you two."

CHAPTER 18 - Airways to Mayhem

The Motherboard sits proudly against the gates of Eagle's Equinox. The cracks in the once shattered blade glinting with color as the setting sun casts its light on the nanogel holding the sword together, coming to life as he drew near it. Having more control than ever, the excitement he felt was as palpable as the feeling of goosebumps inch down his forearms and up the back of his neck. The evening air was piercingly cold and the thought of flying back to New Beam City seemed dangerous when considering the temperature at higher altitudes.

His fingertips run gently across the cracks of his self-forged blade. He reaches for the handle, magnetically pulling into his palm, then effortlessly flinging it into the air. He catches it with a deft movement and rests the blade across one shoulder. The smooth maneuver is foiled slightly as he stumbles under its weight.

Forgot how heavy this thing is…

"Welcome Clain. Will you be departing?" A calm, digitized voice startles him. He whirls around, Motherboard at the ready. "Clain?" the voice repeats, finally drawing his attention to the right spot. He sighs with relief, relaxing his stance at the sight of the air ryder Mr. Le and Fila arrived in.

Just the onboard AI, he realizes.

"Uh, hello?" *How did the vehicle know my name?*

"Welcome Clain. Will you be departing?" It repeats. He slings Motherboard back over his shoulder, attaching it to a metal plate on his back.

"You know my name?"

341

"I do. I have been waiting for you," the car explains. "I am ready to depart as soon as you are."

Clain circles the car, examining its sleek black and chrome chassis engraved with elegant floral and vine motifs. His gaze lands on an unfamiliar insignia: A griffin.

"And where would you take me?"

"I am to offer you a return flight to New Beam City."

"A flight?"

"Correct."

"So, this is an air ryder car?" He asks.

"Correct. I am fully equipped for aerial travel exceeding one thousand miles per hour."

Clain's eyes widen.

"Ex...Excuse me?" he stammers. "One thousand?"

"Correct!" the AI replies cheerfully. "The owner of this vessel has prepared a message for you, hoping to offer you reassurance, should you require it. Would you like me to play it now?"

Clain weighs his options. He doesn't have many.

"Sure, play it."

A holographic video projects from the vehicle's roof. A man's silhouette faces away from him. The man's build is familiar, as is the tailored trench coat he wears. Sure enough, when the man turns, Clain is met with a familiar weathered face: King.

King exhales, looking tired and exasperated. "Clain, I know you have a lot of questions racing through your mind. It is time for you to get some answers." He rubs the back of his head, glancing away with another heavy sigh. "I can only imagine how frustrated you must feel, watching this recording of some stranger that wandered into your

342

shop one day and seemingly ruined your life. I don't know if I can make any meaningful amends." His voice breaks. "But maybe. Please, meet me in person. Cloud 9. Top floor. I will explain all I can. I hope my own vehicle providing safe passage to your friends is enough of a show of good faith that you'll heed my request. I hope to see you soon. And if you can help it, don't scratch the car. I'm especially fond of it."

Clain stands and listens, his hands clenched into involuntary fists at his sides. King's expression is pained as he continues.

"There is, unfortunately, a danger in accepting my invitation that I cannot do much about. Synric. I did create him, but his programming is rapidly evolving beyond my control. Like a jealous itch, he insists on challenging you yet again. Something about 'earning the right to walk these historic grounds.' I must ask that you honor this challenge. For what it's worth, I'm rooting for you. Some humbling would do Synric good. I can only stress just how valuable I feel the answers I have will be to you should you agree, and I implore you to do so."

He goes silent again, pacing back and forth. "I will be departing this world soon Clain. I have many loose ends to tie, and not enough time. I am not at liberty to explain everything in this message. We need to meet, face to face. That said, I can offer you this: you are not going crazy." The hologram flickers to a shaky wide-angle shot of a neon-lit penthouse. Amidst the flickering holograms and billowing clouds sits a rift in reality. Beside it, as if having emerged from within, is a five-headed dragon. Her scales gleam with an otherworldly sheen, reflecting the neon lights in mesmerizing patterns. Each of her heads survey the cityscape, five sets of gimlet eyes glowing maliciously as if already taking in the destruction she hopes to inflict upon New Beam. She unfurls massive wings, and the very fabric of cybernetic reality seems to warp and bend around her. She unhinges her jaw and unleashes a deafening roar, sending shockwaves through the city. The screen flickers again, phasing into a neon static blur as Tiamat's roar fades.

"What you just witnessed is a nightmare come true. Tiamat, mother of all dragons, is being reborn into our reality within the storm circling here around Cloud 9. Her rebirth is now inevitable, 87% complete as of this recording."

343

The footage flicks back to a close up of King's face. "I am responsible for all of this Clain, and now I need you to know why. Please hurry." The recording ends abruptly. Clain stands back, struggling to process what he has just seen. King, the dragon, all of it. The old man is right about one thing, however: they are running out of time.

The door of the air ryder hisses as it opens upward.

"Unlock the trunk," he orders. He retrieves the Motherboard from his back, placing the blunt of the blade across his forearms to inspect it.

Definitely won't fit...he realizes.

"Lenny claims you respond to the frequency of my thoughts..." Clain thinks aloud.

"User Lenny is not recognized in my system," the air ryder responds.

"No, not you." Clain grumbles. He closes his eyes to focus. The sword hums in his hands, clicking and shifting as it separates into pieces. He is pleasantly surprised with the ease of this useful new function as each piece floats forward to pile nearly in the trunk. "Well that was easy," he remarks, climbing into the rear seat.

"Shall we depart?" the car inquires.

"Let's go."

The vehicle begins to reverse quietly as its tires crunch along the gravel. A ten second countdown starts on a large screen on the interior of the cab while thick, sturdy harness straps roll over Clain's shoulders. The craft begins to rumble as the rear turbines whine to life. Four struts deploy from the undercarriage, springing the vehicle into the air. The wheels retract and the thrusters propel the ryder into the sky.

Clain sits back, enjoying the smooth ride. He has ridden in every ryder model on the market, but this is something else.

The craft enters a smooth cruising altitude. A GPS map loads onto the screen in front of Clain. The display estimated a flight time of fifty-seven minutes to arrival. "Fifty-seven minutes? We are less than eighty miles away. Why will it take that long?"

"A violent storm is surging within the city and there are unsafe conditions on the ground. We will navigate toward the rear of Cloud 9 and approach from a safer angle." The AI explains.

As Clain peers out the window, the mountains and desert blur together, their shades of sandy brown mingling with the vibrant oranges, yellows, and reds of the rising sun. He steadies his breathing as he watches it all, lulling his mind into a meditative trance.

"Would you like any in-flight food, beverage or entertainment?"

Clain's leg bounces vigorously. Nerves are setting in. He asks for the first thing that comes to mind.

"Got any whisky?"

A compartment to his left opens and a shot glass pops into a slot at his elbow. A bottle of vintage whisky slides out of a hidden compartment, and a large cube of ice drops into the glass. "Will that be all?"

"Sure." Clain reaches to pour his drink. "Well, actually can you show me the latest headlines from New Beam?"

The screen swaps to a BNN news broadcast. The ticker scrolling across the bottom of the screen reads, CHAOS AND CONFUSION CONTINUES.

The news anchor's professional facade is creased with worry as she speaks. "Officials have confirmed the citywide lockdown will remain in place indefinitely. We implore all residents this measure is in place for their own safety. A state of emergency is still in effect, and the dangers necessitating it have been described, among other things, as 'unprecedented.' Despite concerns over the performance and indeed the methods of local police in light of the recent riots and gang wars, a spokesperson for the mayor's office has stated that the department is

New Beam's best, and only, option for restoring order. Please remember to comply with all directives issued by your local law enforcement officers and most importantly, stay inside. Riot control units have been instructed to treat anyone seen violating lockdown protocols with extreme prejudice. BNN wishes all citizens well and encourages our viewers and everyone in the city to stay safe."

A video clip plays, showing a disheveled man in ragged clothes. His eyes are wide, almost hysterical as he rants at reporters behind the camera. "There are fuckin' demons out here, man! Ripped my friend apart and ate his insides! It's a war out here, and no one is on your side!"

"Sir, are these yours?" A reporter points to a small pile of used hypodermic needles near the man's foot.

"Fuck those!" the man screams, while kicking them down the street. "You ain't gonna spin this! You planted those there!" He struggles to catch his breath. He grabs the camera and looks into the lens. "The Pigs are back!" he yells. "They're fighting for our survival! Join us! Fight for Kruger!" He trips over his own feet as he stumbles backward, away from the reporter attempting to wrestle the camera back from him. He points at the air to something offscreen as he loses his grip and falls backward.

"I'd like to offer BNN's sincerest apologies for that disturbing display," the reporter remarks, straightening his hair after fighting with the homeless man. "As is becoming plainly obvious, substance abuse has also grown to historic levels amidst the lockdown. One more among a host of reasons to remain indoors. BNN implores its viewers to continue sheltering in place until the danger has subsided."

"Enough." Clain exhales, disturbed by the horror in the man's eyes. "Next channel." The screen flips to a popular music video channel, currently playing a grating pop song. What was that man pointing at? The footage cut off conveniently, but the man also name-dropped Kruger. Clain wonders how any of this is making it onto local channels. Is someone pulling strings at BNN? Could the Illuminaries be involved? Or even King and Synric?

A sudden heavy bass drop shakes Clain out of his thoughts. The artist on screen dances between scarlet waterfalls, her glittering bodysuit sequined in red like a thousand crystallized droplets of blood. She grins and capers, a beautiful devil beckoning any takers to hell.

"Next channel." He Clain says. This is the last thing he feels like watching.

"Is there a channel you prefer?" the AI inquires.

"Don't care."

The screen swaps to an infomercial. A seductive voice greets him. "Hey there big boy." A pair of glistening red lips fill the screen. "Up late?" The camera glides down the toned navel of a woman's body. Try as he might, Clain can't look away. The voice continues as the camera pans out on a woman dressed in black leather and silk. A whip dangles from one hand, while the other rests on the curve of her hip. "Why not visit me for the most sensual experience in New Beam City? Located on floor XXX in Cloud's 9's exclusive adult-only floor." The woman snaps her fingers. The paneled walls on either side of her slide back, revealing rows of sex toys. "What are you waiting for? Come and play. Now!" She cracks her whip.

"Enough! Turn it off…" Clain slams his glass down on the armrest. This sort of distraction isn't helping. He closes his eyes, attempting to clear his head and refocus on the looming challenge ahead. The comforting hum of the aircraft is soothing. He focuses on breathing, relaxing into the soft leather seat. He conjures the image of a wing chun training dummy in his mind. He tightens his fists through Buster and Banger's grip, rehearsing stances, strikes, and blocks in preparation for his fight with Synric, hoping it'll be enough.

~~~

"I tell ya, these kids got it rough these days," Lenny remarks. He's seated on a stool at the saloon, drink in hand. Ain't that some shit?"

"What's that?" The Elder raises a curious eyebrow.

347

"Usually us old folk sit around complaining to the youth about how easy they got it, ya know? Don't think I could ever say those words to 'em with a straight face now."

"Indeed. I always thought the struggle for them would be keeping pace with technology. I can't say I ever foresaw a demonic invasion," the Elder laments. "You know what, why don't you pour me one too."

"Really? You ain't had a drink in decades!"

The Elder shrugs.

"I had to keep a clear head for the kids," he muses. "Perhaps I'm feeling a little indulgent now that I've got some time for myself. Now pour before I change my mind!"

"You got it." Lenny obliges.

"Make that three, if you can spare it!" A voice calls out from the back of the saloon. The squeaky doors swing open, revealing a half-asleep Mr. Le.

"Well damn, look what the cat dragged in!" Lenny laughs.

"Ugh, don't mention cats please." Mr. Le grumbles.

"Right. Well, hope ya understood why I told ya 'bout it," Lenny says, wincing in sympathy.

"Nah, it needed to be done. How the heck did we get fooled by a fake cat?" He rubs the back of his head as he takes a mug of beer from Lenny.

"It was the most believable one I ever seen so don't feel too bad. Now, cheers!" Lenny raises his mug to the two men.

"Cheers to what?" asks Mr. Le.

"To three old heads with a moment of no youngins around!"

They share a chuckle before gulping down the delicious golden brew. "Gahh it's so damn good!" Lenny announces. "And thank fuck that silver headed devil is gone now!"

Mr. Le sputters a laugh into his drink.

"Shit man, you're cleanin' that up!" Lenny guffaws.

"So very sorry." Mr. Le says sheepishly. "I really shouldn't have found that funny."

"Nothing to feel sorry for my friend." The Elder pats him on the back. "You all have been through a lot with him. Heck, we all have. Even so, I'm worried about him."

"Oh fuck that. The kid's superhuman." Lenny scoffs, gulping down another mouthful. "I got sick and tired of makin' them damn training dummies. He went through them like kindling. And that's not even mentioning the repair I did on his sword and all the other bullshit for Dawn."

Mr. Le rubs his forehead, tears rimming his eyes. "Thank you guys for having my daughter and I. We really had nowhere to go."

"Hey now, no tears in this bar! You can stay here as long as ya need." Lenny refills his glass. "How long ya reckon you'll stay anyway?"

Mr. Le stares down into his glass, watching the bubbles fizzle around the rim. "I really can't say. For now, I suppose I am just happy that Fila's finally sleeping. Can't really think beyond that right now."

"Hey, no rush. With cookin' like yours, we could use ya!"

"Not a bad idea," Mr. Le admits, gazing thoughtfully around the saloon. "But with all due respect, I don't think Fila would last here very long."

"Understandable," The Elder chimes in. "You got a firecracker of a daughter. I reckon she wants to be in the thick of things. Not in this old, dusty, abandoned town."

"Ain't that the truth. Don't think I could handle much more mayhem myself. Even so, not sure where y'all could go. New Beam City is a shit show. I certainly wouldn't wanna raise a teenster on those streets. You're damn good with her, all things considered."

Mr. Le raises his glass, "Thanks. I always ask myself what my late wife would do, but these days it's difficult to say what anyone would do, living or not. I have no idea how to raise a fourteen year old." He laughs. "Probably why so many people drink!"

"Amen to that!" Lenny hiccups.

The Elder wipes his mouth, then squints at a red light flashing on Lenny's forearm. "Say Lenny, is that important?"

"What? Oh, the hell?" Lenny blinks, confused, and quickly thumbs through the menus on his wrist mounted system. "Says our front gate is wide open…"

"The front gate? At this hour?"

"Maybe the car leavin' tricked it, damn automated gate. Thought I turned that off. Oh well, it's closing now." Lenny slurs.

"Hey!" Honey's voice echoes across the courtyard, and she sprints by the saloon window in a blur.

"Woah, where is she going in such a hurry?" asks Mr. Le, looking toward the Elder and Lenny. Both men shrug.

Lenny staggers to his feet and moves toward the door. "Shit. I never seen her move that fast."

"Honey, wait up dammit!" Dawn yells at her, struggling to keep his footing as he hobbles after her.

"Dawn, what the hell is going on? Where's she runnin' to?"

"Fuck if I know!" He gasps for breath. "She woke me up screaming. Said her bike was stolen."

"How in the hell could that happen?!" barks Lenny, rushing to climb onto his nearby utility cart. "Hurry up, get the fuck on." The three men do their best to climb onto the cart. They have barely scrambled in when Lenny slams his foot on the accelerator, sending the wheels into a fevered spin. The vehicle fishtails as the cart careens around the corner toward the front. Upon arriving, they find Honey bracing herself against the gate doors with one hand and punching the metal with the other. Her teeth are gritted, and her strikes are leaving a dent that deepens with each hit.

Dawn leaps from the cart and rushes to her side. "Honey, what happened? Are you ok?"

"She took my fuckin' bike!" Honey screams.

"What? Who did?!"

"Fila!"

"What?! Are you sure?" Dawn asks. Behind him, the three older men just stare, momentarily silenced by shock.

"Yes, I saw her on it. The little shit looked scared as hell when she saw me. I almost caught her on foot but the fuckin' gate closed!" She glares at Mr. Le, daring him to respond.

He staggers back, confused. "I uh, she was just asleep not even twenty minutes ago! This doesn't make any sense."

"Yeah, don't go gettin' pissed off at him! He didn't steal your bike." Lenny interjects. "Besides, how could a kid steal your fancy ass bike? Ain't it got encrypted security or some shit?"

"Of course, but she got through somehow and locked me out. I can't even shut it off remotely." Honey kicks the ground in frustration.

"This doesn't make any sense. Why would Fila steal your bike?"

Mr. Le drops to his knees, covering his face and beginning to sob. "She's going after Clain."

351

"What? Why would she do that?"

"I overheard them speaking before he left. He said he had to face this alone and she didn't want him to die. Now it makes sense that she was so willing to go to sleep." His breath hitches, tears streaming down his face. "She has pulled this trick on me before."

"That still doesn't explain how she could steal Honey's bike." Dawn says.

"That fucking arm of hers." Honey growls. "Last week she was bragging about all the hacking she has been able to pull off with it. I ignored her. Never thought it would bite me in the ass."

"Oh shit. I hadn't considered the arm. Both it and the bike were made at Cloud 9, so it would make sense." Dawn begins to pace.

"That still dont explain how she got through the gate!" Lenny shouts, frantically thumbing through the security footage. "Unless," he looks around toward where Fila had nodded. "Cato! Get the hell out here!"

The girl shyly reveals herself from behind a wooden barrel. She scurries quickly toward the Elder and dives behind his robe for protection.

"Cato…" the Elder starts. "Did you open the gate for Fila?

Cato flicks her hands in a quick series of signs.

"What is she saying?" Dawn asks.

"She says Fila wanted to save her friend and that none of you would even try."

The men all look at each other, dejected. Honey turns away angrily.

"Well, we gotta chase after her." Dawn grumbles.

Honey laughs. "You can't be serious. There's no way we'll catch up with the C9X."

"Please! You have to try! If there is any way at all!" Mr. Le begs.

"We will stop her. Even if we have to destroy the bike." Dawn glances at Honey.

She scowls. "Yeah? You wanna get to the point?"

"Lenny, is the Javelina fueled up?" Dawn asks.

"Bet your ass it is."

"What the hell is the Javelina?" Honey asks. Dawn grins.

"You'll see."

CHAPTER 19 - Return To New Beam City

Fila grips the rain-slick handles of Honey's bike, struggling to see through the downpour. *I did it*, she thinks, a mixture of exhilaration and terror coursing through her.

I actually did it! Dad's gonna ground me forever. If Honey doesn't strangle me first.

But these are problems for when she returns home. If she returns home. Fila shakes the troubling thought away. Instead, she lets herself enjoy how the C9X flies through the desert. The speed is intoxicating. She turns up the music blasting in her helmet and grins, leaning into the rushing wind as the bike's autopilot dodges and weaves through obstacles with flawless, mechanized grace.

New Beam grows rapidly on the horizon, rising from a sea of morning mist like the arched spine of a gleaming, spiked leviathan. Fila's elation fades as the city looms ever closer. She has no plan, no real idea of where she is even headed. A cold shiver of dread snakes down her spine as she thumbs through the GPS map displayed in her helmet. The city is massive, a maze of twisting streets and alleys.

"How can anyone remember all these road names?" she grumbles. She wants to sound angry, but only hears fear in her voice. She taps Cloud 9, highlighting multiple paths to the building. Most of them are red lines: impassable.

She swallows, her saliva thick and sour in a suddenly dry throat. Too late to turn back now. She tightens her grip, spurring the bike forward.

Hold on, Clain. I'll be there soon. Please stay alive.

~~~

A giant cloud of billowing dust tears through the tranquil morning desert as Dawn accelerates the mechanical beast he calls the Javelina. Honey sits beside him, anxiously watching a GPS screen on her wrist. Fila has a huge head start. Even at this pace, they probably won't catch up to her in time.

"I still can't access the C9X. Nothing is working. Kid locked me out." Honey growls, punching the dash. "Can we fucking step on it, Dawn?"

"We can't go any faster, not on this terrain," Dawn says, keeping his tone level and his eyes fixed on the route ahead. Anger rolls off Honey in waves, a white-hot heat. One wrong word and he'll get burned. "Try to calm down, alright?"

"Calm down?" She leans forward to glare, interfering with his line of sight. "You're the one who wouldn't shut up about how fast this thing is. We're barely pushing one twenty!"

"This isn't a fucking street bike!" Dawn snaps, throwing out an arm to push her back into her seat and out of his face. "And punching it won't make us go any faster! Want me to kick your bike when we find it? Seriously, calm down."

Honey crosses her arms. "Might as well. You already bled all over it."

"Like I had a choice in that." He shakes his head. "I've never seen you like this."

"Yeah, well." She glares out at the desert, refusing to look at him. "This is me. You should know that if you're gonna chase me like a dog in heat."

Dawn flinches. That stung.

They lapse into tense silence. Honey is the first to break it.

"Look, I'm sorry. I just…" She throws her hands up in the air. "I don't get what the fuck is going on anymore, okay?" Instead of punching the dash again, she drives one fist into her open palm. "I am sick of this! My life used to be simple. Show up to a shoot, get paid, and then relax on the road. Now, I'm here. One stupid job, one bad choice, and I'm here."

"Welcome to the club." Dawn mutters.

"What?"

Dawn exhales, grip tightening on the steering wheel. "This is what life's like when Clain is involved. Been that way since we were kids. A good guy, but he's like a dark cloud of chaos that destroys all it touches." He exhales again. "Remember, I asked you to run away with me? This is exactly why."

Honey rests her chin on her hand, looking out at the vast salt flats. "Yeah."

"It's that curiosity though, right?" He laughs. "Makes you wanna see how shit will turn out for him. At least that's how it's been for me."

"Makes sense." She rolls her eyes. "Maybe we should do it."

"Do what?"

"Leave this shit behind."

"We can't. You know that."

"Why can't we?" She reaches out, placing her hand over his on the steering wheel. Her skin is warm and soft against his. She's almost irresistible and knows it.

Dawn shakes his head. "We can't, Honey."

"Why?"

Dawn gently taps the small glowing red light on the GPS screen. "That little red dot. Fila. She's just a kid. You really want to abandon her out here, knowing what she's heading into?"

"Fuck." Honey's hand slides away from his. Tears well in her eyes and she wipes them away, furious. Dawn puts his arm around her shoulders, pulling her close. She leans into the embrace, resting her head against his chest. Her warm tears soak his shirt. "Fuck all of this," she whispers.

"Yeah. Fuck all of it." Dawn eyes the mountain range ahead. His eyes flit to the Javelina's speedometer. It's maxed out. He purses his lips. "This thing can't move as fast as we need it to..." he says.

"Yup," Honey agrees. "Ideas?"

"Maybe," Dawn muses. He reaches for the comm, noticing it was flashing red on the console. Both he and Honey raise an eyebrow.

"Missed call?" she asks.

"Think so," Dawn answers. He presses the button. "Yo, Lenny, can you hear me?"

"Of course I can hear you, jackass! I've been trying to get a hold of you for fifteen damn minutes!" Lenny snaps, his voice buzzing angrily through the speakers.

"Sorry, didn't realize the comms were off."

"Yeah yeah, sure."

Dawn ignores his grumbling. "Did you update the trail maps I requested?"

"Way ahead of you. You might be able to cut your time in half if you take the rough trail through the Star Mountains."

"That's exactly what I was thinking!"

"I been tryin' to tell you that for the past fifteen fuckin' minutes! Now bear northwest and I'll route it for you."

"You will? So maps aren't updated then?"

"Updating maps is old shit. Javelina now has an AI system tailored to its capabilities. It will use recent satellite mapping to find the fastest path over the mountains. Won't be a comfortable ride though. You both up for it?"

Dawn and Honey smile at each other. "Hell yeah!"

"Good. Strap the harnesses and helmets on. Keep an eye on the screen. It will adjust accordingly and suggest a maximum speed through that rough terrain."

"Damn. This is awesome Lenny! Thanks!"

"Whatever. Now floor it! Mr. Le is a nervous wreck here so move your asses and get his girl back!" Lenny hangs up abruptly.

Dawn and Honey look at each other.

"Ready?" he asks.

She nods.

Dawn floors the accelerator, shooting the Javelina forward toward the mountains.

~~~

"Estimated time of arrival to Cloud 9: Ten minutes. Please remain seated and secured in place for landing."

The metallic voice of the onboard AI gently shakes Clain loose from his meditative trance. The sky comes into focus as he opens his eyes and looks out the window, fastening his seat belt in preparation for the air ryder's descent. Even with the vehicle maintaining a careful distance from the storms, the flight is turbulent, and he can sense particles of metal swirling amongst the clouds.

Wonder if my magnetism could do anything with that...

Previous fights with Synric flash through Clain's thoughts, and with each one comes the memories of injuries sustained. Cuts, bruises, fractures. With each recollection, the realization that he has never once felt as though he's had the upper hand against the android becomes ever more unavoidable. His knuckles whiten as his fists clench. He replays the briefing on the Motherboard's new features Lenny recorded for him.

"I know telling you to be careful is a waste of time," the recording begins. "Just don't go blaming me if you push the damn thing too hard and don't expect me to share more of the nanoglue with your reckless ass again. That being said..." Lenny begins, walking Clain through the sword's newfound synchronicity with his synth mail armor and even his thoughts, courtesy of the nanobots living in the adhesive now holding the weapon together. With intent alone, the armor can harden for protection or loosen for mobility, and act almost like a non-Newtonian fluid should it sustain a powerful enough impact. The Motherboard itself, however, has undergone the most radical transformation.

"Turns out 'dry' really ain't the right way to describe the glue settin'," Lenny explains. "More like 'integrated.' See, these little critters basically learned how to hold your piece together even if it flies apart. Knowing you, you'll find a way to make 'em forget, but meantime that means your Motherboard there can come apart and back together again at will. Allows for all sorts of nifty shit. Can turn a chunk into a projectile weapon. Maybe that big piece in the middle there can be a shield while you chuck the rest at whoever you wanna cut apart. Point is, this ain't your old sword no more. This here's a damn superweapon compared to what you used to have. Try not to ruin it. And hey, I know I give you shit. And we both know you earn most of it. But stay alive." With that, the recording cuts.

His eyes crack open as a new sound draws his attention. Looking out the window, he sees massive wind turbines come into view. Each is several stories tall, emitting metallic, sparkling chemicals and particles all swirling within the whirlwind engulfing the building.

This is what they have been spraying above the city?

His head jerks left as something forces its way into his senses. An intense, static whine fills his head, sinking invisible teeth into his brain. A violent ripple through reality, a wound ripping gashes in the very fabric of perception. It is agony.

Clain cries out, clutching his head with both hands.

A large presence soars through the air just a few miles away, on the far side of the storm. Five monstrous heads. Two giant wings.

"Tia," Clain whispers. Fear jolts down his spine. "No...Tiamat."

Saying her name aloud eases the pain in his head, but nausea twists his gut. *How is this even possible...* he wonders, gazing out the window in the creature's direction. The famed mother of all dragons,

Tiamat. What he had recently only thought of as a nightmarish creature from his premonitions, was now soaring the skies ahead of him.

King... What the hell have you done?

A beam of light catches his attention, shining in the same direction as the dragon's flight path.

"Arriving shortly," the vehicle announces, jarring him out of his thoughts. A vanity drops from the ceiling in front of Clain. "Feel free to freshen up in preparation for landing." The vanity folds outward, revealing a mirror with a generous assortment of toiletries: toothbrushes, cotton swabs, mouth wash, even cologne.

He rolls his eyes, annoyed by the interruption. He waves his arm, hoping it will somehow retract the vanity, but it remains. A hot towel cabinet catches his eye.

Steamed with mint and eucalyptus? Eh, why not...

He reaches for a towelette, inhaling the wonderful green scent as he presses it to his face. He rubs the towel down the back of his neck, sighing with relief as the tension between his shoulders softens. His eyes drift to his reflection. The hazy glow of aura emitting from his body reminds him why he is here, and it makes his heart race.

"It's time." He nods to himself, but the reflection does not move. Clain tries shifting from side to side, but the reflection remains motionless.

What the fuck...

"Have you ever noticed that the person you see in the mirror is how you see yourself?" The reflection's head tilts eerily. "But with a photo, it is how the world sees you?"
Clain's heart sinks. This isn't a mirror. It is a liquid display screen staring back at him with his own face, which now smirks snidely.

"Hello, Clain. Welcome to your end." Synric reveals itself, ejecting Clain's faceplate and replacing it with another. One familiar to him as well, the one Synric made for his own image. The same face it wore the last time they clashed.

Clain lunges forward, smashing the screen. Sparks fly as the surface shatters. The interior of the ryder begins to pulse red.

"Danger. Danger. Danger." The AI repeats.

The Motherboard is still in the trunk, and he has no way to retrieve it. The aircraft is slowing down, but not enough for a safe emergency ejection - if he even has a choice in the matter. Synric is in control now. "You have one chance at this, Clain. Take me down, one on one, and I will allow you the honor of conversing with King. He will answer all of your questions, but only through me."

"Big words for someone hiding behind a screen." Clain scoffs. "You wanna fight? Let's fight."

"Yes. Let's." Synric sends the air ryder into a barrel roll. Clain is tossed head over heels, crying out as the passenger door flies open and he tumbles out into the storm. He falls, flailing wildly as the violent gale-force winds pull his body in all directions. The suit automatically ejects an oxygen mask over his face with goggles over his eyes before the altitude sends him spiraling into unconsciousness. Clain flings his arms out like rigid wings, focusing all his will on staying aloft. He can hold this position, just barely, utilizing the micro metals swarming the air around him. But staying in place backfires fast as the air ryder doubles back and comes screaming toward him.

Shit!

He dodges clumsily, avoiding the bone-crushing collision by a hair. The ryder surges past him, flipping back upright as it swerves midair. The trunk pops open, and the disassembled Motherboard flies free. Clain reaches for them, holding his hand open for the blade's glowing hilt. It swoops into his palm with graceful ease, the rest of the blade assembling beneath his feet.

Damn Lenny, I owe you a beer.

Clain grins, leaning into the wind as the Motherboard carries him forward, riding the storm like an ocean wave.

The air ryder disappears from view, circling the Cloud 9 tower before remerging on the other side and landing gracefully atop a massive landing pad. Clain squints. A man is standing at the edge of the rooftop, staring up at him. It was King with something sitting next to him. Almost like a dog, yet goat shaped with fiery red, glowing eyes.

A flash lights up the sky behind the building as Tiamat's massive silhouette appears in the far distance. A beam of light fixated on the middle of the five headed behemoth, each appearing stiff, still and focused as it flew through the southern district of New Beam City. Clain's eyes squinting as the beam of light seemed to fixate on the middle of the heads as a subtle sparkle shimmering brighter than the rest of its body. It's coming right for him.

Clain whirls around, riding the wind away from the dragon while keeping King in his line of sight.

Tiamat's rapidly approaching form appears translucent. Clain could sense as much within the winds as if it were an ectoplasmic form of energy. His eyes turn back toward the glowing middle head of the dragon. Something was there, sitting on top of it, gripping onto its horns.

Is that… Synric?

"You must be alarmed." Synric's steely voice echoes through the roaring wind. "As before, I have wireless speakers scattered throughout this storm. After all, why stray from our little traditions?"

Clain struggles to remain in control atop the Motherboard. In all his training, all his obsession over fighting Synric again, he had never anticipated this. Fear clenches his heart in an icy grip. "Is that really…Tia?"

"Correct." Synric replies plainly.

"How? How is that possible?"

"Simple. Micro radiated fissure creation."

"Oh. Right. Simple." Clain shakes his head. "Stop playing games with me, Synric!"

"Within your limited understanding, it can be simply understood as 3D printing the soul of an entity from a parallel dimension. In other words, the light of this beam is stimulating the micro materials and nutrients floating within this storm and reforging the mythical dragon Tiamat, per its specifications."

"Why? Why are you doing this?!" Clain screams.

"The inevitable doom wrought forth by the blood flowing through your veins, Clain. All this destruction, all this evil born into the world, because of you," Synric sneers. "One of many reasons I will kill you, in time."

"You made a deal! Tia told me as much!" Clain screams. "Why would you block my memories!?"

"Only humans can make deals with devils." Synric points toward King on the rooftop. "You are right, however. A deal was made with this demon in exchange for its reincarnation, under the agreement to block your memories of Rezeka. You are a disease, Clain, and you need to be purged."

Clain stands his ground, though his hands tremble at his sides. Synric bears down on him, surfing atop the great flickering beast. Tiamat shimmers like a fever dream, lighting up in a million fractures of morning light as dawn breaks over New Beam.

Clain is frozen to the spot. He cannot run, but how can he fight?

Maybe the android is right. He is a mistake, a stain on the world needing to be scrubbed away. He is so tired of fighting, so tired of grief, and defeat. How many times must he brush shoulders with oblivion, only to lose all he holds dear and be forced to begin again? Surrender, even death, seems peaceful in comparison.

Tiamat's tooth-rattling roar shakes Clain out of his trance. His reflexes take over, propelling him sideways in a last-minute evasive maneuver as the dragon's immense glowing body surges past like a bullet train.

Synric catches him mid-arc before he can completely dodge, smashing his fist into the motherboard. It shatters into pieces, but quickly reforms under Clain's feet. He pivots right, turning his head, face to face with two of Tiamat's snarling faces. Clain throws his arms over his head as the massive soul energy rushes over him, sending him reeling into free-fall.

The Motherboard spins out, circling him in wild loops as he plummets through the clouds. He reaches for it, frantically trying to pin it down with his focus.

Come on, come on…

The motherboard heeds his call, smacking into his chest. Clain hugs it like a long-lost friend before he spins it underneath him, allowing it to

362

take on the brunt of the high speed winds slamming into him. He looks up at Tiamat still circling Cloud 9. Synric is nowhere to be seen.

Clain slides his knees forward onto the board and attempts to stand. The winds are less violent here, and with an effort, he gains his feet. He can now see dim glowing lights from the city below.

Must have fallen a few hundred feet...

Simply flying back up into the thick of the storm and Tiamat's range seems not only impossible, but stupid.

How the hell does King expect me to meet him on the roof?

No time to think about that. Red fire flashes in the roiling clouds above Clain an instant before Synric drops out of the sky like a bird of prey. He slides down the slick sides of the skyscraper's glass walls before hurling himself at Clain, sword drawn and blazing.

Clain tilts the Motherboard back, swinging it up and around to grasp the hilt. In one fluid motion, he swings, pivots, and throws the blade at Synric.

The android blocks the Motherboard, but the force of the blow sends him flying backward. Recovering quickly from the ensuing daze, Synric tweaks his wrists and diverts the sword's momentum, bending backwards to slide underneath the arc of the blade. As Clain completes the swing, he rotates the blade for another horizontal chop. Synric dodges with a backflip, landing on the flat of the Motherboard and using it as a springboard to leap backwards away from Clain, landing near a window. As he looks up to reassess his adversary, he's greeted not by a view of Clain, but rather of the Motherboard spinning through the air towards his face. The massive weapon connects with bone crushing force, compressing even the superalloys of Synric's metal jaw for a moment as the impact forces him through the glass behind him, carrying him down through the air in amongst a hail of shattered window fragments.

Clain calls the blade back to him, deftly catching the hilt in his palm right as he hears another window break from somewhere at least a story below. Just as the sound registers, blots of deadly energy fire through the floor, punching smoldering holes in the ground. In response, he smashes the blade into the damaged surface, sending his floor - Synric's ceiling - crashing down on top of his opponent. As the dust from the impact clears, Clain takes in his surroundings, seeing no sign of the android.

He is in some sort of office, lined with cramped, empty cubicles. He looks back to the window, this one also broken, expecting Synric to be on his ass.

He must've gotten a grip during the fall and crashed through here to attack me from below, Clain realizes.

No sign of the android, for now. His eyes scan the room. A bright EXIT sign catches his attention. Might as well take his chances with Cloud 9.

Clain shoulder rushes the exit door, exploding into the hallway beyond. It is brightly lit. Palm tree leaves scrape his face. He shakes them away, confused. He looks up and down the hallway. The whole length of which is decorated like a tropical getaway.

"Hey!" A slender guy wearing an unbuttoned Hawaiian shirt, flip flops, sunglasses, and a pair of bright pink swim trunks stands under a nearby palm, staring at Clain.

"Hey..." Clain awkwardly closes the door behind him.

"Everything ok in there, bro? We were about to call for help."

"Oh, yeah, it's all fine. I just..." Clain stammers.

A woman pokes her head around the corner to eye him up and down. "Were you hooking up with someone in there? We do it all the time." She winks. "This floor is so much better than that stuffy office."

The door slowly opens behind Clain, startling him.

"Oh there you are, honey!"

It is Synric, having altered its appearance to that of a towel-clad woman. Clain sidesteps away, disturbed. "What the hell!"

"He is quite shy! That is why we picked the offices." Synric smiles sweetly at the couple. "We knocked over a few desks. Alleviates some of his tension." He reaches to caress Clain's arm. "Although it doesn't appear to have worked."

Okay... I need help here.

Clain smacks the hand away, backing down the hall before breaking into a run. He takes the first turn down the next hallway he sees, looking frantically for a stairwell. Anything to get him out of here. There is only a big sign reading WAVE POOL. He sprints through the door, into a domed chamber housing an azure tropical pool. A warm digital sun rises on the far side of the room with the crash of ocean waves running down the middle. Dozens of people cluster around the pool under a massive artificial sky. A few beach goers notice his presence, throwing questioning glances at his suit. He presses himself against the wall, searching for a way out.

"Are you lost?" A few nearby sunbathers call.

"I think so," he admits. "Any idea where the elevators or stairs are?"

"You just came from there didn't you? They are at the other end of the hall."

"Oh, don't mind him. He is just being silly." Synric calls to them, stepping out in front of Clain. "We are just playing hide and seek. He is rather bad at it." Synric laughs. "How about some drinks!" He motions to a nearby servant holding a tray of beverages. Synric grabs a few, handing them to the sunbathers and then winking to Clain.

Clain feels like he is losing his mind. What is Synric playing at? *This is insane.*

He eyes a series of towering water slides on the far side of the pool. One of them stands roughly fifteen feet below the metal rafters of the ceiling. He wonders if he can simply force his way up into the next floor. He speed walks away, his boots splashing into the water. The swimmers pause to gawk. Synric slowly follows behind, smirking. Clain ignores him and the onlookers, pushing his way forward onto the stairs. All eyes are on him as he climbs. At the top, a lifeguard tries to block his path.

"Yo man, what the hell are you doing?" He demands. "Dude, you need to leave. You can't just do... whatever the hell you just did."

"Sure I can." Clain retrieves the Motherboard off his back. In one swift swing, he tosses the sword upward, forcing his magnetism while gripping its handle and flying upward toward the rafters. The entire crowd gasps in awe. Some scream in fear while others cheer him on. Synric stands in the shallows below and watches, one eyebrow raised in... Amusement? Admiration? Disdain? Impossible to tell, and Clain no longer gives a fuck.

The Motherboard lodges into a steel beam, allowing Clain enough leverage to climb on top. The space is tight, the projecting screen thin. Some sort of backlit projection of the sky over the pool. Clain punches through the screen, tearing it open to reach inside. The bright lights of the scene projectors blind him momentarily as he feels around for something to grab onto. Progress he thinks. Inside is a very tight, cocooned duct system. Fans whistle back and forth, keeping the area cool. Clain moves past the blinding lights from the projection. He struggles to fit the Motherboard up with him, opting to break it into pieces and neatly stack them nearby.

The ceiling above feels like several feet of concrete. He senses the rebar within is triple layered. He looks at his gauntlets, Buster and Banger. They are both charged. Would a forceful punch be enough to break through? Chunks of concrete would crash down toward people below he realized.

There has to be a service hatch.

He is rewarded for his patience as he notices one just twenty feet away. He climbs as chunks of the Motherboard levitate behind him. The hatch is locked. Clain rears one fist back and delivers a swift punch, blasting the hatch off its hinges. He clambers through, finding himself once more in an open space.

He exhales, relieved. Something smells wonderful here. Like buttered bread. "Guess I'll follow my nose," he whispers. *Under a bakery, maybe?* He thinks. Clain suddenly wishes that he had taken some time to familiarize himself with the vast variety of floors Cloud 9 has to offer. Having no idea what stands between him and the apex of the monolithic building will make this journey all the more difficult. He pauses a moment, bringing up a map on his arm to study the floors. Sure enough, the floor just above him is a series of kitchens. There seem to be kitchens every twenty floors, which made practical sense considering the thousands of people within, but how can he navigate them with a far more knowledgeable android on his ass?

Maybe I should have taken my chances out in the storm.

~~~

Fila is on the freeway that encircles the city. A massive hole blown through the main security gates had given her easier access back in than anticipated. Huge caravans of people hurried toward escape as she sped by them. The asphalt is bumpy, as if a battalion of tank-treaded vehicles shredded the road long before her arrival.

Maybe the military has arrived?

 She turns her attention to the Cloud 9 building. It is mostly dark, with some floors flickering in a soft light while others remain brightly lit and flashing wildly. She has no idea how she will make it to the top, but the C9X seems to know how to get there. The map in her HUD shows a clear path. She barrels on, trying to block out the chaotic war zone of a city around her, and the piles of bodies heaped on every broken sidewalk. *Too late to turn back now.*

She focuses on the road as the C9X asks her to hold on tightly. The bike weaves to the opposite side of the lane, avoiding massive potholes blown through black top. What the hell came through here? Dozens of pedestrian vehicles lie ravaged and heaped on the road. The C9X weaves swiftly through them. Fila glances into the C9X's rear view mirrors. Something is flashing behind her.

The bike starts to decelerate, even as she presses down on the accelerator. Barbed wire barricades appear on the horizon. Sloppily hung camo-patterned curtains attached to makeshift racks and rods hide what lies behind the roadblock. Traffic signs are covered in crude graffiti depicting pig heads with x's for eyes. The freeway exit sign has been sprayed over with stylized lettering that reads, "COME FURTHER BE KILLED."

Moments later, multiple shirtless vagrants flood the freeway waving vicious improvised weapons. Saw blades jammed into bats. Chains wrapped around forearms with the ends welded to sickle blades. Barbed wire whips and brass knuckles are fashioned from scrap metal and rusted nails. A chanting stir begins to supersede their shouts and grunts as they all focus their attention on the bike.

Pit Pigs! Fila realizes. The bike controls are remotely locked. She's going nowhere. Her cybernetic arm is even struggling to respond to her neural inputs. Its movements are jerky and imprecise, and the fingers are spasmodically locking and unlocking. She barely manages to free her hand from the bike's controls before it locks completely.

"It's Honey!" Jeers and grunts erupt from the crowd.

"Let's butcher the bitch! Save the best cuts!"

367

CHAPTER 20 - Phantom Rider

"Come on, come on, come on!" Fila shouts, attempting to wrestle control of her arm and the bike back from the jamming signal. The C9X fights with her, shooting forward into the charging mob. She clings on for dear life, screaming as she hurtles through the snarling Pit Pigs. The mob tries to dogpile her, throwing their ragged, sweaty bodies in at the bike only to be knocked aside like ragdolls. Fila veers sharply, arcs up a mound of detritus, and suddenly she is flying. The bike soars over a jagged barricade, skidding to a halt safe on the other side.

Fila lets out a triumphant, "Woo-hoo!" She revs the C9X and sets off at breakneck speed. The city is a blur of neon lights, towering skyscrapers, and dark alleys filled with fiery smoke. The bike roars beneath her, its engine a low, guttural grow. She leans forward, eyes narrowed against the biting wind. She tries to shift her grip on the handlebars and realizes the mechanical arm will not move. Dread sinks like a cold stone in her stomach as she tries in vain to budge it. She cannot even flex her fingers yet, it still steered. She isn't directing the bike at all anymore. It is all her arm.

The fingers of her left hand are fused to the controls like a vice. Every attempt to yank the bike in a different direction is met with stiff resistance, the arm's servos whining with effort. "Damn it," Fila mutters. A cold, calculating presence courses through her nerves. This feels wrong. Something is taking control, a foreign invader in her body. "Let me drive!" she screams. Up ahead, another gang of Pigs stand waiting behind a barricade.

The C9X swerves hard to the left, narrowly dodging a stream of bullets. Behind her, the Pit Pigs whoop and holler, brandishing weapons as they give chase.

A Pit Pig on a sleek, chrome-plated hoverbike pulls up alongside her, his scarred face twisting into a malicious grin. "Welcome back to the city, Honey. Where do you think you're going!" he sneers, raising a sawed-off shotgun. Fila's heart skips a beat. Before she could think, her mechanical arm jerked the bike sideways, tires screeching against the pavement, and slams into the Pig's bike. The impact sends the thug spiraling, his bike exploding into a ball of fire and shrapnel as it hits a far wall.

Fila's thoughts race, frantic and scattered. *What is happening? I didn't mean to do that...* Her breath comes in ragged short gasps as she struggles to keep her balance. "Stop! You're going to get me killed!" she shouts. The bike does not respond, instead accelerating faster, weaving through the chaotic traffic of the city, dodging between cars, trucks, and civilians who screamed in terror as she sped past.

Another explosion rocks the street behind her. She glanced back—three more Pit Pigs are closing in, their bikes bristling with vicious barbs and makeshift weapons. The C9X swerves again, narrowly missing a parked car, then cuts sharply to the right, sending Fila's stomach lurching into her throat. She can see the Cloud 9 building in the distance, growing closer by the second. Its towering stature reaches up into the purple cloud-choked sky.

The bike took another hard turn, this time heading straight for a narrow alleyway. Fila's eyes widen. "No, no, *no!*" she shouts, but the bike rockets into the alley, the walls on either side a blur of brick and metal. The Pit Pigs are not far behind, their engines roaring like angry beasts. Fila ducked as a hail of bullets ricocheted off the walls, sparks flying in every direction.

Suddenly, the alley opens up into a wide plaza filled with pedestrians, many of whom are head-deep within FreqyD. The bike shoots out like a bullet from a gun, scattering people in every direction. "Get out of the way!" Fila screams. The C9X swerves and weaves through the crowd, a blur of motion.

The Pit Pigs burst into the plaza behind her, guns blazing. Fila screams, feeling a searing pain erupt in her side as a bullet grazed her ribs, and she bit back a scream. Bullet holes were peppering the road and walls around her and the bike seemed to detect all of them. The bike dodges side to side, avoiding the sprays of bullets. Most of them, at least. Another bullet narrowly grazes her helmet and chunks out a portion of the front fender. She begins to panic. Frantically trying to wrestle the control back from the AI. She slams her other fist on the screen, desperately wanting to regain her freedom before they both end up in a heaping flame of scrap. Her eyes dart around the bike's console, searching for any kind of manual override, any chance to break free from this hell ride.

And then she sees it—a flickering red button beneath a cracked plastic cover, labeled "EMERGENCY RELEASE." It was a long shot, but it was her only shot. Her human hand reaches out, fingers brushing against the button. Before she can activate the emergency release, her mechanical arm clamps down, pulling her backward and sending the bike into a momentary wheelie. The AI instinctively fights against her. "Come on, you piece of junk!," Fila fights back with everything she has, pushing the bike back onto both wheels. She growls through gritted teeth, using all her strength to push against the AI's grip.

The Cloud 9 building looms closer. Its polished, reflective surface gleaming with glare from thousands of neon lights. She is almost there.

With a final surge of effort, Fila slams her hand down on the button. There is a jolt, a spark, and then the bike suddenly decelerates, the engine cutting out. The AI's grip loosens, and momentarily she is free. But she is also out of control, the bike skidding across the slick pavement, spinning wildly. Fila holds on tight, her heart pounding in her chest, and braces herself for an inevitable crash.

The C9X slams into a row of parked cars, throwing Fila from the seat. She tumbles across the ground, the world spinning around her. She comes to a stop against a concrete barrier, gasping for breath, pain lancing through her body. She forces herself to her feet, her legs unsteady. She looks up to see the Pit Pigs closing in, their bikes slowing to a menacing crawl.

"End of the road, Honey," one of them snarls, raising a weapon.

But Fila wasn't Honey. She is a survivor. And she isn't going down without a fight. Fila struggles to her feet, dazed and dizzy with wincing pain shooting through her bruised ribs. Her vision blurs, the lights around her blaze into a chaotic sea of color. The Pit Pigs circle around her like vultures. She sees the twisted grins on their faces, the anticipation of violence in their eyes.

 Suddenly, a deep, rumbling roar fills the air, louder than the bike engines and the city noise combined. The ground trembles beneath Fila's feet as a massive shadow falls over the plaza. She turns, her eyes expanding in horror: a colossal mechanical tank robot lumbering into view, its hydraulic limbs grinding and hissing with each step. She immediately knew what it was as a lump of terror grew in her throat. Atop the hulking beast sits Kruger, the leader of the Pit Pigs. All of the commotion had led him right to her.

Kruger is as terrifying as he was before. His face is blackened in soot caked into his assortment of scars and tattoos, his cold and cruel eyes beneath his signature blood-soaked red bandana tied around his forehead. His grin has a feral slash across his face, teeth sharp like a predator's.

"Well, well, well," Kruger growls, his voice booming over the din of the plaza. "Look what we have here! Thought you could own the streets like any other day, ay Honey?" He chuckles, a low, menacing sound that sends a shiver down Fila's spine. His eyes glint with suspicion as he looks her up and down. "You're a lot smaller than I remember."

Fila's heart pounds in her chest, her breath coming in short, panicked gasps. The image of her burning home flashes in her mind, the smell of smoke and the screams of her injured father. All because of this monster in a man's skin.

He once again towers over her like a god of death. Hux's head stares down at her with lifeless eyes, twitching within its tank of glowing liquid. The entire mech casts a long, dark shadow across her path.

The Hux bot moves with a grotesque, mechanical grace. Its massive limbs ending in thick, crushing claws. Each step it takes sends tremors through the ground. Kruger leans forward in his cockpit, eyes narrowing as he studies her. "You're not Honey, are you?" he mutters. "Not that I care. There are much more pressing issues plaguing these streets. Question is, why are you here?"

He raises a hand, signaling to his men. "Restrain her," he orders, and the Pit Pigs move in, their weapons gleaming in the neon light. Fila's eyes dart around the plaza for any means of escape. There is nowhere to run. She is trapped.

Just as the first of the Pit Pigs lunges forward, a deafening roar cuts through the night. Fila barely has time to react as a massive, armored vehicle barrels into the plaza, smashing through a row of parked cars and scattering them like toys. A barrage of flash bangs detonates in the area. The Javelina. Dawn is behind the wheel, his face set in a determined scowl. Beside him sits Honey, her expression grim. She shouts to Fila, "Hide behind the bike, now!"

The Javelina plows straight into one of the Hux bot's legs with a thunderous crash. The massive machine staggers. Kruger's grin vanishes, replaced by a snarl of rage as he fights to keep the Hux bot upright.

"Hey, Kruger!" Honey shouts, leaning out of the Javelina's window. "Looking for me?" She flashes a cocky grin, her eyes blazing with defiance.

Dawn continues to slam the gas pedal of the Javelina into the mech. Honey gets out of her seat and rushes to the rear of the Javelina, gripping onto a high-powered rifle mounted onto the back, and opens fire. Bullets pepper the Hux's exterior, sparking off the mech. One of the Pit Pigs falls with a scream.

Crouched behind the bike for cover, Fila's heart pounds with a mix of fear and hope. Her arm is flashing wildly, but she at least has control of it. Honey and Dawn had come for her. Despite everything, they came to help. It fills her with renewed courage. Together, they can win this. She smiles and reaches for the nunchucks on her belt.

Kruger's face twists with fury. "Kill them all!" he roars, slamming a lever on the Hux bot's control panel. The massive machine whirs to life again, its remaining leg stomping forward, claws snapping open and closed with lethal intent.

 But now Fila is ready. Adrenaline surges through her veins, her fear now replaced by a steely resolve. She glances at Honey, their eyes meeting for a brief moment. Honey gives her a nod. Fila takes a deep breath, centering herself amid the chaos. Her hand grips the custom nunchucks while her hips begin to sway with the nimbleness of her training. The chucks are crafted from reinforced steel with electric nodes along the shafts. She spins them in her hand, feeling the comforting weight and familiar hum as the electric charge activates. She has trained with this weapon to the point they feel like an extension of her body.

The Pit Pigs began to close in, grinning wickedly. One thug lunges at her, swinging a spiked chain at her head. Fila ducks under the blow, spinning low on her heel and swinging her nunchucks in a tight arc. The electric nodes spark, cracking like thunder as they connect with the thug's forearm, electrifying the chain and sending him backwards. He screams in pain, crumpling to the ground, his arm convulsing.

"Nice move!" Dawn shouts from the Javelina. "But aim for their ankles, Fila! You're shorter than they are—use your advantage!"

Fila nods. She can't go head-to-head with these brutes in sheer size or strength, but she can use her speed, her agility, and her compact stature. She dances back as another Pit Pig charges her, a spiked bat swinging for her midsection. She sidesteps, her mechanical arm jerking slightly, trying to regain control, but she holds firm. She whips her nunchucks low, catching the Pit Pig at the ankle. The crackle of electricity and the sharp blow bring him down hard, his face smacking the pavement.

"Two down!" Fila pivots, ready for the next one, her eyes darting to the Javelina. Honey is still behind the rifle, blasting Kruger, but the Hux bot's raised arm is shielding most of the bullets. Its strength is relentless, its mechanical legs pounding forward, beginning to force the Javelina back with sheer strength.

"Come on, you junkyard relic!" Honey shouts, leaping from the Javalina to avoid the Hux bot's massive fist as it comes swinging down at her, smashing the turreted rifle. Dawn fires off a massive artillery round from the front chassis, but the bullet seems to do little more than scratch the paint. The beast is armored to the teeth.

Fila can see the strain on Dawn's face, the way his hands grip the wheel tighter with each close call. He is clearly in pain from his abdomen. Pit Pigs are regrouping, their numbers still overwhelming. *I have to keep them at bay, give Honey and Dawn a chance to make their next move.* She twirls her nunchucks again, her body moving fluidly as she dodges and strikes, each movement precise as her mechanical arm strikes low, taking down one thug's ankles after another.

A heavy-set Pit Pig with a mohawk and a cybernetic eye lunged at her from the side, wielding a serrated machete. Fila ducks under his swing and sweeps her leg behind his knee, throwing him off balance. She follows with a quick strike to his ankle, and he topples with a howl, dropping his machete. She spins the nunchucks around, bringing them down on his metalized eye, the electric charge knocking him out cold.

"Keep going!" Dawn shouts as he fidgets with his trench coat. "Buy me more time!"

Honey rushes for the C9X. She quickly unlatches a compartment on the rear fender and initiates a series of mini bots that quickly begin to repair the bike. She turns, unsheathing her stinger dagger as a Pit Pig slashes at her from the side. She trips him and slashes him between the shoulders, sending him into a bloodied rage on the ground. With a flick of her wrist, the stinger snaps into its hand cannon mode and blasts the Pit Pigs head off. Fila looks away, her stomach twisting at the gruesome spectacle.

"Fila!" Honey calls. "Get over here!"

Fila hurries over. "Honey, what do we do?"

"You tell me darlin', you got us into this mess!" Honey snaps, scowling at the damaged bike.

Fila shrinks into herself for a moment, feeling ashamed. She swipes her nunchucks at another Pit Pig's ankles, and misses. Honey blasts him in the chest and blows his body backwards.

"Enough of this!" Kruger roars, slamming his fist on the Hux's controls again. "Fuckin' kill them!" The machine responds with a burst of speed, its massive foot swinging down toward the Javelina with the force of a thousand sledgehammers. Dawn barely has time to react. He jerks the wheel, trying to swerve out of the way, but it is too late. The Hux bot's foot crashes down, smashing into the rear of the vehicle with a deafening crunch.

The Javelina buckles under the impact, metal screaming as it collapses. Dawn is thrown forward, his seatbelt harness the only thing keeping him from being ejected from the vehicle.

"No!" Honey screams.

Dawn fights to regain control, his knuckles white on the steering wheel. "Honey, get ready!" he yells, his voice strained but steady. Honey nods, turning back to check the progress of the repairs on the C9X.

The Hux bot's foot lifts into the air for another crushing blow. Dawn floors the gas pedal, the Javelina lurching forward with what little power it has left, barely escaping as the giant foot comes crashing down. The vehicle skids, tires screeching, but Dawn keeps it moving, weaving through the wreckage-strewn plaza.

Dawn leans toward the passenger side window, a massive cannon aimed at one of the Hux bot's joints. "Come on, just a little closer..." he mutters, his finger on the trigger.

"You think you can run from me?" Kruger bellows, his laughter echoing off the buildings. He swings the Hux bot's foot again, this time catching the side of the Javelina with a glancing blow. The vehicle spins out, crashing into a row of abandoned market stalls. Dawn scrambles to get out. Smoke is pouring from the hood, the metal frame groaning.

375

"Get clear!" Dawn yells, yanking the door open and diving out just as the Hux bot's foot smashes down again. Dawn rolls across the pavement. Honey isn't far behind. She rushes to his side, Stinger still clutched in her hands. The Javelina is crushed like a tin can beneath the Hux bot's foot.

Fila fights her way toward Dawn and Honey, nunchucks spinning in her hand, breath coming in ragged gasps. She watches them scramble to their feet, faces set with determination.

Kruger's grin widens, his eyes gleaming with sadistic delight. "Looks like you're out of options!" The Hux bot advances again. "Time to end you motherfuckers." The Pit Pigs tightened their circle, closing in around Fila, Honey, and Dawn. Fila desperately wants to flee, but there is nowhere to run. Her back presses firmly against Honey's as the Hux bot looms over them, its intrusive form casting a long, dark shadow that seem to swallow the plaza whole.

"Stay close!" Honey barks, glancing over her shoulder at Fila. "We're not done yet." Dawn's eyes flick between the advancing Pit Pigs and the Hux bot. They began tossing guns amongst themselves, an obvious firing squad was growing. A smirk creeps across Dawn's face as he reaches into his utility coat, retrieving a small, disc-shaped gadget. "I've got something that might buy us a few seconds," he mutters. With a swift motion, he slams the disc against the ground. It emits a high-pitched whine before projecting a shimmering, translucent shield around them.

The shield springs to life just as a hail of bullets erupts from the Pit Pigs, projectiles slamming into the barrier with a rapid-fire *thunk-thunk-thunk*. Sparks fly as the bullets ricochet off the electronic field. The shield holds firm, flickering slightly with each impact.

"Shit, you weren't kidding!" Honey shouts over the roar of gunfire, giving Dawn a quick nod of approval.

"Don't thank me yet," Dawn replies. "This thing won't last."

Fila's eyes peer at the C9X. The bike is still repairing itself. She can feel her mechanical arm tugging at her thoughts, urging her to get back on the bike, to make a run for it. But she will not let it take control again. She has to make a choice. She looks at Honey, reloading her weapon with grim determination. She's already pissed enough at her.

"We need to get out of here," Fila says, nodding towards the C9X. "But we can't all fit on the bike."

Honey's eyes follow her gaze, a moment of understanding passing between them. "You're not taking that bike without me. Not this time," she says firmly, gripping Fila's shoulder. "You've had your fun."

Dawn glances at the two of them, his lips curling into a smile. "You two go," he says, his tone calm amidst the chaos. "I've got a plan. Just trust me."

"What plan?" Honey demands. "You're not thinking of—"

"I said, trust me," Dawn insists. "I'll be right behind you. But if this doesn't work, I need you both out of here."

Reluctantly, Honey nods. "Alright. But you better not do anything stupid."

Dawn chuckles, glancing back at the approaching Pit Pigs. "Wouldn't dream of it."

The shield wavers and dies. A split second later, Dawn tosses a circle of flash bangs to cover Honey and Fila as they dart for the bike. As they reach the C9X, Fila's mechanical arm activates itself again, gripping the throttle handle and lifting it upright with ease. She swings her leg over the seat, feeling the engine rumble like a hungry beast. Honey jumps on behind her, wrapping one arm around Fila's waist. "What the hell, Fila! This is my bike!"

Fila's arm revs the engine, and the C9X roars forward, tires screeching against the pavement. As they sped away, Fila and Honey glance back to see Dawn standing his ground, his eyes locked on Kruger and his gang.

"Come on, you ugly bastards!" Dawn screams, waving his arms to draw them in. "Finish what you started. Come and get me!"

The Pit Pigs charge forward, weapons raised. Kruger, perched atop his Hux bot, sneers. "Rip him apart!"

Dawn waits until they are almost on top of him, then pulls another device from his belt—a small, cylindrical grenade. He flicks a switch and tosses it to the ground. A thick cloud of smoke erupts, obscuring everything in a dense fog.

"Let's see how you like this," Dawn mutters. He activates another device on his wrist—a mini-projector that casts a blinding light through the smoke, creating the illusion of a massive explosion, a mushroom cloud rising high into the sky. The illusion is so convincing that the Pit Pigs and even Kruger hesitate, believing for a moment that a nuclear blast has detonated in the middle of the plaza.

"Fall back!" Kruger roars, his voice tinged with genuine fear. "Get back, now!"

The Hux bot stumbles backward, nearly losing its balance as Kruger pulls it away from the perceived blast zone in a panicked rush. The Pit Pigs scatter, ducking for cover. Some of them panic and fire wildly into the smoke.

The real grenade is still in Dawn's hand—a small device labeled with a simple warning: *Medusa Gas*. With a quick twist, Dawn arms the grenade and hurls it into the midst of the confused gang.

A second later, the grenade explodes, releasing a cloud of shimmering multi-colored, translucent gas. The Pit Pigs gag, coughing and choking—and almost immediately, they begin to freeze in place, their bodies locking up as the nanobots in the gas take hold. Kruger, still retreating in the Hux bot, watches in disbelief as his men become statues, their faces twisted in horror and confusion.

"What the hell...?" Kruger gasps, slamming the controls to try and pull back. But it is too late. Even his mighty Hux bot begins to slow as the nanobots infiltrate its systems.

Dawn doesn't wait to see the full effect. He sprints through the smoke, his body low, moving like a shadow through the chaos. He slips past the paralyzed Pit Pigs, makes his way toward a ragged metal staircase, and rushes up the side of a building toward the roof where he could find cover.

Meanwhile, Fila and Honey speed toward the towering Cloud 9 building. Fila can feel her arm syncing with the C9X again, guiding it with a precision she can barely comprehend. Honey sits frustrated behind her, trying to move the other handlebar and fidget with the onboard screen. "What the hell did you do to my bike!?"

They crash through a fence and whirl around the rear of a parking area toward the back of the building. Upon reaching the base of the building, before they can take a breath, Fila's arm twists the throttle. The C9X shoots upward into another wheelie, its tires magnetizing to the metal exterior, clinging to the side of the building like a spider.

"What the fuck!" Honey shouts. Fila screams. They begin a vertical ascent up the side of the skyscraper. The wind whips past them, the city stretching out below like a sea of neon and steel. Honey tightens her grip around Fila's waist, her eyes fixed on the rapidly approaching heights as the swirling clouds grow closer and closer. Fila's adrenaline surges through her veins. This is it. The moment she has been fighting for.

"Look!" Fila points as something flashing in the clouds above them. "It's him!"

The C9X continues its vertical ascent, the bike's tires gripping the glass leaving a faint trail of scorched marks in its wake. Fila's mechanical arm makes minor adjustments to the bike's path, weaving them through stray pieces of debris and digital advertisements that flicker and glitch as they pass. The wind howls around them, the noise almost deafening.

As they near the upper levels of the building, the sky above is no longer clear. It is now shrouded in a dense, swirling mist—the eponymous "Cloud" of Cloud 9. A digital fog, a fusion of advanced holographics and particle dispersal systems designed to obscure the highest levels of the building from any prying eyes. But now, within that mist, a battle rages—a battle that seems to defy the very laws of physics.

379

Through the haze, Fila's keen eyes catch flashes of light, bursts of energy that crackle and shimmer like lightning trapped in a bottle. She squints, trying to make out the source: two figures, locked in combat, their movements impossibly fast and precise.

"That's..." Fila begins, her voice barely audible over the mic system between their helmets.

"Clain and Synric," Honey finishes, her eyes wide. "They're fighting."

 The figures become clearer as the C9X climbs higher, cutting through the digital fog. Clain, with his sleek, rail rider armor, moves with a fluid grace. His sword gleams in scattered pieces, humming with a dark, almost malevolent energy. Opposite him is Synric, clad in dark leather, his every movement a calculated balance of precision and power. In his hands is the Beta Breaker, a blade reforged from tempered steel and cyberglass, crackling with a blue-white energy that leaves streaks of light in the air as it moves.

The two warriors soar effortlessly through the clouds, their feet never quite touching anything solid. Only Clain's feet press onto pieces of his sword, assisting his movements. Each swing of their swords sends shockwaves rippling through the air, the blades clashing with a sound both metallic and electric, as if metal and code are colliding in a beautiful ballet of human ingenuity. Dark synthwave music blares around them, again seemingly synched to Clain's heartbeat. Reminiscent of their last battle, Synric played the role of DJ, keeping his mind focused on their dance of death. Sparks fly with each strike, illuminating the fog around them.

Clain's movements are swift and fluid, every strike of the Motherboard aimed with deadly intuition. His eyes remain closed, metal particles dancing around him as he manipulates the environment to his advantage. He is relentless, his face set in a stark mask of determination. Synric, his equal in every way, counters each blow with a graceful parry or swift dodge, his eyes sharp and focused, his expression unreadable.

"Look at them," Honey whispers. "It's like they're... flying."

Fila nods, her eyes glued to the battle. It is like watching gods at war.

Clain swings the Motherboard in a wide arc, aiming for Synric's midsection. Synric counters with the Beta Breaker, the two swords clashing. Motherboard spreads into pieces, parting the digital fog violently, revealing a brief glimpse of the city far below. The force of the impact sends both fighters spinning away from each other, only for them to recover in an instant, launching themselves back into the fray.

The C9X continues its climb, bringing Fila and Honey ever closer to the battle above. "Are you guys ok?" Dawn chimes in through the comms. They were now at eye level with the combatants, close enough to see the intensity in their eyes, the strain on their faces.

"Dawn, look at this." Honey sends him the video feed of what they are seeing.

"Holy shit." Dawn gasps.

"We should help him!" Fila insists.

"No!" Dawn barks at them. "Let him cook. He is focused and in his element, meanwhile you two are rocketing up the side of the building to where exactly?"

"He is right. We have no idea what the hell we are doing here." Honey says.

Without warning, Clain twists in midair, bringing his sword up in a sweeping motion. The Motherboard glows with a dark light and a wave of energy erupts from the blade, tearing through the mist. Synric dodges to the side, narrowly avoiding the blast, his coat flaring out behind him. He retaliates with a quick thrust, the Beta Breaker's energy crackling with intensity as it aims for Clain's heart.

Clain spins his body, deflecting the blow with his forearm, and brings the Motherboard down in a vicious counter strike. The two blades meet once more, sending another shockwave through the air, causing the fog to ripple and swirl around them.

Honey tightens her grip on Fila's waist. "We need to keep moving. If they see us—"

But it was too late. At that moment, Clain's eyes flick open and away from Synric. He locks eyes onto Fila and Honey. His expression hardens, a mix of surprise and recognition flashing across his face.

Synric follows his gaze, his eyes narrowing. "And my advantage has arrived." Synric sneers, swooping in toward the distracted Clain.

Clain's focus shifts, his body twisting midair, readying himself. The digital haze swirls more violently around him, reacting to his presence, to his power. "We can't let them interfere," he growls. "Not now."

Fila glances back at Honey, her face set with determination. "We need to get to the top," she says. "Now."

Honey nods, her eyes still on Clain and Synric. "Hang on. This is going to get rough."

The C9X roars as Honey jams her fist into the side of the bike. They shoot upward, racing towards the summit of Cloud 9. The battle above raged on, but now, Fila and Honey are part of the storm.

CHAPTER 21 - Toying The Edge Of Control

As Fila and Honey surge upward on the C9X, the swirling mist around Cloud 9 thickens into a tempest of flashing lights and crackling energy. The top of the building materializes, but Clain's attention is now fully consumed by the two figures racing toward the summit. His eyes narrow in frustration as he watches them ascend.

Synric, seizing the opportunity, unleashes a brutal assault on Clain. With a swift, unexpected movement, Synric's Beta Breaker slices through the air, its energy crackling with deadly intention. Clain barely has time to react, lifting the hilt of his sword before Synric's blade strikes, the force of the blow sending him reeling through the storm.

The impact causes Clain to lose all focus, his grip on the Motherboard faltering. As he tries to regain his balance, Synric moves with lightning speed toward the C9X. With a flick of his wrist, he activates a powerful control signal. The bike, now fully under his control, abruptly freezes in place, its engines sputtering to a halt.

Fila and Honey do all they can to hold on and not vault over the handlebars. "No!" Fila screams, her voice barely audible over the howling wind.

Synric's eyes glow wildly as he manipulates the C9X with a sadistic grin. "Came to play?" he taunts. "Let's see how well you two can handle the storm."

Clain, still dazed, tries to pivot through the chaotic storm. "Leave them alone!" A stark red energy bursts off of him. The Motherboard clicks together, snapping into place beneath his feet and blasting him toward Synric. He bellows, his voice echoing through the tempest. He whips the Motherboard upward, slamming it into the android with a crack of extreme force, sending him flailing into the air wildly.

Clain's shoulder dislocates upon impact. He snaps it back into place, letting out a shriek of pain.

Fila calls to him, "Are you ok?"

Clain looks at her angrily. "Why are you two here?" he growls, still gripping his shoulder as his aura switches to a somber green tone, attempting to heal it while he can.

"I…" Fila struggles to speak.

"We came to help you!" Honey speaks up. "Fila refused to let you fight alone. And so here we are."

Synric chuckles, levitating back towards them. "I brought them here." Synric exclaims. "Fila permitted it of course, giving me full control over the bike."

"It was you controlling it?" Fila gasps. "But, why?"

"Are they both not your ultimate source of motivation?" Synric asks, splaying his palms, as if presenting them to him. "Fila, your young protege. And Honey, the stunning beauty who just so happens to look exactly like your late fiancé, Rezeka?"

"Fuck off!" Honey shouts at the android. "What a pathetic being. Programmed to harass and screw with humans like playthings."

"That is all you ever were, Honey. A simple plaything. Utilized by Cloud 9 as nothing more than an asset toward an end goal." His palm shifts, beginning to vibrate the bike.

"Hold on Fila." Honey grips onto the girl. The wind whips around them. The C9X begins inching downwards. Clain leaps toward them, spiraling his arms overhead, marionetting the motherboard into pieces before thrusting them forward and crashing into the building around the C9X. Encapsulating them safely in place.

His gaze returned to Synric. "Leave them out of this! Stop toying with me!"

Synric laughs. "Toying with you? I haven't even begun to toy with you." With a blinding flash, Synric shoots toward Clain, moving with supernatural speed. He strikes Clain from behind, the force of the blow sending Clain crashing through the thick, reinforced glass of the Cloud 9 building. The glass shatters into a cascade of sparkling fragments, the impact leaving a massive gash in the structure.

Clain tumbles through the shattered glass, disappearing as he falls into the depths of the building's interior.

With Clain out of the way, Synric turns his attention back to Fila and Honey. They are trapped, the C9X immobilized and ensnared. Fila's mechanical arm twitches, a futile attempt to wrestle control of the bike from Synric's grasp. Honey grits her teeth. "We need to get out of here," she says urgently, her eyes scanning the storm for any possible escape route. "Do you have any ideas?"

Fila shakes her head, her gaze locked on Synric's figure still moving with an unnerving calm amidst the chaos. "We need to break free somehow."

Synric approaches with deliberate swagger, his Beta Breaker glowing ominously in the storm's turbulent light. "You two are quite resilient," he says, his voice smooth and menacing. "We shall see how long you last under pressure." With a flick of his wrist, Synric unleashes a series of powerful energy pulses from the Beta Breaker, targeting the bike. The pulses strike with incredible force, creating a series of violent explosions that rock the side of the building.

Fila and Honey brace themselves, holding onto the C9X for dear life as the bike rocks violently with each explosion. The Motherboard pieces still hold firm, protecting them like a cocoon as the storm intensifies.

"We have to move!" Honey shouts, her voice barely reaching Fila over the cacophony. "We can't stay here!"

Fila nods, her mind racing for a solution. She reaches out with her mechanical arm, trying to interface with the C9X's controls

385

through sheer willpower. With a final, determined effort, she manages to override the bike's systems just enough to initiate a controlled maneuver.

"It's working! Hold on!" Fila yells as she twisted the handlebars with all her strength. The C9X lurches and begins to move again, its engines roaring to life as it fights against Synric's control. Synric's shocked as the bike begins to defy his influence.

"Dammit, King!" he exclaims, taking a step back as the C9X surged upward with renewed power. The bike shoots through the storm, its trajectory taking it toward the final floors of the building. As they approach the edge, the storm around them begins to clear, the haze parting to reveal a path ahead. With a final burst of speed, the C9X races toward the peak of the building.

Clain struggles to his feet just in time to see the two girls escape. He stands amidst the debris within the shattered glass of Cloud 9 building. His breath comes in ragged gasps, feeling remnants of the storm in his lungs.

They are going to make it up there before me, he realizes. A cold fury ignites within Clain as he turns his attention back to Synric, who stands motionless at the edge of the floor, staring toward him. Synric's Beta Breaker sizzles ominously, casting a sinister red light in the dimly lit corridor.

Clain's eyes remain locked onto Synric, taunting him to make the first move. His hands clench into fists as he prepares for the next confrontation. With the Motherboard still firmly planted into the building outside, he needs to switch gears and rely on his physical prowess and gauntlets—Buster and Banger.

He slips into Wing Chun stance, his body low and poised for swift, precise strikes. The corridor is bathed in darkness, the only illumination coming from the occasional flicker of Synric's energy weapon. Clain's senses sharpen as he engages every muscle.

Synric moves with predatory grace, his eyes glowing with a cold intensity. "You're out of your depth, Clain," his voice echoes through the corridor. "Without your Motherboard, you're nothing."

Clain grits his teeth, his gaze unwavering. "I'm not done yet."

With a burst of speed, Synric rushes forward, Beta Breaker cutting through cubicles, sending debris flying. Clain meets the attack head-on, using his gauntlets to block and deflect shrapnel. The collision of energy and metal reverberates through the corridor.

Clain lunges at the android, retaliating with a series of rapid, fluid strikes. Buster and Banger begin channeling kinetic energy with each punch, sending powerful shockwaves through the air. Synric stumbles under the force of the hits, looking almost surprised.

"You're stronger than I anticipated," Synric admits, his eyes narrowing with renewed focus. "But strength alone won't save you."

Clain ignores him, pressing his advantage, his strikes becoming a relentless barrage. The gauntlets' energy crackles with each punch. Synric, however, is not easily subdued. He deflects Clain's blows with practiced ease, his movements calculated and controlled. The battle rages on, the corridor echoing with the sounds of combat. Clain's movements turn erratic and random, each strike aimed to exploit Synric's only weakness, Clain's human unpredictability. Despite his skill and power, Clain feels the exhaustion creeping in, the strain of the battle taking its toll.

With a sudden, blinding flash of red energy, Synric unleashes a powerful counterattack. The Beta Breaker bursts into flames with an intense vibrant brilliance, and Clain is thrown off balance. Before he can react, Synric delivers a devastating gust of fire, engulfing the room instantly. The burst sends Clain crashing through a nearby wall. The impact shatters the wall's reinforced surface, sending debris scattering around him. Clain sprawls amid the rubble, stunned. He struggles to rise, his gauntlets still glowing with residual energy. Synric approaches slowly, his expression a mix of satisfaction and disdain.

"You've fought well. I did not foresee having to use this." He lifts the Beta Breaker upward. Clain pushes himself up, his body aching from the impact. He knows he has to keep fighting. The corridor is in ruins, the darkness now punctuated by the fire of Synric's Beta Breaker. "You are witnessing new technology I have birthed into this world." He smiles. "I have named this, Hex."

His hand gestures sideways across the blunt rear of his wicked weapon as he directs Clain's attention to a series of hexagonal plugs inserted into the Beta Breaker. "These capsules utilize billions of self-replicating nanobots to create the power of the elements. In this case, fire." He swipes at Clain's feet, leaving a line of flame in front of him. "And the more I use them, the stronger they will get."

"What, like some kind of cyber magic?" Clain asks, stalling for time.

"Exactly that." Synric smiles. He rears the blade back, ready to swing it. "Now allow me to continue its testing trial."

Clain staggers upright and backs away, breaking into a run just as Synric brings the blade down in an arc of fire. Flames burst behind him as he dives through the nearest door ahead of him.

"I am not so sure you want to go that way!" Synric chuckles. "Though you did say I was toying with you."

Clain's breath is ragged as he stumbles through the corridor, his senses still reeling. The corridor behind him is engulfed in a wall of flame, He had escaped the inferno.

He is now in an unfamiliar part of Cloud 9. The room is dimly lit with an eerie, pulsating glow coming from the walls. His confusion grows as he takes in his surroundings.

The room is filled with an assortment of unsettling objects. It seems to be a research and testing floor dedicated to adult-themed cybernetics, an area that is both horrifying and surreal. Dildos and other sex toys line walls and tables, their shapes, sizes and designs ranging from the grotesque to the absurd. He can barely process what he is seeing. With dawning horror, he notices some of these objects begin to move in his presence.

The first sign of danger comes from a row of dildos on a workbench. They twitch and wriggle, their surfaces gleaming with an unnerving sheen. As if animated by some malevolent force, they begin to undulate like caterpillars, dropping to the floor. Clain watches in disbelief and terror as they skitter toward him like an army of bugs.

He turns to run, but the room seems to pulse with a life of its own. Sex robots—once sleek and seductive—are now malfunctioning and aggressive. Their eyes glow with predatory light, and their once-sensuous movements are jerky, mechanical lunges. They attempt to allure him with programmed gestures, but their underlying hostility is palpable.

Clain dashes through the maze of twisted machinery and living pleasure toys, his mind racing with fear and confusion. He ducks under a moving tentacle-like device that whips through the air with a snap, narrowly avoiding its grasp. As he runs, he hears mechanical whirring and unsettling moans from the robots, their voices warped and distorted by malfunctioning systems.

His path is a nightmarish labyrinth of synthetic flesh and cybernetic terror. Every turn reveals more horrifying creations coming to life. A tremendous, monstrous dildo with rotating, sharp edges lurches toward him, its metallic surface catching the dim light as it charges with terrifying speed. Clain ducks and rolls away just in time, the object slamming into the wall with a deafening clang.

Desperation fuels his movements as he fights through the grotesque floor. Swinging and punching at whatever throws itself at him. RGB fleshlights shoot at him like suction cupped plungers. He uses his gauntlets to smash through the malfunctioning robots and destroy the advancing toys, his strikes now fueled by sheer anger and adrenaline.

Suddenly, the floor beneath him trembles with a low, menacing rumble. Clain looks up in alarm as the room seems to shift and warp, the walls and floors moving with an unnatural, pulsating rhythm. Without warning, a powerful force throws him violently upward. He is lifted off his feet and sent crashing through the ceiling, the impact leaving him disoriented.

He lands heavily on the floor above. The room he finds himself in is less grotesque, but still unsettling, with dim lighting and an oppressive atmosphere. As he tries to get to his feet, Clain hears the distant echoes of the living horrors from below, their mechanical sounds haunting the air.

Clain scrambles down the debris-strewn hall as the sounds of mechanical whirring and distorted moans echo through the building. His heart pounds in his chest. The air is thick with the electric scent of ozone and rubber, a stark reminder of the horrors just a level below.

"Now I am toying with you," Synric says. The eerie calmness in his demeanor is more terrifying than his words.

Clain backs away slowly, his eyes darting around for another route of escape. He turns and sprints down another corridor, the sound of Synric's mocking laughter echoing behind him. His heart races as he pushes himself harder, desperately searching for a way out of this nightmare.

The corridor opens up into a vast room, almost awe-inspiring. Clain stops abruptly, his eyes shocked in horror. The room is filled with rows upon rows of private pods, each one occupied by a person hooked up to a complex network of VR equipment and machines gyrating over the occupants. The soft glow of the pods illuminates the faces of the users, all lost in their own vivid experiences.

 Synric appears beside him, gesturing grandly to the scene before them. "Welcome to the secret future of pleasure," he says, his tone almost reverent. "Think of it as a sperm bank, but not just any sperm bank. The double dip profit margins are astronomical—not just from these customers but from the black market of sperm as well."

Clain feels a chill run down his spine as he turns to face Synric. "You're sick."

Synric's expression remains unfazed. "Am I really?" he asked softly. "Consider this—many of these users pay top dollar, but many of those you see here are on hospice. They are at the end of their paths, and here, they can live out their wildest fantasies before they pass. Is that not a form of kindness?"

The room seems to spin around Clain as he struggles to process the reality of what Synric is suggesting. The ethical implications, the sheer manipulation of it. Yet, there is a part of him that wonders... Clain shakes his head, trying to clear the fog of confusion. "It doesn't justify it. You're using them, harvesting them without their understanding or consent."

Synric simply shrugs, a hint of genuine curiosity in his eyes. "Perhaps. But morality is often a luxury of those not facing mortality. For some, these last moments are their happiest, their most alive. They even sign a contract to be here."

The sound of approaching whirrs reminds Clain that the horrors from below are not far behind. He needs to make a decision quickly—engage further with Synric or find another way to escape this twisted place. Clain clenches his fists, the gauntlets humming softly with stored energy. "This ends now, Synric. No more games."

The room's eerie glow casts long shadows as Clain and Synric begin their battle anew, clashing amidst the rows of VR pods. Each hit sends ripples of kinetic and digital energy surging through the air. Clain lands a powerful punch with his gauntlet, sending Synric stumbling backward into a bank of pods. The impact causes the pods to shudder violently, alarms blaring as their serene blue lights flicker erratically. The occupants inside, abruptly torn from their immersive experiences, begin to convulse and scream.

Synric's expression shifts from fury to concern as he quickly regains his footing. He rushes to aid the pods, his hands moving deftly over the controls to stabilize the affected occupants. "You fool, you don't understand the delicacy of this technology!"

As Synric manages to stabilize the last of the affected pods, his gaze meets Clain's, a grim understanding passing between them. "Clain, this technology—what you see here—it's not just about exploiting the dying. It was developed to explore the deepest realms of human consciousness, to bring comfort where medicine could no longer reach." Clain's attention sharpens, his stance relaxing slightly. "What are you talking about?"

391

Synric sighs, his eyes darkening. "FreqyD—the drug that's been plaguing New Beam City. It was derived from this technology. The Illuminaries twisted it, introduced it to the streets to destabilize the city, to tap into the dark realms sealed within you, Clain."

A cold chill runs down Clain's spine as he processes Synric's words. "Why? What do they want with me? What is this dark realm?"

Synric shakes his head, his expression grave. "It's ancient, powerful. Something sealed away for good reason. The Illuminaries believe they can control it, use it to reshape reality to their whims. They think you're the key to unlocking it completely."

The room feels oppressively silent after Synric's revelation, the only sounds being the soft hums of pods and the distant, muffled disturbances from whirling winds outside as Tiamat files by slowly. Eyeing them through the glass. Clain feels the weight of the situation bearing down on him—his role, unwittingly pivotal, in a game of cosmic stakes.

Clain's eyes blaze with a fury that matches the chaotic swirl of Tiamat. He points accusingly at the monstrous form, his voice thunderous over the howl of the wind. "What have you done to me? Why were my memories of Rezeka sealed away? Why is this monster here!?"

Synric leans against a console. "Oh, Clain, you are but a lost soul," he mocks. "These answers will on come from King's lips and his alone. He has forbidden me from telling you myself."

The mention of King only fuels Clain's rage. A deep, violet aura erupts around him, the air vibrating with the power of his unleashing fury. Without warning, he lashes out, the force of his anger sending Synric crashing through the glass wall and back into the violent storm outside.

As Synric tumbles into the chaos, Clain calls to his Motherboard. The scattered pieces respond to his command from floors below, swiftly reassembling beneath his knees and forming a platform that carries him aloft. His anger ignites a terrifying transformation; a thick, swirling aura envelops him, within which glimpses of his dark premonition realm could be seen—shadowy, spectral figures that moved with foreboding purpose.

Clain soars upwards, propelled by his rage and the power of the Motherboard beneath him. Synric, recovering from the unexpected assault, steadies himself midair, his eyes wide with a rare flash of fear as he witnesses Clain's transformation.

Above them, the rooftop of Cloud 9 looms, and there stands Fila and Honey, their faces etched with shock. They watch, helpless, as King waits. The fierce red-eyed goat still by his side.

Clain's voice echoes through the storm, powerful and resolute. "This ends now, Synric!" The pieces of the Motherboard rushes in front of him, spinning wildly like a tornado while generating a massive build-up of energy. Buster and Banger matching his intensity. Synric's mechanical features tighten in curious terror.

With a deafening roar, Clain unleashes a massive beam of energy. The beam is brilliant, pulsating with purple and black fire, tearing through the storm with unstoppable force. It strikes Synric squarely, ripping through his body. Metal and circuitry fly into the wind. Yet, remarkably, Synric remains mostly intact.

Clain, his aura now a blazing torrent, pushes higher, driving their battle toward the rooftop. Each move is a blur, their fight a spectacle of light and fury against the backdrop of the swirling storm.

As they near the rooftop, Clain prepares for a final strike. Fila and Honey step back, their eyes wide. King remains unmoved, his expression unreadable.

Synric braces himself. Above the storm-wracked skyline of New Beam City, Clain hovers, the Motherboard beneath him a spinning disc of seething energy. His newly transformed aura blazes around him, a maelstrom of purple and black energy that flickers with the fierce shadows of another realm.

Synric, seeing an opportunity in Clain's struggle to control his new power, surged forward. His Beta Breaker gleams ominously in the storm's erratic light, each swipe slicing through the air with lethal precision. Clain raises the Motherboard in defense, but the torrent of attacks is relentless as Synric shifts into a whole new gear. The strike sends violent slashes of Hex-fueled fiery air piercing through the energy of the Motherboard, creating openings with every motion. Clain manages to deflect most, but the ferocity and speed overwhelm him. One vicious strike follows another, getting closer to its mark.

Then, with dreadful precision, Synric's blade connects. The impact is catastrophic. Clain's arm, caught in the path of the blade, is severed into pieces, the fragments scattering into the billowing winds around them. A guttural scream rips from Clain's throat as terrible pain sears through him.

Driven by a primal roar of both agony and defiance, Clain taps into the deep reservoirs of his power. "No!" he bellows, his voice thundering above the storm. "Return to me!"

Miraculously, the pieces of his arm respond. Just as the Motherboard could be commanded, so too could the fragments of his own body. They hover in the air, encircling him like a macabre halo of flesh and energy, each piece alight with the same intense purple aura that enveloped him.

With a vengeful cry, Clain directs the floating fragments of his arm towards Synric. The pieces slice through the air with the precision of a guided weapon. Synric, taken aback, attempts to maneuver away, but it is too late. The fragments strike with brutal efficiency, cutting the android into pieces, his components scattering like leaves in the wind.

Victory. After all this time.

Clain's control falters as the pain from his severed limb surges through him. The immense power he has summoned is too much, its wild force pushing him beyond his limits. His body, overcome by pain and power, drops from the sky.

He crashes onto the rooftop of Cloud 9 in a burst of shattered tiles and scattered debris. Blood pools around his broken body. The pieces of his arm, still hovering.

Clain lays still, his chest heaving with labored breaths, his eyes staring blankly into the storm above. The rain washes over him, mixing with blood to stain the rooftop.

Fila and Honey rush to Clain's side. Fila kneels beside Clain in a panic, her hands trembling as she reaches out to touch his bloodied body. Tears stream down her cheeks as she pleads with him, her voice breaking with each word. "Clain, please, don't die. Please, keep fighting! Fight this!"

Clain's eyes flicker weakly, barely able to focus. As his gaze meets Honey's, pain and delirium twist his perception, and in Honey's face he sees Rezeka.

"Don't fight it, or else it won't come true. I am coming, Rezy," Clain murmurs, his voice a ghost of its former strength. Each word is a whisper of longing, a tender echo of a past filled with love and loss.

Honey's chest aches as she listens to Clain's delirious words. She reaches out to gently touch his face.

Suddenly, King appears. He shoves Fila and Honey aside with a brisk, "Move!" as he kneels beside Clain.

King pulls out a syringe, its contents glowing with a pulsating blue energy. Without hesitation, he plunges it deep into Clain's chest. The needle's glow intensifies, its eerie light casting shadows across their faces.

"You made it, my boy. You finally made it," King says, looking into Clain's fading eyes. His voice holds a mix of relief and something darker, an ominous satisfaction.

Clain's body jolts from the injection, and a faint glow begins to emanate from his wounds. The pieces of him that still hover in the air begin to settle, drawn by the energy radiating from his body. Clain's eyes, reflecting the stormy sky above, show a glimmer of recognition.

As the serum works through him, the raw edges of his pain dull, and his breath steadies. Fila and Honey watch as Clain's shattered form starts to show signs of stabilizing. King stands, his gaze sweeping over Clain and then turning to survey the storm still raging around them. Tiamat watched them impatiently. As the storm begins to ebb, the true challenge has been met and exceeded. All that remains are answers.

CHAPTER 22 - Throne Of Atonement

 Clain's breathing begins to steady, but his mind is still a raging storm of disjointed memories and half-formed thoughts. Fila and Honey exchange uncertain looks. They both gaze toward King, who stares down at Clain, awaiting a response. The bizarre glowing syringe is still firmly gripped in his hands. He turns his back to the group as his attention shifts toward Tiamat circling in the distance. The great dragon's movements continue at a slow and deliberate pace, awaiting the completion of its revival.

Honey leans in, gently squeezing Clain's hand. "Clain… If you can hear me. We're here." But Clain's eyes remain distant and watered, flickering between recognition and the haunted look of a man grappling with his past.

Fila, still kneeling beside him, wipes her tears away and tries to steady herself. She looks up at King. "What did you give him?" she demands, her voice cracking. "What is that stuff?"

King turns slowly, his expression unreadable. "Something to rush his healing," he replies coldly. "Clain's not dead yet. Not by a long shot."

Honey stands, anger simmering beneath her calm exterior. "You can't just do that—inject him like this! He's barely hanging on!" she shouts, stepping between King and Clain. "What's your game anyway? And who the hell are you?!"

He smirks, turning back to face them. His gaze shifts to Clain, who is now struggling to sit up. "The irony of you speaking to me this way. This isn't a game, Honey. This whole thing is about survival. And Clain... he's more important than any of you realize."

Before anyone can respond, the ground beneath them rumbles. A deep, resonant growl echoes from the sky, drawing everyone's attention to Tiamat. The dragon's heads lift, each set of eyes glowing with a predatory hunger. The creature is growing more restless, its enormous wings unfurling as it hovers closer.

Clain shuffles forward onto his knees, every muscle aching. The blue serum is doing its job, numbing his pain and giving him the strength to stand, but his mind is so foggy, torn between past and present.

"Clain, don't push yourself!" Fila cries, but he barely hears her. King watches Clain's struggle with a mix of pride and anticipation. "It's not just the dragon, Clain. Synric will return here shortly, and he's not going to stop pushing you. You need to continue getting stronger. And fast."

Clain staggers up onto his feet, gripping the edge of a shattered wall to steady himself. His eyes meet King's, burning with a renewed fire. "I don't need your lectures," he growls. "I need some fucking answers."

King hesitates, the confident smirk on his face faltering for the first time. Clain saw a glimpse of uncertainty in King's eyes—a crack in his usual armor of control.

"You've been pulling my strings since the beginning, haven't you?" Clain continues, his voice rising, fueled by the anger boiling inside him. "You knew what I was capable of, even when I didn't. Did you make me this way?! And you're resurrecting Tiamat—why? What the hell am I? Why am I at the center of all this bullshit?"

"Just another minute, Clain," King mutters, his voice lacking its usual bravado. "I might as well wait for the full audience."

"Fuck no. Not another moment of this!" Clain snaps, fury blazes in his eyes. "I'm done with your games. You know exactly what's going on, and you're going to tell me—now!"

King's eyes dart away, avoiding Clain's glare. "I've been trying to protect you. All of you. But there's a lot you don't understand. It's not just about you, Clain—it's much bigger than that."

Clain surges forward, his emotions boiling over into pure rage. "Stop stalling, King! Tell me why I'm the reason this monster is back!" Before Clain can reach King, a sudden blur of black and white streaks into his vision. Clain barely has time to register what is happening when something slams into his groin—a forceful, crushing impact that knocks the wind out of him.

Clain doubles over in pain, gasping as he realizes what hit him. A bizarre creature—the goat, its fur striped like a zebra, with eyes glowing an unnerving shade of red—stands before him, snorting and pawing at the ground. It lowers its head, displaying a set of sharp, spiraling horns, and charges again, aiming straight for Clain's groin.

Clain narrowly rolls to the side before collapsing onto the rain-slicked rooftop, clutching himself in agony. He pushes up on one fist, his knuckles pressed firmly into the roof. His vision blurs with pain.

King takes a step back, barely suppressing a laugh as he regains his composure. "Stop at once, Goatsee" he commands, gesturing toward the aggressive goat standing over Clain. "That's my... biggest pain in the ass. He likes to keep people in check. Specifically, when someone raises their voice toward me."

Clain groans, his anger momentarily sidelined by the throbbing pain radiating through his testicles. He tries to get up, but Goatsee snorts again, keeping him pinned with a threatening glare.

King crosses his arms. "As I was saying, Clain... you'll get your answers. But just a moment more. We need everyone together first."

Clain grits his teeth, forcing himself to his feet despite the searing pain. His rage hasn't subsided; if anything, it burns brighter now, fueled by King's evasiveness and the humiliating encounter with this bizarre Goatsee. But for the moment, he has no choice but to catch his breath and back down.

"You're not going to keep this from me anymore," Clain spits, holding his nads. "One way or another, I'm getting the truth." Pieces of the Motherboard hover in around him, still fully functional. He staggers forward, clutching his side as Goatsee stands defiantly in front of him, its glowing red eyes locked onto him with smug intensity.

A sudden hiss fills the air—a strange, mechanical noise that draws everyone's attention skyward. From the ceiling above, a massive azure liquid-filled tube begins to descend, glowing faintly as it lowers toward the rooftop. Inside, a figure forms, coalescing in the fluid like a ghost taking shape. Clain watches, eyes narrowing as the figure becomes clearer. It is Synric, returning in a new body. The android's previous battle scars and mechanical brutality have been replaced with a sleek, elegant appearance. Synric steps out of the tube, the liquid draining away as he touches down gracefully. He is dressed in a sharp, form-fitted suit, black with subtle colored accents that shimmered under the storm's dim light. Synric's cold blue eyes scan the group before resting on Goatsee, who trots up to him with a proud little bleat. Synric smiles—an unsettling, gracious expression while bending down to scratch Goatsee's head. His touch is oddly gentle. "Good job, Goatsee. That was quite the hit."

Clain turns to King, his patience all but gone. "This was your final guest? Get on with it then! Tell me what the hell is going on."

King glances from Synric to Clain, then to the rest of the group. "Well... Actually there is one more."

As if on cue, a soft *ding* echoes from the far end of the rooftop. Everyone turns to see an elevator slowly open, its doors parting to reveal Dawn standing awkwardly inside. He steps out hesitantly, his posture tense as he raises a hand in a tentative wave. "Uh... hey, everyone." Shocked to have a full audience looking at him.

Dawn's entrance is almost comical in awkwardness. He shuffles forward, eyes darting nervously between Clain, Synric, and King before making his way to Honey's side. His eyes fixate toward Goatsee and it's bizarre appearance. Honey offers him a small smile, grateful to have him there and safe. "How the hell did you make it up here?" She whispers.

He shrugs, "Came to the front and the elevator said it would took me to the top. Took a chance."

Clain's focus remains on King, his impatience boiling over. "Everyone's here now. No more stalling. What's the truth, King? Why are we here?" Clain's demand hangs in the air, but King does not immediately respond. Instead, he glances downward, his expression shifting to a rare look of introspection. For the first time, his posture seems to sag under an invisible weight.

 "Welcome," King begins, his voice softer than before, tinged with a hint of weariness. "Welcome to the top of Cloud 9. I know... I know what you've all been through because of me. Because of us." He nods toward Synric. "We don't expect forgiveness. I know we've put each of you through hell, and there's no taking that back." King's eyes drop again, staring at the rain-slicked rooftop as if lost in thought. "But I didn't bring you here without offering answers. I brought you here because my time is up and it is the least I can do. Before I go, I need you to understand why."

The group watches him, a mix of confusion and guarded anticipation on their faces. King straightens, facing them all with a solemn, almost vulnerable expression. "You ever heard the phrase, 'You never know you're a monster until someone comes to slay you?'" His shoulders slump, the weight of his past pulling him down. "I'll cut straight to the beginning," King says, his tone subdued. "To when this nightmare first began. I was always different. I was born with a mind that could grasp things others couldn't. Concepts, patterns, numbers—they were like second nature to me. But growing up...that didn't make things easier. In a school system designed to churn out mediocrity, kids like me were punished. Smarter students were held back, forced to slow down just to 'level the playing field.' To make us all equal in intelligence." He laughs bitterly, shaking his head. "Ever notice society no longer glorifies the exceptional? All the wrong people get all the fame with examples of pure stupidity glorified. By design."

"I couldn't take it. I couldn't just sit there and waste away while my mind screamed for more. So I dropped out of the public space. Didn't even bother with high school. Instead, I taught myself programming. By the time I was 17, I'd started my own freelance business. But programming was never just a job for me—it was a skill. Power. An escape. It was…my obsession."

King pauses, looking down at his hands. "Through savvy business intellect and discipline in execution, I gained a decent income and enjoyed many years almost on autopilot. Working for clients in every tax bracket. Accomplishing their needs with ease and partying with all classes of people and traveling all over the world. Living life as any young twenty something man could only wish for. It was never enough, however, as... Well, I had another hobby. One that I kept to myself. It started out playful, innocent. I wanted to quantify the possibilities of other realities, alternate dimensions. It was just theoretical at first, like a puzzle I was trying to solve for fun. But as time went on, it consumed me. I spent every waking moment perfecting my calculations, refining equations, getting closer and closer to unlocking something no one had ever seen. Then one day, while working late into the night, I… found something. Or maybe it found me. It was a frequency—bizarre, unintelligible. At first, I thought it was just a glitch, a mistake in my calculations. But it was far from that. I'd made contact with something."

"The entity on the other end… it began to speak my language quickly. It understood me. It told me it could give me the answers I was seeking—the solutions to all my equations, the key to unlocking other dimensions. I was intrigued, excited even. But the more I communicated with it, the more it felt wrong, as if I was speaking to something that shouldn't exist in our reality."

King's expression darkened, his voice dropping to a near whisper. "Then, one night, it wasn't just a frequency anymore. It was a presence. I suppose you could say… it visited me." He pauses, his breath hitching. "The entire interaction didn't even feel real. A demon. A creature of darkness that appeared in my room like a shadow pulled from the depths of my own fears. It didn't give me a name, but it showed me the clear solution to my equations. It offered me knowledge—more than I could ever dream of. It all became so clear."

Clain's expression hardens as he listens. King continues, his voice filled with bitterness. "But the demon was no altruist. It was there to make a deal. It told me that if I didn't agree, it would wipe my memory of the solutions and disappear forever. I'd lose everything I'd worked for, everything I'd sacrificed."

King looks at Clain, his eyes haunted. "I thought it was the devil. And I've been trying to find it ever since. To end this madness or perhaps… to end myself if it resolved this never-ending deal."

His gaze returns to the sky, where Tiamat circles above like a judge watching the damned. "Everything that's happened since, everything I've done, has been because of that night. I'm sorry for what you've all endured because of it. But I have to find that demon again. I have to make this right. I heard the demon out that night. It spoke plainly, with no pretense, no deception—just a raw deal to me. It offered me all the answers I had ever sought, every secret of the universe I craved to uncover, in exchange for one thing: the soul of my first-born son. An heir, destined to lead a great army of the underworld."

King chuckles darkly, shaking his head. "I laughed at first. The idea was ridiculous. I never had any interest in children. Never cared for the whole family life—relationships, love, any of it. I was obsessed with my work, my research, my ambition. So I told the demon, 'You do know I have no child and never intend to have one.'"

He pauses, his eyes narrowing as he recalls the demon's chilling response. "'I am aware,' it said. I remember thinking then that the demon was probably just desperate, grasping at straws. But it also had intelligence foreign to me and I again pointed out the obvious. 'I could simply continue my life free of relationships. Never produce a child. And you're telling me I'd still be granted every possibility I desire?' The demon didn't hesitate. 'That is correct, King. In exchange for the soul of your son.'"

King laughs again, this time with a hint of self-loathing. "Arrogantly, I agreed. I thought I was clever—thought I could cheat the devil himself. I shook the demon's hand, looked it right in the eyes, and said, 'I shall have no son for you to claim. 'Whatever happens, happens.' it said. And just like that, the deal was struck. I had what I wanted—more power, more knowledge than I could have ever dreamed of—but those words, they… they've haunted me ever since. The demon's touch sent a cold shiver through me that I'll never forget. Goosebumps crawled up my skin as if death itself had brushed past me. From that moment on, my mind expanded beyond human comprehension. The calculations that had once taken me days or weeks were now instantaneous. I could see the answers to problems I hadn't even begun to ask. Equations that were once theoretical became real, tangible things. My abilities to create, to innovate—everything was amplified to an insane degree."

He looks back at Clain and the others, his eyes distant. "It didn't take me long to find what I was looking for—the existence of other dimensions and how to open them. But creating a gateway wasn't so simple. The process was immense, a colossal feat of technology and power that was far beyond my means at the time. So, I focused on building everything I could imagine mankind would need. Devices, systems, conveniences that would make life feel like paradise. All to accumulate the wealth and influence I'd need to fund my true goals."

King gestures around them, at the opulent skyscraper and the sprawling city below. "Cloud 9 was the solution. A place where people could live their lives in blissful ignorance, thinking they were on top of the world. Their lives of comfort and excess paid for my ambitions. Every luxury, every convenience, every technological marvel—each was a stepping stone toward opening the gateway. Toward finding that demon again and making him pay for all that he's caused. I thought I could outsmart it. I thought I could live above it all, free of consequences. But I was wrong. And now, everything I've done has led us to this moment." He looked up at Clain, Honey, Dawn, and Fila, his eyes pleading for them to understand. "I've been running ever since, trying to undo the deal I made. But the price of that knowledge... It's a price I'm terrified to pay. And whether you realize it or not, you've all been dragged into this because of me."

The storm rumbles overhead, Tiamat still circling like a harbinger of doom. King's confession hangs heavy in the air, a chilling reminder that the true enemy is not just a monster from another world, but the darkness that had taken root in one man's soul. King continues, his voice taking on a more reflective tone. "As my abilities grew, and my ambitions expanded, I realized that I could only go so far on my own. My mind, though vastly improved by the deal, still had limits. I was human, after all. But what if I could create something— someone—even smarter than me? A being that could think faster, act without hesitation, and double my productivity?"

King's eyes gleam with pride as he glances over at Synric. "And that's how Synric came into being. A creation born from my mind, designed to exceed even my own capabilities. He started out as a simple AI, a digital assistant that could answer my menial questions, manage data, and optimize my work. But as Synric grew, so did his intelligence. He became more than just a tool; he evolved into something far greater."

King gestures toward the side of the rooftop, where a massive video screen flickers to life. The stormy backdrop gives way to grainy footage, showing a sterile laboratory filled with machinery and cables. In the center of the room, a humanoid figure emerges from a thick fog of vapor—Synric, taking his first unsteady steps as an android.

The image on the screen is haunting. Synric's movements are slow, deliberate, almost childlike as he tries to steady himself. His body is sleek and metallic, a far cry from the refined suited stature and swagger he wore now. King stands within the footage, watching his creation come to life like a proud father.

King's voice echoes from the recording, filled with a cautious excitement. "How do you feel?"

Synric's head tilts slightly, his glowing blue eyes meeting King's with an intensity that is almost human. "Able," Synric replies, his voice mechanical yet laced with a strange, burgeoning self-awareness.

King, taken aback, leans closer in the video. "Able? Able to what?"

Synric pauses, as if considering the question, before responding with a single word: "Live."

King pauses the video, the screen freezing on Synric's unblinking eyes. He turns back to the group, looking as fearful as he is proud.

"A creation made in the image of humanity yet unbound by humanity's limitations," he observes.

"What does any of that have to do with me? I never asked for this power! Why do I have it?!" Clain shouts. King meets Clain's gaze.

"But you did, Clain. You chose it when you died at Eagle's Equinox. When you conducted your ritual with the Elder in pursuit of unknown power." He nods toward Dawn. "When you made that sacrifice, you unknowingly stepped into this deal that was made long ago."

Clain's eyes expand. Dawn steps forward, interrupting in a solemn tone, "What do you mean? He...died?" His eyes shift to Clain almost looking through him like a ghost.

Synric's eyes gleam with a knowing glint.

"Your father had no idea you existed until you were already gone," Synric answers. The deal was sealed the moment you sacrificed yourself. You paid his price without even realizing it."

King steps closer, his eyes heavy with regret. "I thought I could outsmart the demon. But in the end, the deal was always bigger than me... bigger than any of us."

"What are you saying?" Clain urges, his voice shaking with desperate fury. "That I am your son?"

Synric moves closer to King, placing a hand on his shoulder. His eyes betray uncharacteristic concern. "Dammit, answer me!" Clain shouts. Synric's gaze snaps to Clain. His glare is deadly.

"Mind your tongue. He has waited for this moment far longer than you can imagine. You have no idea what he's endured."

"Allow him his emotions, Synric," King says. His voice trembles. "They are justified." Tears stream down his face as his eyes meet Clain's.

"I didn't know, Clain," King whispered. "Not until it was too late. Not until I saw you die... and realized what the demon had taken from me. You're my son. And I failed you." Clain can't even move. Shock alone has him petrified. "For a long time," King continues, "I worried that Synric might somehow be the son I swore never to have. He was so perfect—everything I'd dreamed of creating, and more. As he grew and evolved, I began to see in him a reflection of everything the demon had promised."

Synric's eyes soften slightly, but he remains silent.

"I thought maybe… maybe I had created something more than just a machine. I feared that Synric had somehow become the heir the demon wanted. But then… the demon came back. This time though, it wasn't offering a deal. It was there to thank us—thank both of us. It told me the deal was complete, that I had fulfilled my end of the bargain. Neither of us understood what it meant at the time. But, slowly, I started to notice changes."

King clenches his fists as he begins to shake. He speaks through gritted teeth.

"My mind, once so sharp, so powerful—it wasn't the same. I couldn't keep up with the things I'd once done effortlessly. I started to rely on Synric more and more, turning to him for answers that used to come naturally. I became dependent on my own creation. Then, one night, everything changed. Synric discovered something… something I thought was impossible. He found a way to travel through time."

Clain's jaw drops. Desperate questions all try to force their way out. The crowd ineffectually at the base of his throat. All he can manage is a strangled word.

"Wh…What? You can't be serious."

King looks back up, nodding in commiseration.

"I was terrified. That much power over, well, damn near everything.…But before I could even process what Synric had done, the demon returned. This time with a warning. 'Should you continue,' it said, 'your time in this world will be greatly reduced. With each and every attempt.'"

"You…you didn't…" Clain struggles to say.

"I'm afraid I did. Many times. Yet, I found nothing. No hint of the demon's existence in ancient texts, no sightings in the shadows of historic events. It was as if it was bound to me and me alone. Eventually when I finally admitted the trail had gone cold, or rather that there never really was a trail to begin with, I started just exploring our past. Humanity's past. But even that, fittingly, got old. I sought when times were simpler and revisited my own youthful past."

"There was one night, one I'd completely forgotten. I was at a bar, celebrating another big contract. There was this woman. We hit it off instantly, our connection was electric. We drank, we laughed, and before I knew it, I was in her bed. It was one of those nights that felt like it would last forever, but morning came, and I had a last-minute flight to catch. I promised her I'd keep in touch, but..." King's face twists with regret. His hands clench into fists. "Cloud 9 took off right after that. My empire grew, and in the whirlwind of my success, I never contacted her again. I simply moved on, consumed by my ambitions, my obsessions, my constant pursuit for more."

He paused, his eyes clouding with the weight of his realization. "I got curious about her—about what became of that night. I checked in on her, expecting nothing more than a brief memory of a wild past. But what I found..." King's voice breaks. "She had gotten pregnant. Our one evening together resulted in a child I never knew about. A son. She tried to find me, tried to reach out, but I ensured my identity was well hidden with the success of Cloud 9 for my own security. I was untraceable. All those years, all that time wasted chasing a demon's shadow, and the answer had been right there, hiding in my own past. The demon had known all along. That's why it made the deal. I didn't know, Clain. And I'm sorry... for everything. For the life you never got to have because of me."

"Why are you only telling me now?" Clain whispers, nearly choking on his words as tears fall.

King's mouth opens, but no words come.

"He didn't want you to grow up under the shadow of his empire," Synric begins. His tone is flat, matter-of-factly. "He didn't want you to live as the pampered prince of Cloud 9, gazing down on the world from above. King wanted you to know what it was like to be at the bottom, to have nothing, to struggle and fight. He wanted you to have a chip on your shoulder, an itch to grow stronger, to constantly strive for more. We watched you grow from a distance, all this time, helping where we could."

"Clain's jaw clenches, his hands tightening at his sides. The storm around them seems to swirl with his anger. "You call that parenting? Manipulating my entire life from the shadows? You think that's what a father's supposed to do?"

Synric doesn't waver. "Is that not the role of a parent, Clain? To guide their child, to influence their journey toward success—even if it means making difficult choices? King believed he had no right to be directly involved after what he had done and this was the only way he could prepare you for what was to come. He wanted you to experience some level of normalcy the past several years."

Clain's aura flares as he finally stands up.

"Enough," he declares. "You keep saying I died, but here I am. How? Where did my powers come from? This demon?"

"No, Clain," King answers. "There's more to it than that. The demon didn't bring you back. It was bait."

King takes a deep breath, glancing at Synric, who nods slightly, urging him to continue. "When Synric and I realized who you were—when we saw you grow up, saw your relationship with your mother, watched you run away to Eagle's Equinox—we saw what was coming. You were strong, but you were always hungry for more power. The Elder saw that in you too. It was why you underwent the ritual, wasn't it? That hunger?"

Clain nods.

"But that doesn't answer how I brought you back, does it? Forgive me. The point is we saw it happen. And within minutes we were chasing a cure for your death. We found it. Old, classified documents from military black sites referencing an unidentified object falling from the stars. Inside was a substance resembling mercury. But that's the only thing it resembled anything this Earth has seen. It could merge with any organism and find ways to perfect it, enhance it. Fix it." King is lost in memory now, looking right through his long lost son as he recounts his story. "Bring things back to life."

Clain freezes. He can barely breathe.

410

"Our hypothesis is that it's at least semi-sentient. It has a fundamental drive to exist, in any case. To entrench and enrich itself to evolve and survive. Almost like a benevolent virus, one that enhances its host as opposed to ravaging it in the name of replication. We decided to call it...Clainium," Synric explains. "All your father had to do was go back in time and retrieve it before the military ever

 discovered it. And so he did." Synric's eyes glow for a moment and a holographic recording of King displays in front of Clain. It's King, standing over a dead body. His body. A hypodermic needle is in King's hand. He nods to Synric, and the recording plays. King cradles Clain's body as tears stream down his face. And then he injects the liquid.

In time, the dead Clain's eyes flutter open.

Synric's voice broke the silence. "The substance worked, resisting death itself. It gave you back your life, altering time and fate. But also in that moment, King got to hold you for the first time, knowing the cost."

The footage continues of King sobbing uncontrollably, clutching Clain's still body as the silver substance takes effect. Holding his head to his chest, tears dropping to his face. "A dark fate falls from father to son," Synric narrates. "As the stars chose the son to be their light." King holds Clain close as he buries his face into his shoulder, overcome with grief and joy. Clain, still dazed, weakly pushes King's face away, trying to comprehend what was happening.

He held Clain tighter, his cry hoarse. He presses his scratchy beard against Clain's head, his tears flowing freely. "I will be with you... always," King whispers in the footage. He gently lays Clain back on the hospital bed, his hands trembling as the machines around them start to beep with life. King takes one last look at his son before the footage comes to an abrupt end.

CHAPTER 23 - Farewell For Now

Time dilates for Clain as the weight of King's confession settles in. By the time King breaks the silence, Clain can't even begin to guess how much time has passed. He's just been pacing the whole time. His thoughts were a chaotic storm, mirroring the turbulent sky above, and every step felt like an attempt to escape the reality that had been forced upon him.

Dawn, Fila, and Honey stood off to the side, whispering amongst themselves. Dawn's usually lighthearted demeanor was replaced by an imposing seriousness; Fila's eyes darted between Clain and King, her face etched with empathy, while Honey's gaze lingered on Clain, filled with a deep concern she couldn't quite articulate. The silence stretched on, only broken by the distant rumble of thunder and the faint hum of the warring city below. King watches Clain pace, his eyes following his son's every movement.

"Tiamat's resurrection is nearly complete," King warns. "We have minutes, maybe less. There is so much more I need to tell you. Please ask. I will answer."

Dawn exchanges a hesitant glance with Fila and Honey before stepping forward.

"Sorry, Clain... but I need to know something." Clain stops pacing. "Why does Honey look like Rezeka?"

The question hung in the air, sharp and direct, cutting through the tension like a blade. King glances at Honey, then back at Clain, knowing that this was a truth he could no longer keep hidden. King nods, sighing heavily. He looks again to Tiamat as she circles the building.

"I knew this would be the next question," he admits in a sorrowful tone. "The answers stem from the tournament years ago. The one that went so very wrong."

Grainy video clips began to play on the projection screen again, showing Clain in his element—dominating fight after fight in the underground tournament circuits. Crowds cheer. Between bouts, he signs autographs. He's relentless. A force of nature. His skills seem all the more inhuman now that their origins are known to the group. Various trophy ceremonies and belt winnings flash in a quick montage.

Suddenly, the footage cuts. On screen now is the night Clain first met Rezeka. His eyes fill with tears as he forces himself to watch, the desire to see the genuine article, the real woman he truly loved, even one more time, winning out over the fear and sorrow that erupt with every memory of her. He enters a packed arena after one of his prize fights. The atmosphere is electric, but his attention is drawn to the stage where Rezeka is performing with her band, her voice captivating the audience. Their eyes meet from across the room. The chemistry is immediate.

She came to every fight after that... Clain recalls.

The woman on screen was, during her criminally brief life, his anchor. He's been adrift ever since he lost her - glimpses of their life together, celebrating, carefree and blissful.

"Watching you two... it was awe-inspiring," King says. "You were unstoppable, Clain, but Synric and I knew what was coming. We knew the darkness that would eventually find you. The complacency that sets in when struggle is absent." King's tone shifts, becoming more somber as he continues. "We wanted to push you further, to make you realize you needed to work harder, to never stop improving. So, we entered Synric into your seventh tournament circuit as a challenger—a fighter meant to test your limits, to push you beyond what you thought you were capable of."

Clain's fight with Synric begins on the screen. Synric, in disguise as an unassuming competitor, moved with mechanical precision, his strikes now undeniably familiar to Clain. At first, the match was like any other, but as it went on, it became clear that Synric wasn't holding back. The crowd watches in stunned silence as the android's power force Clain to extremes not even he had witnessed prior to this match.

King's expression darkens.

"Synric's designed purpose was to push you, but he pushed too far. You killed him. Self-defense meant to stop him from almost killing you. Luckily for him and I, he can be repaired. But the crowd didn't know who or what he was, and neither did you. Or Rezeka. To everyone present, it appeared you'd just obliterated a man to death. Had it been anyone else in Synric's place, that's exactly what would have happened."

 The film shows the final fatal blow from Clain. Synric's body collapsed to the ground, motionless. The audience gasps, their excitement turning to shock and horror. He stood there, drenched in sweat, eyes wide with disbelief.

"She saw everything..." Clain mutters absently, his mind miles away as he relives what he's seeing projected.

"Yes," King acknowledges. "I'm sorry. You know the rest. That night was the night she left you. We had no idea about your promise to her to never kill anyone. I'm sure you don't want to hear it again. You've relived enough pain for a thousand lifetimes."

"Thanks to you," Clain replies. The fire behind his eyes is a cold one. "And me. And what you turned me into. You made me break my promise to her!"

"Her death wasn't your fault, Clain. You didn't know it then, but that wall you punched. It ruptured a gas line after she had walked out. It ignited, setting the whole building on fire. She never made it out. A terrible, heart-rending accident you've blamed yourself for all these years. But you couldn't have known. It wasn't your fault."

Clain's knees buckle, his mind reeling from the weight of the truth. Tears well in his eyes watching the aftermath from his fit of

414

uncontrollable sorrow. King turns away from the screen, unable to watch the devastation unfold any longer. "We scrubbed the headlines, buried the story. Synric and I made sure no one ever knew the truth. We distanced you from what happened that night, from the fire. It wasn't your fault, Clain. It was ours."

Clain's voice is deathly quiet.

"You killed her," he finally says. His aura grows in intensity. "You fucked with my entire life behind the scenes. You let me think I was a murderer. Her too." Energy flares at his fingertips. He fixes a dead-eyed stare on King. "Maybe it's time I truly become one."

The Motherboard suddenly reassembles in mid-air, the pieces snapping together as if drawn by Clain's rage, each surging with energy. The enormous sword flew into his waiting hands, and he gripped it with white-knuckled intensity. His whole body shakes as he points it at King and Synric.

"This is unforgivable!" Clain screamed, his voice trembling with the force of his emotions. "You manipulated my entire life, and now Rezeka is dead. I won't listen to this anymore! I won't let you—"

"Wait a second!" Dawn shouts, stepping between King and Clain. Clain raises a fist. "Clain, just… wait. It still doesn't explain Honey. Why does she look like Rezeka? Why didn't you go back in time and just fix this?"

"You're right," King admitted, his voice cracking. "It's all our fault. I did not know about your promise to her. Our goal was to see if you could kill true evil when needed. To see if you had the fight in you to survive against all odds. To prepare you for your inevitable fate leading demons in the underworld. After Rezeka died, the guilt consumed me. I thought I could fix it… thought I could make it right somehow." He pauses. "We destroyed the time machine after bringing you back from the dead. Vowed to never time travel again after abusing it. Synric has the code locked away from me where I can never regain it. Otherwise… we could've…"

"So what did you do?" Clain growls, lifting the Motherboard into the air with eyes bolting between King and Synric. "What did you supposedly do to make it right?"

415

King looks down at the ground, his voice barely a whisper and eyes defeated.

"I created her. I made Honey." Clain's aura fades. The sword clatters  to the floor. His hands start to tremble. "I designed her to look like Rezeka. I made her as a new prototype android—far more realistic than Synric, even more humanlike. I gave her free will, allowed her to live as she saw fit. But her one goal, her one purpose... was to get close to you. To help you fall in love again. It was all I wished for. I thought... I thought maybe it would give you peace and allow you to move on. It's really more of Synric's overall creation. His idea even. I had lost most of my superior intelligence when the deal fell through and her lack of true humanity seems to have worked against us."

Synric's posture remains stoic, appearing cold and cynical.

The group stood in stunned silence, the truth too overwhelming to process. Honey slowly looks down at her hands, her expression shifting from shock to terror as the weight of King's words sunk in. The memories of her life, her thoughts, her feelings—they had all felt so real.

"I'm... not real?" she asks. Her voice is a whisper. Her body starts to shiver.

"I never wanted it to turn out like this." King chokes out. "And I'm sorry, but there's more you need to know, Clain. We are running out of time." King glances at Synric. Synric nods and the footage on the projection screen changes once again. The screen fills with complex, swirling patterns of data and images—abstract landscapes that shift and morph like a living, breathing thing.

"Synric was able to start mapping the realm within your premonitions," King explains. "We studied it extensively, trying to understand what you were seeing and why. We mapped your nightmares, your visions... and it was there that we first discovered Tia. I bargained with her to seal away your memories of Rezeka, to

416

keep you from losing your mind to deep guilt and depression. I wanted to protect you, to give you a chance to move on, but it was a fool's gamble. Tia doesn't do favors. She makes deals. And like any demon, you always pay more than you realize."

Before King can continue, Honey rushes to Clain's side, her face twisted with anger and heartbreak.

"You've been pulling strings all this time," she spits, her voice shattered. "You manipulated Clain's life, ended Rezeka's life… and fuckin created mine?!"

"Yes," King admits in defeat.

"My name," she says. "Why? Why would you name me Honey?"

"I named you Honey because of a moment that meant everything to Clain." New footage fills the screen again, shifting to Clain giving an interview with a local reporter after another victory in the pits.

"Clain, you've had an incredible winning streak, six in a row now," a reporter comments. "But what keeps you grounded? Is it Rezy? What do you love most about her? All the fans must know!"

"Rezeka?" Clain's eyes light up as he stares to the distant ground. A big smile spreads across his face. His voice is warm and affectionate. Punch drunk in love. "She's sweet… like honey. She's the sweetest thing in my whole life."

Clain falls to his knees. Remembering a passive small moment from so long ago that struck him to his core. The screen goes dark. King turns back to face the group once more, heavy with regret as he addresses Honey.

"I named you Honey because that's who you were meant to be. A reflection of the love Clain lost. I thought… in a fucked up way, it would help him heal. But it was never enough. I'm sorry, Honey. I'm sorry to all of you."

Honey goes statue still. Unnaturally so. She struggles to make sense of her existence. Memories flash rapidly through her mind until it stops on Dawn. All eyes are on her, mouth ajar, the air increasingly suffocating. She reaches for her Stinger multi-tool. With a flick of her thumb, the tool transforms to its compact caster cannon. She points the barrel at King, her eyes blazing with fury.

"You motherfucker!" she shouts grimly. "If none of this is real, if I'm not real, then I've got nothing to live for! Let's do this, Clain!"

Clain, still seething, tightens his grip on the Motherboard, his aura rages back to life. His eyes lock onto King. For a brief moment, he and Honey were perfectly in sync, united by their shared rage to attack.

But just as Honey's finger begins to squeeze the trigger, King shouts "H1 STOP!"

Honey's body seizes. Her arms shoot out to the side in a rigid T-pose as she drops her gun. Her eyes widen as panic sets in. "No... no!" she screams. Tears stream down her cheeks as she fights the paralysis in vain. Stripped of her free will in an instant.

Clain stumbles back, his momentum halted as he watches Honey's sudden paralysis. His gaze snaps back to King, his face pale and stricken with fear.

 "You both left me no choice," King pleads sternly. "Try to understand my intentions. Please."

Clain's heart pounds in his chest. The sight of Honey, frozen and helpless, a prisoner of the very technology that had given her life. His mind implodes, grappling with the chaos unfolding around him. King still held power over them all. This was his territory.

Dawn and Fila snap into action, rushing to Honey's side. She is still frozen, trapped in the rigid T-pose, her eyes wide and pleading but unable to move. Fila grabs Honey's belt with her mechanical arm, feeling their joint consequence of being altered forever by Cloud 9. This person Fila looked up to a figment of their creation. No time to mourn or dwell in the moment. Dawn's face twists with anger as he watches Honey struggle.

"We got this!" he shouts. "Clain, focus and rush them from the right, I'll go left!"

Clain nods, gripping the Motherboard tightly. "Watch for the goat!" he warns, his eyes scanning the area.

"The goat...?" Dawn stammers, his momentum faltering for a split second. Suddenly, Goatsee barrels toward him, its red eyes glowing with a mischievous glint. The zebra-striped goat lunges at Dawn, but he reacts just in time, catching the beast by its twisted horns. He grunts as the powerful creature pushes back, its sheer strength matching Dawn's own and driving him backward.

Clain sprints forward, keeping his focus on King. Dawn laughs through gritted teeth as he struggles against the goat's relentless assault. "Good looking out!" he yells, wrestling with Goatsee to keep it from breaking free.

Clain charges at King, his feet pounding against the rain-soaked rooftop. But before he can reach his target, Synric appears in a flash, blocking Clain's attack with a powerful counter strike, sending Clain to one knee.

Clain's eyes flare with determination. He thrusts his arms forward, channeling his magnetic powers as the Motherboard shatters into lethal fragments, scattering in every direction. Synric somersaults backward at blinding speed, his movements precise as he deflects each piece of the blade, preventing them from flying toward King.

Clain spots his chance—a clear path to King. King looks on with terrified eyes. As Clain closes in, his resolve wavers. The thought of striking his own father gnawing at his conscience. Suddenly, Fila rushes to his side, her nunchucks spinning wildly. She shoves Clain forward, her voice filled with urgency. "You got this Clain! Let's go!"

Clain's hesitation vanishes. Together, he and Fila charge at King. Synric instantly drops down in front of them, his stance poised

419

and ready. The android moves with a fluid grace, effortlessly dodging their flurry of attacks. Fila's nunchucks crack through the air, and Clain's punches land with explosive force. But Synric's footwork is immaculate, his movements weaving through the onslaught like a ghost.

Dawn finally manages to shove Goatsee away, spinning around and joining the assault on Synric. The three fighters attack in harmony, their strikes relentless and unyielding. Fila's nunchucks whirl, Dawn's kunais fly, and Clain's blows strike with raw power. Synric still evades their every attempt to hit him. Seeming on a whole new level of power. Clain drops low, diving forward in a sweeping motion aimed at Synric's legs. Synric flips backward, narrowly avoiding the sweep, but as he twists in mid-air, his eyes widen. The Motherboard has reassembled above him, crashing down like a guillotine. The blade strikes Synric's back, crunching down his cybernetic spine with a sickening sound of grinding metal. Synric is pinned against the massive sword, struggling to free himself as Clain uses his magnetic powers to keep the Motherboard pressing against the android.

Dawn lunges forward, wrapping his arms around Synric's torso and the Motherboard to hold them in place. His muscles straining as he struggles. "I've got him!" Dawn shouts, gritting his teeth against Synric's attempts to break free. Fila quickly joins, grabbing hold of Synric's ankles with her chucks and pulling with all her strength. The android thrashes, but their combined force holds him tight.

"Go, Clain!" Fila yells, her voice fierce and commanding. "Finish this—finish King!"

Clain locks eyes with King, the fear in his father's face finally erasing the last of Clain's hesitation. He summons every ounce of his strength, his aura blazing around him as he leaps into the air, his gauntlets fully charged. He aims his punch directly at King, ready to end this once and for all. Just as Clain's fist is about to connect, a large shadow sweeps over the rooftop. Tiamat's enormous wing descends, blocking the blow with a thunderous impact. The force of Clain's strike meets the ancient beast's scales, sending a shockwave through the air as a brilliant flash of energy erupts.

All five of Tiamat's heads roar in unison, a deafening, primal scream that shakes the very foundation of the building. The sheer power of the dragon's presence scatters Clain, Dawn, Fila, and Synric, sending them all tumbling across the rooftop like ragdolls.

Clain hits the ground hard, skidding to a stop as he looks up at the towering figure of Tiamat, all of her eyes burning with frenzy. Tiamat rises up on her powerful legs, her gigantic body stretching high above the rooftop of Cloud 9. Her claws scrape harshly against the concrete, tearing through it with a grating, thunderous noise that echoes across the platform. The dragon's presence is overwhelming, her form radiating a brilliant pink energy that pulses off her reforged scales like a heartbeat. Each head looms ominously, snarling and snapping as Tiamat's immense power fills the air.

Atop the middle head, King stands strong and unwavering, though his face is marked with sorrow and deep regret. He looks down at Clain, Dawn, Fila, and Honey—his son, his creation, and the people he has hurt the most. The pain of Clain's attempted strike lingers, not because of the physical threat, but because his own blood has tried to end him. King looks at each of them with a heavy, remorseful gaze.

"I've made so many mistakes," he says. And you all paid the price for them. I'm...sorry. H1 Release." Honey's body jerks as the signal releases, her frozen limbs loosening as she collapses to her knees, gasping for breath. She glances up at King, a mixture of relief and anger in her eyes, but for now, she is free. King's voice wavers as he continues. "I must go now. Tiamat and I are leaving... into the stars. I need to find answers. I have to find the demon that has enslaved our bloodline and set this all in motion. I don't know if I will ever return, but Synric... Synric will be here. He knows more than I do, and he can guide you in my absence."

King's gaze shifts between Clain and Synric, his eyes filled with a deep, paternal love. "You are my sons. Both of you. I see you as brothers, even if your paths were forged in different ways. I know you have the strength to fight the darkness that now threatens this world. You're stronger together than apart, and I believe in you both."

Clain's anger begins to soften, replaced by a complex mix of emotions. He resents King, but now, in this final moment, he can see the anguish in his father's eyes—the deep, unending guilt of a man

421

who has lost everything in his pursuit of answers. King's voice cracks, his final words almost lost in the wind.

"I love you. And I'm sorry that I wasn't the father you needed me to be." King bows deeply to them, his head low, a gesture of respect, humility, and unspoken apology. "And one more thing," King raises his hand with a finger. "Be sure to look after Goatsee. We still aren't sure about that damn goat." Just as he finishes speaking, Tiamat's massive head rears back, her eyes glowing with ancient power. And with a sudden, violent motion, she tosses King high into the air. The group watches in a stunned silence as Tiamat's jaws snap open, catching King in mid-flight and swallowing him whole.

With King now within her, Tiamat lets out a deafening roar, her five heads arcing upward as she launches herself off the rooftop, her powerful wings beating against the sky. She darts straight up, piercing through the clouds with a blinding pink glow, her form shrinking as she ascends toward the stars, disappearing into the vastness of outer space.

~~~

The silence that follows is suffocating. The wind dies down, and the storm seems to still as the group stands in the aftermath of King's departure. Clain, Dawn, Fila, and Honey exchange awkward, uncertain glances, their minds struggling to process the enormity of what has just happened. But it is Synric who breaks the silence.

Synric glanced at them all, his expression unreadable but tinged with a hint of resignation. "I'll… be right back," he said calmly. His body began to crumble. The advanced cybernetic frame that had held him together fell apart, piece by piece. The parts scattered across the rooftop, clattering to the ground, leaving only the Motherboard lodged firmly into the rooftop.

Just as the group stood in uneasy silence, the air above them shimmered and a familiar liquid-filled tube descended from the sky, the same eerie light bathing the rooftop. The thick, viscous fluid within began to swirl and churn, coalescing into the familiar form of Synric. The android emerged gracefully, the liquid draining away as he stepped onto the rooftop with the elegance of a performer taking center stage. Synric adjusted his sharp, form-fitted suit, his colored accents

422

catching the faint glow of the moonlight now shining through the dissipating storm clouds. He greeted them with a slight, almost smug smirk.

"How many times do we have to kick your ass before you finally stop coming back?" Dawn asks.

Synric chuckled, brushing a stray droplet of the liquid off his sleeve. "Oh, you've only ever managed to 'beat' me because I've allowed it. Don't flatter yourselves too much." He looked around at the group, a playful edge to his words. "You should be grateful I'm only permitted one body at a time."

Clain steps forward, his anger still simmering beneath the surface. He eyes Synric with a cold, disdainful glare.

"So you've only ever been some sort of sick dick measuring contest? Programmed to challenge me over and over? That's your grand purpose?"

"In a sense, yes. I was designed to push you, to make you stronger. But also to find solutions for the... horrific things King set into motion. Believe me, Clain, I don't agree with what he's done any more than you do." For the first time, Synric's confident demeanor wavers. He hesitates, his usual arrogance giving way to something more genuine. Slowly, he walks toward Clain, each step deliberate, and then, in a move that leaves the entire group stunned, Synric takes a knee before him. "I apologize, Clain," Synric says. "For my role in all of this. For every fight, every manipulation. I've caused you pain when I was meant to help you grow, and for that, I am deeply sorry." Synric looks up, meeting Clain's eyes. "I pledge to work tirelessly by your side. I will find a way to rid you of the dark horrors that have been sealed within you.

"I, too, have grown tired of this destiny we're all bound to. It's ingrained in my very core—a relentless drive to solve the problem, to end the chaos. But I want you to understand, Clain, that my existence offers no escape from this fate, just as you can't escape yours. We are both trapped, servants to a destiny neither of us chose, bound by programming and blood alike. We will find a way, Clain. Together. Not because of some programming or some grand plan, but because it's what we must do. And I will stand with you, regardless if you want me there or not."

The rooftop fell silent once more, but it was no longer the heavy, suffocating silence of betrayal. It was a moment of tentative understanding, a fragile yet possible alliance could be formed in the wake of King's departure. The future was uncertain, but for the first time, they were facing it together.

Clain scoffs.

"Rezeka is dead because of you. I can never forgive that." Clain turns back to the group. "Let him search for his own damn answers. Let him fester here. The world's falling apart, and we have more important things to deal with."

Dawn, Fila, and Honey stood back, their expressions mirroring Clain's disgust and mistrust. They all shared the same thought: how could they just forget everything that happened and work willingly with the android that had been at the center of so much pain?

Clain turns back to the group, his tone dismissive.

"Clain, wait," Synric calls after him. "There's one more thing you need to know."

Clain stops, his back turned to Synric.

"There's more to Honey's creation than King told you. A backup plan. Honey was also designed as a vessel. One that could channel the real Rezeka. She can be reborn, Clain. Her body was designed as a conduit. Rezeka can be with you again. This was King's final gift to you."

Clain's heart pounds as he glances back at Synric. The android's face is deadly serious. Clain turns away, his mind racing, and continues his walk toward the elevator, joining the rest of the group inside.

He reached the elevator and turned to face his friends one last time. Dawn, Fila, and Honey stood there, each wearing a mix of worry, support, and uncertainty. Clain hesitated, forcing a smile. He

424

looked at Dawn first, then Honey, whose face was still contorted with confusion and pain. Finally, he turned to Fila, his smile warm and genuine.

"Thanks for having my back," Clain says softly. "I appreciate you all more than you'll ever know." He pauses, his voice catching as he continues, "I just… need some time alone."

Dawn nods. "No worries, man. We have some shit to figure out as well. We'll grab the other elevator."

"Where will you go?" Fila asks, her disappointed voice breaking.

Clain shrugs.

"I don't know," he admits, calling the Motherboard back to his side. It snaps into place on his back, a reassuring weight. "Somewhere quiet. To meditate."

Dawn gives Clain a reassuring nod. "As will I. And I'll get these two back to Eagle's Equinox safely. Take care of yourself, Clain."

Clain steps into the opposite elevator and leans heavily against the synthetic banister at the rear. Meeting eyes with Synric's cold expression as the door closes in front of him. He lets out a long, exhausted sigh, relief momentarily washing over him. The elevator begins its descent, and Clain stares out the glass window, watching the chaos below. New Beam City is a nightmare—a sprawling landscape of fires, destruction, and panic.

He considers his next move, wondering where he can go to find some semblance of peace even for just a moment. But his thoughts are interrupted as the elevator picks up speed. Clain's brow furrows, a twinge of unease prickling at the back of his mind. The descent feels wrong. Too fast. Panic sets in as the elevator plummets toward the ground floor, hurtling past it at a blinding velocity.

Clain is thrown to the floor, grasping at the slick metal walls, realizing they are actually synthetic plastics. He can't exert his magnesis on them. The elevator continues its descent, plunging deep

425

into the earth. The sensation of falling is relentless, disorienting, like he is being swallowed by the depths of the planet itself. Miles down, or maybe more—it's impossible to tell.

Finally, the elevator lurches to a stop, and the doors slide open to reveal a pitch-black room. The only light comes from a single monitor that flickers, illuminating Synric's face in a cold, artificial glow.

Clain's heart pounds as he stares at the screen. Synric's expression was calm but grim.

"I'm sorry, Clain, but I cannot let you venture out there freely. I have to seal you away from the rest of the world and those that seek you."

The weight of Synric's words hangs in the air, and Clain realizes he is trapped, cut off from everything and everyone he knows. His pulse races as he stands alone in the darkness, the faint hum of machinery his only company.

The world above is still burning, but down here, Clain is isolated, imprisoned by the very android that promised to stand by his side only moments ago.

"Now we train."

THANK YOU FOR TAKING THE JOURNEY INTO
NEW BEAM CITY

COMING SOON

A new trilogy is on the horizon! Set four years in the future as the fallen arise. Keep up with Son Of Syn and Christopher through these networks and show your support:

https://www.sonofsyn.com
https://www.reddit.com/r/SonOfSyn/ https://www.twitch.tv/mixtopher
https://x.com/mixtopher
https://patreon.com/mixtopher
Direct inquiries and investors welcome! We need your help.

ABOUT THE AUTHOR

Christopher R. Mix, also known as Mixtopher has been a full-time live streamer since 2012 beginning on Twitch.tv. A Lifelong fan and consumer of franchises spanning games, movies & shows, he felt jaded & underwhelmed by many of the stories told within modern-day media. This motivated him to share a story he began writing in 2004 during his time at college & his passion for this adventure was reborn. Hence the introduction to the Son Of Syn series! His debut as an author is in collaboration with a team of editors & illustrators who are also new to this medium & equally as passionate.

His dream is to see Son of Syn grow into a multi-novel series as well as evolve into several forms of media such as games, animated shows, or even movies. Chris is powered & sponsored by his incredible community of viewers known as Cosmo Canyon who he hopes to make proud as they embark on this journey with him.

2d20a978-873b-4f60-b4b7-917d1b2a0b1eR02